Church Girl
Gone Wild

Church Girl
Gone Wild

Ni'chelle Genovese

www.urbanbooks.net

Urban Books, LLC
97 N18th Street
Wyandanch, NY 11798

Church Girl Gone Wild

ISBN 13: 978-1-62286-970-1
ISBN 10: 1-62286-970-2

First Mass Market Printing June 2016
First Trade Paperback Printing October 2014
Printed in the United States of America

10 9 8 7 6 5 4 3 2 1

This is a work of fiction. Any references or similarities to actual events, real people, living or dead, or to real locales are intended to give the novel a sense of reality. Any similarity in other names, characters, places, and incidents is entirely coincidental.

Distributed by Kensington Publishing Corp.
Submit orders to:
Customer Service
400 Hahn Road
Westminster, MD 21157-4627
Phone: 1-800-733-3000
Fax: 1-800-659-2436

London Borough of Barking & Dagenham	
90600000141092	
Askews & Holts	14-Nov-2016
AF GNR	£5.99
BDBAR	

Church Girl
Gone Wild

Ni'chelle Genovese

This one is for you Grandma Dorothy

Prologue

"I will also send wild beasts among you,
which shall rob you of your children."

-Leviticus 26:22

1998

My body felt heavy and weighted down like all of gravity was working against me. I struggled to sit up, wincing when I scraped my forehead against something rough and grainy. That hard mess was all around me, scratching me in the places where my Mulan sheets should have been. It pressed against my back through my thin night-shirt, scraped against the back of my forearms and legs. Blinking didn't help bring anything into focus. I couldn't even see my nose on my own face because it was so dark.

"Momma Rose?" I called out, praying she'd answer me. "Momma Rose!" My voice bounced around me hurting my own ears.

The only response I got was a soft tapping sound. Even though I was ten I'd still have nightmares.

The kind that'd make me shoot awake with my heart in my throat. They were usually about the night two-years ago that got me and Leslie taken away and put with Momma Rose and Deacon. Momma Rose always came and prayed over me until I'd fall back asleep. But this wasn't one of my nightmares, this was real.

The fact that we'd all just had dinner and then gone to bed as usual had me three levels past confused making my head throb. And here I'd always thought a headache was something Momma Rose made up for the times when Sue was being extra annoying. Tsukiko or Sue, as we called her, was Deacon's half-past-crazy Japanese cleaning lady. At least that's the lie that he told everybody. She was really his second wife. As far as I knew, a man wasn't supposed to have two wives at the same time, but Deacon did a lot of things most people didn't do.

If Momma Rose was a warm fluffy towel fresh out the dryer, then Sue was a cold sopping wet one, twisted up tight at the ends ready to snap at you. Sue stuck her little pointy nose up in the air at us from day one. She even went as far as changing her doorknob to one that locks with a key from the outside. Ain't nobody want anything of hers, but you couldn't tell her that.

I squinted into the blackness so hard my eyes started hurting. The air was warm and heavy, like trying to breathe with a blanket over my face.

"Momma Rose! Sue? This isn't funny I can't breathe," I wailed into the dark.

This felt like another one of Sue's stupid lessons that never made sense because she didn't speak enough English to explain. She once locked me inside the toy chest in my bedroom for no reason at all. Whenever she was having one of her moments I'd just try to keep close to Momma Rose.

This was nothing like the inside of my toy chest though. At least that was wider and there were gaps at the hinges so I could see out. There was no escaping the pitch-black box that Sue found for me this time. I could imagine her pasty bone-white face, giggling at me, doing that stupid thing where she covers her mouth when she laughs. *She knows good and well she can hear and understand me.* I'd eavesdropped on enough conversations to notice her English wasn't always jacked up. Especially not when she was asking Deacon to buy her more of that bird crap she liked to put on her face all day. Real bird poo, the bottle even said nightingale poo. Anyone crazy enough to walk around with dried bird poo on their face was definitely crazy enough to think this would be funny. *We'll see how she likes me flushing all her face-poo down the dern toilet.*

Sweat rolled down my neck and shoulders as I took shallow raspy breaths. There was no telling how long it'd be before Momma Rose got up and noticed I wasn't in my bed. I squeezed my eyes shut against the tight feeling in my chest. It swelled up like a moon-bounce-castle. My heart jumped and bumped all over it. *Lord, please help me. I promise to stop listening to things I'm not supposed to and I'll learn something useful, like how to Houdini myself out of boxes.*

The tapping was getting louder and closer. When it finally occurred to me what I was hearing the blood froze in my veins, thawed and rushed to the center of my chest in a tiny explosion. My eyes snapped open. I knew that sound. It sounded like winter, like wood popping and crackling in a fireplace. The air was even starting to smell like smoke. It reminded me of the whole pigs daddy would roast on his smoker every Fourth of July. He swore by alder wood because it kept the best heat. And it burned the longest.

The few shaky breaths I took made me cough so hard I gagged. Painful hacking coughs ripped their way up my throat. My stomach heaved dredging up banana now-and-laters mixed with ketchup smothered meatloaf. Vomit burned its way up my throat gushing out of my nose and when my stomach was empty I kept dry-heaving so hard I peed on myself. Embarrassed frustrated tears rushed down my face running into my ears. It felt like I was inside a pressure cooker. Sue had finally gone and completely lost her mind. I tensed; the wood underneath me was starting to get hot. She was trying to cook me to death. No, she wasn't *trying*, she was burning me alive.

I blindly pounded my fists and kicked trying to fight my way out. Smoke mixed with foul smelling banana-meatloaf scented vomit was all around me. It was running down my neck and getting into my hair. The eerie crumbled skeletons of just about every mummified Eskimo and caveman I'd ever seen on TV flashed through my head. By the time anyone found me, I'd just be burnt bones. The thought made me want to crawl inside myself and cry until I fell asleep, but it was getting so hot I could barely breathe.

Every breath made my lungs beg for fresh air. I couldn't get enough the wind to scream out loud so I screamed over and over in my head. My toes were stinging and my fists hurt. There was nowhere to go.

I'm supposed to watch out for Leslie and keep her safe. She's gonna grow up and think I abandoned her just like momma and daddy abandoned us.

Cool air shot across my cheeks whipping up the smell of stomach bile and burnt candle wicks. I felt light as a feather and stiff as a board as someone scooped me up. I took in huge gulps of fresh air. Opening my eyes felt impossible. It was like sandpaper was attached to the insides of my eye lids. When I finally managed to force them open I was lying on a table with the night sky staring back at me. The moon hid behind cotton-ball fluffed clouds. Cicadas buzzed in the treetops and the trees rustled with the wind. All through a big jagged opening where the roof should have been.

"Hey honey-bee."

A man's voice came out of nowhere with all the gruff cheerfulness of an evil Santa collecting bad kids.

He stood at the foot of the table swallowing up all kinds of space with his wide-barrel chest. He was just big and wide all over. My eyes swept the room searching for something familiar. There was no Sue and no Momma Rose; I didn't know where I was or who he was. Shivers zigzagged across my spine. The old folk always said that meant someone had walked across my grave. This definitely wasn't the time to think about a superstition like that. Grimacing, I realized it was just me and this blocky man who could have passed for that ugly purple McDonalds blob called Grimace. Grimace with big Toro the bull from Bugs Bunny nostrils.

He leaned down over me until his nose was barely touching mine. Everything on him smelled like rotten eggs, even the warm air blasting me in the face from his double-barrel nostrils smelled foul. Turning away from him I squeezed my eyes shut.

"I pulled you out, but if you say a word about any of this *to anybody* you can go back in that box any time. *And you will burn.* Understand?"

His voice crawled into my ear in a rotten whisper making me shake so hard my bones hurt.

My stomach turned and tightened until I thought I'd be sick all over again. Grimace grabbed my chin forcing me to look up into his dark-blobish face. My heart was going a hundred miles an hour. Out the corner of my eye I could see the box he'd pulled me out of sitting on bricks in a corner. I couldn't hold back the gasp that slipped from in between my lips. It wasn't a box that I was pulled out of; it was a small wooden coffin. It was still smoldering, slowly turning black. The thought of being back in there and never getting out made me nod that I understood even though I didn't.

He smiled. "We gonna have us a good time Eva. You be a good girl and you can have the world. I promise."

He knows my name? How does he know my name? My eyes darted from corner to corner searching for a way out. Wide wooden doors like the ones I'd seen on barns were a few feet away. The walls were knotty slats of wood, with zero windows. And from what I could tell there was no way other way out. Grimace grabbed my wrists and started tying them together with a rough rope. My hands pumped open and closed into sweaty fists. A gloomy sinking feeling wisped around me, it mixed with the drifting branches of smoke that danced out of the coffin.

"John 15:16," Deacon's voice floated in from the shadows.

Grimace froze.

It's a wonder I didn't do a happy wiggle at the sound of his voice. I waited for him to pray the gates of hell open on this funky fool for what he'd done to me.

"Deacon," my voice cracked over my scratchy raw throat. I squirmed trying to get my eyes on him. I wanted to see him take this idiot down.

For the first time ever, my ears actually perked up at the sound of Deacon's signature slow shuffle. As much as Momma Rose stayed fussing at me about picking up my feet. You'd think she'd eventually get sick enough of hearing his spiky ostrich dress shoes shush from room to room that she'd say something to him.

He shuffled himself over until he was shoulder to shoulder with Grimace. He stared at me with his eyes glowing like creepy glass marbles in his head. When he nodded at Grimace my expression went from hopeful to hopeless. Two dressed up religious guys in a temple of cob webs and rotting wood couldn't mean anything good. A breeze caught hold of a writing spider's web over Deacon's head. I could have sworn I saw Charlotte the spider up there weaving the words, "I'm sorry honey."

"You did not choose me," Deacon whispered in an intense voice that sent his sunflower-yellow bowtie bobbing up and down. "For I chose you and appointed you so that you should go and bear fruit. This is your choosing ceremony Eva. Papa Psion fought the flames for your life and has claimed you. You are his."

"He wh . . . I'm . . . this is my what?" My words came out in a confused croak.

A new set of footsteps moved closer from somewhere behind me at the head of the table. My brain sent nervous pings down my neck that ran into my heart charging its ways up my throat. The footsteps stopped, but whoever it was, was still outside of where I could see them. Warm drops of water splattered down over my face and a hard round peppercorn fell in my mouth. The tip of my tongue pressed the hard kernel across my lips. I tried blinking through the splashes as they stung my eyes. The rabbit came into view above me with its blood red fur at the same time as I recognized the salty-sweet taste in my mouth. I screamed so loud my voice cut was cut off by my stomach clenching into another round of dry-heaves. My sides were starting to hurt worst than my wrists burning against the ropes.

Derian, one of the men from Deacon's church stepped closer. He had the meanest darkest eyes. He frowned down at me with the poor rabbit dangling from his hand by its feet. Its insides were shiny yellow and grayish white balloons with tiny black pebbles.

"Derian, next time you attend one of my ceremonies," Deacon paused with his lips twitching like he was fighting to stay calm. "Remove the filth from the beast or I'll have you strapped down and fed rabbit shit until you remember."

Derian's shrug was followed by a nonchalant nod.

I looked at Deacon and Grimace at my feet, begging them in my head to just stop all of this and take me home. I'd gotten out of a box just to get boxed in. Papa Psion wrapped his fat-sausage fingers tight around my ankle yanking me towards him. It took everything I had trying to kick him lose but he wasn't budging. I gave Deacon my biggest kitten-in-distress, hurt-puppy dog, please-help-me face. He didn't even blink. And here he was supposed to be my guardian and he wasn't guarding anything.

Papa Psion's hands were heavy black tarantulas creeping up underneath my night shirt. His fat barrel stomach pressed against my stomach and my chest making it impossible for me to take a breath.

"Girl, you smell like a truck stop shit house, but it's all good. I'll be in and out nice and easy."

He tried to squeeze his fingers in between my legs. I wiggled my hands up from their pinned position between his stomach and my chest. If Deacon wasn't gonna help me then it was up to me to make him stop. The rope cut into my wrists like razor wire but I kept wiggling. There was no way I'd lie still and let this happen. My fingers got near the sweaty flabby skin under his neck and I grabbed onto it squeezing as hard as I could.

"Stop touching me," I hissed between my teeth.

Caught off guard, Papa Psion roared up in pain. The table rocked on unsteady legs.

Deacon's bony fingers dug into my ribs.

"You aren't special Eva. Every woman offered must go through the choosing ceremony," he growled in between strained grunts.

My lip curled up into a furious snarl. No one had ever told me about any of this. None of the other girls ever said anything about something like this happening. If they thought I was just gonna play possum and lay there all nice and calm they were wrong. I was smaller and they were stronger but it didn't mean anything. Before I was taken away animal control would stop by my mom's and get possums all the time. But if anyone had a raccoon loose in the yard or attic they wouldn't come out at all. A special animal catcher had to come out and half the time the raccoons got away because they put up the nastiest meanest fight. Just like those raccoons, I was gonna' fight until I got loose.

"So after all these years, you and your boys still playin' with little girls in the dark huh?"

The shuffling, scuffling, and clawing stopped. We all froze with our eyes bulging out of our heads and our chests heaving.

"Mommy?" My voice was a cracked whisper.

The last time I'd seen her I was trying to press a towel over the bullet hole in her stomach.

"Ava? Is that you?" Papa Psion was the first to find his voice. "I, um . . . it's been a while sis. You know I, uh . . . I was really sorry to hear about you and D.J. splitting up, given the circumstances." He stumbled over his words sounding embarrassed and awkward.

As soon as his grip loosened up, I squirmed myself free scooting down off the table. Bits of old straw and gritty dirt met my feet. Derian crossed his arms over his chest. Deacon and Papa Psion stood frozen like they were waiting on someone to tag them back in.

"It was long overdue Psi. But I'm not your sis or sister-in law. You can't call me family anymore. And you obviously ain't too sorry from what I'm seein'."

Squinting against the blinding glare from the flashlight I edged around the mess from the rabbit on the floor. She was standing just inside the double wide doors that led outside. I had a thousand questions to ask her, starting with whether or not what Papa Psion was saying was true but my head wasn't ready to process any of that. Now, I was the one doing the shuffling because my legs were too shaky to take full steps. I still couldn't believe it was her. I'd had so many dreams about seeing her again and I wasted all kinds of time daydreaming about the day she came back. She was a familiar stranger that I'd loved and re-hated over and over again in my head. I cast a sideways glance in Deacon and Papa Psion's direction. Worry that they'd thaw from their positions and grab me before I could get to her made me shuffle faster.

Everyone said she'd disappeared, and once my daddy got out of jail for shooting her, he went to work out of state. The girls at church told me that when old folk say somebody's daddy "works out of state," it was always code for, he found a new family. The story came in as many different versions as the mouths telling it, but everyone ended with momma and daddy somewhere minus me and Leslie.

I stared at her so hard she got blurry and came in clear again. I couldn't figure out if seeing her and hearing her voice meant I was safe or if I was already dead and didn't know it.

"It's okay baby girl, I got you. You're okay."

Her voice floated over the sound of the cicadas and Papa Psion's loud mouth breathing.

My chest tightened with so much relief I thought
I'd pop. That was the voice that used to tuck me
in at night and apologize when I didn't get exactly
what I wanted for Christmas. My legs ate up the
short distance in between us. I crashed into her
hip wishing I could wrap my arms around her.
Something was different about her. I had to compare mental memory notes to be sure she
was the same person. I remembered old pen-
nies at the bottom of a purse and fresh clothes
dried outside on a line. Those were the smells
I remembered. But now she smelled like really
strong cinnamon perfume that clogged up my
nose. She brushed long, pearly, fake claw-looking
nails across my cheek. She used to hate fake nails.

Deacon let out a long sigh. "Okay, what is this
Ava? You know what the scripture says about—" his
tone was flat, almost bored.

"No *Ozias*," she snapped at him.

Ozias? I mouthed Deacon's real name. Nobody
called him that, not even Momma Rose, he was
Deacon to everyone. The air crackled from the
heated look that came over his face.

Momma's foot went to tapping as she sucked
her teeth. "I don't give a fuck about your conceptu-
alized scriptures. I know what my bank statement
says. You've missed *three* mothafuckin' drops in a
gotdamn row. *That* wasn't the damn deal. You ain't
gettin' over on no gotdamn-nobody. I've come to
take my kids back."

Her words echoed inside my head. They were far from what I was expecting her to say. Then I realized she wasn't hugging me or crying a thousand happy tears at the sight of me. She didn't even bother with untying my wrists. Her hand was painfully tight on my shoulder. Her fingers were frigid icicles against my skin, colder than my soaked nightgown. My lower lip quivered as my feelings double-dutched between loves her and loves her not.

"You were never one for manners. Your sister was always the polite one. *In case* you ever wonder why I married Rose instead of you. A woman in a position of power has to be polite. Genteel." Deacon kept his cool distant composure but the meaning of his words carried a ton of heat.

Her fingers clenched into icy needles in my skin.

I gave her a nervous side glance. *Eeew, I know she didn't date Deacon's old crotchety baldy black behind?*

Her spiky-black spider-leg lashes lowered into a nasty glare.

"Hold on now Deac," Papa Psion huffed. He leaned towards Deacon lowering his voice. His argument came out in a rush of hushed words that carried across the empty room. "You just had me tear into a flaming coffin with my bare hands. And that's *after* I gave you what I know was damn near five times what any of the brother's say they've ever paid for one of your *virgin* brides of the church. Look man, our deal is a deal . . . but maybe a different girl —"

Deacon raised a hand stopping him mid-sentence. "We still good Psi."

His eyes were blank and cold as he stared a hole into momma over the top of my head.

"I think Ava here, just got confused about our agreement." He still managed to look rigid and calm, like a master salesman going over a basic lay-a-way plan. "I mean, Ava I did graciously take in your newborn, who's two now in case you didn't remember. *And,* this one here who puts food away like she has an army of tapeworms in her gut. The choosing ceremony is a mandate of the church; it's also me doing you a financial favor. I'm taking care of the debt you owe with the money I get for her."

"What kind of favor is this? I don't want favors. I want my money on time, like we discussed. Don't make me tell *all* your secrets," Ava hissed. "How your fake ass is the furthest thing from sanctified and Derian would probably burn if he ever stepped foot in a *real* church. And Psi we all know you wouldn't be shit if your daddy didn't leave you his church. I'll tell everyone how y'all lie, buy, and sell little girls . . ."

Deacon was in front of us with his hand around her throat before she could finish her sentence. She let me go, to grab pitifully at his hand around her neck. They were locked eye to eye.

"You know good and well when you make deals with the devil, you accept the devil's terms," he whispered. "There's *nothing* to tell Ava," Deacon exploded, shaking her so hard I was worried her neck would snap. Sweat rolled down the sides of his face. He dragged his free-hand back across the light-grey stubble on top of his head flinging sweat to the ground.

I waited to hear it sizzle.

His tongue snaked nervously across his fat lips.

Papa Psion, shifted from foot to foot. Derian, rocked back and forth, still holding the bloody rabbit. My momma had just gone from hero to zero and I was shaking like the room was below freezing.

Deacon patted the top of Ava's head. "Now you can make yourself useful and hold her down while Papa Psion consummates his choosing *or* you can take her place."

She swayed on her feet before straightening up with her shoulders shaking. "Take her," she said without so much as even looking in my direction.

Just as easily as she let me go before, she let me go again. I tried to make a run for the door tripping over my own feet with my vision on underwater exploration. The hem of my pee soaked nightshirt itched the back of my heels. I crumbled to the floor, scraping my knees, but I didn't even feel it over the pain of what she'd just said stabbing me in my chest. Now I could never call her mommy aga~ not after this. She'd just be Ava, as far as I coul~ tell I didn't have a mommy anymore.

Deacon chuckled as he turned towards the men in the room. "Oh, no no no, Ava. That wasn't a question for you. Papa Psion will make the decision."

The sound that came out of the Ava was like the wicked-witch, her monkeys, *and* the tornado were all about to come flying out of her mouth. Her eyes locked on me and I'd swear she hated me in that stare.

Papa Psion's fat bullfrog face split into an ugly grin. He turned to Derian announcing in a loud croak, "take the girl home so she can get cleaned up. She smells like shit. He winked at me. "Our little party's cancelled for now. So no boys honey-bee, you're already engaged. I'll just keep it in the family until you're old enough to appreciate all this."

Derian, dropped his nasty rabbit. He snatched me to my feet and marched me out into the humid musky night air.

I stared through the rearview as the forest swallowed up the orange glow from the shack. Everything I'd ever felt for Ava vanished with that light.

Chapter 1

-Heavenly Father, if I Have Daughters Bless them with the Ability to Peep Game

June 2004

My birthday was only a couple of days away. Turning sixteen should have had me on some mess like cake, car, and party. But since I was stuck living under Deacon's ever watchful third, fourth, and invisible eye, with Papa Psion coming any day now, the only thing I wanted was to get away. You see, in Deacon's church you didn't follow the bible; you followed his interpretation of it or what he liked to call Deacon's Law.

People would give everything they had in offering. Deacon would use his connections to answer their so called prayers. The church was full of business folk, itching the left hand of the person beside them so they could scratch it in the church's pocket. They'd help find you a better job, house, life, it didn't matter. They knew as soon as you started getting what you asked for, you'd tithe more out of thanks. Because law number one was, "anything multiplied by zero is zero."

The Church of Kings would never build wit
somebody that "ain't got" to begin with. And i
didn't even have to be money. You could roll up
like Ava offering your own children too for the
choosing. Choosing could happen at any age,
but Deacon liked to start as early as five or six.
Kids even came with fake adoption paperwork
so neighbors wouldn't get suspicious. That's how
crooked, conniving, and sideways Deacon's church
really was.

Deacon's views on women could get even more
twisted and complex than the Jacob's Ladders
Leslie was obsessed with making out of string. I
was stretched out on my back pretending that
I was paying attention and not trying to take a
nap. Leslie was stretched out on top of me using
my boobs to rest the back of her head.

"And this one is breastbone and ribs," she
announced proudly.

The blue yarn was looped a gazillion times
around each of her little fingers. I nodded, giving
her a mumbled 'mmm hmm.' Each and every one
of those things looked like tangled yarn, or straight
up knots to me.

"Eva, I don't want boobs."

I frowned down over the natural arch of her
eyebrows towards her sandy-brown lashes. She
had no idea how much she reminded me of our
parents. Those brows were all Ava. My girl Storie

ped mine up in the bathroom at school. At
st it stopped everyone from calling me Attila the
un. But then they replaced it with Attila the Nun,
s in don't even try to date me because you will get
none. Not that anyone was every actually checking
for my eyebrows anymore. My chest usually caught
everyone's attention before the rest of me.

I don't even know how it happened. One day
I was five 'one, flat as a board and straight as an
arrow. The next day my boobs were hurting so bad
I'd have sworn Momma Rose was beating them in
my sleep. Yes, on some straight-up African breast
ironing mess. A few weeks later I was still five 'one,
but my hips were wider, my breasts grew, and my
ass had even gotten bigger.

My growth spurt went all out instead of up.
And it made me wish Leslie would stay a kid forever. She'd be super pissed, like Claudia the little
vampire girl that couldn't age from Interview with
a Vampire. I loved the book so much I forgot to
return it to the library on purpose. Had to pay forty-five dollars for a twelve dollar book but that was
easier than letting Deacon find out I'd borrowed
it. But the thought of Leslie with eye-catching,
attention-grabbing, chest-pillows made me shift
uncomfortably.

"Is there a way to just not grow any?" Leslie
asked.

"Why would you say something like that? Ev[e]
girl wants boobs."

"I'm not every girl. And Momma Rose sa[id]
you're leaving us. Sue said if you don't go you'[ll]
turn into Onibaba, the demon witch. And that
you'd start tryin' to eat my skin. But Momma Rose
said it's because you need a man to take care of you
and keep other men off your goodies." She rocked
her head back and forth between my breasts. "I'm
pretty sure she was talking about *your boobs*. So, I
just don't want no man or no goodies. And since I
ain't got any now I can take care of you, Eva."

As usual, whenever my choosing was brought up
my throat would shrink to about the size of a rice
grain. All these years I did everything to protect
her and now she was one talking about protecting
me. I pressed my lips to the top of her thick wavy
hair. Who was she gonna' protect when she still
smelled like a damn baby? Momma Rose had
caked so much Just For Me detangler in her hair it
probably came out her pores when she sweat.

"Les, I told you not to listen to Sue and what in
the world would you do—"

"Why is my TV on channel twenty-two?" Deacon
snatched the bedroom door open letting it bang
against the wall. He stood in the doorway making
his crazed with religion face at us.

*Maybe it's because, I was watching MTV when
you weren't home.* I needed to think up a quick lie

fore he decided to snatch the coaxial cable right
ut the wall to beat us with it. We'd just gotten
cable back in the house from the last time he did
exactly that. He was good for turning a broken rule
into a punishment. It didn't make any sense for me
to be able to have a husband and babies, when I
wasn't even trusted basic cable. There wasn't even
a lock on my bedroom door. Which I was reminded
of every time he just bust right in.

"Because, Momma Rose sits on the remote. And,
sometimes she don't even know it's underneath
her."

Leslie was right on it.

"Yeah, and you sound like you don't have any
sense or upbringing when you use don't instead
of doesn't. Both of you up and dressed in thirty.
Dinner with Ava. In honor of Eva's birthday and
all." He spat his orders and shuffled away yelling
through the house for Sue to get off the phone.

She'd started using telemarketers to practice her
English whenever they called. They'd get stuck on
the phone with her for hours in a reverse outsourc-
ing call center hell.

My breath was already gone and Leslie going
into excited kiddie overdrive on top of me didn't
help. I just stared at the spinning blades of the
ceiling fan until they faded from sight. The thought
of being in the same room with Ava made me see
black. My breath hitched and there was the linger-

ing smell of burning wood and misery. All the ti. hairs on my arms were standing at attention. *Who made Ava, think I'd want to be anywhere near her? Oh, no what if this is it and Papa Psion's ass is there too*. I was getting light-headed from the thought of finally facing it all.

Leslie propped herself up, jabbing me in the stomach with her bony elbows.

"Hello Earth to Eva? I asked you if you think momma will like me. Why aren't you smiling? She used to like me when I was a baby right? What should I wear? Do you think she's with daddy and they want us back? That would mean you wouldn't have to leave Eva." She was out of control with all her questions.

Considering the way things went down the last time I'd seen Ava I could only imagine what this whole dinner thing was going to be about. *Me or money*. Especially since she'd single handedly shut down my bullshit choosing ceremony. I might have seen Papa Psion once or twice since. It left me wanting to hate and hug her for distracting him, even though she hadn't done it by choice.

Leslie was still going on and on about "mommy-this and does-mommy-that facts.

"Damn Leslie, how many times do we have to go over this?" My voice came out harsher than I meant it to. "It's just us and it's always been that way. If I hadn't told you, you wouldn't know a thing about daddy or Ava —" I took a deep breath. "Let's just go pick you out something cute and do something with all this hair okay?"

Half an hour and five arguments later we were dressed. Leslie finally lost the fifth argument on why she couldn't wear her hair in a wavy afro. After taming her mane, I decided that we'd both dress as informal as possible so I picked out stone wash jeans, black t-shirt, and beat up black Chucks for me. Leslie was my twin except her Chucks and her t-shirt dark blue. It was my version of a silent mutiny. Deacon, Momma Rose, and Sue were all dressed like we were going to a formal dinner party.

"What in the world, are we going to a dinner or out fishing?" Momma Rose stared us up and down violently shaking her head. "Where are the sundresses I got y'all when I went to Potomac Mills. We have a reputation to keep up ladies, I can't have ya'll —,"

"It's just Ava, they look better than the condition we got them in. So it's fine," Deacon interrupted her.

As we made the two-hour long drive towards Franklin and Mecklenburg County on what had to be the hottest day in June, they were the ones looking stuffy and overdressed.

Part of me wanted to know what Ava had been up to and why she'd moved all the way out bum-fuck-Egypt. On the other hand I could have cared less. I'd spent six years listening to the gospel. And eavesdropping in on the "nigga-news" at night, trying to figure out who or what Ava was doing before I stopped caring about her not caring about us.

The nigga-news was usually started by somebody that seen what happened and they hooked up the story a little bit before retelling it. By the time it got to you you'd have to pick the pieces apart to find the truth. Like the time they said Ava was hookin' on High Street for a pimp named Reena. That just sounded completely made up, everyone knew women weren't pimps. The gospel was the sanctified, cleaned up version passed down the pew on Sundays. Ava resurfacing was like a punch in the nose. It hurt like hell that'd she waited so long to see us but I kept blinking back tears waiting for that feel-good sneeze that never came. Leslie had been driving me crazy with questions and now she could just ask Ava herself.

We drove for what seemed like hours passing a sprinkling of abandoned wooden shacks.

"That looks like those vampire nests from that movie we watched," Leslie open-loud mouth whispered against my ear.

I tried to melt into the side paneling of the car and peek out the window at them. My toes involuntarily curled into the bottom of my shoe, my chest got that achy heavy feeling. They were rotting reminders with their shutters barely hanging by a nail set against the graying cloudy sky boarded up with old rotted wooden boards. Each shack could have been the perfect safe haven for a vampire, serial killer, or choosing ceremony.

"Deacon, why don't they just tear those creepy things down?" I asked when I couldn't stand the sight of them anymore.

He never took his eyes off the road. It was as if his answer was rehearsed.

"Those houses are older than freedom itself."

What he meant was that they were probably from the slavery days.

We finally pulled up in front of a small wooden greenish-yellow house with rickety shutters. It was all by itself in the middle of the woods at the edge of town. All the spit dried up until my tongue felt like I'd bitten into one of the unripe persimmons Sue had given me one day.

It wasn't the tear-soaking, "I'm sorry and I take it all back" greeting I'd been secretly hoping for. This woman who was supposed to be my mother methodically unhooked the latch on her raggedy screen door. The springs creaked like we about to walk into a crypt. Without saying a word she stepped aside and let us in. Her eyes were red and tired, like she'd been awake for days at a time and was about to fall asleep any minute. I could still see they were the same Jupiter-round light brown eyes as mine, and the same spiky-spider-leg thick lashes. I was expecting her to have wider hips maybe put on some weight, but her orange sundress fit her like a second skin. It tapered in at her tiny waist that was still small as if not smaller than mine.

Her house was dark for the middle of the day. The bare hardwood floor creaked and groaned with every step. Everything was covered in a layer of dust. You could even see the particles in the air as they floated through the tiny slivers of sun that managed to squeak between the aged yellowed blinds. Ava wasn't acting nice, motherly, or even friendly. For all intents and purposes I wasn't going to jump back and forth between her periods of solitude and suddenly wanting to be a part of our lives.

"It's a dirty dirty bird that won't keep its own nest clean," Momma Rose whispered behind her hand to Deacon as we filed into the squelching heat of a tiny windowless kitchen. Leslie, held onto my hand with a vice grip. She stared at Ava in awe and fear. If she wasn't going to speak to me, the least she could have done was acknowledged Leslie. I wanted to scoop her up in a big hug and apologize on Ava's behalf but knew it would be best to just wait until we got back home. Sue was the only one that wasn't the least bit bothered. The other day, I'd overheard Deacon promising her everything from shoes to a cruise. He wanted her to suck his thing in the study and go somewhere, now I know where that "somewhere" was. That was one snooping session I could have done without.

A black bucket sat by the stove with fruit flies hovering over it. I glanced in it and gagged.

"That's for the hogs around back. It's a slop bucket. I don't waste anything. Old food to me is good food to them." Ava spoke to me for the first time since the last time I'd seen her. It wasn't exactly what I imagined our first words to be and if I wasn't mistaken her tone was a little snippy. *I can't help if I've never seen a bucket full of rotten slop. And what happened to all that money Deacon supposedly been giving her?*

We all crowded in Ava's kitchen, waiting to be offered a seat, taking one on our own when we realized she wasn't going to offer. Roaches scurried underneath the cabinets and thick cob webs waved from where they hung in the corners. My Motorola flip-phone dinged in my back pocket. I already knew it was Storie, asking for an update. Trying to make sure I hadn't killed anyone yet. Deacon cleared his throat shaking his head at me. He was strict about my phone and would take it in a heartbeat if he thought I was being disrespectful.

The air was so thick with the smell of salted pork, hickory wood, and mildew I could feel it seeping into my pores banding together to plot a secret blackhead attack. The smell was worse than cigarette smoke and fried chicken grease combined. It was liable to be in my hair and my clothes for at least a full two day stretch. I picked invisible lint off my jeans nodding at the thought that of treating the smell like skunk spray, using tomato juice to get it out.

Once we were all seated at the small wooden dinner table, Ava laid out what I guess was her best. The plates were chipped and cracked and the blue designs that might have been flowers or birds were all worn off. We sat in an uncomfortable silence with the plates clacking against the table like we were strangers with those "hello-my-name-is" stickers on our chests. I quietly scrutinized her as she moved mechanically around the kitchen. I was expecting apologies and instinctive sparks of love to come shooting back. But, watching Ava, with gray starting to creep into her temples and worry lines creasing her forehead, I felt more curiosity about her than anything else.

She didn't look at me or Leslie. Ava didn't look at any of us or say another word as she scooted into the seat across from me. The chair groaned under even her tiny bit of weight. Her back went drill-instructor straight. The veins snaked along underneath the skin on her hands and forearms as she folded her napkin into her lap. *I wonder if that means she has high blood pressure or diabetes. She'll probably get pissed if I ask. Don't ask.*

She glared at my napkin on the table before tilting her head and then glaring down at my lap waiting for me to do the same. I snapped it off the table with so much gusto I'd have made a magician proud. The thin coarse material rested lightly on my lap. This cheap heffa didn't even have real napkins. They were old as day thrift store men's handkerchiefs. *Boy, she had some nerve, have us sitting up in the middle of a pigsty while she's acting like she'd been trained at the academy for spoiled rich bitches.* Ava's eyes were hardened like someone used to having things held just out of her reach. I kept staring at her looking for something, anything to make me feel love or some kind of connection but I couldn't find it.

My stomach complained extra loud. At least the food smelled good. Ava could always cook. She used to turn powdered milk and eggs into a five star breakfast. Dinner definitely was not what I'd consider much of a birthday feast. Mostly because none of the foods were things I liked and they didn't really go together. There were candied yams, Mexican corn with cheese and cayenne, nasty bitter turnip greens which none of us liked, but I remember them being Ava's favorite. She'd made two small glazed hams with pineapple rings and a cherry top. From my angle one looked kind of charred. The other one didn't look as bad which is probably why there were two. Deacon said grace and Ava insisted on fixing our plates. As we ate, it was so quiet you could hear the cob webs shifting in the corners.

I was trying to work down a stubborn piece of ham when Momma Rose's fork clattered to her plate. She started pointing wildly, tapping Deacon's arm. Leslie and I both giggled when she spit her food into her napkin, I looked over curious to see if she'd bitten into a roach. Now, that would have been priceless. Deacon's fork clattered to the table then Sue's. I stopped mid-chew. My fork was frozen in a death grip. My brain was telling my mouth that only Daddies came with tattoos that read, "Do Royal Deeds or Pay Royal Dues," not hams. I got that watery feeling in my mouth around the piece of mystery man-meat. It was the same lettering, spacing, even the same size as the tattoo I'd seen on my daddy's upper thigh.

Deacon bucked up out of his seat. "Ava! Tell me this is your idea of a sick joke. Tell me this isn't what I think it is!"

A brief smile flashed across Ava's face as she raised her fork to take another bite. She pointed the bent prongs at Deacon.

"No Deacon, not what, but *who* you think it is. Psi with his all his lies, he was never good enough to marry our baby-girl and you know it. I was hoping you'd choke on his stinking ass. That *is* where the meat came from since he was mostly fat." She stood up and slapped her hip.

"Your *what*?" Momma Rose suddenly blurt out. Her chest was heaving as she stared between Ava and Deacon.

Sue launched into what must have been every Japanese curse word in the book.

The rickety wooden chair splintered when Deacon slung it out of his way. He charged around the table with the greasy carving knife gleaming in his hand.

My mouth unhinged in slow-motion. The achy hole that'd just opened up in my soul blocked out the sound of Leslie crying next to me. I used the back of my hand to wipe my eyes.

Ava laughed. It was more like a stole-the-winning-base cackle. "Oh, let me guess. You never told Rose about us. Never told her Eva is *your* daughter?" She teased him, dancing out of his reach with more oomph than we'd seen the entire meal. "Don't look so shocked sis. Ain't like you was ever good with men, but you *always* had a way with money. Ozias, you could talk a nun out of her habit and into a bad one couldn't you Deac? So, how much of our inheritance did you sink into this black hole of a nigga Rose?"

"Enough!" Deacon roared lunging at her with the knife.

Ava twirled away from him. She spun past the counter turning to face him with the black barrel from memories past pointed at the center of his chest.

That was the same gun from my real life nightmare all those years ago.

It was too much to process at once. I stared at the sliver of Papa Psion meat on Deacon's plate back to the piece of my daddy on my own. The salty ham but not quite ham taste was becoming more obvious by the second. My chest felt tight. He wasn't my daddy. Deacon was my daddy.

Ava waved the gun around taunting Deacon.

I wavered between wanting her to shoot him and fear that a stray bullet would hit me or Leslie.

The room spun, everything went black. And suddenly I was eight-years old again standing outside our old house in Norfolk.

A scream came from inside. It split the air open like a vocal lightning bolt, spooking the finches out of their nest in a nearby snowball bush. Sweat tickled its way down my forehead. It burned my eyes as I squinted up at the white hot ball of heat in the sky. The flimsy crown I'd been braiding out of dandelions dangled from my fingers. If there was anyone in this world crazy enough to hurt the Devil, it was my momma. I'd never heard a man yell like that in all my life. He sounded like he was hurtin' so bad it made my stomach hurt for him. She'd brought the Devil in and was just a smiling all in my face. Then she ordered me outside to play.

It wasn't fair. Leslie got to stay inside. She was taking a nap in her crib where my Polly-Pocket princess castles used to be. Momma gave away half my toys to make room for "the new baby." Then she spanked me and made me promise not to give the new baby away. I'd tried twice. The mailman laughed at me and walked off shaking his head. Mrs. Tomlinson, the lady next door took her just so she could call my momma and give her back. She had three babies in diapers; one more wasn't gonna make a difference. Snitch. Nobody even bothered asking if I wanted a new baby.

"Hey pretty girl, your momma inside?"

Trisha, momma's old best friend, slinked from around the side of the green truck parked in our driveway, the Devil's truck. Her sugary-sweet voice didn't match the hard look on her face.

I started to nod but stopped. She hadn't been coming over since the day I heard momma call her the b-word on the phone.

She stopped in front of me long enough to pull her bright gold weave back into a black scrungee. It matched her baggy black sweatsuit.

I looked from her to the bomb-pop-blue sky and back.

"Don't lie to me, little girl. You can burn in hell for lying. Is your momma in there? I just wanna' ask her about my shit over here in y'alls drive-way." Her face furled up into an ugly frown as she stared at the truck blocking my usual play space.

"She's busy." I lied, I don't know why momma had Trisha's man inside but if momma didn't like her anymore, I didn't like her either.

"Busy? I bet they busy." She laughed. "Stay your little ass right here."

My answer had the opposite effect of what I'd hoped for.

Trisha went barging up into the house and I waited for the roof to blow off. Minutes ticked by and I dreaded the moment the door would open again. Now I'd catch it from Momma for letting her in and from Trisha for lying.

A tiny squeak slipped out of my mouth as hands grabbed me around the waist lifting me off the ground.

"Why is my Poodah-poo out here sulking all by her lonesome?"

The sound of Daddy's voice made my cheeks feel like they were about to explode from smiling so hard. I squealed. "It's not chicken chow-mein day yet. You're back early." I squirmed around until I could wrap my arms and legs around him like a baby koala. The Navy had sent him away for work right after Leslie was born and it felt like he'd been gone forever.

A deep laugh rumbled up through his chest. "Chicken chow-mein day, girl?"

I pulled my face out of the warmth of his neck. He smelled like iron ships and soapy aftershave.

"Yeah, I was using my school lunch calendar to cross off the days until you got back."

"Well, I flew in ahead of the ship. Couldn't wait to surprise my three ladies. Where's your momma and the baby?"

He sat me down scooping up his big sand-colored sea-bag. The sun made the perfect waves in his hair look like black ocean water. He still had on his dark blue work t-shirt and matching camouflage pants.

I glanced towards the house twisting up my mouth. "It's non-denominational pizza day. She was beating up the devil, and then Trisha came over. She seemed kinda mad." I eyed his sea-bag curiously.

He eyed the green truck.

I poked at the bag in his hand. "So, did you surprise us with surprises too, Daddy?"

He quirked an eyebrow up in my direction and started walking. "You'll see. Tell me where you learned a word like non-denomina . . . wait, what is your momma doing?"

I shrugged taking two steps to match one of his. "You missed it. We had a spelling bee at school, I won first place. Non-denominational was my word. The Devil brought yucky from-anywhere pizza, it just says "pizza" on the box. Not Pizza Hut or anything. I didn't see who he is though. The doorbell rang and momma handed me the pizza and told me put it in the kitchen." I scrunched up my nose for emphasis at the frown creasing his forehead.

His cream-soda complexion was turning about as bright red as the greasy pepperonis I'd just been subjected to. He looked like he could tear down the walls with his bare hands.

"Then she said, I had to eat my pizza out here so she could watch a movie. I don't know what movie he brought. But, when Momma opened the front door I heard her say, 'you are the devil.'" I mocked her voice. "Just like that, and then I went out in the backyard but came up here because there's only dirt back there. No flowers. Then Trisha came over."

He dropped his duffle bag and skipped all four of the stone steps landing square on the front porch. He glared back at me, holding up his hand like Willie-fo-five the hall monitor at school. Willie got a paper badge that said he was supposed to count to five whenever a class lined up to drink out the water fountain. That made him act like *he was directing four lanes of traffic with a five-point sheriffs' badge pinned to his shirt.*

"Stay out here Eva. I'll come get you in a few minutes."

At least he didn't say five minutes. That would have made me scream. I sulked kicking a dirt clod into the side of the house. It was quiet, too quiet. Daddy had probably sat down and started watching the movie or worst, giving out presents.

The storm door was noiseless as I slid inside closing it softly. The living room was semi-dark with the blinds closed and the curtains drawn. The TV wasn't even on which was weird. I tip-toed down the hall, the purple barettes at the end of my pigtails clicked together with each step.

The sound of the shower running was all I could hear while standing outside my parents' room. The door was cracked just enough for me to not be able to see a dern thing. I tipped closer pressing my face up to the gap so I could peek inside. The smell of cherry blossom body wash drifted through the room. Steam crept out of the bathroom. I'd turned to go see if Daddy and Trisha were in my room with Leslie when I heard a weird bumping sound. Somebody was breathing super-heavy in between each thump.

I inched into their bedroom like I was walking on a tight rope.

Clunk, clunk, clunk.

My heart synced up thudding heavily with each thump even though I couldn't figure out what in the world the sound was.

Momma was soaking wet, sitting naked on the lid of the toilet. She usually pinned her weave up when she took showers but it was plastered to her forehead hanging down her shoulders like black seaweed. She rocked back and forth holding herself tight.

I jerked to a stop like I had on an invisible leash.

Her big midnight-black devil was butt-naked with Trisha limp underneath him on the bathroom floor. His shoulders heaved. He banged her head against the tile one last time. She was limp in hands, her head lulled from side to side. Trisha's bright gold hair was this fiery reddish orange. My eyes played connect the dots with the streaks of blood smeared all over the tile. Daddy was sitting propped against the wall. He looked like an old G.I. Joe someone got tired of playing with. His head was down with is chin on his chest.

The devil's back was to me as he walked over and stared down into his face.

"See what you just made me do soldier boy? You want to be playing detective from all the way out there in the middle of the damn ocean? Why would you tell my side woman to come to my other woman's house all disrespectful like that?" The devil questioned him.

Daddy groaned.

The devil shook his head. "C'mon D.J.," he called him by the letters in our last name. Desjardin. "I know you ain't think Ava was all yours. We've been watering the same hole for years bruh. She's carrying my seed right now. Tell the man sweetheart." He tilted his head waiting for her respond.

She swallowed hard before finding her voice. "He . . . he's right."

Her eyes were wide and blank as she stared at the wall in front of her. When I dragged my eyes back momma's devil had pulled a gun from I don't know where and pressed it to daddy's forehead.

"Let's make a deal D.J. I help you turn over your half of what you'd inherit from your father's church to your big brother Psi and I won't even charge you for Trish."

The devil turned the gun towards momma. The crack that the bullet made as it jumped out of the gun was so loud it shook the house, made my spine tingle, and my ears ring. He was a black blur that knocked the wind out of me when he came bulldozing out of the bathroom.

When I came to, Ava's screams from my memory were still ringing in my ears as she squirmed on the bathroom floor. The way her blood looked soaking through her towel as it turned my hands bright red was fading away. All hell was breaking loose around me. I didn't want to wrap my head around Deacon being the devil without a face from way back then but he was and he was more so the devil now. Everything slowly came together in my brain as the bright spots faded from in front of my eyes.

I tried to focus on the bristly-black stubble on the chin of the paramedic leaning over me. My eyes nearly crossed.

"Welcome back Sleeping Beauty." His voice was warm and friendly.

I pushed myself up into a sitting position in the floor. Lord knows when it had been mopped last. Dirt sifted through dark cracks in the splintered floorboards down onto mice and whatever else I could hear scurrying beneath me. Black grit and grime clung to the palms of my hands and I wiped them on legs of my jeans. My stomach made gurgling and bubbling noises as I grimaced up past grease and dark brown stains that I didn't even want to try and identify on the mahogany legs of Ava's table.

"Hi Eva, my name is Quinn. I'm a volunteer paramedic. How are you feeling?" He asked.

Police officers, paramedics, and men in suits marched from room to room. *How am I feeling? I just ate a man-sandwich, learned the devil is my daddy, and he framed the guy I called dad so Papa Psion could inherit a church. I feel sick.*

I croaked out a weak okay over the sound of Deacon's agitated voice carrying from the living room. He was giving his version of what'd happened all over the sound of Ava laughing like she was completely out of her damn mind.

Over channels of static on one of the Officer's scanners someone yelled, "get the Chief back here. I've never seen anything like this! We've got three bodies so far!"

Heavy footsteps thumped towards me. A forensics agent grabbed me by my elbow all but shoving me outside. I stumbled down the three steps planting myself beside the rickety porch with everyone else. Mosquito's whined in my ear and the cicadas were buzzing so loud it felt like they were screaming in terror. Every time the screen door slammed against the wooden frame of the house my heart jerked against my chest. My eyes would search the dark interior and I'd stop breathing, waiting to see if a headless corpse was coming to get me for eating his body. The chatter from the police's scanners in their cars mingled with the beeps and blips from the radios on their shoulders. More cars crunched up the gravel driveway swirling clouds of dust.

My mind was quickly becoming a painful black hole, collapsing into feeding on and possibly destroying itself. Leslie held onto me like a human life preserver. Snot trailed down her nose and around her thumb lodged into her mouth. She hiccupped and cried, soaking my leg through my jeans. My own tears mingled with the human-ham-vomit aftertaste in my mouth were making me feel sick all over again. The police wouldn't even let us get a glass of water for fear we'd contaminate anything from the kitchen to the smokehouse. Ava was led past us to a waiting car. Her expression was blank, like she wasn't even with us anymore. As soon as the officer started reading her rights she turned to Deacon with her eyes blazing.

"Hey, Ozias! You feed us the blood and body of Christ so that we can be more holy. *Right?!* Well, I gave my baby-girls the sinners. So they can be more like the fake-ass, lying, mothafuckas that walk this Earth. Eva, Leslie? Ya'll hear me? " She screamed at us spraying flecks of spit into the air.

The officer tried to lead her towards the car but she jerked away from him. "DJ, and Psi won't no damn saints. Y'all betta run and ruin these niggas! No nigga will eva' run a daughter of mine. *Ever*," Ava wailed throwing herself down to the red dirt like her legs wouldn't carry her anymore. They had to get someone to grab her by each arm so she could be dragged into the back of the waiting van. I didn't even ask which institution they were taking her to.

Chapter 2

Blow me Away

August 2006

The sky was rolling itself into the same dark gray as the sidewalk stretched out in front of us. It looked like the sky on the day of Ava's reckoning. That's what I called it in my head, because none of us were allowed to speak about it since it happened. They identified the bodies as Warren Desjardin the man I'd always call daddy and Papa Psion's ass. But the third body was a mystery still. We were all under investigation for a while basically because Ava kept insisting that she'd done it all for us. Eventually they gave her life in an institution. I didn't even bother going to her sentencing or asking the name of the asylum she was put in. She'd done enough damage to my life in the name of help. I ignored the tight feeling in my throat. I was over Ava.

The only person who'd still come out winning was Deacon. He'd managed to convert most of Papa Psion's followers and he even had the nerve to start planning Leslie's choosing ceremony.

thing had changed but at the end of the day
ything was still exactly the same. It was still
. Leslie and I, no one else, and it was up to me
protect her.

I squelched all the feelings of wrong tugging at
the back of my mind focusing instead on getting
us as far away from Virginia and Deacon as I
could. I was also storming away from a full-tuition
scholarship at Norfolk State. Registration was on
Tuesday and it sucked to think about missing my
freshman year. It cut me to the core not to be able
to tell Storie where I was going, but if she got questioned and cracked, that would be it. No part of
me wanted anything to do with Deacon especially
since my scholarship was probably just a favor
someone owed him. As soon as we got where we
were going I'd start applying for some community
colleges or something.

I marched past all the shops, pubs, and bars that
I'd never get to sneak into. I had a taxi pick us up
just outside of our neighborhood in Portsmouth.
Just in case Deacon went all private-eye on the
outgoing calls, I didn't want him figuring out
where we were headed. The cab driver kept giving
suspicious looks through the mirror the entire
time. I'm surprised he didn't snatch my backpack
to see if I'd stolen all the silverware and jewelry.
I'd never been happier to finally tip and be rid of
somebody.

"Are you sure the two of you are supposed t
out here alone?" He asked as we climbed out.

I nodded. "Yeah, my aunt has a brownstone n
too far from here. And I go to Norfolk State, this i
home for us." I lied.

Satisfied, he pulled off.

For once I was happy with the cool weather even
though it was August. It made it easier to walk
however many blocks we had to go. I kept busy
by admiring all the old historic buildings, that'd
been restored into new storefronts. Even the 7-11
seemed kind of fancy with its old Victorian style
storefront with lanterns and pointed archways.
We wound up on Boush street. Across the street,
park benches and bright pink Dogwood trees
lined the familiar brackish brown-green edge of
the Elizabeth River. A feeling sank into the pit of
my stomach that pulled at the backs of my eyelids
where tears hide.

Leslie was doing the damn march of a thousand
deaths beside me, dragging her feet like she had
cinderblocks tied around her ankles.

She rubbed the back of her hand across her eyes.
"Eva, where we goin'? I don't feel good and all this
walkin' . . . *what* are we walkin' for? You couldn't
get Momma Rose to just drive us to wherever it is?
Urrggh."

*I swear this little girl had one more time to
moan, groan, or growl at me.* I chewed even

...er on the strings of my hoodie to keep the ...d from whipping it off. Bad habit, but I didn't ...ve any gum and Leslie was about to get on every ...st one of my frazzled nerves. We were excused ...rom church because she was sick, not play sick but for real sick. It honestly just sounded like she was coming down with a cold. I'd promised to stay home and take care of her. Since Momma Rose hated missing the chance to show off one of her new outfits she was more than appreciative. There wouldn't be many opportunities for me to be alone with Leslie before Deacon started brainwashing her into choosing ceremony.

I gave her hand a soft squeeze. "We're goin' to the Amtrak station and taking a train to Atlanta. You can sleep all the way there, I promise."

After months of what I'd call "borrowing" from the church's collection I finally felt like I had enough to get us away. Three thousand should get our tickets and get us into an apartment until I could start working. *I hope.* At least this way the money could go towards something useful. It was usually put towards Deacon's mortgage or Sue and Momma Rose's massage or shopping expenses anyway.

"Dang, Eva slow down. What's in Atlanta? Are Deacon and Momma Rose meetin' us there? Eva?"

My backpack cut into my shoulder but I couldn't slow down to adjust it or to accommodate Leslie.

All her questions and whining were ann[oying] me. We only had another couple of hours be[fore] Deacon and Momma Rose got home from chu[rch] and discovered us gone and even less time th[an] that before the sky opened up.

It'd have been nice if I had a car. We were kep[t] under too tight of a leash for that kind of freedom. Deacon had stood in the doorway of my bedroom for a good thirty-two seconds with his lip twisted up in sour disapproval when he found out we'd miss service. He finally gave in, ordering me to check on Momma Rose's navy beans and ham simmering in the crock-pot. Then he rolled out taking my damn cell phone with him. Times like this made me wish I'd learned how to hot-wire a car.

I didn't want to catch another cab or take a bus to the station. The less people we dealt with on our way out of town the better off we'd be. I'd planned on walking but it was already creeping past ten-fifteen and we needed to be there by eleven-thirty.

"Eva? What in the world are you doing out here in this weather?"

I physically deflated at the sight of Derian. He stepped out of the Towne Bank's revolving doors directly in front of us. My grip tightened protectively on Leslie's hand. The last time I eavesdropped on one of Deacon's meetings it was this grown-ass pervert that started asking about a choosing for Leslie.

quinted past him like I hadn't heard a word just said. The wind whipped his tie in all ctions like a cloth viper. His old ass stayed the middle of women's business, clucking and arting more mess than a man should. Anything I aid could and would be misconstrued to make me sound like I was up to worst than no good, so the less I said the better.

I put on my best fake-friendly voice. "Can't talk, running errands for Sue . . ."

For the first time in history the mean, calculating look left his eyes. He focused on something behind me. The smile fell from his face. He turned into a live-action marionette with a bad ventriloquist. His mouth was moving, but someone put him on mute. My fingers went cold and numb. I was too scared to turn around. Scared that Deacon was standing there holding up that bloody crime-scene'esque choosing rabbit.

People trickled out of the buildings and stopped their cars in the street. They rushed by us, their faces were masks of confused panic. Nature's weather-man turned the wind up from weave-destroyer to full blown wind-tunnel. It was as if someone lifted a train out of the station and dropped it right behind me. Leslie and I both jumped from the sudden clap of thunder, she started pulling hard on my hand.

"Please just take me back home now Eva," Leslie begged.

She sounded terrified over the sound of b[...] rushing to my ears. Out just past the boardw[...] and the docks where the ocean went on for miles, [...] funnel stretched down from clouds into the water[...] This wasn't anything like those videos from storm chasers. The videos didn't make me feel conflicted for staring in awe while terror was seizing my insides, pulling at my feet to move.

"I've never seen a water spout," Derian whispered in awe.

The word water spout didn't even sound like something that would look like God's finger reaching down to stir up a body of water. It looked more like a water-tornado. Shame on Deacon, he just had to take my frickin' phone. Everyone rushed out to snap pictures of what I overheard one lady behind me say was an anomaly on the east coast. The Navy ships docked next to the Nauticus museum groaned against their chains. They dipped and rocked from the wind stirred up by the funnel of gray clouds and water churning out in the middle of the river.

Lightening crackling across the sky followed by monster-raindrops was my sign to get us back on course. Leslie was already sick, the last thing I needed was for her to come down with pneumonia or something crazy and it be my fault. We left Derian standing slack-jawed along with everyone else. The rain started coming down sideways in

ding sheets overflowing the gutters. It never
k much to make Downtown Norfolk flood. I
xed my toes against the squishy wetness of my
cks inside my sneakers. Deacon's ears should
ave been ringing from all the names I called
him in my head. And that's when the screaming
started. Without even thinking or looking to see
what had happened, I scooped Leslie up into my
arms. *Big mistake.*

With her head over my shoulder she could see
everything. She shrieked, cried, and screamed ear
splitting gibberish in my ear. I sprinted, chanting
like a marathon runner on the last steps of a 5K
run. We were just a few feet away from a squat
brick building. People were tripping over each
other. Someone was even driving on the sidewalk
trying to bypass all the other cars. The wind picked
up until it felt impossible to run against it with
Leslie's weight. Huge nervous bubbles swelled up
in my stomach turning me into a human lava lamp.
I glanced back for one second, and felt the glass
around my lava lamp go to pieces.

The water spout had decided to grow itself some
legs, turning into a nightmarish blackish-gray
churning tornado. I tripped up onto the sidewalk
in front of a small brick diner. My hands slipped
off the handles as I tried to yank the doors open. A
small lady with short reddish-brown hair stood on
the other side of the glass staring back at me.

"Open the door," I shouted over the wind w
realized it was locked.

She stared at me with Leslie in my arms. I
Bambi-wide eyes were apologetic and full of fear
she raised her trembling fingers to cover her lips
I could see people crouched behind counters and
table tops behind her.

Fire blitzed through my veins hot enough to
dry the rain off my skin. I sucked in a quick breath
and moved on to find a safe place away from
glass and bricks. My chest felt like my rib cage had
shrunk five times over. Leslie had her arms and legs
wrapped around me so tight she was starting to cut
off my air.

I stopped underneath an awning. The entrance
of the building was nowhere in sight and I needed
to get somewhere fast so I could take a knee before
I passed out. My eyes flew to a part of the sidewalk
where four crumbling cement steps led down to a
flat brick wall. It looked like it might have led down
to an old doorway that was walled up with bricks.
Pushing my drenched hair back from my face I
coaxed Leslie down tucking my backpack beside
us.

I kneeled pulling her tight into my chest. The
sky swirled black behind her, hail the size of waffle
balls bounced to the ground and the wind was
finally so loud it hurt my ears. Squeezing my eyes
shut, I focused on using my body to shield hers.

et out! You bitches get the fuck out!"

y eyes snapped open at the sound of the high hed yell.

Derian, of all people was running right at us.

The brick building across the street crumbled like a graham cracker before he threw himself at us. His elbow connected with my eye.

Pain seared across the bridge of my nose shooting down the back of my neck.

He snatched up my backpack throwing it out into the wind and I felt something far worse than my aching face.

"I said get the fuck out!" He screamed, not even sounding like himself.

The space wasn't big enough for all three of us. This time he grabbed for Leslie. Before he could get his hands around her he was snatched up onto the sidewalk.

"What the fuck is wrong with you? She's got a little girl with her. Take this storm and this ass whoopin' like a man nigga. You don't fuck with women and children. *Now*, put your hands on me, c'mon." The man who yoked Derian's ass up pounded away at him like an angry grizzly bear. He accented each word with a punch or a knee to his face or his stomach. By the time he was done the tornado was gone.

I climbed up the steps, speechless at how different the street looked. The rain slowed to a drizzle

and the wind was barely blowing. The
with the little diner was nothing but a pile c
bled bricks. Hot miserable tears filled my
They didn't deserve my tears but I still felt sor
them even as I scanned the street for my backp
All of my money was in there and without it t
storm might as well have done us in. I pressed n
fingers to the bridge of my nose and stood there
shaking my head at my situation. Derian's legs
might as well have been made of rubber. He was
trying to stand but kept toppling back down to the
concrete.

Our rescuer brushed off his jeans and smoothed
the wrinkles out of his soaked olive-green polo
shirt. He wasn't even out of breath as he made his
way over to us. "I think this makes the second time
I've saved you. So you owe me a date."

My face hurt so bad I couldn't even frown at the
man. "All I owe you is a thank you. And you've got
me confused with--"

"No, I know you. You're mom is Hannah Lecter --"

I snatched up Leslie's hand and started walking.
The lava lamp was back except this time I could
feel myself turning bright red. How long would I
have to be connected to Ava this or Ava that?

"I'm sorry. I didn't mean it that way. I'm Quinn.
The paramedic that felt ashamed for staring at
this beautiful sixteen year-old for the good part of
thirty-minutes . . ." his voice trailed off.

gave my hand a soft squeeze whispering,
he wants your goodies."

...ing at her out the corner of my eye I sub-
...ally told her to shut the hell up before calling
...over my shoulder, "well there's nothing to feel
...amed about now. I'm eighteen."

"Well, let me take you and the little miss to
...et some lunch." Quinn nodded giving Leslie an
award-winning smile.

I was two-steps from ripping out all one-hun-
dred and thirty-two of her super-thick lashes
when she batted yes, batted her eyes up at him.

"We would like that. But you mean real food like
a restaurant right?" She asked in a haughty tone I'd
never heard her use before.

"I wouldn't take you anywhere else," he answered.

And I balked. When did my baby sister end up
with more game than me?

With that we all said a silent prayer as Quinn led
us in the direction of his car. Hopefully it was still
in one piece. And if it was, hopefully there weren't
any pieces of anything on top of it.

"Bad fruit begets bad seeds," Derian called out
after us.

I glanced back at him on the ground with his cell
phone pressed to his head.

"Yeah Eva, Deac gonna love hearing how you
just following right along in Ava's footsteps."
Derian called after us. "Hey Deacon, sorry to
interrupt you during service . . ."

I clenched my teeth against the pain in m[...] that was already heavy from the weight of f[...] pressing down on me. If it wasn't for him we [...] on our train to a new life. Now, we were stuck c[...] crash-course with the devil himself.

Chapter 3

Deacon's and Demons Run my Life

I un-did my seatbelt and sat staring out the window at the house that was both a prison and palace. Service normally ended around four-thirty. The bright white numbers on the dashboard of Quinn's Audi were yelling at me, saying I had a half an hour to come up with an exit strategy. He still didn't have a real idea of what I was running from, or that I was even running. Our conversation was catered more to Leslie, which was fine by me. There were too many things buzzing around in my head, all I could do was make polite conversation.

It'd started drizzling earlier while we ate and hadn't stopped. The only reason Leslie wasn't talking our ears off was because she'd dozed off. She talked a hole in Quinn's head after asking for restaurant food and then begging to go to the Pizza Hut buffet. It didn't matter one way or the other to me, my appetite was shot from the moment three-thousand dollars slipped through my fingers.

"Never would have expected to see a water spout and a tornado in one day. Kind of like a life altering

experience," Quinn started saying. He was givir.
me that after-school special look. The kind of loo:
the coach or counselor has just before they tell you
to keep straight and push ahead. He leaned his
head back against the headrest while he sorted out
whatever he was trying to say. His Adam's apple
bobbed up and down. "Back there at Pizza Hut you
said something about going to Norfolk State. Well
what if—"

The door was yanked open, I was snatched out
the car before I could even hear what the "if" was.
Deacon's first connected with all the impact of a
cannon ball hitting me in the face. My head snapped
to the side, blood went pulsing back towards my eye
and poured from my nose at full strength. Momma
Rose's voice combined with Leslie shrieking was
all just a bunch of squawking over the ringing in
my ears. I could feel my knees going out of service
and I braced myself. I could feel myself falling
but, Deacon's hand around my neck kept me from
hitting the ground. If my eye wasn't black yet it was
slowly getting there. His fist went up again and I
willed myself to pass out.

Quinn stepped between me and Deacon. He was
so close Deacon's arm was almost resting on his
shoulder.

"Every punch you land is about to come right
back to you times a thousand old man. I been on an
ass-whoopin' spree today," Quinn growled.

Deacon's fingers tightened around my throat in a quick warning squeeze before he let go. Maybe he figured out Quinn was the same guy that put Derian on his ass earlier. Quinn pushed me out of the way as Momma Rose rushed over in a flurry of apologies with her fingers going all over my sore face.

"I'm sorry Eva. Why would you do something like this? You know how he gets," Momma Rose cooed at me with her eyes full of worry. "Sue! Sue, take the baby in the house and get me some ice ready for Eva."

I watched Deacon and Quinn over Momma Rose's shoulder. The words police, and child protective services floated towards me over the sound of Leslie whining about being called a baby. She immediately launched into telling Sue how we'd just gone on our first date with a man, her sickness long forgotten.

Momma Rose cupped my cheeks with onion and lemon dish soap scented fingers saying whatever grown folk say to make you feel special after you get hit like you're nothing. I didn't listen. I stared at the space just above her eyes at the reddish-brown frame surrounding her face. Her foundation was about two shades lighter than the rest of her and her eyes were all done up with silver and blue eye shadow. That was her look.

"We talked and sometimes I just let that fool have his way so I can go about my busin in peace. But I can't let this one go and he isr hearing a thing I say."

I squinted at Momma Rose, trying to understand what she was saying or apologizing for. Her whole demeanor was off.

"Deacon only offered you in the choosing to get you out of the house before I found out you were his."

One by one my muscles locked into place. I tensed up as flashes of my choosing and then Ava's dinner flashed across my mind. It's a damn shame we can't delete memories. If there was a way to get a sorbet spoon and just dig those memories out I would.

Momma Rose went on, "Deac has decided to keep Leslie for himself. I'm not sure when he plans to have her ceremony but his mind is all but made up." Her voice cracked.

I clenched my hands into fists so tight my knuckles cracked. Heat rushed up my neck flooding my cheeks and exploding behind my eyelids in bright red flashes of pain and hatred.

"Don't do it Eva," Momma Rose whispered her warning. "He controls too many people who will turn their eyes and call you a runaway if he decides to put you back in that box. Just do what me and your momma didn't. Go to school and be smart

ugh to know when you should and shouldn't
t. Leslie will be fine."

Quinn had started walking toward us. His face
as just as stormy if not more so than mine. It
lidn't take Momma Rose but a half a glance in
Deacon's direction before she dropped her eyes to
the ground and bustled over to patch up his ego.

All the air deflated from my chest as I leaned
back against Quinn's car.

"You over here lookin' like someone just robbed
you of your favorite puppy," Quinn said with a
smile before leaning on the car beside me. He
nodded in Deacon's direction. "So, I got that nigga
to see things my way. He knows not to lay a hand
on you or I'll come for him when it's nice and dark
and he can't identify me to the cops."

A weak smile was the best I could do. It wasn't
me that Deacon wanted to put his hands on. It was
Leslie.

"Oh and I don't think he liked hearing how I
was the volunteer EMT who rode with your mother
from the jail to the asylum after her sentencing.
Before she was sedated, she kept saying, *Deacons
and demons run my life, three lost father's three
lost daughters,* over and over."

My head was about to explode from T.M.I., too
much information overload. Why did everything
have to revolve around this Deacon and the invisible chain he'd managed to wrap around my life?

It didn't surprise me at all, knowing he just u
Ava. His finger pulled the trigger in the bathro
all those years ago. If he didn't care about the ba
Ava was carrying when he shot her, I know h
wouldn't give a damn about Leslie even if she end
up being his third wife.

Quinn put his arm around my shoulders. I
leaned into his side, wishing I could absorb some
of his heat and strength.

"It'll be fine. You sure you don't need to go to the
hospital?" Quinn asked.

I slowly shook my head to keep my brain from
banging around and making things hurt even
more.

"We'll figure this out and in the mean time
you've got me. By the way, I teach a course on
campus, sign up for it and I'll make sure you're
good. And call me Que."

Chapter 4

Like Sugar for Candy

May

A storm was coming. Battleship-gray clouds churned into a dark unified wall outside the office window. Nothing about spring or summer rains appealed to me, not the damp muddy smell in the air or the way the clouds hovered over the buildings like a scene right out of *Ghostbusters*. The few pigeons flying around that were brave or too stupid to find cover fought against the wind like tiny black kites. It brought back memories from the day Ava dragged us into her insanity. From my experience, storms never brought in anything good.

"Eva?"

I jerked my attention away from the window back to Mrs. Porter, the assistant dean, who was busy studying me through the haze of her hazel contacts.

So much for keeping my head out of the clouds. The only time someone got called into the assistant dean's office was for an award or an accusation and I wasn't too thrilled about finding out which one I was up for. I had been trying not to fidget while politely waiting for her to finish looking over my file. It must have been written in Latin based on how long it'd taken her to read over it. During that time I'd absentmindedly folded into myself in the chair across from her. My ankles were crossed and my legs were as far back under the chair as I could get them. A fake smile stretched the corners of her bright red lips upward as she propped her elbows up on the arms of her chair and began tapping her steepled fingers together. Mrs. Porter brought to mind all the well-to-do women I saw in church, which automatically put her on my "phony fake" list. I'd seen too many women smile that same smile all up in Momma Rose's face only to hear about them trying to talk "privately" in Deacon's office later. Those heffa's had no idea he told Momma Rose everything. Momma Rose and Deacon had no idea I could hear everything they said through the vent in my bedroom floor.

"Eva, I know this is a sensitive subject." Mrs. Porter leaned forward giving her best "fake care" face. "Most freshmen have the misconception that dating a professor will help them get ahead, but that is not the case. I don't want you to feel pressured but is there anything you would like to tell me about any of your professors?"

My heart did a swan dive into my toes. Granted yes, I'd been secretly seeing Que who was now my political science professor, but we were always careful. I still had Deacon and his "no men outside of the church" policy and the fact that messing up on my part meant a rushed ceremony with Leslie on his part. He'd been letting it hang over my head until the situation was darker than the clouds outside the window. The last thing I needed was to have mine and Leslie's situation jacked up by someone who complained because they got a lower grade point average than they thought they deserved.

Leaning forward I looked at her with real concern on my face. "No, ma'am. Why, is one of my professors some kind of pervy serial student humper?"

She pursed her lips together looking down at the papers on her desk before answering. "No, Eva, but if there's anything you'd like to tell me about any of your professors please don't hesitate. Your family's church goes way back with Norfolk State and they make generous donations to our programs." She paused and her massive Reebok Pump orange bosom expanded, straining against the buttons on her suit jacket. "Programs that pay scholarships such as yours. Needless to say it's imperative that you and I work together to ensure your collegiate career stays its course. That will be all if you don't have anything to add."

With that I gave her a quick nod and
myself on up out of there before she pop,
started in with more questions. *I couldn't m*
through my first year without any drama?
enough I get stuck living at home instead of
campus. Get on the ball, girl, you've got to g
on the ball.

My brain was telling me to get to my next class
so I wouldn't get caught in the rain but I'd been
ignoring my brain a lot lately. Skipping Mr. Jiel's
review in statistics right before our big exam was
about to be number two on my list of dumbest
decisions ever. The number one spot couldn't even
go to me whipping out my phone and texting Que
to meet me ASAP.

When I left the house that morning, it was sunny
and almost seventy. Now the wind had picked
up bringing an unseasonal chill; it was whipping
the mess out of my 1b shoulder-length curls. I'd
meticulously placed every curl so they framed
my naturally round face perfectly. I didn't grab
an umbrella or a hoodie, and instantly regretted
leaving the house in nothing more than a fitted
V-neck T-shirt. It was the one Deacon hated with
the word JUICY across the back in big pink letters. A
mischievous grin spread across my face as I hiked
across campus toward my car, thankful that I'd at
least worn jeans.

ttle champagne-brown beater Protégé
e first grownup thing I could feel proud
acon had no choice but agree when I said I
getting myself a car. He didn't have the time
shuttle me back and forth between classes.
slie and I would be out of here as soon as I
ould save up enough. No more stealing. Some
poor guy named Morris got blamed for all the
money I'd taken. Deacon even pressed charges and
everything without seeing him do it. All because he
had low friends in high places.

I hoisted my backpack over into the passenger
seat and prayed the window wouldn't fall like it
was prone to do.

"I've got one hour. Get in," Que called out from
his car behind me.

I whirled around at the sound of his voice, uncertainty making me hesitate for a half of a breath
before getting in. Everyone was in class so the
street was virtually empty. His voice still made me
feel like the day of that freak tornado. Like there
were spiders crawling all over themselves inside
my stomach. I settled into the passenger seat
happy that the seat warmer was on. He always did
thoughtful things like that.

Que treated his car like a baby and although
he'd given me enough to buy a nicer ride I settled
on the Mazda, saving the rest for the day Leslie
and I could officially jump ship. There was never a

speck of dust or so much as a receipt lying around inside of his platinum-silver Infiniti. Not even ash or the minty tobacco odor lingered from the long brown Nat Sherman cigarettes he smoked every blue moon.

"Did you wake up with me this morning?" He licked his lips, locking me into his hypnotic brown gaze. He always asked that same question whenever we saw each other and it always had the same effect on my senses. My skin tingled and my pulse would stutter in my chest. Breathless, I leaned across the armrest lightly brushing my heart-shaped lips to his. He pressed forward like a starving wolf, parting my lips and our tongues made frenzied circles around each other. The prickling from his goatee against my face combined with the leathery roughness of his firm lips made my panties wet. As if he could read my thoughts he broke away and started eying me up and down.

"I wanna taste you. Take your pants off." He sucked his bottom lip between his teeth. His words made me hotter than steam.

I shook my head. "Um, no, sir, not here. And we have to talk. I got called into the assistant dean's office and she didn't exactly say your name or how she knows but—"

"Shhh. Pants off," Que ordered while putting the car in drive.

I gave him one last eye-popping glance before obliging. My fingers were shaking so bad I had to bite my bottom lip just so I could focus. I didn't even bother untying my DCs and slipped them off my feet.

He wasn't the handsomest man in the world and he for damn sure wasn't the most articulate, but how many science nerdy types were? At five foot one, Professor Quinn, or Que as I called him, was shorter than me by a good inch. He had a rough, gravelly voice, bushy eyebrows, he could beat anyone's ass and his sex game was insane. Not in an Ava kind of insane but in a good way, if that made sense.

Most women probably took one look and went in the other direction when they saw his splotchy beetle-brown skin scarred from years of not eating right and battling bad acne. He actually brought to mind one of those short stocky beetles that fly into everything at night. He wasn't fat, but he wasn't in the best of shape either. None of my friends knew about him and I sure as day wasn't trying to let the school or my church find out. If anyone ever asked what or why I was even doing this fool in the first place I could try to explain all day but they wouldn't understand.

Que would strut into the lecture hall in wrinkled blazers with worn-out elbow patches. He dressed like work attire meant rolling out of bed, grabbing something off his floor, and splashing coffee in a cup. His facial hair was always grizzled and unkempt but confidence surrounded him like a force field. That confidence, combined with the goose bump–inducing gleam in his eyes, was what made me accept his invitation to lunch the first time he asked and I was glad I did.

He started flipping through radio stations before giving up and switching to his favorite custom mix in the CD changer. I wiggled my bottom out of my jeans taking the time fold them neatly to hide my nervousness. We parked on the top level of a parking garage off Bank Street. It was hard for me to get out at night since I involuntarily volunteered at church most evenings and worked in the church bookstore on others. Que had gotten good at finding places outside of hotels close to campus for us to play.

Usher serenaded us: "Can you handle it if I go there, baby, with you?"

The lyrics hit me dead center. At some point I'd gotten tired of hearing all my girl's dicktales and sexcapades. Deacon would kill me and Momma Rose would pray for Jesus to raise me up so she could kill me all over again, if either of them found out I was dealing with someone outside of the church. I wanted my first to be my decision not theirs. They'd agreed not to make me do another Choosing Ceremony; I thought they were more afraid of Ava breaking out of her asylum if she got word. Ever since October we'd managed to sneak away at least three times a month. Every time he taught me something new or did something completely unexpected, I could feel myself slipping into love.

I climbed into the back seat expecting him to follow when he shook his head at me. "Get on your knees facing the back window and slide your panties down."

Since the upper level was outside I was beyond thankful for the dark window tint. Thunder roared across the sky rattling the car. The air hummed silently in its wake before fat droplets of rain came hissing down. There was the familiar crackling of a wrapper being torn as I slid my panties off and assumed the position. *Good thing I'm already wet.* My breath got caught somewhere between my throat and my lungs. My nails dug into the black leather seats like we were going a hundred miles an hour and I was holding on for life.

Que rubbed himself across my lips before easing in. He felt rock solid, surprisingly cool. His arms wrapped around my body so he could tease and play with my nipples. Confusion swept across my face as he eased back and began slurping and sucking his way down from the base of my spine. I was trying hard to process how he could be inside me and simultaneously nibbling my left butt cheek.

He paused. "You'd better not drop my candy bar, Eva; it needed a little more sugar."

His voice broke through the sex haze over my head. I caught a glimpse of a Milky Way wrapper before his hands spread my cheeks apart and his mouth went back to setting my skin on fire.

Oh he isn't about to lick my . . . I need to stop him before that tongue hits the deodorant I put in my butt crack. Embarrassed I reached back and he swatted my hand. I know putting deodorant in your booty crack sounds weird but it was a habit I'd picked up ever since I hit puberty and my booty decided it wanted to sweat like an armpit. Momma Rose used to have a fit about buying me both Dove and Secret but I was too ashamed to tell her the real secret behind the extra Secret deodorant. One swipe every morning and I stayed dry and cucumber-melon fresh all day.

My eyes widened and my mouth froze into the shape of Pluto. Invisible fingers tap danced down my spine, involuntarily arching my back. Something along the lines of a whimper and a gasp managed to slip through my lips. Que made head-spinning laps with his tongue around parts of me that'd never seen the light of day let alone another person. I was buck-naked in the back of a man's car in the middle of the day with a Milky Way in my lady bits. It made me feel like the dirtiest woman in the world and secretly I loved it.

My fingers were cramping from clutching at the seats. "Que . . . Daddy, please."

He barely slowed down. "Please what? Say it."

He slid his candy bar deeper before easing it out torturously slow. I squirmed backward whining at the empty achiness. The soft shushing sound of skin sliding against danced up to my ears and I visualized his hand sliding up and down the length of his rigid shaft. He was just waiting on me to tell him what I wanted. The shushing stopped and my mind stopped as his thick, warm fingers danced in the slick puddle between my legs. He dragged a calloused finger across my throbbing pearl, stiffened his tongue and went in trying to get all the sugary goodness out of my cookie.

I pushed desperately against his face and fingers. "Take it, daddy, make me cum please." I broke down begging, talking dirty like he wanted.

Thin, breathless moans eased from my lips mixing with the storm outside and Trey Songz's "In the Middle."

Veins of white-hot lightning spread across the sky shooting through the clouds. I glanced back. He licked my juices off the candy bar easing himself deep into my center hitting my G-spot on the way in and then again out.

I could feel a different kind of lightning firing up inside me and I closed my eyes.

Que groaned. "My good girl, like that good dick down. You ready to cum for me, baby?"

I could barely nod. I was beyond ready. His fingers dug into my hips as he slammed into me over and over like a man possessed. I was feeling the sweetest torture, stuck somewhere between heaven and not wanting to go to hell. Fat moonshine-clear tears of feel good, ran down my face. Liquid heat coated my insides.

The words "I love you" climbed their way up my body pulsing, winding, and finally tightening into a solid convulsion that launched them into the air as I gave in to the power of my own release.

The second scream that tore its way up my throat was from the hooded figure that'd manifested from the mist of the rain stinging the ground. Azrael, the death angel, stood with the open-mouthed barrel of a gun pointed directly at us.

Chapter 5

Words Are Weapons

Glass shattered, flying like sparks; I dropped down drawing my knees into my chest pressing my naked back against the cold leather of the back seat in terror.

"Oh shit, oh shit, oh shit," Que chanted. "She done lost her fuckin' mind." He scrambled into the driver's seat.

"What's the matter, Quinn? I know you ain't think you could run around without somebody lettin' me know. You can't hide from home, nigga, you . . ."

I stuck my nose over the back seat, trying to catch a quick glimpse of this murder mood wrecker without getting my head blown off. The wind had lifted the hood off her head but that didn't do anything to cool her temper as she got closer to the car. I hit the floor. Another bullet took the side mirror off Que's car. Her words were drowned out by the sound of the squealing tires and the wind howling over the car as we sped away.

Blood trickled down the side of Que's neck. I'd never seen anyone get shot except on TV, so unless she had a really powerful dart gun it was probably from the broken glass.

"Who the hell was that, Que?" My voice trembled. The icy, vengeful gleam in her eyes replayed in my head. She looked like she was on some kind of hit woman for hire mess. I shimmied my panties up, straining to reach over the center console for my pants on the floor in the front.

Que slammed his fist into the steering wheel blasting air out of his scuba-wide flared nostrils.

"It's not what you think, Eva. That was Cameron, my wife . . . soon to be ex-wife now. I can't believe she just tried to shoot me."

I stopped mid-shimmy and stared at him in slack-jawed disbelief. The rain soaked my hair through the rear window but I was oblivious to it. The churning in my stomach mixed with the feeling of gritty hostility rising up the back of my throat had me fighting to swallow. I cracked my knuckles. The ugly "worried about his wife trying to kill him" face he was making pissed me off more by the second. He didn't wear a ring, never said anything about a wife; he even answered his phone no matter what time of day or night I called or texted. Blood rushed up to my neck and face. The reality of being played hit my ass like a blazing injection of jealousy. It started at my toes creeping its way up my body.

Something was howling in my ears. It was louder than the wind through the windows and sharper than any of Mariah Carey's highest notes. It was my own voice. Tears slashed their way across my cheeks blinding me. Screaming, I clawed my way across the back seat jerking the steering wheel in his hands. Que must have thought I was having a typical hysterical female moment until the second my fingers wrapped the steering wheel.

"Eva! What the fuck?"

Metal grated against concrete. Sparks shot from underneath the car. Que managed to pry my fingers off the steering wheel. I then wrapped them around his neck as best I could. We bounced across the median into the oncoming traffic on the other side. High beams flashed and horns blared. We zigzagged and weaved but I was not letting his ass go. Sweat rolled down his face making his neck slick and hot.

It was different when I was eight. I couldn't do anything about the ball of bitterness in my chest when they brought Leslie home. This wasn't even the same as when Psi put his fat, nasty-ass hands on me.

"I gave myself to you and you lied to me," I screamed against his face. "I want you to hurt. I want you to die."

Que turned to look at me over his shoulder and I noticed we'd stopped on the side of the road. I wasn't expecting the hurt and resentment that I saw in his eyes. I almost killed us, but hearing it bothered him more than me doing it.

I took my hands off of him and forced myself to breathe until we got back. Ava had said, "Don't get played, don't be a fool," and I'd done just that.

I grabbed my shoes feeling perfectly fine with sitting in the back seat until we got to my car. There was nothing in me that wanted to be close to him without killing him.

Cameron, Que's wife, was supermodel tall. Even with her hair slicked down in a matted black mess and her mascara running down her cheeks she was still beautiful. I wasn't runway size or sample petite; on a good day my ass was at least a size ten.

We pulled to a stop beside my car. Que turned to me with sad eyes. "Eva, I'm sorry you had to be a part of that. This doesn't mean anything changes. My marriage was over long before I met you. I'm gonna see you again right?"

The reckless me from moments before was gone and now I felt shy, almost embarrassed. Unable to look him directly in the eye I shrugged. "I'm not sure and I've got classes, work, and—"

"Here." He pressed his money clip toward me packed with hundreds. "I can be all the work you need and then some."

Shaking my head at him, I started reaching for the door handle. It was beyond tempting, but I had my pride. *On second thought if his wife puts me on blast I might have to haul ass in the middle of the night. I'll make sure to tithe extra out of it on Sunday.* I grabbed the money clip stuffing it into the back pocket of my jeans.

Making the rest of my classes was the furthest thing from my mind. I just wanted to get home, shower, and go to bed.

My phone rang and I answered without looking. "What is it?" I snapped thinking it was Que.

"Damn, homie. Well, since my bestie-boo didn't show up for Mr. Jiel's review I recorded the lecture. What's the matter?" Storie asked.

Growing up Momma Rose would tell me over and over to pray for discernment so I'd know the difference between friends and friendly folk. She'd say, "Fall and watch what happens. Friendly folk'll stand back sayin', 'I'm prayin' for you.' Friends won't be worried about where you are, what time it is, or getting their knees dirty. A friend will get down, pray, and then pull you up." Storie was no part of friendly folk; she was a friend. I felt low for not letting her in on what just happened but I didn't have the strength to put it into words yet.

I put on my best front. "Everything's fine, girl. Leslie has been blowing up my phone texting about going to the movies or something, I thought it was her. Let me call you when I get in the house. I'm driving."

Thankfully, she seemed preoccupied enough not to notice my voice cracking. Storie looked stuck-up but she was cool as hell once you got to know her and she had zero filter. Her thoughts hit her brain and then they fell right out her mouth; that's how it worked. She'd been my ride-or-die guardian angel since ninth grade when she beat Big Keish up for me in the girls' locker room. These days she spent more time fighting with Bear, her boyfriend, who according to her was only useful in the bedroom.

By the time I got home, the rain had gotten worse and the street was only minutes away from being classified as a murky raging river. Not even fazed by the weather I pulled into the end of the driveway and dragged myself out of the car and squished my way through the front door. My thoughts were pin-balling back and forth between Que and his pop-up wife. *Does he touch her the same way he touches me, kiss her the same? Out of all the people to give my virginity to, I picked a married one.* The whole thing was making my head hurt.

"Eva, you're home just in time." Momma Rose floated toward me. "Where is your jacket and umbrella? You're drippin' all over the floor. Let me get you a towel. You trying to catch your death out there, baby?"

A shadow of a smile played across my lips as she fussed to herself. She dashed toward the laundry room drawing my eyes toward Deacon sitting on the couch. I hadn't even noticed they had company and was glad I could blame the way I looked on the foul weather. Momma Rose always did her best to be a better mother to Leslie and myself than the one we had. Deacon on the other hand was always looking for an arm or a leg to help pull him to a higher level of the barrel.

He nodded at the guy sitting across from him. "Eva, meet Dontay. The church is offering him a home for a couple of weeks."

My eyes whipped from Deacon to the stranger sitting in our living room. Leslie was only eleven and starting to get boobs and all that good stuff. What if he was a pedophile? Even though Deacon probably wouldn't have turned him away even if he was. Deacon was disgustingly committed to appearances. I forgot about Que and the hollow hole in my chest for a split second. I assessed this so-called homeless guy that "the church," or in plain English Deacon, was taking in.

Thank you, sweet little seven pound eight ounce Baby Jesus for bringing chocolate colossus out of the arena and into my living room. Dontay was sitting forward with his elbows propped up on his long legs. He was probably being put to sleep with all of Deacon's rambling but under the surface of

boredom he seemed alert. Good thing my girl Sto[...]
wasn't here because she'd have marched over an[...]
rubbed her panties on him to mark her territory. [...]
barely got a half of a smile when he finally decided
to acknowledge me. His bright granite-gray eyes
met mine briefly and he nodded before turning
his attention back to Deacon. It might have been
my imagination, but I'd have sworn his expression
mirrored how I was feeling inside. He looked like
he'd lost or was missing someone too.

Chapter 6

Dontay
Gardens Always Attract
Wild Thieves and Other Wild Things

Eva had walked in looking like she'd just won a campus wet T-shirt contest. I did my best to look at anything other than her mermaid-like figure with her jean-busting hips. It only took a glance at the sullen expression hidden under all that soaked hair to see something was wrong. She squeaked and squished past us nearly slipping and falling on her face. My lips quivered as I fought back a grin and I forced myself to refocus. I had bigger problems to deal with. Deac was talking about whatever when all a nigga really wanted to know was where I could lay my head.

This church mouse shit wasn't conducive to getting my Cali green, or daily dose of THC. Even though that's what got me in this mess in the first place. The white boy I used to buy my shit from hooked me up every time he came back from visiting his people out in Cali. His moms was the trophy wife of this dude who hopped on the Oregon Trail and got rich growing for them medicinal marijuana farms. White Boy hated his stepfather for reasons he never disclosed. But he would get the best shit from out there, roll it into these little cigarillos, seal the box, and walk right through the airport with it. That wasn't major; the major part was the robbery we were planning. I'd gotten my crazy-ass homeboy who moved to VA from Staten Island, or up top as we called it.

The way I figure it, every dude has to evaluate the face value of another one. If a nigga says he ain't, can't, or don't, he's lying. I don't mean we go into detail like analyzing a dude's eyes and ass. It's a bare-minimum basic scale that alerts your man senses to the niggas you'd better not leave your woman alone with down to the ones you shouldn't go toe to toe with. Capo was someone I'd categorize as a triple threat. He looked like he just walked out of somebody's prison rockin' them G-Unit tank tops all year round to show that shit off. Even when he wore a button up, all the buttons would be undone. My homeboy Bear would say it was because the dude ain't know how to fasten buttons. On top of the being prison strong, with paper stacked, Capone was officially board-certified, sealed, and probably never released, crazy as fuck.

Deac was saying something about the backyard and how it got overrun with frogs in summer. It made me think back to the night that got me up in here.

Crickets and frogs chirped in unison around us. The moon spied on us through the trees as if it were God's eerie silver all-seeing eye. We were on the outskirts of the field and already surrounded by the dank evergreen aroma like ground-up pine needles with a little oomph. Adrenaline was pumping through my system tightening my chest making my ears ring. I adjusted my camouflaged, insulated jacket making sure my piece was ready to go at my hip. My body temperature was already abnormally high but now it was going through the roof. I duct taped sticks and branches to my arms and legs before pulling down my insulated face mask.

Capo walked over looking like Swamp Thing. The corners of his mouth turned down into his traditional scowl. He always looked like he was mid-scratching the back of his throat or about to hack something up.

"Nigga, that must be a harvest moon up there, because we about to rack up out this bitch." Capo tried to whisper but he had one of those gruff voices that made it damn near impossible.

I was just as excited as he was but I intended to stay focused until we'd seen the plan through. Adrenaline had me on ten. My blood was rushing to my ears until they went on sonar trying to pick up any non-forest-like sounds. Capo taped shrubs to my back and I returned the favor. We worked quickly and silently layering ice from the bucket we'd dragged up from the truck into the inside of our jackets and pants. It was White Boy's idea to use those face masks chicks put over their eyes for dark circles. Ain't even ask how he knew what they were for, or why. I just figured it was a white boy thing. We wore those underneath our skullies.

Cali law only lets niggas grow five plants per person so the growers would band together and form collectives. Most guarded their crops stupid close. I'm talking shotguns, Rottis, or Pits, but not White Boy's people. There were thermal imaging cameras somewhere above our heads pointed at the field in front of us. This collective monitored their crops from the comfort of their own homes. Big mistake. With our body temperatures lowered we were damn near invisible, and the shrubs taped to our clothes would break up any heat signature making us look less like men and more like deer or dogs. The shit we were about to cake up on was thirty-five people deep and well worth freezing my balls off for. That was a good 175 plants pushing at the max a pound each. And since a pound could go for three to four Gs. Shiiiiit.

White Boy was waiting at the edge of the woods with a produce truck Capo "found." The plan was simple. We were going to layer the plants one by one onto a tarp we'd hiked in, wrap 'em up and Capo's prison-strong ass could lug 'em out.

"Tay, I heard somethin'." Capo crouched down with his hand on his piece.

I didn't hear shit, but I still crouched with my head cocked trying to pick up on what he heard just to be safe. We needed to get moving, I could feel a thousand pinpricks on my skin as the ice settled against my body.

"I don't hear anything, Capo man, we're good. Let's get started in case we need to hit up a gas station for more ice."

The whites of his eyes shifted around nervously under the blue glow of the moon. He rolled his head from side to side cracking his neck; it sounded like snapping twigs. We stayed crouched down and made our way into our field of green. The scent was even more powerful and I wanted to light up and kick back. Capo pulled the first plant out of the ground and we silently celebrated. I wrapped my gloved fingers around a plant and tugged.

"Gaba-ga."

I whipped toward Capo. "Nigga, da fuck? Was that you? Stop playing, man."

He was bug-eyed. "Fuck no, I thought that was you."

You know niggas don't do woods, or forests, camping, or nature in general. The field was now tomb quiet as even the crickets were too scared to chirp. We waited like twin warrior statues ready to spring to life and take down anything that crossed our paths. After several moments of complete silence I let out an exasperated breath and went to pull another plant. My sweat mingled with the smell of my fear and anxiety as I ripped yet another Jurassic fern from the ground. Capo did the same tugging wildly at a particularly stubborn plant.

"Pick a different one, nigga. This ice is melting faster than I thought; we ain't gonna be invisible for long," I hissed in his direction.

Refusing to be beat by a plant he yanked hard. The roots ripped free from the ground with a loud crunching sound.

"Gobble-ga!"

The sound pierced the air like a phantom Indian war cry.

"Hey, hey, what the fuck." Capo shot up from his crouched position, dropping our money trees and pulling out his piece.

My lips barely moved. "Don't shoot unless you want every armed cowboy, hillbilly, and hippie within earshot to come straight here."

Soulless onyx-black eyes attached to what looked like a vulture in a Triple Fat Goose bubble coat headed straight for me. I rolled to the side dodging the devil bird and it set its sights on Capo.

"Wha . . . wa . . . wait . . . Hold up." He let out a chilling, bloodcurdling scream hitting the ground so hard it shook. He writhed in pain clutching his *junk with one hand. He'd pulled his piece back out from his waistband with the other hitting the wild turkey. "It tried to eat my dick." "Gobble, gobble, gobble, gobble, gobble!"*

All the noise spooked the entire flock. Turkeys as tall as my waist and so big around they'd have put Charlie Brown's great pumpkin to shame burst through the foliage. When I was a kid, one Thanksgiving I watched a special on National Geographic. All I could recall was that everything on 'em was sharp. Their night vision wasn't worth a damn though. That would explain why they were everywhere, running into and pecking wildly at each other. Pain shot up my leg as one of their beaks caught my ankle going Lord knows how deep. Capo dragged himself up off the ground. We were outnumbered and ill-prepared, leaving us no alternative but to limp away defeated in disbelief.

White Boy fucked up. His people didn't have dogs, or guards, because they didn't need anything more than cameras. The only things standing between me and my field of dreams were forty twenty-five-pound Thanksgiving dinners with ball-height beaks. To make matters worse Capo got pinched for that produce truck on the way back to VA. I'd become public enemy number one on his shit list.

"Dontay? Dontay?" Deac snapped his fingers to get my attention.

I blinked rapidly clearing my mind.

"Well it looks like I've bored you into la-la land." Deac stood with a sigh and I followed his lead welcoming the chance to stretch my legs.

"Okay, let's get you to your room. Should be nice having another man around the house. Keep in mind I have a machete. I'll chop it off and be forgiven before it"—he nodded in the direction of my manhood—"ever hits the floor."

I swallowed hard at his threat and shoved my hands deep into my pockets. I was trying to ignore Eva who'd paused long enough to wink in my direction as she tiptoed across the hallway wearing nothing but a towel.

Chapter 7

Eva
The Ruler

"The lazy and the wicked will not inherit nor inhabit any parts of the Kingdom of God," Deacon's voice boomed over me.

I snapped one eye open, sadly realizing that I was not dreaming. It was Wednesday morning. Leslie was screaming her head off of her shoulders in the bathroom with Momma Rose. She was having a full-blown temper tantrum over her hair. You could talk yourself blue in the face trying to convince her she had good hair. Something had given her the impression "good hair" should be bone straight. I'm sure that something was probably Sue. But no amount of brushing or combing would ever straighten out that naturally wavy mane she had going on, but that didn't stop her from being pissed about it.

The sky was still painted in the royal purple hues of night outside my bedroom window so it was somewhere around five; my alarm was set for five-thirty. *Here this fool goes, on ten all extra early.* I sat up with a sigh. That last good thirty minutes of sleep would have me hurting and evil later on. As my eyes adjusted I could see his hand wrapped tight around the end of The Ruler. It was splintered from the trunk of a petrified tree forged from the fires of hell and, if you let Deacon tell it, sacred. No, in reality it just felt that way when you got hit. Ironically, even somewhat idiotically, it was a yardstick he affectionately called The Ruler. It wasn't meant for measuring a damn thing except the number of strikes needed to rein in your unruly senses.

I sent up a couple of silent prayers, hoping he was just holding it for dramatic effect. *Figure the odds of that.* The only thing I had to protect me was my camisole and boy shorts. My eyes drifted down to my pitiful blanket in a heap beside my father's spit-polished cognac-tinted Stacy Adams. They were so clean I could almost see my *Fraggle Rock*–looking reflection with my hair going in all directions because I didn't have that good grade stuff like Leslie and no matter how well I tied my scarves I always woke up without them.

He stared down at me with a steely expression that was void of all the love and admiration he rained onto his church friends; he actually looked sad.

"Do you ever forget to eat?" he asked.

Confused I looked around like the answer was hanging out of my closet or about to jump out my top dresser drawer. Momma Rose must have been using the brain this morning. That's why he was asking such a dumb rhetorical question after the day I'd had. Oh yes, I'd convinced myself a long time ago that they shared one brain or they at least acted that way. The catch was that only one of them could use it at any given time and the result was something like asking me at o'dark thirty if I ever forget to eat. The Ruler started tapping a steady rhythmic countdown against the hardwood floor heating up the cold silence that floated between us. I cursed silently for not knowing the answer or purpose of his riddle and shook my head no.

Ennnnh. The buzzer sounded. That definitely wasn't the right answer.

He let loose with all of the bluster and fierceness of a thunderclap yelling down into my face. "Then how come . . ."

In one fluid motion he leaned back, slicing the ruler through the air, it landed with a painful, searing crack against my bare upper thigh. I jumped, wincing at the blood rushing to the red welt forming on my skin. The Ruler and I went way back; we been good friends since I was eight. No matter how many times I tried, I was never prepared and could never figure out *how* to prepare for that first strike. That was always the one that got the worst reaction that in some sadistic way would make him unleash the strike team. Every other word got its very own searing, painful exclamation point in the form of The Ruler. He started hacking away taking his anger and frustration out on my skin with the ruler, no different than someone hacking through the jungle to clear a path. He must have found out about Que. I'd already cried myself to sleep over that jack-ass and now this. If Deacon knew about him then it meant that Mrs. Porter was probably Mrs. Quinn's sorority sister. She was the only one who knew who I was.

"You act like we don't eat and live off of this family's reputation. If I can't lead and control my own family why would they think I have any right to lead them? You will not plant that seed of doubt into my sheep—"

"Chill out, Deac." Dontay barreled into the room in nothing more than some green plaid boxers. He slammed into Deacon pushing him back against the far wall. Dontay pinned him against the wall grabbing hold of him until he dropped his precious ruler.

"You wanna hit somebody, you hit me. We don't do that woman-beating shit, Deac. Not as long as I'm around," he growled through clenched teeth, the ropey muscles in his upper back and shoulder flexed in response.

He dropped his hands away from Deacon taking a step back almost daring Deacon to pick up the ruler or say something. Winded, breathing loudly through his mouth Deac sniffed, too tired and emotional to fight or say anymore. He stared Dontay down before turning to leave my room barely casting so much as a glance in my direction. The house was so quiet his nose breathing was the only sound ringing over the uncomfortable silence. Leslie was miraculously mute as a mime. Momma Rose might as well have been a mime since she never spoke up for me. They'd probably sat right there in the living room hearing everything, pretending it was nothing.

I winced; the entire right side of my body felt like one big blazing red welt.

Dontay stared at me with big sad eyes. "Are you good? Let me go get you some ice or some—"

That was the same way Que looked and just about the same thing Que'd asked when he helped me that first day. He should have been here saving me but he was probably spooning his wife or giving her a damn candy bar.

It came out of nowhere. Shoulder-racking sobs like my world was ending. I curled into a tight ball turning away from Dontay. Of course I wasn't good, and I didn't like anyone to see me cry especially someone I didn't know. The bedsprings creaked against the extra weight. Dontay wrapped his arms around me pulling me back against the heat of his chest. He felt perfect, like we were meant to fit together. Sadly I wanted Que's arms around me; he was the one who'd managed to melt and scoop out a piece of my raspberry sorbet heart. My mind went on repeat telling me the same thing over and over like a spoiled five-year-old. Dontay wasn't Que and Que wasn't available.

"You okay, Eva?" Leslie whispered from around the bedroom door.

At the sound of her voice Dontay scooted to a safe distance and I pulled myself together with a few deep breaths.

"I'm good, Leslie-boo. You know that mess don't bother me," I told her.

She poked her little heart-shaped face around the door. Two Pocahontas braids dangled from the both sides of her head, they flopped against the middle of her back. Her little nose wrinkled up at me. She stepped closer eying all the red marks all over my skin like typos in a term paper. They felt even worse under her scrutiny. Embarrassment at being beaten into a teary ball in my underclothes had me feeling too mortified to look Dontay or my little sister in the eye.

"Okay, well." She hesitated. "Deacon sent me to tell you that he wants French toast for breakfast."

I quirked my eyebrow at that. "Does Deacon want it or do you want it, Leslie?"

"We want it." She shrugged. "He kind of suggested it and I agree." She'd started to take herself off when she turned back eyeing Dontay curiously. "And now I see why he said you're doing redemption service at church tonight. There's a boy in your room; that's against the rules. Serve and obey, Eva." With that she left.

Dontay cleared his throat while watching me with an awkward expression out the corner of his eye.

"Excuse my Stepford baby sister. The brainwashing has already started. After Ava . . ." I stopped myself. I wasn't ready to tell him about our family dinner that changed our lives just yet. "Sometimes she acts like her head is stuck up Deacon's ass. It's my job to get all that religious bullshit off of her. You know reverse the brainwashing."

His voice rumbled like bottled thunder. "What the fuck is Deac's problem?"

I told Dontay about Deacon's infamous rags to bitch-assness story. How he was so poor he'd catch frogs so they'd have dinner. How one day his grandma made him walk his four-year-old brother to a neighbor's house to ask if they wanted a little boy. Come to find out the neighbors weren't so great. Deacon had to watch his baby brother grow up being abused by a couple of crazies. All the not having and taking away may have changed him into a Godly man, but it made him a sad, tyrannical hypocrite at home.

"Why are you still staying up in here if it's this bad?" Dontay asked softly.

I shrugged. I'd asked myself that same question plenty of times. Que had my savings account beyond nice and I was a good legal eighteen. But that feeling of losing everything in one blow made me want more than just a nice amount of money.

"Probably because if I leave, no one will be here to take care of my little sister."

"Guess that means I'll have to stick around to take care of you then huh?"

His words brought a small smile to my face. They weren't what I'd expected or the answer I wanted but they helped.

Later that night I was getting ready for church when Que decided to start calling my phone back to back. It already sucked for me to stand and attend to Sister Bealiah. Redemption service was Deacon's second-favorite punishment next to The Ruler. You got assigned to a church member and you were pretty much their servant for the night.

Once I'd gotten Brother Beasley who wanted his feet rubbed the entire service. Not one person batted an eye. They couldn't see the stiff finger of applause he was giving me in his pants or the cum stain when I finished.

Sister Bealiah was sitting in a hospital-sign blue skirt suit with some poor animal's fur lining the collar and sleeves. That old chest of hers puffed up as she looked back and forth between me and my phone buzzing in the pocket of my skirt. Her lips folded down into a dissatisfied frown making the creases on either side of her mouth deepen into sad faces on top of her sad face. It made her big chubby cheeks stand out even more. It looked like she had asses on both sides of her face.

"I graduated from Norfolk State top of my class with honors. In my day women earned their degrees with their head. I guess your generation interpreted that a little differently." Her eyebrow went up until it almost touched her hairline. "Then again you are your mother's child."

Several ladies within hearing distance all nodded simultaneously. My fingers twitched from the temptation of laying them all across the round ass cheeks on her face. Instead I excused myself to the bathroom. I slammed the cover down taking a seat in the last stall. *How does Sister Bealiah know? How else would she know? Either Dean Porter told her or she's cool with Que's wife.*

My cell buzzed with what had to be the twenty-second call from Que. I forced myself to ignore it.

"Is that why I can't get a hold of you?" Que's head appeared under the stall.

I jumped up with a gasp. My phone fell, and the floor dismantled it. Pieces went flying in different directions.

I glared at Que. "What are you doing in here? Do you know how much trouble you could get me into?" I slammed the door open.

He was blocking my only way out of the stall and he knew it. I could feel the bathroom shrinking around me until it felt like a broom closet. Deacon would kill me, he would definitely kill me. Que moved towards me backing me up until I was pressed in a corner of the stall with the wall against my back. Reaching behind him, he locked the door with a click. He was all yummified with his beard trimmed and a fresh edge-up. There were even creases in his khakis and not a single wrinkle in his black knit polo shirt. But then again, for all I knew his wife could have picked all that out for him.

"I've been trying to apologize but you ain't making it easy, Eva. Daddy misses his girl. He needs her."

I put my hand against his chest to stop him from getting any closer or saying anymore. "No, Que, this isn't—"

"Eva?" Sister Bealiah's voice echoed through the bathroom.

My eyes went wide and round.

Que whispered, "Kiss me and I'll cooperate."

"Eva, girl, don't make me come get you. I don't take well to lazy cherrun."

"Hurry up before she gets closer." Que pulled his bottom lip in between his teeth.

Adrenaline had my head spinning and I could feel the armpits of my blouse getting damp. My hand clenched into a fist against his chest. I let him pull me in. My knees felt wobbly from the shock of pleasure that shot through me when his tongue tangled with mine. He shoved his hand up my skirt pushing my panties to the side. All my senses shot to ten. I was sweating, wet, angry, and I still wanted him. I couldn't even hold back the moan that slipped its way out of my mouth.

"Dern cell phone all over the place; are you sick, girl?"

Sister Bealiah's voice sounded like she was two stalls down. Alarm whistles went off in my head. Que pulled away from me. He never took his eyes off of me. He licked my juices off his finger all while slamming the stall door open. All five stalls shook from the dull thump on the other side.

Sister Bealiah crumpled to the floor.

Chapter 8

Eva
Ain't No Party Like a No-panties Party

We rode home in complete silence. Deacon wasn't convinced that I hadn't tried to kill the woman. Que was able to slip out without being seen while I went to get help. I called Storie as soon as I got in the house and could get my cell phone pieced back together.

"Why do I feel like you've been avoiding me?" Storie asked.

"Well hello to you too. I'm surprised you noticed since you only come out from under your Bear blanket for food and water."

Storie faked gasped into the phone. "Boo, girl. I'm shocked that you'd think that. One, I had to break my own bed to teach him how to break my damn back. So B, That means I've got to get it while he's still motivated. And third, what's this rumor about some man candy stayin' up in your house?"

"That's what I was calling to tell . . . Wait, break your bed? How'd you break your bed?" I couldn't keep the disbelief out of my voice.

"Yes; let me school you right quick. Loosen the lug nuts on the bed frame. Start gettin' in and when the bed collapses into shrapnel you blame Bae. Bae feels guilty and buys you a new bed frame. Now every chance you get, remind Bae about that time he broke the bed frame. Ta-da, Bae will work extra, extra hard trying to break the new one."

I laughed so loud I had to set the phone down.

Leslie interrupted my conversation. "Deacon said you should be praying and meditating for Sister Bealiah." She paused giving me a wary stare. "He was holding The Ruler."

I twisted my mouth up at her. Dontay was still out somewhere with his friends so it was best if I didn't press my luck.

"Girl, I'll call you later. I've got to go help Leslie with her homework."

I lied to Storie about most of the things that went on in our house. If a person wasn't part of our household they didn't need to know what went on within it.

"Ugh. Whatever with you and all that blasé blah. Come to my party. I miss my bestie and need to see her face to make sure I'm not talking to an imposter," Storie whined.

She sounded pitiful enough that I actually agreed. Plus I really did want to talk about Que and all his craziness.

I dragged myself up white cobblestone steps of a porch big enough to park my car on. Leaning against one of the support columns I closed my eyes and sighed. It was too hot for all this mess. *Storie's party better be all that she'd said it would be.* I needed something to keep my mind off Que's hundred and whatever phone calls and texts. I was deleting them at first but then he'd just call and call, so now they sat in my voicemail box keeping it too full to receive any more messages. His class had become a no-fly zone; not only did I not bother with going to take the final but I dared him to fail me.

"Lick" by Joi and Sleepy Brown thumped through the wall in front of me. That song made me only imagine the kinds of nasty and wrong that was going on behind that door. The two-story house was the last one on the cul-de-sac surrounded by trees the size of skyscrapers. The hard plastic of my bright gold Mardi Gras mask was making my face hot but I wasn't about to remove it. That and the long fire-burst red wig I picked out would hopefully keep me from being recognized.

Why do I let myself get talked into stuff like this? Know good and well I should be in church or at home.

Changing in the car was harder than I thought it would be so I took a minute to do a last-minute check on the drape of the black sheet I'd fashioned into an above-the-knee toga. I'd left the house in jeans and an oversize sweater to keep everyone from being suspicious.

"Who the hell is that lookin' like a chocolate Greek Goddess? Eva, is that you?"

My friend Laurence could go under witness protection and you'd still know it was her. I'd been so lost in my head I didn't even hear her walk up with her boo. She was unmistakable in her loose-fitted black toga with a short gold wreath on her low-cut fade. Why she even bothered with her little solid black mask was beyond me. Laurence could bench more than half the dudes I knew and she ran eight miles a day. Laurence was cut with these magazine-worthy abs that she showed off as often as possible. She made straight girls self-conscious about being able to pinch a little extra. How she managed to drape her toga so low you could see the cut of her abs dipping into her hips on the side was beyond me.

I tried to hide my nervousness behind a shaky smile. "Yeah, it's me; how in the world could you tell?" I asked.

"First off everybody's already here and second we saw some of your little peep show before you got out of your crooked-as-hell Jesus freak mobile over there. I told you them custom plates get you recognized. You are 'Blssd2B' caught out there, woman," Laurence joked.

I popped my tongue at her. "Whatever. Ring the doorbell; this wig is making me hot. And um FYI, you know sports bras and Air Max ain't proper toga attire right?"

Her girlfriend Charmaine jumped in the convo. She was posted up close enough to be Laurence's Siamese twin.

"Girl, I tried telling her that; you know she don't listen worth a damn. But she still look good so fuck it."

She had a weird half smile on the part of her pinched face that I could see from under her mask. Charmaine had always been a little too clingy for my liking, but if Laurence wanted a warden, who was I to argue about it?

Laurence sucked her teeth, looking back and forth between the two of us. She was about to say something smart, but the door was flung open. Apple coconut–scented fog wafted into the hallway. Storie made me go to five different party stores just to find the stuff to make the smoke machine fog smell pretty. At least it worked; it'd have been tragic if the place smelled like a haunted weed house all night.

"Everybody been in here for a minute and I already know that's you, Laurence; you can't masquerade worth shit. I should make you take them shoes off before you come in my uncle's spot. I'll leave you be, this time. Hi, Charmaine.

And, is that Eva?" Storie let out an exaggerated gasp. "Wait, Doctor, does this mean what I think it means? I'm no longer contagious with the bubonic plague or whatever it was that had my best friend avoiding me?"

She definitely knew how to make a person feel guilty for just needing a little space.

I smiled big and bright. "And here I am making it up to you even though I said I'd never come to one of your freak parties. I just had a lot of stuff going on in my head. I'm sorry."

"Oh well, let momma see if you actually *came* or if you're just here."

Storie sashayed out onto the porch with a plume of smoke from inside billowing behind her like a ghost. Before I knew what she was up to, her hand was up under my toga. I jumped back in shock smacking her arm.

"Really, girl, what the hell? I thought I'd at least make it inside before I started getting felt up."

"Oooh, Eva, and you shaved. Good girl," Storie replied with a content nod and a wink.

Charmaine and Laurence gave each other the look, and I rolled my eyes at them all. It was a costume no-panties party and they weren't about to joke me for the rest of my life for wearing some.

"Just because I didn't wear my panties doesn't mean I have to do something, damn."

Storie held up her hand. "Eva, I'm the last person you have to justify yourself to. I don't judge remember?"

"Nope, me neither," Laurence added.

I waved them both off motioning for Storie to lead me inside. She paused long enough to hold out her hand showing us folded slips of paper.

"Take one and don't look. Everyone inside pulled out of a bowl before you got here and the last one is mine. It's about to go down. I want me a random Bearless fizuck."

We'd all concluded that Storie's momma was a little eccentric; that's why she actually named her after the stories, or the soaps. She couldn't pick one character so she just went all out. What she ended up with was an all-out daughter. It was a tradition Storie started back in high school. At the start of summer, my bestie would throw her no-panties party when her even more eccentric uncle went out of town.

It was mostly for single people but couples with no boundaries and cheaters and everything in between would be there. Storie personally made the invitation list herself. She just had to approve of everyone's guest. Everybody showed up in whatever theme she came up with and the rest was never talked about. Last year it was bathrobes, and the year before that hospital gowns, this year she wanted black togas which in black folk language was basically a black sheet. Nobody wore panties or drawers and from the things I'd heard, just about anything went.

"Well, y'all are the last of my guests, so, let's get this shit going," Storie called out, clapping her hands together and leading the way.

Laurence unceremoniously pushed me forward and I stumbled into the dark sour and fog-clouded main entrance. It was the first time I'd ever seen her uncle's place and since I'd never met the man eccentric definitely fit. Storie locked the door and I could see an army of at least thirty people in togas mingling throughout the first floor. Storie led us through a wide-open seating area. Bright gold and purple throw rugs and walls lined with oversized cushions. The walls were painted deep purple and every now and again the candles would flicker showing off tiny gold flecks in the paint. It was her uncle's private hookah lounge.

We stepped into the living room and my jaw hit the floor. I was transported to a penthouse loft on the highest floor in New York. Every wall was wallpapered from floor to ceiling with a mural overlooking the city at sunset. The real country appeal of his VA view was blotted away, hidden behind thick silvery velvet drapes. I could see a glass-encased fireplace glowing with a soft blue and green flame toward back of the living room.

Storie positioned herself in front of a flat-screen television that looked like it was just floating in midair and I don't mean on a stand or mounted to the wall. It must have been on invisible wires or something. The guys she'd gathered for her party came in every shape and size of appealing and I visually crotch raped them to my heart's content. Ever since Que's pocket-size short self pulled out his thick and long panty dropper I couldn't keep my eyes from dropping. Some of their togas didn't leave a lot to figure out unless they were growers.

Storie made a hand motion and the music automatically lowered itself. A guy no taller than me brought her a box setting it down on the *Star Trek*—looking coffee table with its pretty blue crystal in the middle.

Storie addressed the room: "All right, we are about to play a new game. I call it Indulgence. Take out your slips of paper. Unfold that shit."

I did as she directed, reading what looked like some kind of perverted fortune cookie.

AND I'M GONNA KISS YOU, SUCK YOU, TASTE YOU, RIDE YOU, FEEL YOU DEEP INSIDE ME OOH

"You have a piece of a song," Storie stated. "Someone else has another part. Walk around and sing until you find your match."

Everyone jumped into action singing parts of songs I'd never known existed. I'd just finished shaking my head at this one girl singing to me about put it in her mouth when I bumped into Laurence.

I poked her in the side showing her my lyrics. "Girl, what song is this?" Without the music the words meant nothing if it wasn't one of the songs I'd heard on Que's playlist.

"That's Janet, 'Would You Mind.' Damn you got a good one. I got Adina Howard."

After a quick rundown on how my song was supposed to go, I didn't feel so out of place anymore. I was about to tell Storie her game was janky when someone made the hairs stand up on the back of my neck.

"'I just wanna touch you, tease you, lick you, please you. Love you, hold you, make love to you,'" he sang from behind me.

What am I supposed to do again? Sing back? I couldn't make a sound. Without turning around I held up my slip of paper so he could see we had the same song. Before I had a chance to recover from that sensual serenade handcuffs were slapped around my left wrist and his right. I stared at Storie in shocked horror as she went around the room with that box, handcuffing everyone to their song partner.

"Now, for the indulgence part of the night." She giggled and continued, "There are three ways to get out of your cuffs. You can drink twenty shots of jungle juice." She pointed toward the black granite counter tops in the kitchen. Two huge Gatorade coolers like the ones the football team used during games were waiting. Little paper Dixie cups were filled on the table beside them. Everyone started whispering back and forth trying to figure out what the hell jungle juice even was and which partner would drink the shots.

Storie clapped her hands together, jerking the taller girl's arm she'd managed to get cuffed to. "The second way to get free is to make out with your cuff buddy or help your cuff buddy make out with someone else. Otherwise you're stuck and yes, you will be using the bathroom together and you can't leave until you get un-cuffed so . . ."

We all rushed the jungle juice at the same time. I silently toasted my cuff buddy in his movie-like full Batman mask and we did shot number one. Storie must have mixed straight Everclear with watered down mango-peach juice. It burned all the way down and made options two and three seem less formidable compared to a second and third shot let alone twenty. Bottled water was purposefully removed from the stainless steel fridge and replaced with beers, Mike's Hard Lemonade, and liquor. The ice trays, filled with strawberries in rum, Jell-O shots, and fruit soaked in liquor, were strategically placed throughout the kitchen beside liquor-infused cans of whipped cream.

The entire concept of the party was pretty obvious; it wasn't meant for anyone to make it to twenty shots. We managed to fight down two more shots of jungle juice and three Jell-O shots that were surprisingly hella stronger than the jungle juice but a lot easier to get down. I needed to sit down because the room was spinning and he needed to pee. We compromised and I sat on the edge of the counter closest to the toilet. I closed my eyes for what felt like the briefest second. My arm moved just enough to snap me out of my tipsy power nap and when I looked up good old toga-clad Batman was standing in front of me stroking his bat cane.

"What the hell are you doing?" I asked scooting myself as far back as I could with the limitation of my cuffed wrist.

He responded by biting his lower lip, sliding his hand faster up and over, again and again. It was more exciting than scary. I focused on the dimple in his chin and told my eyes not to go any lower, but since when did they ever listen? My lips dried and I couldn't close my mouth to wet them because all the wetness in me had decided to just pour itself from in between my legs. Why was it so hard to just be good, do right, and have as little sinful sex as possible?

Maybe I need to get some stuff out of my system and then things will go back to normal. No strings, no problems, nothing. I nodded at my masked crusader and he took a step forward standing directly in between my thighs. I scooted to the edge of the counter until I could feel the heat from his skin just inches away. Before I could think about it anymore or feel guilty, I imagined Que doing this very thing with his wife and I surprised Batman and myself. Pushing off the counter, I took the seat he'd been so proudly showing off.

He groaned. I hissed through my teeth. Batman felt thicker and longer than Que, and he hurt so good I was gasping. He gripped my ass roughly guiding me up and down his bat stick. I was on the best standing rodeo ride of my life, hanging on with my one free arm around his thick neck. We could hear voices getting closer to the bathroom door and my heart started hammering away between my thighs. The excitement of getting caught combined with his perfectly deep strokes was all I needed. The first wave came crashing in. It was one of those beach-destroying waves. The kind that takes the old sand makes new islands, making me say things like:

"Oh Willoughby shit," I panted.

It felt like he was trying to push me up but I'd locked my thighs around his waist slamming down against him.

My simple behind was coming and by the time I realized we didn't use a condom I could feel him throbbing and painting my insides with white gold. Shock and panic made me lift myself up off his johnson in a rush. My bracelet caught the back of his mask. I pulled away taking it over his head. My own mask had gotten knocked crooked as I was unceremoniously dumped onto the floor. I sat there with my legs still shaking from post-climatic tremors staring up in shock at Dontay.

Chapter 9

Eva
Batman Begins

Shocked I tried to recover squeezing my eyes shut as if it would help me un-see and un-feel every bit of Dontay that I'd just experienced. If I'd been paying attention I'd have noticed he was the only person in the room with a mask that hid his eyes.

Feeling foolish I glared at him. I picked myself up off the floor snatching some toilet paper off the roll to catch the wet heat running down my thigh.

"What the fuck are you doing here, Eva?"

"What am *I* doing here? You can't question me. I was invited. What the hell are you doing trolling my homegirl's party?" I snapped back at him.

His nostrils flared. "I'm not the deacon's daughter. Bear is my nigga; he invited me. I just came to window shop."

"Then what the hell was all that?" I slashed my hands through the air referring to what we'd just done.

"What was what? Us fuckin' just now? That was me having some kinky voyeuristic fun in front of a complete stranger so I wouldn't have any slip-ups out there. I didn't know it was you, and I sure as hell ain't know you'd just hop on. Wait, you thought I was this Willoughby nigga?"

My eyes widened in horror. *What did I just do?*

Dontay reached down between our wrists, his fingers grazed my skin, and I felt myself blush. He pressed along the inside of his cuff and they fell off like magic.

"No, I didn't think you were someone else." *I just wished it.* "I meant um, Willoughby spit, it's a beach that a hurricane pretty much spit in the middle of, never mind."

"I'll give you some time to get cleaned up." He winked and grinned down at me. "You do got some good pussy though."

A wicked chill ran down my spine as he eased through the door. My mouth dropped open and snapped shut. I was at a complete loss for words. Leaning on the sink I stared at myself in the mirror trying to process what'd just happened. I twisted the knob, splashing cold water on my cheeks. I needed to find something to clean myself off and out. Que'd had a vasectomy so babies and birth control weren't even on my radar with him. Dontay tapped lightly on the door. *Hopefully he found me a washcloth, some paper towels, hell some spermicidal cream.*

I clicked the lock and in burst none other than Que. Seeing him sent me from happy to hate so fast it had to be a world record. He was in full toga attire with a Zorro mask tied around his eyes and a bandanna covering his mouth. How no one else recognized him was beyond me; maybe it was the sex that made him look familiar even in a disguise.

He pulled the bandana down letting it hang around his neck. "Eva, baby, I've missed you so much."

Que took a pleading step toward me and I took an anxious step back. Seeing him and hearing his voice had me reliving all of our moments over again in my head. He was my first everything down to my first heartache.

My voice was shaky. "I don't know how you got in here." I lifted my chin so my eyes would be higher than his. "But you need to leave before I tell everyone who you are and then have Bear whoop your ass."

His lips shook. "It doesn't matter. What do you think I'd do without you? Nothing. I'm not even at the school anymore. I quit that bullshit job and my wife for you." Que stared me in my eyes. The bandana around his neck had him looking like a booty bandit or a heart bandit.

He was saying everything I needed to hear. I just didn't feel like I could believe him or trust him.

"Que, what you did was unforgiv—"

Before the words were out of my mouth his lips were on mine. Que didn't spark the same feeling I'd just had with Dontay. Que gave me a sense of urgent familiarity. His kisses always felt like he was trying to climb into my soul, through my lips. They made me feel weak and breathless. I melted into him, feeling him grow rock solid against my stomach.

"You were a bad girl weren't you?" he whispered against my lips.

Confused tears slid down my cheeks. On the one hand it felt good to know he still wanted me; on the other I felt like I was playing myself if I took him back. He pinched my nipples into tight points underneath my toga. I tried looking every which way but at him, scared he'd see the answer before I could decide on a lie.

"Answer me." He bit my bottom lip.

I gave him a pitiful nod. His lies hurt me and my truth could hurt him, but I wanted him to feel every bit as hurt as I'd felt. Que rolled his tongue around the inside of his mouth. He was too quiet for my liking. We were alone in the bathroom and there was no telling what was going through his mind. The music out in the party area was so loud no one would even hear me if I screamed. I squeezed my eyes tight fighting a silent debate on whether I should go for the door or ask him if he was okay.

The room spun or at least it felt like it. In one fluid motion Que lifted me throwing my legs over his shoulders. His mouth felt like molten lava on my kitty. I grabbed his head closer and then I tried pushing at him away. *Oh no, oh no, oh no. Please, God, don't let him kill me.* He held me hostage with my back pinned against the wall; my head was just inches away from the ceiling. I was on the verge of a heart attack or hyperventilation. If he hadn't tasted Dontay yet he was about to. Panicked I did a combo of slapping his head and trying to squirm away. Que sucked and slurped on my lips like he hadn't eating anything since the last time we'd seen each other.

"Mmm hmm, I knew it. You been real bad without daddy around," he sighed into my kitten.

It was coming. I tensed waiting for that zero-gravity freefall as I was dropped or thrown to the floor. He growled, digging his fingers so hard into my thighs I'd be wearing pants for a month to hide the bruises. He snaked his tongue deep inside me churning it back and forth devouring every drop of mixed nectar he came in contact with.

He paused just long enough to ask, "You still love me, baby?" He pressed his nose and upper lip into my pearl shaking his head from side to side while tonguing me. He slowed to an almost torturous stop waiting on his answer.

I softly knocked the back of my head against the wall in frustration, so close it was killing me. "You know I love you. I missed you; please don't play right now."

I moved my hips grinding into his lips, riding his face. Satisfied with my response he went back to work. Sparks were shooting off behind my eyelids; my legs locked shakily around his ears. My back arched so hard I couldn't make a sound if I wanted to.

Que alternated between planting soft kisses on my inner thighs and I peeled my eyes open slowly. The river was still there, crackling and roaring in my ears as my senses came back.

"Fuck me sideways on a Sunday, my girl is a freeeeeak." Storie stood in the bathroom doorway grinning like I'd just won a gold medal in the Freak Olympics.

My humiliated gaze shifted from her to the rest of the party behind her clapping and cheering over the music. Everyone except Batman, who stood with his arms crossed over his chest. Que eased me down the wall with his fingers digging hard and deep into my side. I winced.

It felt like he'd crack at least two of my ribs. He slid his bandana back into place before leaning close to my ear whispering, "This my pussy. Don't give my shit away again."

Chapter 10

Dontay
Cake . . .

After the wild shit I'd seen at that party I needed to get out and get some action to erase the action I'd gotten. I still couldn't stomach the fact that a nigga was face-deep eating it up after I'd just finished. But Eva let him do it. That's what Storie's parties were for. They were so all the freaks could freak out together.

Messing around with Eva whether intentionally or unintentionally was by no means a good idea. I was supposed to be keeping my nose out of trouble while staying with Deac. Problem with that situation was that Eva seemed to stay on my mind more than she should've been and nobody told me Deac was plum fuckin' nuts. When I got a text from White Boy it didn't take much to make me consider his new wild-ass idea. I rolled out of one freak party and right up into another one. Except this one was a hustle.

I met White Boy outside a house in Great Bridge. From the outside it looked like it had been plucked out of a French fairy tale.

"What up, White Boy? What the hell kind of setup is this?" I asked eyeing our newest mark.

He casually strolled over swinging his long, lanky arms looking like his usual stoner self. "I promise, dawg, once we get in you'll see. The guy who owns this place is royalty or some shit. He flew a plane of my stepdad's shit in just for this party. Does it every year; and we can get in on that dough or dro, stacks or triple stacks, my dude."

I rubbed my hands together in agreement. If we didn't walk out paid we could at least get in good with a connect.

We were given twenty minutes to change and then Gaius, our ambiguously gay chaperone, was keeping an almighty enthusiastic and uncomfortable eye on us from the side of the large banquet hall. I cut my eyes at White Boy as I tried to hide my saddle swag as I did my best to make my rounds. Saddle swag is when you walk like a cowboy who's just ridden a wide-backed cactus across the Painted Desert. My balls was not liking the material of the man thongs they put us in. It was chafing and rubbing me in all the wrong ways. Every time I got close enough to White Boy I had to keep myself from reaching out and wringing his damn neck.

We were both at the side bar refilling our trays. There were about twenty of us all together.

The others were spread out enough for me to chew his ass out.

"You ain't tell me we was gonna be damn near butt-ass naked serving these mufuckas and shit." I gritted my teeth.

"Just chill and keep an eye out for a chance to explore or talk business."

"Business? Looking like this? When have you ever seen a mufucka talkin' business at a dinner with the hired help?"

"You two." Gaius flagged us down. "Away, away you go. I need you servicing."

Checking out the table had me doing my best not to try servicing the French pouty-lipped piece sitting at the table I was entertaining. They had the most shit at their table; she did a couple of lines of coke but I didn't see her reach for anything else. From the way her light pink dress fell her off her in waves, to the way her hair was pinned to show off the soft olive-brown swoop of her neck, I knew she was either important or her man beside her was. Old boy was on that pimped-out Prince Charming shit, with the white high-collared military jacket, red trim and gold medals pinned on the shoulders. They both sat like they had metal rods implanted in their spines. God must have molded her for Himself and then put her on earth so He wouldn't be tempted. That was the only reason He'd make someone who looked like her.

I couldn't stop watching her out the corner of my eye. Her man kept whispering in her ear and cutting up her food. He had this tick with his right eye like it wanted to blink all by itself and he was fighting that shit hard. So this dude looked mad intense, important, and insane, squinting that one eye at people while they talked to him. He was listening to a chick who I'd swear was a dude in a blond and blue wig when I caught his wifey or whatever staring me down. She waved me over with a flick of her finger and a blank expression. My tray had these weird little pastries with apricot and kiwi glaze with crushed-up ecstasy powder on top.

Disgusted I stared down at my junk in its silk black sling. *Chill, my dude, we'll get you right when we get home. Just stay down so I can get us paid and get out of here.* I clenched my embarrassingly bare ass cheeks together and gritted my teeth. Because of my height my junk was pretty much shoulder and eye level every time I walked my tray around. I tried to make my trips as quick and brief as possible. This was the first time she'd called me over as everyone else had gotten a kick out of having me stand there while they debated over pastry A that looked exactly like pastry B. All the while they were really covertly examining "pastry me" under the tray.

I shifted from one foot to the other trying not to notice the plunge in the neckline on the front of her gown now that I was actually up close. It looked like it went clear down to her belly button. Somewhere a metal tray clattered against the marble floor snapping my eyes out her dress and back to the moment. She had this Queen Midas attitude from the way she sat at the center of the table with her solid gold skeleton bracelet. Boney ring extensions covered every finger. It was creepy and sexy in its own way. I waited until Skeletor Princess of the Rich made her selection. Turning with my dignity still intact I'd almost gotten away when, *smack*, the sting of a warm palm cracked against my bare-ass cheek. Now I know how chicks feel when someone grabbed they ass in the club.

"*Gâteau*," she murmured with a gleam in her eye. Everyone at the table chuckled.

Gaius stepped out of the shadows. "She says 'cake,'" he answered with a wave.

"The fuck she mean by cake?" I asked glaring between her and Gaius.

She looked right through me and answered Gaius, "*J'aime celui-ci, il a foutre.*"

Everyone at the table laughed at whatever comment she'd obviously made insulting me or about me. They were the money; and only because I had a feeling she could get me a meeting with the nigga in charge did I let her slide.

***

After the longest, highest dinner party I'd ever seen we were shown to rooms so we could change. White Boy was acting like he'd eaten one too many of those pastries. He was across the room touching every part of the wall like an idiot looking for a hidden panel.

"Dontay, I'm telling you. What if there was one in here and it led to some unexplored crazy shit? Imagine if we found some scrolls or an alchemist's diary."

I gave him the blankest of blank stares. "I don't even know where you come up with this shit. Don't talk to me unless I can smoke it or spend it."

I was trying not the mess up the lines in the carpet. At the crib Eva hated it if after she vacuumed you dragged your feet erasing all her neat little lines. Every now and again I'd do it on purpose for fun and Leslie would help, but this wasn't my house. I shot her a text to check on her even though I'd told myself it was going to be Eva free for the rest of the night.

WYD woman?

Still at Storie's place. Someone stole my car.

Someone did what?! I stared at my phone waiting for her to reply.

White Boy jumped halfway across the room when someone knocked on the door.

"Dontay, come with me please," Gaius purred in his French American accent.

I frowned in White Boy's direction and he responded with his eyebrows shooting up to his hairline as he shrugged his shoulders. Shaking my head to myself, I bristled up and marched out behind the little Frenchman. He talked about the history of the different pictures on the wall. They were of different battles and queens, who built what where, who killed themselves, who died where. There were even actual hidden passages in the place that went from the master bedroom to his mistress's chamber. You couldn't do anything like that with a black woman. First I'd like to see you move the mistress in and second trying to have a secret anything under the same roof would be damn near impossible.

"So, Gaius, tell me what your girl said about me back there that everyone thought was so funny?" I asked.

"Oh, your ass, she liked it, called it cake and she also said you had spunk. So, we are here. Enjoy your night. *Bonsoir*." Gaius's fairy tale ended with a mystery. He knocked lightly on the solid oak door in front of us and walked away whistling.

Spunk? What the hell is that supposed to mean? It sure as hell ain't sound funny. Not one for games, I'd have walked off myself if I knew how to get back to my room. We'd walked down so many hallways and corridors it would take me days to find the front door.

"Hello, brute, come in." She spoke in surprisingly perfect English.

The pretty thing with the important man toy from dinner stood in the doorway and for whatever reason that annoyed me. All I wanted to do was find this paper and get out without a ton of people recognizing or seeing my face. I agreed to be eye candy and serve dinner and it was all I'd agreed to do. So this shit she was pulling right here was only adding insult to injury. None too pleased with the turn of events I looked in the direction Gaius had just gone, wondering where the hell it led.

"I wanted to pay you in person and apologize for earlier. I am Bellamy-George Saunier. Please call me Bellamy."

She stepped aside and reluctantly I walked in. Our rooms were night and day. Hers seemed to stretch back farther than the eye could see with giant arched floor-to-ceiling windows taking up two entire walls. My eyes focused on the way her hips moved under the knee-length oversized men's dress shirt she was wearing. *And she had the nerve to talk about my cake; I see them rounds poking out.* Bellamy walked with a natural quirky bounce that made her wavy ass-length hair float like a dark river behind her. It was hypnotizing to watch. I forced my eyes and my thoughts away.

"Yeah, I noticed a lot of recreational product out there. You looking for a partner?"

"No, that's something he wanted to talk to you about." She nodded toward the bed.

I could vaguely make out a man's form in the shadows.

"He liked you," she said, smiling and slapping a bundle of hundreds wrapped in a gold band marked $10,000.

I shook my head. "Nah, I don't know what impression y'all got. But I don't get down go down or even point in that direction I'm sorry."

Captain Face Down spoke. "You like her, do you? So how about you and her then; I just watch no?" he asked and his sleazy creepo voice echoed around the room.

So y'all can knock me over the head and ass rape a nigga or sell me to one of those sex slave hostels. I done watched enough movies to know the brother never makes it.

My feet started backing me in the direction of the door as I locked eyes with the little princess. "No, I'm sorry."

Her gaze dropped to the floor and her shoulders slumped in obvious disappointment but not before I caught what looked like a tiny smile cross her face. Her boy wasn't as good at taking rejection as she was.

"You American swill. You dare insult us? You aren't even worth the money we generously throw at you. I will have you and I will fuck your face until you gag and swallow my *jouir*," he shrieked like a little bitch.

And I stuck around just long enough to see hands tighten into fists as he yanked and tugged against the knotted sheets around his wrists.

Chapter 11

Eva
A Token of My Take Back

Panic set in as I glanced down to look at the time on my phone. It was after midnight. The kicker was that Momma Rose and Deacon thought I was on campus. I'd told them I'd volunteered to stay on campus overnight to help with freshman orientation tour for high school kids. Deacon couldn't stand Storie. I'd say it was because she was twenty-one and acting wild, but he didn't like anyone.

"Girl." Storie stopped pacing long enough to turn toward me. "Are you sure the doors were locked? There ain't no glass on the ground or anything."

I nodded and stopped with a blank stare on my face. "He took my car back." I blurted it out before I realized who I was standing in front of.

"Who took your shit? Deacon? Deacon's bitch ass does not own you, Eva. Come on." She chirped the alarm off of her Explorer climbing her tipsy behind in.

I opened the passenger side door. "Storie, we can't leave, girl; the police are coming."

"And it ain't like they rushing to get here. We called over an hour ago. Get in and—"

"And it wasn't Deacon. It was Que, Professor Quinn. He bought it for me, we kind of broke up, and I think he just took it back."

I dropped into the passenger seat and sulked into the neck of the big sweatshirt she'd given me. All my clothes were still in my car and I wasn't about to stand around outside in nothing but toga. I could see Storie's mouth hanging open out the corner of my eye.

"Damn, explains why he asked me for an invite then," she blurted out after a few quiet seconds. "I guess we'll just have to go get your shit back. I'm pretty sure he'll give it to you. I doubt he'd want his wife seeing you this time of night."

"Wait. You knew he was married?

"Girl, yes. I done been there, almost got shot, and instead of a T-shirt or a degree Dean Porter expelled me for giving someone Tylenol. She said I was distributing blah blah blah, some made-up shit."

It was apparent I wasn't the only one keeping secrets from my bestie.

***

We pulled up in front of Que's place. I didn't expect the pang of jealousy that hit me. His car was parked beside what I assumed was his wife's. They had a cute two-story brick house with a little jetty and a small boat docked off to the side. My car was nowhere in sight.

"What are you waiting for?" I asked Storie. "Go ring the doorbell."

"I'm waiting for Bear. I texted him on the way over. He should be here in a few minutes. Quinn might try to get stupid. You already know Mrs. Quinn stay locked and loaded. She didn't take too kindly to catching me with her husband. I'd hate for her to have a flashback."

Shoot, I wasn't taking too kindly to hearing or even thinking about her being with Que. How many girls had he been with before me? How many of us was he seeing right now? Imagining him doing what we did with anyone else set my insides on fire.

"There he is." She nodded toward the rearview.

A silver Acura pulled up behind us. Bear got out along with two other guys. I cursed under my breath. Dontay's tall frame unfolded out of the car followed by a skinny white guy. They lined up on Storie's side of the SUV like soldiers waiting for a command.

"Where's your car?" Bear asked looking through the window toward the house.

Storie answered for me. "We think it's in the garage."

"Y'all think? So you don't even know if this nigga stole her car?" Bear all but growled at us through the window.

Dontay stepped in. "Don't worry about it. We got this. Y'all just stay here. Let us know if you see anyone coming."

The guys crept toward the house splitting up at the garage. Dontay went around the side and Bear tried to look through the windows. I had the whole truck rocking from bouncing both of my knees up and down.

Storie stuck her upper lip up to her nose. "I can see now that I'll have to train Bear to not include his boys on a solo mission. I didn't know he'd bring Bumbles and Fuck Shit Up with him, my bad girl."

"Who and what?" I asked her.

"Gracious, Eva, how the nigga staying in your house and you don't know nothing about him? Dontay and White Boy got a reputation for bumbling and fucking up all kinds of shit. Neither one of them wants to do right, but they done smoked up too many brain cells to realize they get caught out there every time they try to do wrong."

An all-black car crept up to a slow stop behind us with its headlights out. We simultaneously swiveled our heads toward the back.

"The GPS shows it's in here." A short, pale man who could have been a Napoleon impersonator got out and tried the doors on Bear's car.

"What the hell is all that?" I asked Storie.

She barely moved. "I don't know but I bet Bumbles or Fuck Shit Up did it. Hopefully they find whatever it is and leave before . . ."

There wasn't a breath taken between the two of us as we watched Napoleon take a small package out of the car. He leaned down and neither of us could see what he was doing. Flames licked at the inside of Bear's Acura.

"Yo! That's my shit. What the . . . Who the fuck?" Bear ran across Que's perfectly landscaped yard toward the street.

"Tell your friend I am not to be fucked with," Napoleon called out.

The front door swung open and both Quinn and his wife stormed outside. My heart slammed into my lungs. Mrs. Quinn's hand was already reaching into the pocket of her robe. We could only imagine the size of the gun she was about to pull out of it.

Storie panicked. She threw the truck in drive and took off with the tires squealing.

"We can't leave the guys. What about Bear's car?" I sounded out of breath.

"They got legs. To hell with gettin' shot. If Quinn and wifcy don't see us the guys can say anything and still walk away."

***

The guys walked away all right. I'd just settled down from Deacon's religious tirade when it sounded like the garbage man was running a late-night pickup outside my window. These fools climbed out of my car looking like three urban desperados. Dontay tapped lightly on my bedroom door.

"I rescued your cat, ma'am." He tipped an imaginary hat at me.

I giggled. "However in the world did you find my kitty?"

"I kind of stole it back. You might have to scrape those not-so-nice people's garage door off your back bumper in the morning but you'll be fine." He ran his tongue over his lower lip.

I ate him up in eyefuls, digesting every little detail. I let my imaginary fingers trace all along his lips while I replayed how good they felt at the party. He smelled like power and Armani For Him. How I never noticed all that before was beyond me, but in the few seconds we stood side by side I'd imagined our first date all the way to us walking down the dern aisle. The man looked flawless. So what if his ears were a little big? I could look past that.

My eyes were still watching that mouth of his. "I guess I should thank you for saving my *cat?*" I took a timid step toward him.

He stepped inside closing the door.

I got the teeniest bit of common sense at what was going on. "Deacon might—"

"He won't even know I'm home. Bear took my car."

It was a good enough answer for me. Dontay started kissing his way up my neck as an incentive.

"Did you hear something?" I tried to dodge his lips. I couldn't listen or focus when they were on me.

"Think I just broke through my zipper. My bad, it happens," he joked.

"Well then let me—"

Deacon came through my bedroom door with a team of police like he was on a holy drug raid. Que marched in with a smug look on his face.

"That's her." He pointed in my direction. "She came to my house, broke in, and stole my car after I told her she couldn't borrow it anymore."

Chapter 12

Doers Do While the Watchers Watch

I had to take five deep breaths before I could even try to speak and not blast Que with a thousand curses. The officers marched towards me with their gold badges shining against the black of their uniforms. At least a night in jail could be a night away from the ruler or another redemption service.

"Hold on boys. I think me and this here gentleman can settle this amongst ourselves. No need starting a paper trail," Deacon announced.

Que immediately bristled up. "No, I want a paper trail. You ain't even seen my garage old man. I could care less about –,"

"About your wife asking why you gave this child a car or how you could stain her soul with the sin of the adultery you commit against your own marriage?"

All the anger drained from Que's face. His mouth twisted from side to side before turning into an ugly frown. The look he gave me to everyone else might have just seemed angry, but

I knew better. Que was beyond pissed off and he wouldn't be happy until I paid.

Without a word he turned and stormed out slamming the front door on his way. Deacon looked from Dontay down to me in my tank-top and shorts. He wouldn't say or do anything in front of the officers.

"Strip," Deacon said.

The sound of that single word rolling off his lips grated against my ears like rocks inside a tin can. He shuffled towards my bedroom door and quietly closed it before leaning back with a conceited smirk on his face. Dontay was frowning in confusion. He probably wasn't sure if he'd heard him correctly.

"Mannie, Chuck, give her some incentive," Deacon casually addressed his hired henchmen.

The sound of theirs boots rushing across the room echoed the pounding of my heart in my ears. They each pulled their pistol and the taller of the two stood behind Dontay reaching around to hold his cheeks in his hand.

"Open your mouth nigga," Chuck or Mannie demanded.

I didn't know who was who.

Dontay tried to yank his face away. His lips were balled up so tight they were going white at the corners.

The shorter officer punched Dontay hard in the side and I felt the pain for him. There was a short heated pause where I could have sworn he was calculating his odds on fighting. His lips opened just enough for the officer to angrily shove the barrel between them wedging them wide.

Deacon waved his hand in my direction. "You want to run around acting like a whore, I'll treat you like one. Now strip."

The room clouded over from the tears filling my eyes. I hid behind them as they fell down my face, letting them block everyone from my line of sight. The sound of Dontay's heavy breathing around the metal barrel clanking against his teeth were the only sounds in the room. I wasn't close enough to hit either officer but I considered it. They could shoot Dontay and Deacon would say it was justified before I took two steps.

I clumsily pulled my tank-top over my head before letting my shaky fingers slide down my shorts. My skin blazed from the heat of every eye in the room on my bare body.

"All right stud. Your turn." Deacon's voice was low and mean.

"Deacon, it was all my fault with the car please–" I whispered, bringing my arms up to cover my naked breasts.

"Mannie," Deacon said completely ignoring me. "Help Eva lie down and get comfy while our stud gets ready."

I figured out Mannie was the taller of the two when he stepped away from his post behind Dontay and came towards me with a sketchy grin. His pistol was aimed towards the middle of my chest. I forced my feet in the direction of my bed silently wishing the gun would just go off and end all of this. The sound of Dontay's clothes sliding off washed over me in a wave of disbelief. I was suffocating all over again. The cold sheets pressed against my ass and I swung my legs up feeling awkward and exposed. Goose bumps rose all over my body as the bed creaked from the shaking of my shivers. The barrel of the gun made an icy trail from my big to towards my ankle. I shut my eyes to the world. As long as I was around Deacon, as long as he was alive I'd always be inside that box.

Heat pressed against my skin and I opened my eyes to Dontay leaning over me. The gun to the back of his head only made his expression all the more painful to look at. His arms were shaking as his fists dug into the pillow beside my head.

"I'm so sorry," he whispered before lowering his eyes.

I followed his gaze letting out a sharp exasperated breath. The fact that he could even get hard with three other men in the room and a gun at his head was damn-insane. I rolled my eyes to the ceiling and back again.

"What are you waiting for Thumper?" Deacon asked.

Dontay's cheek clenched, he sat back on his haunches shaking his head no even though part of him was definitely saying yes.

Deacon shuffled towards Chuck pulling a pistol I never knew he had from somewhere underneath the back of the moth-brown suit jacket. It was skinnier than the officer's guns with a longer skinnier barrel. I'd never seen a gun like that but it made Dontay curse under his breath. He came down over me nudging my legs apart in a single movement. There was the briefest most aggravating pain as he pushed his way into my dry skin. I dug my teeth into his bicep muffling my groans from pain. I wasn't gonna be able to pee right for at least a week. Dontay stopped moving as if he'd read my thoughts. His chest pressed against mine and I focused on the heat of his skin blazing hot against mine.

The sounds around me felt amplified in my head. A zipper went down to my right and somewhere to the right of that there was heavy breathing. I didn't want to see who was or wasn't jerking off to this. I for damn sure didn't want to see Deacon or his smug face.

Dontay swelled up inside me surprising even me when he was able to smoothly slide out and back in again. My only escape was by pressing my face into the side of his neck. He stroked and glided back and forth until I forgot all about our audience. It was only when we both came crashing back to reality that we remembered they were there.

"See boys what'd I tell you?" Deacon's voice broke through the haze in my head. "Everyone has a purpose. She's a natural. She can start tomorrow. Any of the boys at the precinct want something other than a financial handout, send them my way. Need to get a few things unders!tood first."

I slowly pulled the sheets up to my chest covering myself. Dontay scooted to the edge of the bed with his back to me as Deacon escorted his uniformed dogs out into the hallway. A sigh of relief had swept over me when he didn't let anyone else touch me. But I still couldn't wrap my mind around everything that happened up to what Deacon hinted at happening.

Deacon shuffled back into the room with his face furled up. "Your mother was one of my top girls. You can exchange that little slut gift you have with people that can benefit the church or the *two of you* can leave my house right now as you are and not come back."

I opened my mouth to say I don't know what but Deacon had turned and marched out of the room before I could find my voice.

"Fuck this, I'm out." The muscles in Dontay's arms flexed as he pushed himself up off the bed. "Come on Eva, let's just leave. Your sister will be fine. He's done more shit to you in the time I've been here and he ain't laid a hand on her once. She'll be fine." He lowered his tone to a hushed whisper. "We can come back and get her when we have a spot and some money. Look, you have to put you first, or you won't be alive to save the one you keep putting yourself second for."

Dontay had the sincerest look in his eyes and his words as right as they were fell with on me with the sound of my world crashing down around me. I twisted and knotted the sheets around my fists untangling them and then wrapping them tighter each time. That's what Deacon was doing to my life. He'd give me a little freedom but every time I thought we could function like a normal father and daughter, he'd wrap some kind of hell tighter and tighter around me.

My lips were trembling and I couldn't swallow past the lump in my throat. I'd never left Leslie, never considered leaving her. But Dontay was right. I wouldn't be able to save her, if I didn't save me first.

Chapter 13

Dontay
Robot Sex

2009 Three years later

Every thick-hipped, round brown sword swallower from damn near every flick I'd ever seen was moaning in head calling my name. They were clawing at the blankets, pulling me by my ears, fighting each other for my attention. I picked one of the many faces and imagined myself pinning her thick legs back to her shoulders. She was lovin', straight-up begging for me to stop suckin' on that plump pearl of hers. She wanted all this sea cucumber. My cheeks all the way down to my chin were soaked from her salty-sweet ocean water telling me that's exactly what she wanted. I could have written the beginner and intermediate courses Sex 101. Slide her the tongue then slide her the tip and she'll beg for a nigga to hit all them walls.

"That's too fast. Slow down, Dontay. Small circles; matter fact just do like lowercase ABCs or something. I can't focus when you're down there acting like you've got a sloppy joe," Eva huffed.

That textbook shit worked on everybody else anyway. My mental mistresses melted away like sugar in warm water. Eva's snippy tone dragged me back to the boring reality of our dark-ass bedroom, with the same tired-ass foreplay. I rolled my eyes repositioning my lips. *It would be nice if a nigga could at least see. I be havin' more fun in my head than in the bedroom. The hell she need to focus for when I'm doing the work anyway?* Eva been on this vampire pitch-black shit since the day Deacon made us friendly-fuck in front of him. At first I thought she just needed someone to break her out of her churchy-ass shell. It swole my ego all the way up to know I'd be that nigga to get all those first time awards. I was her first love, first fuck, first kid, and the first O champion. And in so many years that's *all* I was.

I could tell the pillow was already back over her face from the sound of her muffled humming. *She could probably focus if her crazy ass wasn't doing so much. And, man, I know that ain't that Kenny G shit.*

I spelled out "what the fuck" in lowercase letters when I sure as hell picked what sounded like "G-Bop" by Kenny G. I sped up and started writing a thesis with my tongue on why I hated jazz while Eva hummed even faster tapping her fingernails against the headboard. *The things we do for love, I swear*. There was a point in time when I couldn't even get my lips anywhere near her waistline or she'd clam up on me. Now, she'd launch into a one-woman jam session and after three years I knew what "G-Bop" meant. It meant she was gonna get hers and try to bop her ass right to sleep.

I was goin' straight-up stir crazy on some for real love and hate type shit. Eva was my everything. And now that we had a daughter I wasn't even about to let her cult family take that from me. It took months after we left to keep her from going back for her sister and it took even longer than that to keep her busy enough to not cry about it. I'd found us a nice small spot in Norfolk and when I made enough, I'd get us a real place.

Eva needed to stop worrying about them when they ain't give a damn about her. When she'd called to tell Rose and Leslie about the baby, and they insisted she get married or we were all going to hell. No congratulations, none of that. Shit, Eva couldn't get it into her thick head that Leslie was actually happy. I'd told Eva she had my heart and I'd take care of her and I meant it but lately the shit she'd been doin' was workin' my nerves. It didn't even have to be as complicated or as serious as she was making it. I'm talking about things like scheduling sex three days in advance and it had to be no earlier than nine p.m. and no later than eleven p.m. on weekdays. I ain't even bother trying on Saturdays because as she put it, she ain't "want to feel the stain of sin in church Sunday morning."

We synchronized the calendars in our phones and up until my appointment time I was on eggshells trying not to do or say anything to piss her off or my sex session was cancelled. There was no spontaneity, no doggie style, no hand jobs, no fingering, no talking, and definitely no fucking excitement. Just plain-ass, geriatric, old people eighteenth century vanilla put it in and take it out. If the E is for excitement you can go ahead and take that motherfucka completely out of s-e-x with Eva.

She started humming faster, which meant she was gettin' close. Any kind of touching would throw off her concentration, so my fingers were fisted up in the sheets on either side of her. *We need to wrap this up. I should start humming that shit they play during award shows to cut off the actor's speeches*. The joints in my fingers were getting stiff and uncomfortable and on top of that my jaw and the back of my neck were starting to hurt. I put everything I had into the final stretch of my tongue marathon.

I waited until the humming stopped before wiping my mouth and the sweat out my eyes. Eva squirmed as I worked my way up from underneath the covers. Balancing over her I leaned down to give her a kiss and got a mouthful of pillow. It didn't make any sense. The room was pitch-black plus I was under the damn cover. Everybody always talked all this mess about church girls being the biggest freaks. Myth busted. I had the princess of stone-cold prudishness in my bed every night.

I pulled the pillow off her face. "Baby, you all right?"

"Mmm hmm," Eva sighed.

"You know it'd be nice if I felt all right too," I told her.

I pressed the length of myself against her stomach so she could feel my frustration. She'd done left me high and hard one too many times to count. I could feel the start of the worst concentrated cramp known to man building up in my groin like a pissed off corked bottle of champagne. You don't shake that shit up and just set it down; hell no, you pop the fuckin' bottle and enjoy that champagne shower.

Eva exhaled, giving me a quick apology peck on my shoulder. "And if we did all that I'd have to get up, take a shower, get clean sheets, probably wake the baby up and then I'd have to put her back to sleep. Dontay, baby, I'm tired. And I came too hard; my booty hole got a charley horse," she complained.

My shoulders slumped in disappointment. I pressed my lips to her forehead and rolled over to my side of the bed feeling like I could tear a building down with my bare hands. The sheets on my half were cold but not cold enough. This whole situation was frustrating enough to drive a priest to the bottle. No man wants to walk around feeling like his girl has some kind of dick aversion because she always running away or hiding from it.

Glaring up at the ceiling I wondered if there was a step I'd forgotten or if my game had really just fallen off all together. None of my exes were this hard to crack; hell I used to have make up shit just to get a break from puttin' in work. Frustration was compounding on top of fuckstration. The only way I was going to feel any kind of relief would be from an ice-cold shower.

Eva had already dozed off so I left the lights off, stubbed my toe twice, and hobbled into the shower cursing under my breath. I cursed again when I lathered up with one of her botanical explosion shower gels that smelled like it could make a bee go in heat. *How is it Bath & Body Works can come up with a million ways to remix fruit and flowers but they can't put the men's line in a different shaped bottle?*

When I finally had myself under control I climbed out realizing I ain't have a towel. I snatched one of Eva's out the hamper. She never used the same one more than two days in a row anyway so by my standards it was damn near laundry fresh. I toweled off wishing I knew how to break through her mental block. For a minute I just stood there like a lovesick fool, shaking my head at myself. *How did I go from getting more ass in my parents' crib to living on my own and getting next to none?* I'd retired my player jersey and let my whole stable of on-call super freaks go just for her. Woodsy karo karounde blossoms and soft baie rose scents were imprinted on the fluffed cotton towel from Eva's skin. It was intoxicating and haunting, like the scent of her I'd just washed off my face. I looked down pissed that I'd managed to work myself back up into a frenzy. *Guess I'm gonna have to handle this the old-fashioned way.*

A hand is man's best friend. I revisited my playgirls from earlier, letting them moan and dance in my head. Every dude has a favorite selection of on-demand porn clips in his head. Multitasking would probably be a helluva lot better if we deleted that mental memory file, but we'd probably use that brain power to focus on getting in trouble. In a last-second call to increase the reality and freak level I fought back a moan feeling the first pulls of release. I grabbed panties from the hamper ignoring the crazy weirdo impression anyone would have gotten if I got caught. I needed some freakiness in my life something serious.

The soft pussy-perfumed lace touched my nose and the reaction was instant. My knees almost buckled. Liquid heat splat up against the bathroom wall and Eva's panties landed on my foot. My nostrils were still filled with that unmistakable putrid odor. To a dude it's like sitting in your own fart cloud: you can tolerate it all day easy. But when it ain't your own, it turns your stomach, makes you gag and run for the nearest window. No nigga wants to smell another nigga's spunk.

Hands down, that was the most painfully disgusting and infuriating way to find out Eva was cheating.

Chapter 14

Eva
Thems the Rules

Our apartment complex was one of those starter apartments with two families on each floor and each building goes up three floors. We were somehow lucky enough to have landed on the middle floor underneath a professional mover. No, really, the man above us never stayed still for more than a few minutes at a time. He stomped, paced, or whatever it is you want to call it, from one end of his apartment to the next all day and night. We couldn't hang pictures or mirrors, the walls shook, they'd rattle, jingle, and fall. This was our starter apartment; that's what Dontay called it. I was just happy for once buffalo butt upstairs didn't sound like he was coming through the ceiling and I could finish what Dontay had tried to start.

I was always filled with the guiltiest feeling when we were together. You really don't forget your first and Dontay wasn't giving me any crazy insane comparisons. Sighing, I lay back trying to block out all the sounds of people living on top of people. The pipes clanked in the wall whenever anyone in the building flushed or showered. The moisture also formed a pretty tight seal around the door so you had to yank a few good times to get the door open. Dontay finished his shower and the sound of the bathroom door popping loose broke me completely out of my zone.

And the Didn't Get to Finish for the Second Time in One Night Award goes to none other than yours truly. I eased my vibrator back into its hiding place between the mattresses. He came into the bedroom smelling like gardenia and sweet cassis mixed with manly sandalwood and black coriander, and making way more noise than normal. I peeked at Jada in her crib.

"Shhh. And how many times I gotta remind you to just reach your Stretch Armstrong arms up? You'll find all your shower gels along the top ledge. Because you're, duh, taller," I whispered at him in the dark before rolling over and facing the wall.

After a few minutes when I didn't feel the bed shift or hear him moving around the bed room I realized I was all by my lonesome. Carefully leaning over the side of the bed I scanned the place with my ears on sonar. The living room was still dark but I was able to just barely make him out lying on the couch. He was probably pissed and pouting because he didn't get any booty or head. If he thought throwing a temper tantrum was about to make it happen it wasn't. It wasn't that I didn't want to or didn't like to. We used to sneak and do things all the time all over the place. Something was just, ugh, off.

Like how I couldn't stand his nipple game. He'd latch on like one of those fish that cleans the sides of aquariums. His lips and tongue never really moved; they just sat there around my nipple until it started to become the most annoying feeling in the world. And he forgot there were two nipples so I literally had to pop his face off one only for him to do the same irritating shit to the other side. Teaching didn't work because, just like with his shower gel in the bathroom, he did the same thing every time no matter what. Eventually I just gave up and came up with the "don't touch my nipples" rule.

Dontay's idea of eating coochie was like watching Flick from *A Christmas Story* sticking the tip of his tongue on a frozen flagpole: fearful, timid, tip only, one-spot action. I was pretty sure he got more wet from drooling than from me. Since when had the tip ever satisfied anybody? I hummed so I could keep track of how long his behind had been down there. Humming came in really handy now because it helped me stay focused, too.

The sound of Dontay's phone vibrating against the wooden coffee table echoed through our apartment like a swarm of bees. Those same bees started gathering in the pit of my stomach in the form of an angry feeling. I wasn't the jealous type but then again he wasn't normally the type to sleep on the couch or text late at night either. *What does it mean if I love someone with all my heart but I just don't love it when he touches me?*

I woke up in the same position I fell asleep in. Dontay was making so much noise trying to open the closet door he'd have had better luck just snatching it open. I watched him for a few minutes wondering if maybe I was just taking him for granted. His shoulders were almost as wide as the doorway; he ducked into the closet coming out a few seconds later empty-handed.

It was barely light outside and it sounded like a scene from Alfred Hitchcock's *The Birds* outside. We happened to have the only patch of trees in the entire apartment complex outside of our bedroom window. Most mornings every walk of wildlife would convene out there like I was some kind of urban Cinderella.

"Dontay, you okay, baby?"

"Yeah. I'll be back later; gonna see about this warehouse job." He didn't look in my direction or further acknowledge me before just strolling out.

Where was my good-bye kiss or at least a hug? I grabbed my phone off the charger on the nightstand.

Storie sounded drunk and half asleep. "You okay? My godbaby good?"

"Dontay left and he didn't kiss me or the baby," I told her.

"Girl, I am free and manless. You know Bear been out of town for his job. Do I need me to get my ski mask and come through?" she asked.

"No, I got this. But if you're using my place to creep again, please take your funky-ass drawers with you. I'm tired of doing your stank ho laundry. If I find one more pair of your crusty-cum drawers somewhere crazy I'm taking your key back. You and that side squirtle you humpin' can go to a hotel like regular creepers," I warned her.

She hung up still laughing. Praise the Lord I got home before Dontay because I'd have had one hell of a time trying to explain that. Only because she was like a sister to me did those nasty things not go in the trash. Vicki's ain't cheap so I wrapped them up good in a towel and buried them in the one place Dontay didn't know existed: the laundry hamper. They'd get washed when I went to the laundromat.

Chapter 15

Eva
Bye Bye Alibi

The next morning I stood barefoot in his oversized Sean John T-shirt, the one I'd given him for his birthday to match one of the umpteen hundred pairs of Jordans he owned. His shoes damn near took up an entire wall of the bedroom almost blocking the sliding glass door onto the balcony. Dontay was beyond obsessed with them. Something just ain't right about a man being that gone over some sneakers. They were stacked halfway up the wall, organized according to the color and release date all in their original boxes. Every pair could only be worn once before they were retired to the sacred J burial ground that was slowly taking over our closet. Why he had to have retro shoes in every color if he already had the originals was beyond me. He had more pictures of himself with them stupid shoes than with his own daughter.

He should have known I was mad. Standing in any doorway when I was pissed meant I was a hair of a breath from going slam the heck off if I walked into the same room as whoever had done it. He sat on the couch by the front door quietly pulling on his shoes.

February sunshine slid through the cracks in the blinds. The rays bounced off the chunky diamond in his ear, another gift from yours truly. The sun kissed the thick muscles in his shoulders; his pecs and abs flexed as he sat back. My blood started to run hot from a reason other than anger. I crossed my legs tight to match the current position of my arms. *No, Eva, don't you dare say a damn thing to his ass.* How was it I could notice when he got an edge up from a different barber or did a thinner or thicker beard? Or just stopped shaving all together as he'd been doing this month, face lookin' like some kind of raggedy coochie hair taco meat mess.

Yet he hadn't said a word about my eyebrows I'd just gotten waxed or that he liked my hair parted down the middle hanging halfway down my back. I thought he was aiming for a Rick Ross look but he ain't have the fullness or the complexion for it. He was just too pretty.

Dontay eased his behind up off the couch, threw on his favorite green Under Armour shirt and matching green and gold hoodie and grabbed his gym bag and my car keys off the table. "I'm gonna meet some of the guys so we can get a couple of games in before work. See you when I get off," he stated casually, barely glancing in my direction.

"Hold up, are you sure you aren't off today?" I asked.

"I picked up an overtime shift until one of the other jobs I applied to picks me up. Gotta save to get us a better spot for Jada. Anyway, I'll see you later tonight."

No kiss, no hug, no Happy Valentine's Day. *No, he didn't pick up a shift on damn Valentine's Day of all days.* I was so mad I could spit and it'd probably burn a hole through the floor. That's how heated I was. It'd burn until I could see into Mrs. Kim's apartment below us.

I'd made plans to have the chubby little Korean woman watch Jada for the rest of the night because I thought Dontay was off. Yes, we needed the extra money since he was supposed to be paying the brunt of the bills. Mad notices were starting to come in with past due stamps making me wonder where his money was going or if he just couldn't say it was all too much. But, to go play ball in this kind of cold and during the little time we could've spent together was . . . suspicious.

Now I felt like Boo Boo the fool for wanting to do something special. All this mess was nowhere in my life plan. With a heavy sigh I tiptoed across the bedroom to grab my purse. I stepped over sweaty boxers and work tees, socks and spare change. The clothes hamper wasn't but an arm's reach from where he'd dropped all his mess. *It'll stay*

right there, too. I am not his live-in housekeeper.
I quickly checked his laptop and was disappointed
when it immediately asked me for his password.
When I'd helped him buy it we set up my name as
the password but he'd changed that a long time
ago. Lately he'd started falling asleep on the couch
claiming he was too tired to come to bed.

Jada was still asleep in her crib. I was tempted
to wake her up so she wouldn't be up all night but
that little girl loved two things: sleep and food.
It was probably wrong for me to pray that she'd
eventually grow out of his almond-shaped gray
eyes and that they'd turn wide and brown like
mine. There were plenty of times I stood over her
debating on cutting her ridiculously long daddy
long leg–looking lashes. Those were her damn
daddy's lashes; mine were short and thick. *Leave
that baby alone, Eva.* We'd have our own little
Valentine's dinner and that itis would put her right
back out. I needed to find that receipt for the gift
I'd bought him. When I couldn't find it in my purse
I wound up searching every shred of paper in the
house.

It must have fallen out of his gym bag. The
receipt was from a month ago. It was for a Pandora
bracelet with an engraved charm. The inscription
he requested said U R REAL LOVE. I sank to the
floor. For the first time ever I felt blank. I didn't
even try convincing myself it was a gift he'd bought

to give me later tonight. The overtime he'd been working, the distance between us, even his attitude toward me all pointed at him having a "real love" who apparently wasn't me.

I put the receipt in my purse and stared blankly at the gift I'd bought for him. Tiny diamonds winked up at me. *What you look like giving a man all these diamonds, when you ain't got a single one your damn self?*

The song "Happy" by Tasha Cobbs started blasting from my phone cradled beside the bed. I dove, bouncing across the bed to answer it before Jada woke up hollerin'.

"Hey, pud," I sang into the phone while tryin' to catch my breath.

"Happy Valentine's Day, boo," Storie shouted in my ear.

"Ugh. Ain't no Valentine's Day up over here; you know this fool forgot. So you know I'm takin' his present back after work tomorrow."

"Girl, you need to let that go. Y'all ain't been the same since that night we do not speak of anyway. But just because you got his baby don't meant you need to stay with him, Eva."

"I know, but I ain't make Jada by myself and I'm not trying to raise her that way. I'm gonna talk to him about all that when he gets off work tonight."

"Well hopefully me and Bear will be getting off by then. I ain't gave him none in two weeks and I been using my honey dust powder. It makes your skin and your sweat taste like honey. If it was summer I'd have all kinds of fruit flies and wildlife chasin' behind my ass. He is gonna tear this up. Want us to come pick you and Jada up? Y'all can hang out with us. I'm just not responsible for anything you see or hear though."

"No, girl. I'm not trying to rain on your day since mine is wack."

"Please, it's no big deal. If we have someone else around then he knows he'll have to wait even longer to get this. That'll give me just enough time to take me a vinegar bath and make sure my shit tightens back up. I had a blast from the past and um, Eva, I managed to sneak off and he blasted me away."

Mrs. Kim downstairs was all grins when I dropped Jada off. All her kids were grown and living on the other side of the world. She'd bring Jada up in the morning with her clothes and hair smellin' all like that spicy cabbage and red curry paste she called kimchi. Mrs. Kim barely spoke English. She'd frown and say, "Oh un huh," to everything, like me telling her Jada's feeding schedule for the fiftieth time. I knew she was giving my baby Korean food on the low. Jada always had the worst diapers after a day with Mrs. Kim. But free babysitters are hard to come by and she's right here.

It was too cold for me to think about dressing any cuter than some dark blue jeans that had me looking like that Atlanta housewife with the big ol' big ol' booty. That show was my favorite guilty pleasure. I threw on a tan and dark brown turtleneck with matching dark brown boots and I was ready right as Bear texted to let me know he was outside. I was quiet when we just so happened to pass the court where Dontay said he'd be. All my life functions went on a temporary pause. I could only see a handful of guys in sweats and hoodies; none of them looked like Dontay. I was on the brink of being pissed all over again until I saw my car parked off to the far side of the court. If that wasn't some kind of agonizing relief I didn't know what was.

I tried not to look into it too much.

"You okay? Storie told me what happened. Maybe he's gonna surprise you when he gets off work." Bear reached over and gave my leg a consoling pat.

Chills ran down the back of my neck before he pulled his hand away.

"Okay, Bear, tell me, would you ever buy jewelry for another woman, forget Valentine's Day, and then go play basketball with a bunch of sweaty dudes if you were surprising someone?"

He stared at the road making the "guy code" confusion face. That's the face dudes make when they know you're right but guy code prevents them from admitting it.

"It's all right, don't hurt yourself. At least it looked like he might be at the court we just passed."

"Oh, well yeah, you're good. You should have told me you seen him over there. We could have stopped by so I could have gave him a quick gut check about what day it is."

"Hmm," was my response.

"Hmm what? You saw him right? Because back in the day . . . Never mind."

He got that stupid guy code look again and my mood instantly darkened. "Bear, back in the day we what?"

"Nothin'. Let's go holla at him right quick."

We hit a quick U-turn. I tried to make myself say no but checkin' on Dontay was exactly what I wanted to do. We pulled up behind my car and I held my breath while my eyes roamed over the guys on the court. Not one of them was Dontay.

Chapter 16

Eva
Girl Code Against Guy Code

"Girl, don't look like that. He might have walked off to take a piss or get a Gatorade." Bear had the heat turned up to walking in the Sahara Desert in a sauna suit. *That fool is probably out with his real love.* I had no choice but come out of my coat. *Should have pulled that spare key out and took the car on his MIA behind.*

"Damn, Eva, you get some work done? I mean you're looking real bountiful up top these days. I'm just messing with you. I haven't seen you since what, since we came to the hospital?

The good thing about having a baby was that I went from a B cup to a full D and those ultrasounds with a full bladder make you work until those Kegel muscles are built up like Popeye's forearms. I'd gotten my shape back but my hips were thicker and all my shirts fit a lot snugger now.

"Gonna have to start call you Top Shelf Diva or something."

I punched him in the arm. "Whoa, ho, don't make me pull out the nickname list. You know Storie tells me everything, Papa Pump, oh wait, Dick Slater. I think we need to get you a Dick Slater T-shirt made. I bet you still have those wrestling action figures, too."

We laughed so hard I had tears in my eyes.

"Oh you went way back. That's all right; watching wrestling was like the poor man's karate. I was learning vital survival skills with that."

We stopped at the ABC store and Bear bought enough stuff to last a couple of house parties. He held the door open for me, something Dontay rarely did, not even when I was holding Jada. Storie was my girl but she was definitely being selfish when it came to Bear. She had a really good one, but if you asked her all her men were good ones. The only thing that made them all stand apart was their dongs and which one she wanted as her flavor of the week. My eyes kept drifting to Bear's crotch to see if there was an outline. He was supposedly really long and thick and . . . Lord, she'd given me way too much information. I couldn't think about Bear like that; it was wrong on so many levels. Now I *could* think about Enzo, one of the other guys she was always creepin' with. She'd describe his johnson and you'd think she was talking about a five-course meal. It was juicy and with a big old mushroom tip that she'd go into withdrawal from not having.

I need to get my mind off the random johnsons and on to the one in my house that I hardly liked. Shoot, he'd better hope I don't find one to replace him.

"Eeeh, my twin, I've missed you," Storie squealed and ran to grab me up in a hug as soon as I walked in.

I always felt a tug of envy whenever we were all together.

"Are you ready to get wasted, boo?" She laughed.

I hadn't drunk since before Jada but I nodded and smiled. "I'm so ready to get wasted. But not too much. I'm goin' to first service tomorrow."

Storie responded with an exaggerated finger down her throat and gag. "Can you stop being a Jesus freak and just be a regular freak with the rest of us heathens for one day?" she whined, grabbing me by the shoulders and shaking me until we were both giggling.

"I am a freak for my God and that is it. Wait, that don't sound one bit of right," I said while fighting back a smile.

We started off with vodka shots while Vaughn showed off his bartending skills trying to make us some blue motorcycles. I tried to call Dontay again but his phone was going to voicemail. It was two forty-five and he usually worked from three until midnight. I was hoping he was actually at work.

"You better not be over here callin' that idiot during our Valentine's celebration." I snapped the screen off on my phone setting it on the glass coffee table. I chewed the inside of my cheek debating on even mentioning the basketball court, but if I didn't there was a good chance Bear would bring it up and I'd have to hear her mouth. My recap was four shots long and since neither of us had eaten we were feeling every single one.

Storie put on her serious face. "Well now that we got that out the way, this is your mission should you choose to accept it. I'm gonna have Bear call some of his boys over and every time you mention he who we will not mention anymore, you will take a shot."

"Mission accepte . . . Wait, do you mean every time I mention Jesus or Dontay?"

"Shot! Dontay, girl, why would . . . Never mind. Drink the damn shot, Anna Mae."

By the time Bear's friends showed up with pizza, more liquor, and Red Box movies I would have paid one of them to feed me pizza in my sleep. Guys only hang out with guys who are of greater or equal sexiness. There was Mateo, John, and Enzo. I reached under the couch cushions and pinched Storie's butt when I heard Enzo's name. It was mushroom dong in the flesh. She was messing with one of Bear's homeboys and yes, it was so so wrong but I could see why. Enzo and Bear both towered

over the other two. If either one put you on their
shoulders you'd probably come down with a nose-
bleed. Aside from their height they were night and
day. Bear was clean shaven and lean with creamy
dark skin. Enzo was motor oil gold with a rugged
beard and a little bush of hair peeking out the
collar of his shirt. Enzo looked like he could ride
the hell out of a bike. *Or a woman*. After looking
at him I already knew I wasn't about to remember
anyone else's name. From the way the other two
trailed behind Enzo and Bear they became Shadow
and Shadow Lurker.

After a few drinks Enzo got bolder than a fat-tip
Sharpie. I somehow wound up on his lap and Storie
was surprisingly quiet, which meant she was jealous. *Lighten up, girl; you can't have all the fun*. I
hadn't even planned on doin' anything more than
flirting but her stank attitude was irritating me.

The rest of the guys sounded occupied yelling
and carrying on with their game of pool. They'd
escaped to the little den Bear called his Bear cave
that extended off the back of the kitchen. We, well
he, talked all over the *Fast & Furious 6* movie we
were supposed to be watching, while I fantasized.
Enzo was twenty-whatever; I accidentally replaced
the number with how many ways I wanted him to
make me cum. He had a brother or maybe a sister,
I thought, and he was half black and . . . well I knew
he was mixed.

My fingers gave the thick nape of his neck the same slow, loving devotion that an obsessively compelled neurotic would pay to stroking a kitten. All thoughts of Dontay evaporated the second my own kitten got bumped awake. Enzo smiled and I blushed at what I knew was a big ol' mushroom pokin' me in my butt. Storie should have never relayed that little bit of information. He made big, sweeping circles rubbing my back trying to coerce me to move closer and I leaned my ear closer to his mouth.

Storie sucked her teeth and hopped up bumping the coffee table spilling our unfinished shots from the last round. She grabbed her coat and jetted for the front door. Shock, complete and absolute shock, was the only thing my half-drunk mind could muster. Enzo dumped me on the couch like we weren't just having what I thought was "a moment" and went running off behind her. I crossed my arms and stared at the television playing like I was severely insulted. I seriously didn't want to be the one to tell him his woman was with her other man. Storie didn't walk across the stage at graduation because she beat Tisha Lesner into the hospital just for starting a rumor. Nope, I wasn't about to be spreading real business.

"Damn what's wrong, Eva? Dontay still ain't hit you up? Girl, it's just a phase." Bear asked as he strolled into the living room.

I perked up like we were on *Pee-wee's Playhouse*. "You said the forbidden word. You've got to take a shot." I poured and handed him what I'd learned was a double. He needed to play catch-up anyway. As an afterthought I poured myself one more, hoping it would burn away the sadness that seemed to come up with Dontay's name. I tossed it back fighting my gag reflex and then coughing like crazy as it tried to burn its way back up. Everyone else made that mess look so easy. The devil was a liar.

When I could breathe again I looked over at Bear. "Do you ever feel like you don't know Storie? Like she's changed or she's a completely different person from when you two first got together?"

He made the man version of the duck face, pursing his lips to one side of his face and then the other. He'd been doing that goofy mess ever since we were little.

"No. I know Storie inside and out to the point where I can say that I actually get bored sometimes. I mean, she's not a very complicated person, Eva. Now you on the other hand—"

"Me?"

"Yes, you; you seem like this perfectly evolved stranger. You used to be so cool. I mean cool for a chick who wasn't housebroken. I remember a story about you peeing in my bathroom sink and all."

I gasped. "Whoa now, that's not fair. Dontay told you that? He ran up in the bathroom to take one of those long as sin camel hump horse pees. I had a baby pressing on my bladder, jerk."

"Would it be wrong if I said that's what I like about you?" Bear replied in a low voice.

His words sounded playful but his tone sounded like we'd had too much to drink and he was going in a very strange and very wrong direction.

"So you have a pee-pee fetish?" I teased, trying to lighten the atmosphere. Bear was off-limits and I was not going there. Storie would murder him if I told her what I thought he was hinting at and then she'd probably stab me too.

"No, more like I had an Eva fetish." He did a mock Southern girl voice. "But Eva was in love with Jesus and was gonna marry Jesus and had a Jesus ring and was even gonna pray to have a miracle Jesus baby."

We both cracked up laughing. My sides hurt; that's about exactly what I'd said to any Negro who tried to talk to me before Que and Don—

My punishment wasn't a shot this time. Bear's lips made me feel hotter and tipsier than all the liquor in the house combined. He tasted forbidden. It was this indescribable honeyed sensation. I was licking a nine-volt battery drenched in cinnamon-apple butter and the jolt ran from the tip of my tongue up to the tips of my ears. The more my brain tried to ping on how wrong this all was the more electrifying it became. I could barely catch my breath from all the shocks running through my body.

Is this what it's like when he cheats on me? All this wanting and feeling, is this why he does it? It was probably wrong or unnatural for me to be thinking about Dontay with another woman. But wondering about him only made me want to put it down one hundred times better. Disappointment hit me like a tidal wave when he stopped. I sighed. *Maybe one of us needs to show some common sense.*

"Come with me," Bear stated holding out his hand.

There was a small break in the lust fog and I looked around suspiciously. His Bear man caveamajigger had been awful quiet all this time. "Where are your boys? Shadow and Shadow Lurker?"

"You talking about John and Mateo? They left; they parked on the side of the house by the Bear cave. Went out that way."

Bear led me into the darkness of his man cave with black carpeting and matching leather armchairs. He sat me on the edge of the pool table. I pushed the bright red three ball across the black felt fabric toward the eight. They clinked and separated.

"What about um . . ." I couldn't bring myself to say my best friend's name.

"Oh yeah, y'all's girl code right?" Bear responded, sliding my turtleneck over my head. "You weren't gonna tell me about her and it's cool."

I opened my mouth to defend myself and kisses on my neck and my shoulders stole my breath. I closed my eyes trying to ignore the thoughts spinning along with my head. This was sin on top of sin compounded by betrayal. Storie was my girl, Dontay was my man, I was Eve, and Bear . . . Bear was the apple.

"Eva, you don't think I don't know she's with my boy? We boys damn near brothers. He wasn't about to smash my girl and not tell me. I was the one who gave him the okay. I just let her think she was running that. Like I said, I know what she's gonna do before she does it."

And that was it. I was biting, scratching, and clawing at my apple as the rest of my worries fell away with our clothes. He bent my knees pressing my legs up toward my stomach with one hand. I almost came up off the table when I heard what I thought was a hornet or a bee. His mouth closed over my clit with his tongue vibrating up and down, and around it until I was buzzing on the edge of heaven. He paused just long enough to take his tongue ring back out.

My human blanket covered every square inch of me. He felt like flannel sheets fresh out the dryer with his wide tongue licking all my senses on fire. I didn't know it was possible to want someone as bad as I wanted him and I told him just that.

We were anxious and feverish. I wound my hips toward him trying to get back to the edge of the cliff he'd just yanked me off of. We offered what the other felt was missing at home. I nibbled his shoulders, dragged my nails across his ridiculously perfect ass. *If all this were mine I wouldn't be going anywhere with anybody.*

"Mmmm," I moaned, and he growled when he sat himself at my opening; it sure felt all the hell like a mushroom tip to me. I turned into a human cage, wrapping my arms as tight as I could around his neck and my legs around his waist. *Oh please forgive me.* I wasn't sure whose forgiveness I was asking for in that small window of guilt but the line had already been crossed; scratch that, the line had been completely erased.

I bit his lips, then kissed and sucked the spots I was meant to. Bear eased himself forward going inch by agonizing baby anaconda inch like he was snaking a damn punani drain. I wasn't anywhere near mentally prepared to be stroked like that. This nigga went deeper and was more precise than one of them grandfather clocks that dinged out the hour all loud and long. All I could was bury my face into his neck and gasp. I was on some for real Lois Lane clinging to Superman flying over the city, praying he'd go ahead and drop me off the edge of that cliff he showed me earlier.

Bear crashed into me over and over, perpetual motioning all his bad but so so good sexual energy into me until the nerves in my palms were throbbing. As the saying goes when you don't know what to say or what to pray . . .

"Jesus," I whispered through clenched teeth unsure of whether I was calling on Him, praying to Him, or just out of words all together.

The pool table rocked and I ain't never felt a good so good that tears ran out the corners of my eyes. I begged him to let me go, make me cum, drop me, and throw me off the mountain. I'd never felt that with Dontay, not with his quick super-fast jackrabbit strokes. Bear roared his way to the top like he'd just lifted an entire car off all four tires. It was powerful and sexy and it shattered me from the inside out.

Mission control; come in, mission control. Is there any damage? Neither one of us moved for a minute; my brain was trying to assess the condition of my body. My butt was stinging from rug burns from the table, and my legs felt slick and shaky.

Bear smiled down at me. "Explain to me again why you ain't mine?"

"Because you—"

We almost broke our necks as our heads whipped in the direction of the living room. Enzo and Storie were back.

Chapter 17

Dontay
The Price of Fayme

"Oh bookie-boo, thank you so much for gettin' my feet done." Fayme smiled over at me from the vibrating massage chair.

I picked the nicest shop I could find and treated us both to pedis. Real talk, I liked to get my dogs rubbed and massaged all over. There's nothing worse than climbing in bed with somebody and you couldn't sleep because their heels were scratching up the front of your shins all night. Or someone told you to stop moving your feet because the scratching sound they made across the sheets was too annoying. That's exactly what Fayme said the first night we met up.

She was getting her toes done up in bright cherry red. I got up and kissed the back of her neck earning myself a giggle.

"Getting you to dinner and back to the house with this dress intact ain't gonna be easy," I whispered along the fine hairs at her nape rubbing my lips back and forth across her skin for emphasis.

Fayme shivered. "No, we take Lanvin off, baby; we don't mess that up. But you are gonna be paying for me to get my toes redone if you don't stop. I'm gonna make her mess up," she replied in a breathless voice.

"Mmm, speaking of messing up."

I straightened up slowly like she had a gun pointed at my chest and had just asked for my wallet and keys. "How are you doin', Sister Bealiah?" I asked her in a tired, worn-out voice.

Out of all the nail shops in the entire world she had to march her self-righteous self up into this one. I hadn't run into her since we moved and Eva stopped goin' to Deacon's church. If Eva got wind of this from her of all people, she'd take Jada and throw me on child support.

"Step over here for a moment, Dontay James. I'd like to give you a word." Sister Bealiah's tone was dryer than dry ice and equally as cold.

"What's the matter, Dontay? Is everything all right?"

I gave Fayme a brief nod for an answer before slipping on my coat and following the bluebird of bad news out the doors of the nail shop.

"It's bad enough that we have to see each other on occasion and I have to act favorishly and keep my opinionations to myself," Sister Bealiah huffed in her dignified tone using her made-up words just the same as she did when preaching. "But, I can't take it anymore and unless you want me to tell Eva about you and Oholah the whoreah in there"—she raised her hand shushing me when I started to interrupt—"you keep your . . . your . . . oh, Jesus, give me the words. You put Lillith over there on a short leash with a muzzle. Get her to leave my husband alone."

Sister Bealiah spat the end of her tirade poking me hard in the chest with a white-gloved finger. She glared up at me with her eyes narrowed into slits that made her irises look black. This definitely wasn't the way I expected the conversation to go down. I cleared my throat a few times trying to get over my initial shock and awe at Reverend Matthew's old player ass.

The nail lady stuck her head out the door about to go spastic. "You no pay. He no pay."

I handed her some cash. "Go do her eyebrows, too, or something," I told her nodding in Fayme's direction. The last thing I wanted was for Fayme to come outside asking a ton of questions.

As cold as it was outside, my nerves and what Sister Bealiah was pretty much ordering me to do had me damn near in a sweat. "Sister Bealiah, how do you know Fayme and um, Reverend Matthews are, I mean—"

"Boy, you think a hen doesn't know when her rooster's crowin' on top of another hen house?"

I almost fell out laughin' at her hen analogy. Sister Bealiah would have given Big Bird a run for his money.

"Matthews and all his foolish improprieties, got him leasin' cars for that pigeon nicer than the ones we own. That old buzzard even got her a credit card. The first statement came to our place by mistake instead of going to the house she's living in. That house was supposed to be fixed up and donated to a needy family. I've seen her little raunchified pictures on his computer. He was trying to tell me the walls had termites, that the place was a money pit. She's the only money pit in the picture."

I ran my hand down the back of my neck letting out a long breath. Skirting around Eva on top of trying to get Fayme to steer clear of someone else was a damn suicide mission. Sister Bealiah just put me in one hellafied pussy pickle. My phone went off. It was a serious e-mail I'd been waiting on, putting business front and center and all this play relationship mess to the side.

I gave Sister Bealiah a stern look. "All right, you just make sure Eva doesn't find out about this and we're good."

She stuck her chin up in the air in agreement and stormed past me into the shop almost knocking Fayme over as she came out.

"What was all that, Dontay?" Fayme asked with a look of concern on her face.

My mind went in a million different directions at once trying to find one solid answer. "She just worried about one of my boys sniffing around one of her choir girls. I promised to talk to him."

"Aww, look at you. Being an upstanding role model, I'm so proud of you, bookie-bear."

Fayme stood on her toes to kiss me on the cheek and my stomach bottomed out. I wasn't feeling too proud of me at the moment nor was I in any way feeling enthused about competing with Reverend Matthews.

Chapter 18

Eva
Hoes and Hoeing

I threw together some Cream of Wheat with a little sugar and butter so it would be ready when I went to grab Jada from Mrs. Kim. She'd usually have her up and dressed by six on Sunday morning, so I could get her fed and situated before we headed out to church. I showered and threw on a cute yellow and white knit top with a matching skirt in the same bright yellow and white. Mrs. Kim knocked on the door just as Dontay got up to get ready. He was never a morning person so his growled good mornings didn't bother me anymore.

He was quiet on the ride to church as usual. I didn't even raise an eyebrow when I noticed he forgot Jada's binky. I was just happy I made it home last night in enough time to get myself showered and in bed before he could walk in and see the guilt all over my face.

Storie and Enzo had walked in and Bear, who was obviously quicker at thinking on his feet than I was, shoved me out the side door with my bra and turtleneck balled up in my arms so I could finish getting dressed. There I was in the freezing cold praying his neighbors couldn't see over his fence on the side of the house. Storie thought I'd gotten sick and was out there getting fresh air. When he asked where she'd been and why she left in the first place, well she forgot all about little old me.

Dontay nodded off hard beside me, jumping when he snored his own self awake. I rolled my eyes and turned my attention back to the front.

"Wouldn't be so sleepy if you weren't out doing no good last night," I whispered in a nasty voice. I know what I was out doing, so I could only imagine what he did. Jada snored softly on my shoulder. Her chubby face pressed against my neck had us both sweating. She was sleeping so good I'd be damned if I'd tried to shift or move her. I'd have rather let Jada slobber all down the collar of my shirt and snore in my ear than listen to her holler through the rest of service. After what I did last night I needed a prayer, some forgiveness, and some restraint. My eyes wouldn't stop wandering to the front of every man's pants that walked past me. *How have I never noticed this before? It's like a candy factory with so many different shapes, and colors, and sizes.*

Some guys had small bulges while some were huge. Some of their pants looked smoother than me in a pair of jeans. I thought I smelled Bear's cologne and turned to see if it was him. I tried to pull myself together. *Bear cannot happen again but, Lord, if I can just find me a good substitute or teach Dontay how to do that whole pool table power pump . . .* I snapped myself out of my jacked-up dickmatized thoughts.

I bowed my head trying to see who Dontay had the nerve to start texting in the middle of prayer. Frustrated, I gave up when my eyes crossed and started to hurt from straining. When I opened my eyes I noticed a very pretty petite woman sitting down in the empty seat next to Dontay. I didn't remember ever seeing her at any of our services or functions. She kept leaning over to ask Dontay questions; rude heffa didn't even bother introducing herself.

When she covered her mouth with her hand and leaned in to ask Dontay yet another question I elbowed him in between his ribs.

"Are you going to introduce your little friend to your family sitting right here?" I hissed in his ear.

Dontay shrugged before turning slightly in my direction.

"She wanted to know how long service is. Then she asked what section in the Bible we're on because she can't see the words on the teleprompter."

Something about his answer sounded legit and she smiled politely at me around him before turning her attention to thumbing through her Bible. I talked myself out of being jealous, even though my gut was telling me otherwise. There were a ton of empty seats all over. She didn't have to sit in the one seat that put her damn near in Dontay's lap. Just to be on the safe side I shuffled Jada off my shoulder.

"I've got to run to the ladies' room," I whispered to Dontay.

"Okay, handle your business." He whispered his response back a little too quickly and a little too quietly for my liking.

Plopping Jada onto Dontay's lap I hopped up and darted for the double doors before he could try to hand her back or follow me. *How about that? She might not be able to see the teleprompter but anyone can see that Jada is Dontay's twin.* I stood outside the door peeking at them through the narrow glass. They appeared to be having an actual conversation and I could only imagine what was being said. From a distance it looked just as harmless as it could have been dangerous. My temper simmered just beneath the cool exterior of my composure.

Dontay made a gesture with Jada suggesting he was telling the woman who we were or at least who Jada was to him. I was projecting my own guilt at cheating with Bear onto him. Just because I had a slip-up didn't mean he did too.

"You do know the view is supposed to be better from inside the sanctuary?" A deep voice rang out behind me.

I whirled around ashamed at being caught spying. "Brother Hall, I thought you'd be inside listening to the service. Um, I just needed a moment to myself. It was a little stuffy where I was sitting."

He stared through the door behind me and I could feel his eyes dart to Dontay and the stranger.

"Come take a walk with me, Eva. That's just Toikea sitting beside Jada's father. I don't think she's anyone you need to be worried about. But I get the feeling you may have some things you might want to volley off me."

I nodded even though I had no clue what he meant and walked through the lobby with my head down. Brother Hall nodded to the few ushers wandering the halls or people headed back inside from the restroom. The sermon quietly played over the speakers in the hallway; it was so low you had to strain to hear it. The auditorium was erupting into applause and cheering so just about everyone was inside or rushing to get back inside so they could listen to the service.

There was something I wanted to discuss with Brother Hall but to say the words out loud was so much more intimidating than whispering them in my head. There was this nagging feeling I couldn't shake. I was scared that he'd judge me or not want me to be a part of the church anymore.

The man deals with drug addicts and homeless people in other countries. This ain't nothin'. I took a breath to build up my courage.

"I cheated on Dontay and now I feel like I'm obsessed with it." I blurted it all out together on that same breath.

Brother Hall's expression didn't change. I thought he'd condemn me to hell or make me repent on the spot but instead he looked contemplative, lost in thought.

"Eva, I want you to know that God forgives you and He does not think any less of you for giving in to temptation. The Lord forgives you the moment you ask. Now you just need to get over being obsessed with your sin," he said.

I took a deep breath. "Well you see, it's not that I'm obsessed with the sin or the fact that I even committed one. It's the sex that I'm obsessed with. Like I'm always hungry, can't stop thinking about it."

My eyes went back down to the floor. At that point I couldn't, I didn't want to see what he thought about me.

Brother Hall chuckled. "You don't think I haven't pop-vaulted into the arms of temptation before? I know how you feel, Eva."

I gasped in shock at the confession my ears couldn't believe. I was still in disbelief when my eyes snuck a quick scan over the delicious bulge in the front of his slacks before looking up into his face. We stood about eye level and he didn't look soft or pudgy like most of the men at this church. His powder-blue Polo shirt strained over his wide, broad shoulders, bulging over his chest, tapering at the waist. I tugged on my earlobe to keep my eyes from going back down there again. You could look at him and tell he took pride in his body like he stayed in the gym, like he could pick me up and bench press me. Slamming me down onto his—

"Listen at that. Service is about over. I hear the closing prayer. Come now, let me get you back. Do set yourself up an appointment to come by and speak to me anytime you need to, okay?" Brother Hall said casually.

He pressed his hand to the small of my back to usher me in the direction of the auditorium. My skin tingled. Biting my lower lip at the thick muscles flexing under the thin fabric of his shirt, I stood back and enjoyed the show as he opened the door for me. *Short, thick, stocky ass, reminds me of Que. I'd wrap my legs around them big shoulders and ride those lips.*

Brother Hall turned giving my hand a warm squeeze. "Remember, Eva, anytime you need me you just come by; don't hesitate okay?"

I could only nod. My whole body lit up with want at the invitation he'd just thrown out there into the universe. I'd started to walk in to take my place beside my incomplete family. My kitten was a raging little ball of need and I knew once we got out of there and Dontay took my car, I'd never get the moment back. I licked my lips, took a deep breath.

"Brother Hall, your study. Right now please." My voice was more of a breathy whisper than the erotic command that I wanted it to be but it had the same effect.

He nodded and abruptly looked toward the stage before turning to lead the way. We speed walked through the halls this time, nothing like the leisurely stroll we took the first time. My heart pumped energy throughout my body. It was the same rush I'd gotten at Storie's. It was fear and anxiety, excitement, and painful need rushing through me all at once. This had to be that high that addicts looked for. My stuff throbbed as I waited for him to unlock his office door. All I needed to do was squeeze and I could have come right there on the spot.

Once inside Brother Hall closed and locked the door. I kicked my shoes off onto the thick royal burgundy carpet, sliding my moist panties down along with my stockings. I was so ready I was practically panting. I let him get the door locked and when he turned around I closed the small space in between us.

Brother Hall's thick well-muscled arms encircled me and held me captive. He liked the same rough shit that Bear liked. I squealed wondering exactly how much time I had to get my teeth into his shoulders. How hard I could bite him before I left a mark in his beautiful smoked amber skin. And then I realized the man was literally holding me captive. As in holding me back, away from him, and staring at me like I'd lost my damn mind. *Hmm, too much?* Maybe it was just a teeny bit too much.

The muscle in the side of his cheek flexed super fast as did his pulse in the side of his neck. He took a few deep breaths through his nostrils.

"Eva, I thought you had some kind of urgent happening you wanted to speak about. You know I am married and I am a man of God. I forgive you and I'm gonna act like you didn't just . . ."

Unable to put my actions into words and just as embarrassed as I was we both nodded in silent agreement.

He let me go and I grabbed my panties and stockings off the floor. I tried putting them on just as quickly as I'd slipped them off and wound up putting a run in my hose. I'd never felt so mortified in my entire life. I tripped over my own feet trying to slip my heels back on and took a few calming gulps of air while he unlocked his office door.

"I'm going to pray for you, Eva. You are beautiful and young; slow down. You are looking for urgent, extreme, and temporary connections with effects that last forever. Forever."

I stepped out into the sea of churchgoers leaving service. A few of the single sisters glanced in my direction as I stood outside his door. Not about to appear like the rejected woman I was I gave them a smug smile patting my hair before I started making my way toward the auditorium with my head high. The wide-eyed glances they gave me in return before they started whispering let me know I'd at least accomplished my mission in their minds, even if my pride was on zero.

Chapter 19

Eva
Deliver Eva

The drive back to the house was a quiet one. Dontay seemed preoccupied with something, probably the pretty stranger he'd talked to all service. I was trying to keep my mind off of this new craving I couldn't seem to kick. Even with Brother Hall's eerie warning in my head I was still restless. Almost but not quite getting him had me on the edge of my seat, biting my nails looking for someone who could make the hunger go away. Dontay was a polite stranger. He was nothing more than a roommate who borrowed my car, dirtied my house up, and sometimes if it was cold enough, he'd hold me at night. Now that I'd felt this new thing with Bear I couldn't help but wonder if Dontay and I were just over and neither one of us wanted to admit it.

Jada went into a motion-induced mini coma the moment the heat cut on and the car started moving. She was bobbing and nodding as we rolled toward home. Storie had been surprisingly quiet since her little rendezvous with Enzo. She usually gave me blow-by-blow commentary complete with photos she'd snuck of the poor guy. I texted Storie to see what she was up to.

I was doing my best not to ask about Bear. That night felt like a dream now. It didn't even seem like it had happened. Storie was at the grocery store looking at the produce. That was code for doin' something she ain't have any business doing. That was also all the fuel I needed to text Bear. Why he stayed with her and put up with all that when he was such a good guy was beyond me.

I did a five-second floaty finger dance over my phone suddenly unsure of what to say or what I'd do if he agreed to do something.

"What do you want to do today, Tay?" I asked casually feeling out my situation.

He shrugged. "Work texted during service askin' if I'd cover that dude Tarique's shift. They caught this fool unloadin' cases of merchandise into the trunk of his car. Been watchin' him for like six months and finally pulled him in this morning. He worked the overnights so it's gonna get crazy. Plus we've been shorthanded. That boy Allen got let go for beatin' down the nightshift manager, called him a racist and Santiago went to lunch and never came back. I'll probably take a quick nap and roll out. It'll take me a minute to get used to the new shift."

"So now you're gonna work overnight, Dontay? I won't have a car all night? What happened to finishing school?"

"What's up with all these questions? School ain't payin' the bills, I am. Where the hell you need to go in the middle of the night?" he barked.

I glanced back at Jada but she could sleep through anything. "What if Jada gets sick or I get sick, Dontay?"

"That's what 911 is for. I'll work the car thing out after tonight; damn, it's no big deal, man," he snapped at me indicating the conversation was over.

I smirked. It always worked my last nerve when he called me man, or dude, any of that mess. I texted Bear: Where's Dick Slater?

My phone dinged almost instantly and I hid a smile glancing over at Dontay to make sure he wasn't paying me any attention. Which he wasn't of course. I read Bear's reply.

Waiting to make you lap out again, was that my Bat Signal?

That almost made me lol, good one. Yes, that was your Bat signal

I kept my phone close to me once we got inside. My nerves were making me feel breathless and happy for no reason. The last thing I wanted was for Dontay to walk by my phone and see one of Bear's texts pop up on the screen. I started some lunch for Jada and tried to straighten up while I waited on Bear to reply. Since Dontay would be working six at night until six in the morning it seemed best to just hang out at the house. That way I wouldn't have to bother with a babysitter and we wouldn't have to worry about running into anyone.

I was laid up with Bear on the couch. We were watching a movie when my phone went off making me jump.

"What's wrong?" I blurted out as soon as I hit ANSWER. Storie never called for no reason. Storie was one of those chicks with a $700 phone who acted like all it could do was send texts and troll Facebook. She'd probably text you to tell you that your house was on fire. She literally acted like her phone couldn't make or receive calls.

"Giiiirl, are you sitting down?" she asked in her "cat with feathers hanging out of its mouth" voice.

"No, I'm just watching a movie."

"Giiiirl. Why am I at the Sushi spot on Granby and . . ."

Bear had dozed off. He mumbled in his sleep tightening his arm around my waist. I put my hand over the mouth piece and turned away from him.

"Anyway, let me tell you what a bitch done told me . . . Hold up." She started talking to someone in the background moving the phone away from her mouth. "Is that our waitress? What the hell was her name High Kick . . . Chun Li? They be talkin' about black folk, and these heffas is walkin' around looking like clones. All I want is some more wasabi. Ask one of 'em. . . Oh, anyway so why this bitch just tell me Bear's cheating on me?"

The phone almost slipped out my hand. "Huh? Storie, girl, no, not him. Who . . . what would make someone say something like that? I mean, I thought y'all did that whole open thing first of all. But, what makes you think that? And with who?"

My nerves were immediately on edge. I debated on waking Bear but he felt so comfortable. I was being selfish and I knew it.

"This her, I'ma call you right back, boo."

Storie, clicked over and I was left sitting there stuck in limbo.

I decided to keep Storie's phone call to myself for now. At least until I could figure out everything she knew. Bear woke up and was up. We decided to try a little role playing. I wanted him to pretend to be Brother Hall. He had gotten so into character he was whispering scriptures I didn't even know. He was preachin' while he was strokin' it all in his reverend, doctor, bishop voice taking me to church when Jesus shook the whole building. It hadn't occurred to me that it might be wrong to have someone else's man pretend to be a man of the cloth until I was callin' Jesus and Jesus tried to break the front door down. Once again, Bear demonstrated common sense and to my immediate disappointment hopped up and ran into the front room.

"Eva, I think that was Dontay," Bear called out while peeking out the living room window.

He was just about all the way back in his clothes and Dontay was halfway across the parking lot headed toward the building by the time I got up there to look.

"Oh Jesus," was all I could get out.

I rushed him back toward the bedroom once he got his feet in his feet in his shoes. I slid Jada's crib out and pulled the stick out the sliding glass balcony door. He'd have to find his own way down, but we were only on the second floor he didn't have too far to go. Dontay was pounding at the front door and it was only going to be a matter of time before he kicked through the chain. Bear screamed when he hit the ground. Yes, I was certain that was a scream. I just knew he'd jumped and landed wrong spraining his ankle. Black folk don't usually turn white but when I saw Storie standing there beating him I was pretty sure I lost about three shades of brown. She caught one glimpse of me and went four shades of magenta.

"Hold up, you was up there with my bitch?" she shouted at him punching him in the chest. "Bitch, you supposed to be my bitch. And you got my man up over here climbing out windows and shit? You done fucked and fucked with the wrong one," she screamed up at me.

The front door burst open slamming up against the opposite wall.

Oh dear God, please don't let me get killed today.

"Where you at, Eva?" Dontay shouted through the apartment waking up Jada and I wrapped the sheet from the bed tight around myself before picking her up.

He charged into the bedroom like a crazed maniac. His eyes were bloodshot and the vein in his temple made him look like Frankenstein's monster. He looked at Jada then back at me in nothing but that sheet and went slam the fuck off.

"You was fuckin' that bitch-ass brother whoever motherfucka with my baby up in here, bitch? What you trying to do teach my daughter how to be a fuckin' ho' or some shit?"

Dontay thundered toward me screamin' in my face; fear paralyzed my feet. I shook my head back and forth covering Jada's head. I could barely hear Dontay over her high-pitched shrieks in my ear.

"Answer me!" Dontay screamed.

I was shaking my head no. What other kind of answer did he want? I could barely look at him, let alone answer him. Spit hung from the corners of his mouth hitting my face like burning exclamation points. As if Dontay alone wasn't enough.

Storie's shrill voice rang out from the living room. "Bitch, I'm gonna fucking kill you! I trusted you and this is what the fuck you do? You was like my fuckin' sister. Bear should have been like a brother to your trader backstabbing ass. Where the fuck are you?"

Lord, you delivered Daniel, Jonah, umpteen others; please get me and my baby out of this mess alive. I'm sorry I didn't listen.

"Storie, just stop; it wasn't her it was me, and it ain't like you wasn't doing your own shit. This is between us; let's go." Bear was trying to talk her back out the front door.

"Don't touch me. Your hands smelling like another bitch pussy! You low-life dog-ass mother-fucka, I'm gonna have one of my homeboys put you the fuck down, Vaughn!"

I saw the moment of realization. When Dontay figured out there was no Brother Hall and the actual object of his hatred was now within his reach. His face became stony and emotionless, his eyes glazed over as he looked back toward the living room. And that's when I noticed the gun in his waistband. I didn't even know Dontay had a gun or knew how to shoot one.

"Storie, Bear, just go now please. I'm sorry," I called out to them my voice breaking.

Dontay turned, intending to take his anger out on Bear when Storie flew past him with all her hatred, anger, and bitterness directed at me. She didn't even care that I was holding Jada. Instinctively I backed up and hit the nightstand knocking the candle over. It rolled setting the curtains on fire before rolling into Dontay's mountain of shoes. Dontay and Bear both grabbed Storie. She reached for Tay's gun. It went off and the blast was so loud it might as well have been a freight train going through the walls of the building. Storie's eyes went out of focus and she slumped forward in Bear's arms. There might as well have been a hole in all of our chests. We were all hurt, broken, or torn up in some way. I fell to my knees beside Bear, crying, rocking Jada in my arms. I wound up losing two best friends that day. Storie was gone forever and Dontay was just gone.

ACT II

Chapter 20

Jail Bait Blues

Small white candles flickered on a table off to the side. Inhaling, my senses were bombarded with the scent of lime and coconut.

What in the Lord's name kind of sacrificial mumbo jumbo was this? Tay never lit candles or did any of that romantic foolishness and he especially didn't do it after the baby. We got it in when we could and suffered when we couldn't. There were candles everywhere and they made shadows shift and dance on the walls.

He came to me out of the shadows that were dancing in the corner. It was as if he were a shadow himself. The lone dark figure strode toward me and fear paralyzed my feet, froze my vocal chords. It wasn't until he was standing over me that I got the nerve to look up. I was afraid I'd see the face of death in those shadows, finally coming to take me away. But, there wasn't anything cold or deadly about the man who seemed to have appeared out of the darkness.

He was so tall I had to strain my neck to look up into his face. He smiled and the darkness melted away like fog in the sun. I smiled a shy smile back and instantly fell in love with his cinnamon-brown skin, perfect white teeth, and deep dimples. He stretched out his hand and directed me to have a seat in a chair that seemed to have appeared out of nowhere. I smoothed the back of my dress and did as I was instructed. I was mesmerized as this tall tree of a man knelt down before me. His head was bald and looked baby smooth to the touch.

There was a knowing light in his gray eyes that reassured me in the quiet darkness. My breath caught in my throat as he slowly trailed his hand up my inner thigh. He didn't break eye contact. His fingers followed the tiny goose bumps that rose on my skin like they were Braille instructions. He wasn't shy or nervous; it was as if we'd known each other forever, and I was his. I held my breath as he looked away from me to lower his head.

His lips touched a sensitive spot on the inside of my ankle and it felt like I'd been hidden away for years in a cold, dark cave and his touch was my first sunrise. I closed my eyes, silently telling myself, girl, breathe before you fall out. *His lips felt like warm honey as they trailed wet kisses up my calf and inner thigh. The heat from his long fingers scorched my skin as he began slowly pushing my panties to the side. Involuntarily my*

ıead fell backward and a soft moan somehow
snuck out from between my lips just as I felt his
lips close in on my clit.

Oh, Lord, this nigga was not playing around.
He went straight for the gold. My hands had a
mind of their own and somehow they found their
way to his ears. I caressed them, dug my nails into
the skin around them, and then I was holding on
for dear life. He was busy introducing himself to
my pussy. Telling her she was his favorite color,
and she was his favorite food, and how much
he'd missed her. He said all that with his tongue
in between softly licking and sucking on my clit.
My body was loving his introduction and I pulled
harder on his ears, begging for him to tell my
pussy his life story. Hell, he could tell her about
nuclear physics if he wanted to, just as long as he
didn't stop.

I moaned again, but this time the sound alarmed
me. It sounded like I was outside of my own body,
like the moan came from someone beside me. I
glanced down to see if he'd noticed, but the lighting in the room had changed. The shadows were
back and darker than they were before. It was
too dark for me to see him, but I could still feel the
warmth of his hands and his mouth. I was getting
closer and closer but something was pulling me
away, throwing me off. There was an odor in the
room that I couldn't ignore any longer. It smelled

like sour sweat and old urine. I opened my mouth
to breathe but couldn't get air. Panicked, I tried to
tell him to stop, but I couldn't see him and his head
was no longer in my hands. Reaching out for him
my arms only caught cold, empty air, and I felt a
sharp pain across my cheek.

My dreams were strange now. They'd probably
seem boring to most people maybe, but they were
strangely appealing to me. There were always
candles and soft music or I'd wake up tasting the
sweetness of strawberries and the dry bitterness of
champagne. I'd have these erotic dreams where I'd
take warm glowing bubble baths that smelled like
Hawaiian ginger. I'd float away carried by strong
arms to a bed covered with yellow silk sheets and
gold-dusted rose petals.

My eyes snapped open. Ivory soap-scented fingers were but a half inch under my nose covering
my mouth; nails were digging into my cheek. My
senses were coming to me too slowly. It was cold.
It was dark. My heart was speeding in my chest as
the haziness of the dream I'd been having faded.
Dontay had been there. The rough wool blanket on
the floor underneath me felt scratchy against my
bare skin, but that dull achy feeling was still there.
My storyteller was still talking; I just couldn't see
who it was. I was about to cum and my head rolled
back against something cold, metal, and hard. I
reached out again and my fingers tangled in long,
silky, thick hair.

Smack. It was too dark to see the hand that struck my face.

"You better stop that shit and be quiet." Her voice trailed off as I felt warm breath and fingers spreading me open.

My mind was reeling and the slow throb building between my thighs was clouding my ability to think clearly. With timid fingers I slowly slid the edge of the blanket off my face. Aeron, my cell mate, sucked my clit hard between her lips sending tiny explosions through my body wiping away all the haziness from my sleep at the same time. All the misery from the prior months flooded me in a wave of memories that made me want to curl up into a ball.

Six months ago I was arrested for embezzlement. The FBI came to my office, handcuffed me, and read me my rights in front of my employees, some of whom were people from my church. Did I do it? Of course not, but I should have known from the smug looks on the agents faces down to the disapproving glares of people I worshipped in church with that I'd already been judged.

Apparently I was a millionaire to the tune of around $2.5 million and I didn't even know it. "Ghost money" was what I'd started calling it since no one seemed to know where the hell it had vanished to. Transia was my company. I'd started it my senior year in college. After taking out a small business loan I bought a shipping container and leased a Mack truck. Dontay drove the wheels off of that thing and we undercut the prices of nearly every competitor in the area until we had enough customers to afford another truck. Those two trucks turned into a fleet that serviced the entire US shipping anything from Audis to office equipment. Someone had been stealing money using my company and they were trying to make it look like I was doing it.

It's bad when you have to learn about your alleged crimes one by one, piece by piece as they're laid out in front of you like a mine field. Every time you acknowledge a "mine," a small explosion goes off in the heads of everyone listening, and the shrapnel spells out the word "guilty."

Yes, the company is mine. Yes, the invoices are mine. Yeah, that account has my name on it, but it's not mine. Boom.

"Evaline, Transia invoiced three specific and I dare say affluent warehouses for transit charges, weight fees, and container rental. All of your paperwork shows that this happened. When the warehousing records for those companies are pulled it's peculiar that there were in most cases no pickups by Transia on those days. In addition to that, in the event there was a pickup the amount on your paperwork doesn't match the inflated invoices that these warehouses received and paid,"

Brimmer, the prosecuting attorney, had stated in his condescending high-pitched nasal tone.

The public defender I was assigned turned out to be about as useful as snow to an Eskimo. His off-white dress shirts were stained yellow at the armpits, drawing attention to the rivers of garlic scented sweat that rolled off him at each proceeding. We'd gone over my case briefly; he'd simply nod causing the third chin underneath his second chin to jiggle in agreement. There was no way to explain how funds were wired to various accounts in my name or how invoices were sent out at nearly triple what they should have been.

Jabber Jaws, my public defender, would only tell me but so much, but Dontay was picked up on separate charges and tried separately. They had him for stealing cargo, as well as "assisting me." That idiot sold me out as a plea bargain, he admitted to everything, damning me in the process. That bitter little pill of information settled itself in my stomach and began to slowly poison me with anger from the inside out. I'd sacrificed so much for love and at the end of the day love didn't give a damn about me. The only good thing I'd gotten out of love was my daughter Jada.

I was sentenced to six years in the East River Correctional Facility in Suffolk, Virginia with the option for parole in three. Now, despite everything my life was being ripped away from me slipping through my desperate fingers like smoke rings. Jada was four now and Dontay had missed the first two years after she was born because I was weak in my spirit and in my faith. I cheated on him in anger and I regretted it every day since. He eventually forgave me, said he couldn't live without me, and I forgave him as well. We fell back into our routine like synchronized swimmers.

At the end of the day my forgiveness cost me. Deacon and Momma Rose had disowned me when I'd gotten pregnant, because even though I wasn't killing anyone or doing drugs I was living in sin.

Welcome to my world, ladies and gentlemen, or what's left of it.

Chapter 21

Eva
Night Dreams and Day Mares

I lay momentarily dazed with all my memories pinging me like a damn Highlander going through that quickening thing. I hated falling asleep because I'd wake up and have to remember everything all over again. Bleach, urine, and the lingering smell of mystery meat surrounded me. It was taco day and the brown goop they drizzled into stale, tasteless flour they called soft taco wraps smelled like week-old grease and left a taste in your mouth like licking a sweaty armpit. That smell would linger in your hair, clothes, and in the air for days. I hated smelling food, let alone crappy food when I was trying to sleep. I used to hate Taco Bell but I'd kill for it now; hell I'd pay just to lick the floor of a Taco Bell. We were only allowed to have soft shells because some chick ages ago managed to stab someone in the eye with a damn shard from a taco shell. You'd be amazed at what the hell you could do with something as simple as bread or taco shells.

What I missed more than anything was privacy and peace and quiet. Someone was always watching or peeking or creeping somewhere. Simon says everyone needed to shut up and be still. They needed to hand out ball-gags or radios with headphones at night. The lights came on at seven a.m. no matter what and they shut off twelve hours later no matter what. Those twelve hours when the lights were off meant sitting in my cinderblock cubbyhole trying not to go stir crazy. At home I'd have a fit if the water was drip, drip, dripping in the sink onto a dish or if a clock was ticking too loud. A car with too much bass would have sent me through the roof. At home I couldn't even lie my butt down and attempt sleeping if I had to pee.

Prison will knock all that out of you in a couple of days. Now I had the soothing white noise of coughing, snoring, farting, lesbian sex, self-sex or "I want to do a million pushups" type breathing and sleep grunting all coming out a megaphone. Shitting was something you'd have better gotten out of the way before lights out because no one wanted to hear the toilets flush all night. If you just so happened to be the one that dropped a deuce in the middle of the night you and everyone would have to smell it all night because flushing could get you jumped in the morning. There were a few times when someone's insides would smell so rotten you could hear the girls begging for that heffa to flush and she wouldn't. Best believe she got jumped in the morning for stinking up the place just the same as if she'd have flushed.

The toilets flushed with the same magnified whooshing ferocity like those airplane toilets. They could probably take off an arm. I'd made a note to try flushing my arm next if I wanted to send myself to medical. They were probably designed that way because prison food all by itself would turn you into a clogged brick layer. Candy, chips, and cup noodles from the commissary made me feel "regular" in more ways than one. No one put money in my commissary and it would be another month before I'd get assigned to a work detail. That was just another thing that made Aeron feel like a safety blanket made out of scolding hot chainmail.

Whenever I'd fall asleep I'd dream of every single thing I missed and it'd make me feel "world sick." That was something like homesick but worse. Whenever I'd sleep, Aeron would take the opportunity to let it be known that as long as I shared this cell with her, it meant sharing my body, too. Lord, I didn't know why on first day in after intake, I didn't just walked up in there set my sights on the biggest chick and start swinging away. That's what the girl beside me did after we got stripped down and examined from our roota to our tootas and released into the wild. I might have gotten beat back along with a mark on my record and a bad reputation with the COs but I was pretty sure I wouldn't be another woman's property.

It was bad that Aeron could protect me better than any CO could, but that was reality. Everyone, COs included, had a "leave me alone and I'll leave you alone" policy. The COs' main concern was walking out at the end of their shift with the same numbers of holes they'd walked in with. Usually if there were black or "other" they were harsh as hell because most of us were black or other and they didn't want to relate; or they were just trying to do their eight and hit the gate.

The "good old boys" were a small band of white guards who lived for coming to work and making our lives hell. I could imagine them at home kicking aside empty Budweiser cans with their steel-toed cowboy boots. They'd probably stand in the mirror slapping themselves just to get amped for their workday. The CO I nicknamed Fingerbangs fell in this group. You couldn't tell me she didn't have wolf in her family. Neander Knuckles could probably curl and style her finger bangs if she wanted to, but she was actually known for fingering inmates. Willingly or unwillingly, Fingerbangs didn't really care.

Fingerbangs, the good old boys, and Officer Blakely were dirty. And if you just so happened to have two dirty guards on watch at the same time when something went down there wasn't much of anything that could save you. Keeping up with who was clean and who was dirty was the trickiest part. A clean CO could go dirty in the blink of an eye, and a dirty one could go clean setting you up in the process just to save face and play the hero. We were all segregated into our units depending on race. We'd actually managed to step back into the early sixties. It kept the Latinas from fighting with the sisters; and all the white folk stuck together during scuffles but they still separated themselves by their standards. The Reginas were these three white girls, Beckman, Rebecca, and Carly. You'd think they called themselves that because Regina means "queen" in Latin, but no, they just liked the movie *Mean Girls* and they acted as such. Everyone else just called them "the Beckys."

I used to carry a Bible; until one of the Beckys bumped into me.

"You can't see bitch?" Beckman hissed at me.

I was still shaken up from watching a girl get beat senseless for the first time in my life. The COs had just gone through our personal items throwing away anything they considered contraband. For whatever reason I'd felt brave enough to venture outside my cell that day. I just wanted to make a phone call, try to find Dontay, and figure out how to fix this mess I was dumped in.

Taking one step back I held up my hand. "I'm sorry, I didn't mean—"

She stormed toward me. Amazingly there wasn't a CO at either of end of the long, narrow hallway with the mirror-perfect white floor.

"Yeah, you are sorry. You a piñata or some shit?"

"Am I a what? I don't know what—"

Beckman twisted her neck from side to side making the bones crackle and pop on each side. "Yeah, you look like you got goodies in your ass or in that fucking book. Let me see."

Her upper lip curled into a snarl and she snatched my Bible right out of my hands and started ripping out the pages. I watched in shock and terror. Who carries candy in a Bible? Who tears up a Bible? Nobody, unless they ain't right in the head. I couldn't shake feeling like I'd just stepped into a dangerous game of Chutes and Ladders or some weird country where I didn't speak the language. They needed a prison Rosetta Stone for new convicts.

"Is it New Year's, are y'all havin' a party or some shit? Beckman, why the fuck are you making confetti in my hallway?"

This little she-man, mean-looking CO appeared out of nowhere. Her face was turned up in an ugly frown as she stared between me and Beckman. She looked like she smelled sour milk twenty-four hours a day and, as a result, her face was permanently scrunched up from the smell.

"No problem here, Blakely, I was just having a little theological debate with the Church Fish. She believe Jesus can walk on water and turn it to wine. I asked her if He'd turn these pages into dollars." She scooted a torn sheet toward me with her foot. "Look like it's still paper to me."

My bottom lip was doing that stupid shaky thing and I bit it trying to keep myself from crying.

Blakely turned her stank face up at us like we hadn't bathed in days. "Clean up your mess, Church Girl. It's too early for you to be provoking debates. Beckman, with me."

Beckman rolled her eyes but thankfully left. I picked up the pages and half pages to my Bible. Genesis was still intact and I could tape the rest back together somehow. That's if they even allowed tape up in here.

Only day one and I'd already almost got my ass beat over Jesus.

From that day forward things went missing or got destroyed all because Beckman thought I was carrying or hiding candy or goodies or whatever she was looking for. I had a fourteen-karat gold cross around my neck: a gift from my mom for my sixteenth birthday. I got jumped in the showers for that when Beckman cornered me asking if I'd found her candy. I didn't even know I was supposed to have been looking, but she took my necklace as consolation. Everybody always wanted to mess with the "Church Girl," steal from the "Church Fish"; they knew "Church Mouse" wouldn't fight back. I wasn't made for nobody's prison or jail. I wasn't even a criminal and they knew it.

"Go 'head, princess. Tell momma she the G-O-A-T." Aeron lay down on her side in the shadows facing me from the bunk across the cell. A smug grin was spreading across her face. This was routine with her. First she'd take it, then she'd gloat about it. Fighting her was pointless. It was best to do whatever she wanted so she wouldn't release me or put the word out that I was unclaimed. That would pretty much have me up for grabs like a human yard sale.

Aeron wasn't that bad as long as I stayed on the right side of the invisible fine line that everyone had to walk around her. She had a soft, oval-shaped face, with strong, high-arched brows. She honestly didn't even look like she belonged locked up.

Block 0039, dorm thirty-nine, no matter how you referred to it or tried to spiffy up the name, it was my new home and I wasn't with the black women. They'd moved me out of Neverland away from Reynoo and stuck me in Spanish Harlem. I was out of my element and the black chicks would give me angry side stares like I was a sellout; the Latinas were mad I was invading their space. It was all the politics I'd missed in high school with none of the perks.

"Well am I the greatest or no? I know your ass didn't fall asleep that fast," Aeron whispered from across the cell.

Sighing, I rolled over so I could look up at her across the arm's distance separating us. She was doing her Morticia Addams, sitting up just enough so the light could shine across the upper half of her face. In another lifetime and another place she probably could have passed for a model or some "it" television personality, just like I passed for a business owner. No one would ever see the aggressive bully she could turn into unless they stared into her eyes. Those dark brown stormy windows to her soul were always angry, as if she were coming from an argument or on her way to handle one. She had a way of squinting and raising her eyebrow like she was just daring you to say something, almost anticipating a reason to show you she could whoop your ass. From what I could see with the little bit of lighting there was, that was the look she was giving me.

Defeated, I shifted my cotton prison uniform back on my body and made my way off of the makeshift pallet on the floor. There was no telling what she was thinking and that in itself frazzled my nerves making me move in short jerky motions as I got up and went to her rack. We didn't have real bunks or beds. It was probably a way to save the tax payers money and it also cut down on places to hide contraband or stuff to kill your cellmate. I used to vote and be all for any congressman or legislation that talked about cutting the cost of the prison system. Those decisions were biting me in the ass now, literally as I pulled my thin pillow up off the floor. If you held two fingers up side by side that's about how thick my pillow was; double that and you had my mattress. Lay a four-finger-thick mattress on a slab of concrete that stuck out the wall and you have a rack.

"Yes, you are the greatest of all time, Aeron. Can I get in bed please?" This was our custom. Aeron was bigger and stronger, she was highly respected by the other females in the unit, and as long as I was hers, as long as I was with her, I was safe.

Chapter 22

Dontay
Expensive Taste

I rubbed my knuckles back and forth over the three inches of beard hanging off my chin. Looking down at all the neon blue lights in the Beemer's dashboard made me feel like I'd actually accomplished smoething. Still I debated on whether I was really about to go through with this shit. *To hell with it, I been good long enough. Time to splurge.*

I went into the Uno's in Norfolk ignoring the stares and looks of interest from the single girl galley at the bar. Aside from my mini Rick Ross on my chin, they ain't have to look to let me know I looked like an appetizer on two legs. My black polo fit just tight enough to show I was cut up but not too tight. Ralph Lauren Black Label was my new thing. I wasn't one for having cartoon shit all over my clothes outside of my J 11s, and they only fell in that category because Jordan wore them in *Space Jam*.

I eye checked a couple of niggas at a back table burning some stank cigars. With all the women at the bar they were staring too hard to be anything but gay or wanting trouble.

"Let me get a voodoo lady," I asked the bartender.

"I'll be your voodoo lady, hoodoo woman. Damn."

I smiled at the politely at the pretty thing sitting beside the bar. The bartender was pretty much looking lost. After two precisely proportioned Courvoisier, triple sec, and lemon juice concoctions later I was feeling nice. They were a little too sour from her throwing in an entire shot of lemon juice instead of a splash but that just kept me from tossing them back. After about an hour I checked my watch and went back outside with the smell of garlic knots and Buffalo wings all up in my clothes. To anyone watching it would seem like an ordinary Saturday night, but I'd been on my mad scientist flow lately working on a master plan.

"Dontay?"

I jumped at the sound of my name.

She stepped out of the shadows like she'd hitched a ride and hopped off with the last warm breeze.

"That would be me." I recovered from that millisecond of fear offering her a lopsided smile. The way she'd said my name sounded almost like

Eva and I pushed the thought to the back of my mind. The last thing I needed to do was spook myself and miss out on a good night. I didn't need to think about Eva. I needed to relax.

"Well, did you miss me or what?" she asked with a flirtatious pout.

Fayme looked exactly the way her name sounded, like she could be seriously addictive, expensive, or just plain dangerous. I raised my cigarillo lighting it with a match and taking a long slow methodic draw before releasing the clouds. I didn't want to answer her right away. Sometimes it was just best to let a woman have that air of uncertainty. Plus she'd work harder later on just to make sure I had a reason to miss her; that and her pouts were sexy as fuck.

Fayme grabbed the front of my shirt pulling me toward her as she took a step closer. My eyes were drawn to her big, glossy pink chocolate-mint scented lips of hers. They advertised themselves on her face so well I could hear them screaming, "With lips like this you know the pussy's perfect."

Fayme puckered up and sucked every white wisp of smoke from in between my lips sending my mind into porno subspace. Her black wool trench coat narrowed at her tiny waist and I knew she was naked underneath. My brain was trying to send some kind of warning signal out but blood was already bullet trainin' itself to other areas, diluting the message.

Even the way she blinked up at me through her lashes made me start to get rock solid. She started massaging me through my jeans and I looked past her toward the doors to see if anyone was coming or going. Fayme wasn't like anyone I'd ever met. She thrived on sex, her skin glowed from it, and just being near her made me want her even more. She squeaked when I pressed forward forcing her to take blind backward baby steps in her heels. Dropping my cigarillo I bit my upper lip while stalking her. A tiny gasp escaped from in between her gloss-slick lips when I slipped my arm around her waist. I navigated her into the bushes until her back was flush against the grainy brick wall of the restaurant.

"You have lost your mind. What happened to wine and dinner at the hotel and—"

She shut up when I slid double her usual fee into the pocket of her thin coat. I was already breaking one of my rules by being out in public with her. My jeans were getting uncomfortably tight as I strained against them. Rule number two flew out the window when she slid her arms around my neck and pressed her hips forward grinding into me. Fayme didn't have a problem with kissing but it was a rule I usually stuck to. She lifted her lips up expecting, waiting, pressing into me begging for me to kiss her. The warmth from her fingers brushed my stomach, snaked down the front of my jeans gripping me tight and I groaned. My mind unraveled itself with the motion of stroking me working me better than I did myself.

"It feels like you missed me," she whispered. "I won't believe it until you show me."

Lifting her up I undid the belt of her coat with one hand as I pressed my lips hard against hers. She moaned against my lips and I entwined my tongue with hers, tasting sweet cocoa and mint. She was already wet and ready; I slid two fingers inside moaning my damn self when they were squeezed tight together. As good as her lips felt I couldn't help thinking about who else they might have been on or if she'd swallowed and sucked someone else before meeting me. Careful so the leaves wouldn't rustle, I set her down and turned her toward the wall. My dick was pulsing painfully in my hand when I freed it from my jeans and I said to hell with it. I bent down just enough to let me slide the tip along her lips wetting myself up. When I pressed forward plunging deep into her in one stroke we both hissed at the shock of skin-to-skin contact.

Fayme's eyebrows came together and her forehead creased up as she made that "hurt so good" face. Her eyes were closed tight as she pressed the side of her face against the brick and moaned, "Oh, shiiiiit, Dontay."

I stroked her deeper and faster. We were on my dime and somewhere too public to waste time so if she didn't get hers at least she'd gotten paid. She threw her ass back hard meeting every thrust and my breathing turned into raspy gasps for air. I was seconds away from exploding when Fayme slipped around and down taking me deep into her throat.

She was one of many, but she was the best. Back in the day I'd probably seen a different girl every other week. The only reason I even started was because one of my homeboys had some strippers at a party when we were in high school and they paid her to break me off. I was the virgin-wallflower with no game. They thought they were doing me a favor by payin' for me to get some ass. Eva didn't know anything about it. No one did. I'd been taking it easy lately with Eva going to prison and everything but the need for my secret sexploits was still there.

Chapter 23

Aeron moved to the side and I scooted onto the bunk in front of her. I could hear the women in the cell across from us snickering. The very top and very bottom half of our doors were metal with scratched and chipped-up blue paint. The entire middle was empty space, thick bars, and your cell was as only wide as that door.

I tried my best to ignore the humiliation gnawing at me. I settled awkwardly into Aeron's chest. Soft, warm breasts cushioned my back. The lack of hard pecs and a hard penis made my brain fire warning flares reminding me that something was missing. Every cuddle, every make-out session, every time I looked at Aeron I was reminded that my body wasn't mine. I was stuck in a hamster wheel of wrong and, worse, every day it took place all over again. Aeron draped her arm around my waist pulling me closer.

I didn't really keep track of the days but I knew it was Tuesday. Adams, the stocky white CO with red hair and the deep Southern accent, was usually off and Fingerbangs or Blakely did the rounds in the morning instead of overnight. Normally I'd be getting home from choir rehearsal around this time. On Wednesdays after work I'd go to the church and work with the teen Bible Study group, and on Mondays, Thursdays, and Fridays I'd help with the women's ministry. Those days seemed like a lifetime ago, when it was such a hassle to get out of my office some nights at a reasonable hour.

I'd debate about stopping and picking up something quick and easy or just ordering pizzas because I was too tired to cook. Dontay would complain but of course he'd been home all day and hadn't bothered to fix anything let alone thaw something out. But, my chunky little baby girl would eat anything; she was never picky when it came to food. The memories alone made my eyes and my mouth water. Church was such a huge part of me that no matter how much I prayed on my own, I didn't feel like the one-hour community sermon they held on Sundays in here was enough to get me back into God's good graces. All the religions kind of mish-mashed into one sermon where they didn't really say Jesus, or God; matter of fact I didn't even think they ever said Lord. We'd pile in and the Chaplain would say, "Let us pray," and we pretty much just read from our Bibles the entire time. People who needed someone to talk to could talk to Sister Mavis but she was Catholic or something like that.

"You know I'll be gettin' out of here soon, don't you, *mami?*" Aeron's voice broke into my thoughts, a warm whisper across the back of my neck. She held me in front of her squeezing me like we were longtime lovers. "You won't have anyone to protect you when I'm gone. I really do care about you. I don't want anything bad to happen to you."

I lay listening quietly. Just like Deacon, she didn't like to be interrupted so I was always careful to make sure she was finished before I'd speak. I'd learned that about her quickly after I'd impatiently rushed to answer her a few times. The sting of her hand would stop the words from forming right on the tip of my tongue. Now, I listened patiently and waited before I spoke.

Aeron was at the end of a five-year sentence for larceny, and I looked forward to and also secretly dreading the day that I'd no longer have to share my cell with her. Things were starting to feel like the beginning all over again, and I didn't like it. Never had I ever wanted to end my own life more than my first month in. It felt like karma had pulled my name out of the magical shit delivery hat. Out of all the real "threatening" cellmates I could have gotten, I was stuck in Neverland with a psychotic little Filipino woman with large, wild eyes and stringy blond and black hair that fell past her butt. I thought her name was Reynoo. Well, that's what I called her. I could never understand a word she said because her accent was so thick. The only thing I was certain of at the time was that we were going to starve to death, because the other inmates would steal every bit of food right off our trays during meals. I wasn't stupid. I knew if I so much as slipped a note to a correctional officer about it, I'd get beaten or stabbed to death for being a snitch.

My first few nights in prison were imprinted in my mind forever like the Treasury seal on all those "ghost greenbacks" that got me here. My stomach was in knots from not eating. I huddled on my bunk, watching in horror as Reynoo took her own waste out of the toilet and smeared it in the corners of the cell walls along the floor. She was crawling along on her hands and knees, singing softly in Tagalog. They started yelling for her to shut up; others yelled because of the smell. I buried my head under my pillow to try to block out the horrifying stench. I cried and prayed myself to sleep just knowing she was doing some kind of shitty death ritual so she could kill me in my sleep. My family wouldn't even be able to have an open-casket funeral because she'd probably eat me or something crazy.

Four days later, after having absolutely nothing to eat and no money in my commissary, I watched in absolute disgust while Reynoo gathered several huge roaches. My momma always called them things water bugs when they'd get in her house. They'd hide all day and as soon as company would come over or you'd find yourself in a comfy spot, they'd climb up the wall or perch on the ceiling just to fall and scare the living daylights out of everyone in the room. Everybody and anybody would call themselves gangsta until that water bug started flying. I'd seen the manliest of men go to climbing up on the couch, running around, screaming all girly and whatnot when there's a rogue water bug zipping around the house. They didn't know they could fly until you tried to kill 'em and they never flew away; they always flew right for your forehead.

Reynoo managed to catch six or so that were drawn to her "shit traps." Hunger will make a person fast as all hell, because those things are no joke when it comes to running. She'd trap them in an old sardine can, placing the thin tin lid carefully in place and then hold it over a small candle. It's hard to describe the smell because of all the shit everywhere, but they surprisingly didn't smell any worse than roasting cashews. Or maybe I wanted them to smell that way. I could hear them in there scraping, clawing, and scurrying around for a few seconds, and then it would go silent.

For an entire week I lived off of that filth. I still gave thanks, I still prayed like I was supposed to. I even meditated and chanted. And then one morning, after I'd gone through the breakfast line as I usually did, I set my tray on the table and waited for the vultures to come. The line served soupy apple-cinnamon oatmeal, powdered eggs with cheese, watery grits, and a brittle dry buttered biscuit that morning. It smelled like a buffet. They even used lemon-scented soap in the kitchen because it made me think of lemonade every time I smelled it. I knew it would only be a matter of time before I completely unraveled or died from some type of disease from eating an infected roach.

On that particular morning Stanika, one of the bigger girls, was one of the first to assault my breakfast. Ripe onion and ass: I smelled her before I saw her. She was what the correctional officers called a "habitual hose down," notorious for never taking showers. Her residual funk would get to the point where they'd have to throw her into a holding cell and literally spray her down with the fire hose. I initially just thought she was nasty. I didn't find out until later she had a fear of the showers because she was assaulted and raped in there by a male correctional officer her first week in. The other COs stood by, laughing and recording it on their phones. Just so happened that a phone got stolen out of the CO's car not too long after and was sold to the highest-paying news team. Everyone involved was fired, fined, and punished if you let the media tell it. Fingerbangs, Blakely, and the rest were still there.

Stanika was in the process of reaching for my oatmeal and I was holding my fork in a death grip. Staring down at her fat, grubby fingers, disgust registered instantly on my face at the black dirt accumulating under her nails. An image of her scratching her ass all day floated through my mind and instantly I could smell Reynoo's shit as if it were singed into my nose hairs.

The chatter in the cafeteria clashed against my eardrums sounding like the crunch of roaches as they echoed in my ears every night. No matter how many times I brushed my teeth each day, the dirty, charred taste of them still seemed to coat my tongue permanently from the night before. I hated the antennae and the fine hairs on their legs; they always got stuck in between my teeth and it'd take me all day flossing to get all the tiny segments out.

I was exactly one half of a heartbeat away from jumping off the deep end. Stabbing that fat heffa and anyone else who wanted to step up and try something. It seemed like the only logical solution. If I'd done what I was thinking, I wouldn't have made it out of the cafeteria alive. Thank the Lord, Aeron decided to come over when she did. She offered me her own tray and within the next hour I was out of my shithole hell of cell and moved to hers. I should have known her kindness would come with a price.

"Why so quiet tonight, princess? You don't wanna talk to momma?"

No, I didn't. I wanted to talk to my fiancé. I wanted to talk to my daughter, Jada. "I'm just tired, Aeron. I've got a lot on my mind," I quietly responded.

Satisfied with my answer, she put her arm around my waist and I lay quietly until I could hear the steady sound of her breath going in and out, indicating that she'd fallen asleep. Tears burned slowly down my face, soaking my corner of the pillow we shared. I cried myself to sleep, quietly asking God how I'd ended up in the hell I was in and wondering what I'd done to deserve it.

Hours later I was awakened by clanking and loud yelling. Out of habit I glanced back at the small slat of a window in our cell. It was cloudy, scratched plastic so thick the sky always looked dull white and the sun would look like an orange gumdrop someone mashed onto the other side.

"How many times have I told y'all bitches to keep it separated?" Officer Blakely was standing by the cell door.

"I'm sorry, Officer," I apologized, sitting up, quickly pulling the course blanket up to my chin.

clumsily bumped Aeron in the process and I already knew she was probably glaring up at me for interrupting her sleep. None of this was my fault and yet everyone was taking it out on me. I felt like a weak sapling bowed down under a ton of snow in winter with all of its leaves dying for sun and the roots desperate for warm soil. All of this pressure . . .

"It won't happen again. I got cold and Aeron suggested I sleep in her bunk to stay warm."

"I don't give a fuck. You could tell me it felt like a northern wind was blowin' up a polar bear's ass up in there and I'd still tell ya keep ya ass in ya own fuckin' bed. One more of these and ya ass is in solitary." She turned and marched off.

"All that damn noise for nothing. Waking people up and shit. She need some dick or something up in her life. She'd be a lot nicer if she got her a good piece of ass at least twice a week. Who I gotta roofie or pay to dick her down?" Aeron threw a quick middle finger in the direction Officer Blakely had just stormed off.

Climbing over me off the bunk, she stood facing the scratched metal that served as our mirror and started braiding her long, thick hair. She always wore two long braids that fell down either side of her head; they reminded me of Pocahontas. Man, my head was a hot mess. I self-consciously patted an itch in my own fuzzy cornrows. One of Aeron's homegirls from a different unit braided my hair up

every Wednesday or Thursday and all it was doin'
was making my mess grow thicker and faster.

"Aeron, I need to call my baby sister. Can you
get me a phone call please?"

I felt like I'd switched places with Jada when
she'd bug me for cookies before dinner. My tone
begging and my eyes pleading. I had no choice but
to be reduced to this level and, ashamed, I could
only lower my head and wait for her answer. I
clenched my teeth, telling the stupid tears that
I could already feel starting to burn with every
blink to go away.

I needed to find out where they had Dontay
locked up at. I needed to talk to him. There were
so many unanswered questions, like why he did
what he did and why hadn't he told me. What
was I supposed to do; what were we supposed to
do? Was he in some kind of trouble? He used
to gamble; maybe he'd gotten in over his head
and was trying to pay off a debt. There had to be a
reasonable answer. I couldn't accept the fact that
he'd just throw me under the bus and think he
could get away with it. On top of that I had no idea
what I should consider saying when I sat before the
judge. My trial wasn't scheduled for another four
months and it killed me not knowing when his trial
was, or if he had copped a plea, had already been
sentenced, or what.

"I got you, *mami*. Now, give me a kiss and let's go eat breakfast."

I got up and gave her a small, emotionless peck on the cheek. My lips and hands had gone cold from nervous excitement. I was anxious to finally speak to a familiar voice again.

Chapter 24

Eva
War of Juarez

I dialed my little sister's cell phone number and my heart skipped a beat as it rang. Other than the first time I'd spoken to her, it normally went straight to voicemail, so I was both shocked and excited. I'd heard through the grapevine that Sue put up such a fuss about Deacon wanting a third wife she threatened to kill him. She must have been putting some wonder-head on him because he never touched Leslie. But I still felt a small tug of regret every time I thought of the way I left her all alone.

"Leslie speaking. Who's this?"

"It's me, sweetie, hey." The sound of her voice brought tears to my eyes.

"Oh damn. Hey, Eva. I miss you so much. Are you okay?"

"I need to know where Tay is being held. Have you found out where they put Jada? I feel so cut off from the world in here. This court-appointed lawyer isn't helping me worth a damn, and they seized all my accounts so I don't have any way to pay for a better one."

Leslie giggled on the other end and spoke to someone in a hushed tone. "Boy, stop. I'm on the phone with my sister." She sounded so happy and completely distracted as she turned her attention back to me. "Look, I haven't found out exactly where Tay is, but I heard he might be in the Clinton jail. You know Momma and Deacon ain't want nothing to do with Jada. CPS took her, Eva. I'm sorry."

My heart slammed to a halt in my chest. My baby was with child protective services? My parents weren't shit. They were so Christian and so concerned about their reputation in the eyes of the community. When I was pregnant I'd asked for a few things for the baby and they blatantly ignored me. I'd never gotten any help from them back then and I damn sure couldn't figure out why I was expecting it now. God might have loved me in spite of all my sins, but I sure couldn't say the same for my own flesh and blood.

"Leslie, is there any way you can try to get custody of her? You are her aunt." My voice strained as I tried to speak through my tears. "I don't want my baby being raised by strangers. She doesn't deserve it. I don't even deserve to be here."

"Sis, I tried. But I'm only eighteen. They won't give me custody. I'll think of something, I promise.

I gotta go. Class starts in a few minutes. I signed up for summer sessions so I can get ahead a little in this college game. Call me when you can and I'll fill you in on anything else I find out."

"Okay, I love you." Inside my heart was breaking into a million pieces. I felt hopeless as the call disconnected.

"What up, bitch?" a voice called out from behind me.

I cracked a half smile as Sayzano strolled over to me. She, I mean he, was one of the few people I felt safe talking to. All of the gay and transgendered inmates were housed together in a protective unit, but they were allowed to eat and come out onto the yard with the female unit.

"Hi, Say. I just found out my baby's with child protective services and there's nothing I can do about it." My voice cracked.

Sayzano grabbed me up into a hug and for a second I forgot all about my problems as I was faced with the bigger problem of suffocating between his huge fake breasts.

"Don't you cry, baby girl. I know a couple niggas on the outside. You give me a few days and we'll work shit out. Okay?"

I nodded and Say held my face in between his large hands and looked me in the eyes.

"Look, we gonna go take out these cornrows and braid you up some fresh ones 'cause, bitch, you lookin' like a hot mess, and Say ain't friends with no hot messes. All Say's bitches is thoroughbred, first class, top shelf, neck breakers. Shit, we make haters hate themself. So bring ya ass." Say let my face go and threw his hands in the air dramatically before laughing.

"You need to holla at my girl Bootie and get yourself something to make you feel better. I got mad credit with her. I know you ain't feeling your whole wifey thing; go get you some ding dongs on me."

I laughed for the first time in a long time and followed Say. "Thank you Say, you are way too sweet to be up in here."

"As are you, boo, but we all got our truth and then the man got what he say happened. Hell, I was out there bootin' and tootin' it up for these doctors and lawyers. Hunty, they was payin' thee big dollars to suck it and make it spray and I am not lying. The only thing I couldn't do was let everyone run up in my chocolate starfish. No, what the hell I look like?"

I was momentarily blinded as we walked out of the building and into the yard. The sun felt different when I was feeling it from behind these brick walls. No matter how hard I tried, I just couldn't absorb its warmth. It was mid-July and nearly ninety degrees outside, but I felt as cold as January on the inside. As we approached the area lining the basketball hoops, I could see Aeron standing to the side, towering above most of the females. She gave me a worried glance when she saw me wiping my eyes with my sleeve. She covered the distance between us in several quick, long-legged strides.

"Somebody been fuckin' wit' you again?" She was always quick to defend me and her reputation. If someone messed with me she'd have to step up or she'd look weak.

"No, I just talked to my sister. Everything's fine. I'll be fine."

Aeron took my hand and led me over to a picnic table. She realized what she was doing and dropped it just as quickly. The guards were funny about inmates and body-to-body contact. I sat down and she sat on top of the table with my shoulders between her legs. She pulled a comb from her pocket and started to unbraid my hair.

"Yeah, A, you unbraid that bird's nest and I'ma do it up real nice in just a minute. Say got some bid'ness to handle right quick." Having said that, Sayzano put his hand on his hip and pranced off.

"Aw look at Timone and Pumpa." Aeron giggled in my ear.

Say was busy sashaying over to his boo, a skinny little white guy we all called Milan. He had to be the prettiest man I'd ever seen in my life. He kept his eyebrows arched and his long jet-black hair was always pulled back into a cute little ponytail.

I'd never in my life been around gay men before and never had any idea they could be so feminine. The way that man sashayed around the yard, one would think he was on a Paris runway.

The couple looked so odd yet extremely happy together. Say was tall and chocolate with high cheekbones. I guessed he looked like a real queen on the outside, rocking wigs and makeup with those big pillow breasts. Say had once described a few drag shows that he'd done and I smiled from just picturing it in my head.

I pulled some fresh cherries out of my pocket that I'd snuck from breakfast and popped a few in my mouth. I munched silently as I thought about life before I was locked up. Dontay and I used to always go pick cherries or hit the Strawberry Festival in Pungo. We enjoyed each other's company so much and we also wrecked each other at times. He was my best friend but I knew firsthand how best friends could hurt each other, become complete strangers. I was distracted from my thoughts and the show Say and Milan were putting on, kissing and cooing at each other, when I felt Aeron's breath beside my ear.

"*Mami,* I want to tell you something and I don't want you to get upset okay?"

What in the world did she want? To share me with another one of her cellies? Wouldn't be the first time. Or wait, maybe she wanted to tell me that she'd found some other chick to make her plaything. I didn't know why, but the thought instantly made me a little jealous. I squashed that emotion like an ant. I wasn't gay. I was only doing what I needed to do in order to survive in this place. If she moved on it would be hell without her protection, but God would see me through it.

"Well, what is it?" I tried not to sound impatient.

"My ex works for the sheriff's department in Virginia Beach. I asked her to run your *fiancé's* name." She spat the word "fiancé" out as if it were toxic. She hated thinking of me belonging to anyone but her. "She said she couldn't find anything in the court system on a Dontay James."

"What does that mean? My public defender said he was part of it. He and I were the only ones with administrative accesses to the system to make the kind of changes that were made."

Her hands stilled in my hair and I craned my neck to look back at her anxiously, waiting for her explanation.

"Do you think he could have plea bargained or gotten off? Never even gone to prison? That's what I mean," she replied, giving me a solemn stare down.

My mind was a flurry of activity as I tried to process a thought it kept rejecting. He wouldn't. There was no way Dontay would do no time at all and leave me in here for years.

"Of course I'm sure. What you're saying is unthinkable, unfathomable, unbelievable, un . . . un . . . I can't think of any more 'un' words but you get my point." My voice was getting raspy and it hurt to swallow past the lump forming in my throat. I turned back around, content with staring at a patch of clovers growing next to the bench. A ladybug scuttled across one of the clovers and I'd have given anything to switch places with her.

Aeron rubbed my shoulder compassionately and said, "Anything is possible when money is involved. Money is the undoer of millions of men and women. Look through history; it happens all the time no matter the century or the currency. Money doesn't make a person evil, it just shows us who the evil ones really are, sweetheart. Speaking of money, you're taking over my business when I leave."

She'd gone back to combing out my hair and I cringed whipping my head around catching some of my mess up in the comb. "I don't know anything about your business and knowing my luck I'd get stabbed before I made a dime off it. No."

"You want to survive until you get out with no commissary and no respect or do you want to take over some shit that can get you both overnight? You know the prices: smokes, cash, or real candy. Sell the smokes and candy, add it to the cash and *mí tía,* well she's not my real aunt, she's an old family friend, she'll help you out. You'll go hard because your ass will depend on it, theses *puntas* will respect you because you'll have their shit. We don't sell to everyone, just the bitches that are down. I'll give you a list."

Everything just seemed so overwhelming. Aeron gave my shoulder a soft squeeze. I could tell she was genuinely trying to figure out a way for me to make it without her and find Dontay. That made my heart warm toward her ever so slightly. At least someone in here cared about me.

"Oh shit." Aeron's outburst broke my train of thought as she tensed behind me.

I looked up to see what had her on high alert. Lord knows I wasn't ready for any more drama.

"Speak of evil and I guess it'll stride on over and say hello," Aeron snapped, focusing her attention on Juarez marching across the yard.

Say and Milan stopped chatting and posted up with their arms crossed and lips pursed up as they stood behind Juarez. It looked more like they were Vogueing than protecting anything. I hid a small giggle at my two gay warrior guardian angels.

"What the hell you want, Juarez?" Aeron climbed from behind me to address her older sister. They were identical twins. Antonia was born five minutes earlier, so she claimed the title and bossiness of being the oldest. When Aeron got caught she didn't dare say who her accomplices were. Antonia, on the other hand, decided she wasn't taking the blame alone. She was all too willing to take the witness stand and incriminate her sister for a lesser sentence. Aeron never called her sister by her first name. When I asked why, she said it was to remind her that she was disloyal to her own blood. They were beautiful, angry Amazonian mirror images of each other. It looked like a WWE prison match was about to take place.

"Hey, I come in peace this time. I just wanted to let you know I'd take good care of your, um, kitten when you get out of here," Antonia replied, shooting a slick grin in my direction.

A visible shiver ran through my body at the cold and menacing way she spoke about me. I didn't want to be taken care of by anyone, but I was sure I'd suffer a helluva lot worse if Antonia ever got her hands on me. Aeron bristled up and for a split second I thought she was going to go off and punch Antonia. But her release date was only a week away. She wasn't stupid.

"What?" Sayzano jumped in angrily. "Who the hell you calling a kitten? Ain't nobody got no damn pets up in here. You ain't taken care of no gotdamn body, and I suggest you back da fuck off before I go Cleveland bus driver on ya Amazon ass. I ain't scared to hit a woman."

All eyes focused on us as the yard fell silent at Say's outburst; everyone was anticipating a fight.

Say started to go in before any of us could react. The COs ran over to put a stop to it before anything else could transpire. Say winked at me as he was being led to solitary, and Milan wailed like someone had just died. He'd done all that just to diffuse the situation to keep Aeron from getting caught up in some mess. I'd need to get my guardian boo a present for that. Hopefully Acron's *tía* auntie or whoever would be able to help.

Free time was cut short and we were all led back inside. Antonia shot me a look that made me feel physically ill. It would only be a matter of time before Aeron left and she got to me, and I had no idea what I could do to keep me from the hell that I knew was coming.

As we entered our cell, Aeron pulled me into a tight hug. Her sudden display of affection caught me completely off guard.

"Don't let my sister scare you. She's always been more bark than bite. I promise." She leaned back, still holding me in her arms, and winked.

"Well big or small a bite is still a bite; it hurts all the same." I couldn't bring myself to return her hug and stiffly tried to pull myself away, but she wasn't ready to release me.

"Stop it. I'd give you a kiss to calm you down but I'm allergic to cherries. She isn't going to do anything that you don't allow her to do." She nuzzled the side of my neck with her lips before letting me go. A myriad of emotions swept over me. Regardless of Aeron's reassurance, the thought alone of Antonia scared the hell out of me, and I prayed God would see me out of this before I had to deal with that woman one on one.

Chapter 25

Dontay
Back to Sunday School

We were in a large cabin three winding staircases below the top deck. The area was wide open with mounted flat screens and so far I'd counted fourteen leather lounge chairs surrounding and a fully stocked bar. Somehow salted ocean air still found its way through the heavy cherry wood walls. I couldn't tell if it was a live piano or just a recording coming. I couldn't help nodding along as someone played the hell out of "Bennie and the Jets" or Mary J. Blige's "Deep Inside." Staring out of the giant paneled window as we sliced soundlessly through the black ocean my mind wandered with the chords from the piano to lazier happier days.

There wasn't a cloud in the sky. The Hampton Roads Bridge Tunnel was lit up in the distance and I felt a sad pull in the pit of my stomach, tightening in my chest. Somewhere way out there was a little stretch of beach that Eva and I used to go to and bury our toes in the sand. We saw two shooting stars on a night when the sky looked about as clear as it did now and we made wishes. All I'd wished for was Eva. *So much for that; who knows what she wished for?*

I snapped myself out of my reverie and looked toward my boy Bear who was busy fighting with his bowtie. It had him looking like a little dark chocolate Chippendales dancer. At least mine complemented me, with my height and bald-headed goodness. I'd rather be Mr. Goodbar or Mr. Clean than Lucky the Leprechaun. We were night and day in every way possible, which was probably why we got along so well. Ever since his girl accidentally got shot he'd been on this new-age spiritual journey, even-tempered, neat, and always organized. I was on an all-expenses-paid crash collision course with hell. He didn't even get salty when I took Eva back after being an asshole about it for a couple of years. Shit, Bear was the one with all the real business sense. When she said she wanted to start a business he walked her through building it from the ground up and even helped me on the road with all those bullshit deliveries.

"Is it fucked up that I'm still going through with this even though Destiny ain't make it?"

I was referring to the elaborate yacht party we were about to have that would be followed in a couple of days by an even more elaborate wedding.

He gave me a sideways look. "Sounds like your woman got you doing what she wants to do. Regardless of how it looks or don't look, happy wife happy life." He shrugged. "You gave your daughter a good few months and a proper funeral—"

"A daughter I ain't even know I had until how long ago? On top of being sick she had to think Daddy didn't want her for ten years. I could have fixed that shit sooner, man."

I fell back into one of the many seats, the leather squeaked and the wood groaned. Splaying my long legs out in a wide V in front of me I scowled at the world in the strands of carpet at my feet. I rubbed my forehead like a dry-erase board trying to wipe away my past and the bad memories all at once. *When did things get this complicated?*

"Dontay, man, all you can do is take care of the little girl you got left and don't drink or think yourself crazy behind what went down. I told you join up, let the brothers help. I put in a word or two."

Bear smacked me hard on the shoulder. He was my ace for life; we grew up across the street from each other. Him and his pops stayed in this run-down bamboo-green ranch-style house with gray shutters. He'd always run to my place and hide out. His pops used to beat his ass like nobody's business over any- and everything. When we got to high school he started wrestling, working out, and he got big on that nigga. That's why we called him Bear, he'd raise up and scare the shit out damn every nigga in school. The next time his pop's tried to give him one of those old-school beat downs Bear handled him like light work; I opened my front door to find his Pops was at our door begging for somebody to call the police.

It was only right that he be my best man for this over-the-top dramatic wedding we were gonna have in a couple of days.

"Nigga you betta nod, smile, and get fucked up if you have to. We stuck out here in the middle of this damn water. I wouldn't walk into a room full of them champagne-campaigning friends of the bride to say you've got a cold. Let alone cold feet." Bear huffed at me from his mighty he-nigga stance.

I stood and shoved my hands deep into the pockets of my fitted slacks and stared down studying the bronze buckles on my Cole Haans. You'd have thought I was waiting for them to give me some kind of advice instead of Bear.

Straightening my shoulders I took some breaths and started feeling like 007 in my black tux. I adjusted the lapels of my jacket and strode toward the upper deck faking a sense of confidence and purpose I really didn't feel. The air was super-charged with affluence. The hairs on my arm were standing up like I was cold but there no chill. I could feel it like a winning three-pointer, over the shoulder, at the buzzer from half court, nothing but net, eyes closed.

All the black elite and politicians were invited to celebrate and rub elbows. When I'd called and told Pops about me getting married he gave me the same surprised, disappointed congratulations. He wouldn't be making it to any of the parties or the wedding, on account of the accident he had. One of the ladders he was working off of fell four stories and shattered his vertebrae. Years of back surgeries kept him laid up and medicated most of the time.

The pianist, who was damn good, broke into Alicia Keys' "Diary." I wandered in that direction, stopping in my tracks when my nose caught a familiar scent. If the color pink had a smell it would be the smell of lotus flowers, ginger, and patchouli in the morning. She was the only person I knew who wanted to be buried in Ralph Lauren Romance perfume and the color pink.

Back in the day, Toikea, my stepmom, would get all fancied up and take me to church every single Sunday. Growin' up my family was always on some middle-lower class shit. No matter how hard she tried Toi couldn't accept the karma for stealing and marrying another woman's husband. My family belonged to the race of niggas known as "have-nots." When I was eight Pops started his little side thing with Toi. She was this cinnamon-brown twenty-year-old waitress with a figure that'd make an hourglass jealous. Ironically Pops met Toi when he took my moms to Red Lobster for her birthday. Moms was in the bathroom and Toi hopped on it, in more ways than one. After that me and Moms had even less than our usual.

Someone should have told Pops that house painters with families can't afford side hoes. They cost more than regular corner hoes. Seriously, you could buy some ass for less than what it cost to keep a side woman, who thought she was the main woman, happy. He'd overdraft the bank account on new rims, clothes, and jewelry that we never saw and mad weekend getaways where we didn't see him either. Money my grandparents sent for my birthday or Christmas usually went missing out the envelope; it probably paid Toi's lights or cell phone bill. The penny that brought the house down was when Pops took money out of my mom's savings account so Toi could get an abortion. I guess Toi got mad when he didn't stay the night to take care of her after the procedure. But, hell hath no fury like that of my mom's when she saw Toi had taped her abortion receipt to our front door.

My parents fought and shouted the rafters down. I was sure the neighbor's neighbors knew our business by the end of that night. I was thirteen the night my mother disappeared.

My mother's screams woke me up. They always got a little heated when they argued but they normally kept it down to sharp whispers with occasional shouts. I slid out of my bed at the sound of the front door slamming and crept to the window. The floorboards creaked under my foot and the washing machine rocked downstairs like it was trying to detach itself from the wall. I watched the silent movie out my window as my moms limped after Pops. She was holding her side like she was out of breath or hurt. Frowning, I rubbed the sleep from my eyes and squinted hard through the glass. A panic alarm went off in my head the same blaring red as the stain on the side of her fitted T-shirt. The words JAMAICAN ME CRAZY were barely visible on the back. She was in her house clothes, hair tied up, barefoot. I watched her grab the front of his shirt and he shoved her away.

There was no way in hell I'd let him do that to her. I was sure he'd done it, he'd hurt her, and I just knew it. After all the days we'd scrounged for lights and food. After all the times my moms had to scrape just to make sure I wasn't in school in dirty, holey jeans and my shoes was all right, he had the nerve to hurt her. Me and my mom stood eye to eye and my pops towered over both of us but at that moment anger had me feeling like an oak tree. He'd need some steel and a good fifty swings before he took me down.

I took the stairs two at a time, barefoot, in nothing but my Duke basketball shorts and a black wife beater. Mom's favorite lamp in the living room was busted and the couch was completely turned over. My stomach turned, blood was everywhere, but I kept moving. A trail of blood ran across the couch it dripped over the tan hardwood flooring ending in a puddle where I now stood, in the cul-de-sac exactly where I'd last seen my moms standing. Steam rose off the top of my head as I stared at the two dry, blocky outlines on the pavement. Oil from the leak in Mom's car mingled with rain, dirt, and black rocks. They were both gone.

Mrs. Nikoli came wobbling her old nosey ass over from across the way. "Dontay, sweetheart, you all right, baby? The police on the way; let's get you out of this here rain okay?"

I nodded and walked back toward my house. Mrs. Nikoli was the only white lady on our block and that made her the neighborhood first responder. Not like help, but like the first person to look and then call the police if anything popped off. She'd then be the first one to relay her findings to everyone else.

I tried to take up as much of the doorway as I could and she tried her best to look around me. "I'm good, Mrs. Nikoli. I'll be fine 'til the police get here."

She wasn't budging that easily. Her head shook nonstop from side to side as she pointed her wrinkled hand toward the living room. "You know can't touch anything, sweetheart. If your momma is bad off, they need to see all this," she told me.

Her words made a knot swell up in my throat and my eyes started to burn as images of how I'd seen my moms last flashed in my head. She had a point; Pops needed to get in trouble for this even if I wasn't the one to mete out his punishment. I must have blinked about a hundred times as I peered past Mrs. Nikoli and stepped onto the porch faking like I'd seen a car approaching. I dropped down hard into the little plastic chair that we used in the summer for car watching and enjoying the weather.

Thankfully she was quiet as she took the seat across from mine. We sat and listened to the rain bounce off the roof of the front porch. I kept taking deep, damp, earth-scented breaths to calm myself down. Mrs. Nikoli smelled like black jelly beans and a distillery or Ouzo, that insanely awful liquor her late husband used to make. That's probably why she was so quiet and leaning in her seat every time the wind blew.

It took them bastards almost two hours to show up and they kept asking about my peeps doin' drugs or drinking. As far as I know the only person who'd been drinking was standing right in front of them and she was looking stuff over more thoroughly than they were. I got sent upstairs when Pops surprisingly rolled back up. He stopped in the doorway with a look of disgust on his face and sweat staining the pits of his gray undershirt that he always wore like a regular shirt after work. Mom's blood was a big, blotchy dark red moth on the front. It reminded me of one of those Rorschach patterns they show to crazy people.

There was so much blood in the house the cops wanted to know where my moms was and if she needed a doctor or had gone to see one. He said she'd been flying around behind him trying to run him off the road and he lost her. That's all I could hear with my ear pressed against the grate of the vent in my bedroom floor.

Mom's job called the next day because she didn't show up. She wasn't in any of the hospitals, wasn't at any of my aunts' places. Pops got picked up off and on for a week so he could be questioned when she still hadn't turned up. I was wondering what really happened too. He sat me down one night over his version of spaghetti. It was really just the mess that comes in a can and all he did was heat it up to room temperature. The taste was something like mixing together ketchup and Purplesaurus Rex Kool-Aid with lots of orange hamburger grease on top of it.

"Dontay, me and your mom ain't been one hundred for a minute." He started talking between mouthfuls of noodles. "I know you might be upset with me now and you ain't understanding this shit but she knew we weren't working out and caused that whole scene cutting herself and shit."

Without thinking I yelled across the table, "I saw everything. I watched you push her away."

His chair slid back scraping across the linoleum until it slammed into the cabinets behind him. Just as my airway was cut off by his meaty fist I was pulled to my feet. He lifted me up until we were eye to eye and my toes were dangling above the floor. Pop's eyes shifted back and forth between mine, heat surged out his nostrils up against my skin, and I held my biting the inside of my lower lip. I wasn't about to be inhaling his recycled air. His fingers tightened. It felt like my lungs were about to explode inside of my chest. I struggled for air.

"You listen to me, little nigga. I didn't do a damn thing and if anybody asks, that's exactly what the fuck you say."

Spaghetti grease and spit landed on my nose and cheeks before he dropped me without a second thought. I coughed and held my throat, staring at the knife on the kitchen table. My leg shook from how bad I wanted to slice him for every single shred of hurt he'd caused my moms. For doing whatever he'd done to her. He was saved by an angel in the form of a knock on our front door.

"We've got company. Now, straighten this shit up."

Pops opened the door and that was the night Toi moved herself in. She walked herself up in the house acting like she'd won the top prize in the lottery. They got married a year later; it was the same day the divorce went through and Pops was telling everyone he had his "happily ever after." That shit lasted all the way up until they found Mom's car abandoned out near some woods deep in the country and Pops got picked up on murder charges. We were already barely making it and then Pops borrowed money from Toi, sinking all of it into his lawyer. The investigation and the trial dragged on for a year before Pops got acquitted because they didn't have enough evidence without a body and he wouldn't confess or plea bargain.

He and Toi went through it worse than him and my moms did. Whatever money she had was gone and they stayed at it day and night until they all but hated each other. Toi didn't stay on top of things like my mom had. A little ways before I turned sixteen it was the same shit all over again. Pops was coming home late if he came home at all and since Toi didn't work, money was even tighter than before. I walked onto the back porch one

Sunday. Toi was crying into a mason jar of Long Island Iced Tea. She was talking about killing him. He seemed to have that effect on women. This dude had gone and run off on another one of his weekend "paint jobs" leaving us stranded. Toi finally got it into that head of hers that she wasn't his favorite toy anymore.

Instinctively I sat down on the white wicker love seat that was falling to pieces. My mom had picked it out and since Toi ain't have any decorating sense and her money was all but gone we never got rid of it. On my life, it started with the purest of intentions. Hatred at the man who raised me and the way he treated the women in his life was the only thing on my mind. Then Toi started doing that dramatic drunk crying thing that women do. It felt good to see her hurt for what she'd put my moms through. Toi was clinging to my neck for dear life with her breath hot against my skin. That shit shut down my big brain and rebooted my little one. I was instantly taken somewhere else with the sounds coming from in between her lips.

I'd reacted before I even knew I was reacting and she felt it, but she didn't pull away. She leaned back and I couldn't take my eyes off her grief, swollen lips. I was going to say something; the world would never know what though. Her lips were on mine and they were salty, full, and sad.

In my head I kept telling myself that what I was doing with my stepmom was in some sick crazy way for my real mother.

Every Sunday about as sure as summer Toi would teach me a new position or some new form of foreplay. She had my young ass so far gone. On the few occasions when my pops was home I'd act like I was leavin' the house to hang out with my boys when I was really going to hide in the shower. Toi would come in, lock the door, and we'd let the water run until we couldn't see through the steam.

All that ended the day my moms walked through the front door. Pops was a cold dude, but my moms was a cold beast. She had Pops steppin' out on Toi the moment he'd gotten acquitted. She'd been living out at my great-great-grandparents' abandoned farm not far from where they found her car. She got to lie low, not work, and make Pop's life a living hell all at the same time.

My moms walked up in there with her chin up in the air and in the heat of the moment and to save face Toi had to fly off and announce we were in love. Which yeah, by then I was as much in love as a young nigga could get but I couldn't say the words. Moms whooped her ass while Pops was beatin' on me. They threatened to press charges, but Toi was talking about never leaving

*me alone and I was down for it. They were gonna
ship me off to military school or some kind of
"hand over your kids" program if I didn't agree
to their demands. There wasn't a day that went
by that I didn't think about her, obsess over her,
or try to find her until I decided it was time to get
over her.*

The song ended and Toi got up from the all-
white baby grand in a dark purple skirt with a
lighter-shaded silk tank top. My eyes lit up, at the
unexpected surprise of seeing her. It felt like there
was a magnetic cord stretching across the room
connecting my eyes to hers. We hadn't seen each
other since the day I ran into her at church with
Eva and when she finally reached out to me a year
ago it was to tell me I had a ten-year-old daughter.
Destiny had a tumor and needed all these surgeries
that cost all kinds of stupid money. And we still
lost her.

I clenched and unclenched my hand in my pocket.
Shit was not supposed to go down the way it did.
I'd only taken enough to get Destiny's surgeries and
while keeping both Fayme and Toikea happy and
then everything fell on Eva's head. I couldn't even
speak up on her behalf or I'd sink too. Now I was
trapped. Damned if I said something and a fool if I
ain't take Toi and run. Love or no love my sentence
could have been worse than settling for this marriage
shit. Toi's skin still had that glow I remembered;

she even smelled and smiled the same with her one dimple. I almost hadn't recognized her the first time I'd seen her with her hair in short, choppy, layered pixie cut. It wasn't bad considering she used to only rock this poufy mane of deep wave remy. That mess shed all over the house; it was one of the main reasons I hated when Eva put all that shit in her hair. She was staring up at me smiling from all of her five feet and some change.

I offered her a distracted smile. "What are you doing up here already? I thought you'd still be getting dressed," I finally managed to croak out.

She reached out grabbing me by my pinky. That was always her thing; she'd never hold my hand, just a finger. But Toi had tiny hands to begin with so it actually worked better that way.

She smiled. "I have a surprise for you."

Chapter 26

Dontay
Pipe Dream

"My boat?" I asked Toi again.

She'd led me away from everyone else toward the helm. We were standing in what I'd call a pimped-out wood-grain black leather-clad cockpit. The instrument clusters were all lit up in bright blues and greens outlined with gold bezels. I got rock hard just looking at it and thinking my name was attached to it.

Toi stood on her toes and smiled up at me. She kissed the tip of my nose, wrapping her arms around my shoulders. "It's my wedding present to my future husband." Her voice was barely above a whisper.

I couldn't speak. Hell, I ain't even know we were exchanging gifts and whatnot. My collar was starting to feel extra tight around my neck. I know what she wanted to hear but I was still reeling from the fact that she'd just handed me a boat like a pair of shoes. A nigga ain't even have a job. Not that Toi knew that. There were just so many not-good times to say something; like even now was just not a good time. I'd gotten fired behind some bullshit from my warehouse job.

Mr. Owens was one of those old as hell, twenty cups of coffee drinking fools, with stained brown teeth and shaky hands. He always acted like he had a problem with the boys in the warehouse bay. We got the worst bonuses, shifts, and never got thanked for shit. Last year he married a twenty-something chocolate drop who he met online of all places.

He messed up when he made her the payroll manager setting her up in her own office. Out of 1,000 people in the workplace only thirty were women so all day she's looking at men in all different shapes, sizes, and flavors who ain't her husband. But, I guessed he forgot to tell wifey about the hidden cameras in the office spaces. Mr. Owens caught her getting it in, but he could only see the dude's back. He said he wouldn't divorce her if she'd just tell him who it was. Who do you think matched her secret fucker's build, height, and complexion? He could have at least given me some severance pay. I couldn't even get Fayme to give me a courtesy fuck, but I bet she would if I brought her on this boat.

"What's the matter, pumpkin? You don't like it, we can change anything up here so it's just the way you like it okay?"

I nodded. "I want to name it Destiny then."

Toi rolled her eyes. "See I told that li'l man you'd want something like that. It already has a name: it's the Poseidon's Point. I don't know if we can change it. Something about title, registrations, and stuff, just like a car."

"It's fine. What the hell's in a stupid boat's name anyway?"

I leaned down kissing her hard and deep to show my appreciation. Toi sighed against my lips and melted into me. I had every intention on christening every inch of this boat starting right here. Breaking the kiss long enough nibble her neck, I lifted her up onto the console and positioned myself in between the heat of her thighs. She gasped, and started fumbling with my pants.

Someone cleared their throat and pounded me hard on the back of my shoulder.

"Dontay, I've got someone here for you to meet," Bear interrupted.

I almost groaned out loud. I helped Toi down, looked to the ceiling, and turned around.

"Dontay James, I remember you back in the day, Norfolk State. Power forward, started in every game Deacon once called you a submarine Christian," Reverend Matthews joked. "Said you only surfaced what twice a year Christmas and Easter? Right, am I right?"

Reverend Matthews laughed one of those bois-terous hurt-your-ears-loud Norseman laughs, jabbing me in the arm with his elbow. I crossed my arms tight over my chest not even slightly amused. I didn't feel like entertaining anyone that was connected to Deacon. Sister Bealiah's conversation from the nail shop all those years ago came back to me. I clamped my jaw against the jealous wave of heat that shot up my neck. I didn't want to imagine this fat-fucker touchin' Fayme. I looked by my side and noticed Toi had somehow managed to slip away and that only irritated me further.

"Come on, Dontay, the reverend was about to hear me out on this business model I came up with. He's got a lot of decent investment ideas if you want to get in."

Reverend Matthews ran his fingers over his goatee tilting his head to one side. "You know I can always use somebody at the church. Bodyguards or something high profile in case they try to take me out like that minister in Belly."

Reverend Matthews spun on his heel. My eyes damn near bulged out of my head. Bear made the mean-mug money face, either fist pumping the air or doing a one-man choo choo train.

I whispered, "How the hell he even know what Belly is?"

Bear shrugged.

We went up another level to a smaller deck that was almost identical to the one we'd just left except the skylight was open letting the fresh sea air pour in. Reverend Matthews's shoes tapped against the hardwood floor until then he threw himself into an oversized couch with a sigh. Vaughn and myself took a seat on the couch across from it. Ralph Lauren Romance was all over the fabric.

"So, how do you like your new man cave, Dontay?"

"Haven't got to enjoy it yet; just found out it was mine."

"Toi always been real special; don't mind letting something like this go for someone like her."

Reverend Matthews made a couple of phone calls. And I looked at Bear, my expression saying I was about to murder a reverend. Bear twisted his mouth to the side silently vouching for this dude. Shaking my head my face turned into an ugly scowl. If Toi didn't have the money for Destiny's procedures, she damn sure wouldn't have the money to buy a yacht.

Reverend Matthews reached down beside the couch pulling out a small remote, pointing for us to do the same. We were on some real *Lifestyles of the Rich and Famous,* crazy money nonsense on somebody else's dime. My soon-to-be wife had all but hoed herself out to get me a yacht. The couches had massagers and heaters with like thirty settings. Maybe this was karma for my bad deed.

Reaching down I grabbed the massager control. There was something else in that little leather holder, too. But, I'd switched my seat on ignoring the glass stem with the copper wire filter in the bottom of it. My fingers flew away from the crack pipe like it'd burned me. Bear and Reverend Matthews were both holding theirs when I sat back.

Without hesitating Bear picked up a lighter off the glass table in front of us.

"Nigga?" I gave his stupid ass the side eye, nudging him with my elbow.

"Calm down, Tay? Can I call you Tay? Tay-Tay, Tater-Trot. Look, when we out chea, we does what we does. Don't hurt if it's once in a while."

I stared at Reverend Matthews with my jaw hanging in my lap. He balanced the phone between his ear and shoulder better than Toi in the middle of a gossip session. Lighters flickered beside and in front of me. I'd only seen this shit on TV.

Just get up and walk out. What if he get offended and take the boat back? Really? Nigga, that's crack! What if you turn into a crackhead? Let them do this dumb shit; say you gotta piss and find Toi.

Nodding to myself I ignored the sickening sweet smell of burning plastic around me. Rev leaned forward tapped the table and I squinted trying to read his lips. He was mouthing something to Bear but I could never read lips worth a damn.

And then I was caught off guard dazed and winded from the force of Bear's shoulder colliding with my gut. I was thrown back against the arm of the couch gasping trying to catch my breath. Bear had me pinned like we were on the damn wrestling mat. My mouth was open, about to blast this fool when his mouth closed over mine. He exhaled a lungful of smoke and I roared up against this nigga with everything. He had me locked in some crazy submission shit and didn't budge one bit.

I didn't feel myself inhale like weed or a Black & Mild. When I finally shoved him off with my forearm, I coughed and gulped air trying to clear my lungs and curse him out at the same time. My lips went numb first then my tongue. I forgot all about whooping Vaughn's ass. And instead I sat there shaking my head trying to regain control of my senses. There was this tingling like all the hairs on my legs were marching up my body. They were climbing up my back and pouring out of my pores on my head; it was small though.

Bear loaded the pipe and I sat listening with my supersonic hearing to it crackling as he inhaled. *What the fuck did this Reverend had that would make him get me, his own homeboy fucked up against his will*. At first I didn't react when he leaned in to give me another shotgun. I didn't know a damn thing about working a crack pipe. *Inhale, just inhale and enjoy the high*. Looking at another dude's face that close was weird so I closed my eyes and inhaled.

As I exhaled I could feel the sensual rush climbing up my body underneath my skin; it was pure ecstasy. I put my head back and closed my eyes. There were conflicting emotions going through my mind. If Toi walked in and caught me she'd be pissed. But the shit felt so good I honestly didn't give a fuck. I'd worry about it later when I wasn't high anymore. She loved me enough to get me a boat; she could deal with me doing some dumb shit at least once. I got my ex-fiancée locked up for her. My thoughts were getting fuzzier and harder to hold on to.

Now I wanted Toi for a different reason. I was rock hard and I realized if I stopped thinking so much I could focus. I could feel my hair growing; feel my pulse throb through my entire body. My breath hissed through my teeth. I was on edge of embarrassing myself and messing up my pants. Pulling my eyes open took some work but I managed. I was glad as fuck I snapped them open when I did. Bear's burly ass was in the process of scooting off the couch down onto the floor.

"Bear, what the fuck you doin'?" I asked through barely moving lips.

My slacks were undone and his hand was down my pants. I was disgusted at myself when he adjusted his grip and I got even harder. The nigga completely ignored me and he went back to stroking as if it was his own dick and not mine. I was shaking my head no and squeezing my eyes closed.

Chapter 27

Eva
Innies . . . Outies

Being locked up makes time drag. But, before I knew it, a week had flown by and Aeron was packing her things, chattering away and pacing around our cell in anticipation of being released in the morning. I'd still not heard anything else from my sister, and with Aeron leaving, the heaviness of my situation was starting to wear me down more and more.

"I just don't know what the hell I wanna eat first when I get outta here." Aeron was nervously playing with her hair in our fake metal mirror. I never realized how long it was until now. She rarely wore it out. I envied the way it fell like a black cloud around her shoulders in layers and stopped in the middle of her back.

"I think I'm gonna get my ass some salmon or a large cheese pizza. Hell, they can put the salmon on the damn pizza. Oh shit, and I can't wait to pour myself a big, chilled glass of rosé or Moscato."

Funny, she didn't strike me as the champagne or wine type. Learn something new every day, I guessed.

Despite her chipper mood I chimed in sadly, "Well, just make sure you pour a little on the ground for me. I don't see me lasting more than a week without you."

I hated to admit it, but the realization that I'd finally be alone in here was facing me head-on and I couldn't see a bright outcome no matter how hard I prayed or recited my psalms. Antonia wasn't due to be released for another few months after getting in trouble a few times for starting fights in the yard. She'd gotten a reputation for being a troublemaker and having a short fuse; otherwise, she'd be getting out tomorrow too. Damn my luck.

"Aww, sweetheart, don't talk like that. I can do more for you out there than I could ever do in here." Aeron waved her hand around like she was addressing a grand hall. She walked over and looked up at me, her large eyes wide and excited, her voice filled with exasperation. "How many times do I have to tell you not to worry, *mami?*"

"Aeron, this isn't worry. This is me being realistic." There was just too much for me to process at one time. I couldn't control the tears that fell from my eyes. I was usually so good at hiding my pain or my fear. Storing everything up for late nights when I would cry myself to sleep or in the showers where my tears could roll down my face unnoticed. Yet, this time I just felt so empty and so drained of everything, I couldn't hold them back.

Aeron stared at me in stunned silence. I buried my face in my hands and let go of all the pent-up emotion I'd been holding back. My shoulders were shaking uncontrollably as I felt every last drop of hope leave my body. The bunk sank beside me and I felt Aeron's arm wrap around my shoulders as she pulled me into her chest. I didn't know how long we sat like that. I also didn't know how the kiss started that put an end to my own assuredness about my sexuality.

We'd never actually kissed before. She'd kept most of our encounters controlled and as passionless as possible. My eyes closed and my mind actually went blank. That never happened when Dontay used to kiss me. It was nothing like kissing a man. Her lips were sweet, warm, and soft just like mine. I could taste the salt from my tears as the tip of her tongue traced my bottom lip, timidly at first. It sent shivers along my cheekbones like someone was standing beside me running a feather across my face.

My mind was doing cartwheels bouncing around good and bad, right and wrong. *Bad touch, this is still bad touch*. My grown behind actually reverted to simple childhood logic as some kind of guiding light to keep me from getting lost. They teach you about sexual abuse and how to identify good touches and bad touches, but damn it they never said that a bad touch would feel good.

I couldn't breathe, yet I was breathing super fast at the same time. It was probably the pre-stages of hyperventilation. My lips parted ever so slightly, and she dove in. Our tongues touched. Aeron moaned against my lips. It was the softest, most feminine sound I'd ever heard her make and that sound alone sparked an instantaneous blaze that set my whole body on fire. What used to be the last thing I'd ever wanted from her was now the only thing I could possibly think about.

I'd never felt this way for a woman. My heart was pounding so hard I could feel its beat reverberate through my chest downward to a similar throb building between my legs. She shifted from my lips and drifted a warm, slow kiss along my neck, stopping to suck and lick on a spot just beneath my ear that I never even knew existed.

This is so wrong, I should stop her.

Stop her for what? You might not get this kind of attention for a long time. Might as well enjoy it. I lost out to my own mental argument as my body reacted to her caresses and the flood gates were opened. I could feel it through my thin cotton panties, dampening my cotton pants. I was sure as hell there'd be a wet spot on the bunk if I got up. This was nothing like I'd ever expected. Her hands were soft and warm like heated satin running across my skin. She lifted my shirt just enough to slide under and tease my nipples with her fingers

LLC
Date Due Reminder

Library name: BD Barking
Library (Barking and Dagenham)

Title: Church girl gone wild
Item ID: 90600001410092
Date due: 15/3/2023,23:59

Total issues for session:1
Total issues:1

rough the thin fabric of my bra. I was literally elting. That's the best way to describe the things hat her mouth and hands were doing to my body.

And just as soon as it all started, she stopped. The heat from her mouth was replaced by the cool air. I opened my eyes, confused. Angry at whatever this interruption was.

"We have to stop. As bad as I want you right now, I can't risk not walking out of those doors in the morning. If we get caught . . ."

"I know," was all I could muster up the strength to say.

"I promise if you don't let yourself waste away in here, I'll make it up to you okay?" She tenderly tilted my chin upward until my eyes locked with her deep brown ones.

"What do you mean?" I was confused and horny, and suddenly so damn frustrated the last thing I wanted to do was make false promises.

"Just promise me you'll hang in there. I know I wasn't the nicest to you, but I had to toughen you up. You'll see. Just be strong for me. Let's go to sleep."

I started to lie in my spot beside her on her bunk but she motioned for me to get in mine. In an entire three months together I'd never slept in my own bunk and the feeling isolated and empowered me at the same time.

***

The lights switched on, an indication it w.
morning. I stretched and almost fell off my bunk a
my eyes focused on Aeron in the mirror. She was
dressed in a pair of skin-tight black jeggings. I never
followed fashion but the equally skin-tight tank top
she was rocking looked like an Emilio Pucci design
I once saw when I was on Nordstrom's Web site.
Couldn't be; the top I'd looked at cost damn near
$900. I mentally shook my head and shamelessly
continued my visual scan, admiring her new look.
Were those red bottom heels? Probably knockoffs,
but either way she looked like she'd just stepped
out of a magazine.

"Well good morning, my sweetness. Like what
you see?"

I was staring in stunned amazement at the
transformation she'd made. "Where the heazy did
you get those clothes? You look beautiful."

"My cousin dropped 'em off. And don't say
'heazy' ever again, it sounds weak. I don't know
why you just don't say 'hell'; you say it any other
time. We're all going there anyway." She rolled
her eyes and huffed at me before continuing. "I
couldn't be seen walking out of here in anything
less than spectacular; believe it or not, I do have an
image to uphold, *mami*." She giggled and twirled
like a little girl. Her hair spiraled around her like
the women in the shampoo commercials.

I was momentarily shell-shocked by the fact that Aeron, the no-nonsense, take-charge bad girl, actually giggled.

"Well hell. I guess you'll be turning heads all up and down the cell block. You're gonna need an armed escort." I swung my legs over the side of the bunk and just stared at her in wide-eyed awe.

"You know, my first assignment as soon as I step foot on free ground is to look for your baby and your man. I promise. Okay?"

I could only nod as I climbed down off the bunk feeling drab and small compared to her. "You don't have to do anything for me. But I'd appreciate it." I refused to cry. There was no reason for me to cry and get all emotional over someone leaving who was practically a complete stranger who made me do unspeakable things. I took a deep breath. *Suck it up, girl. You ain't about to be crying over no grown-tail woman.* I pep talked my tears away.

Aeron handed me a strip of paper. "On Saturday mornings there will be a medium-sized rock in the yard by the south wall. They fly it over Friday night when the guards are all watching television or falling asleep. That's your stash; it comes every Friday night no matter what. You got this, sweetheart."

"Aeron, will I have to bag it or mix it or—"

"Well ain't you just a fuckin' ray of sunshine? C'mon, princess, bring ya ass. Your damn carriage is waiting outside and it's blocking my damn gate."

Officer Blakely's scrunched-faced self appeared out of nowhere and unlocked the cell door.

Aeron gave me a huge, cheesy grin, grabbed up a few of her things, telling me I could keep everything else, and she left. We didn't say good-bye, we didn't hug, and inwardly I couldn't help feeling empty, like I'd just lost my best friend . . . or even my lover.

Chapter 28

I spent most of the day alone in my cell. It was almost time for dinner and fear and depression kept me from eating or joining everyone out in the yard. My stomach rumbled loudly in protest. I'd made up my mind to at least try to eat something. Beckman glared at me pounding her fist into her palm and my hands got sweaty under my tray. Today was not the day I needed to be tested. There was snickering and whispering as I went through the line but no one stepped to me and I was surprised to see Say sitting at a table with Milan.

"Hey, my little solar panel. You look like you've lost all your sunshine and um Beckman's lookin' she wants to play ball or fist you to death. And I don't mean the good kind of fisting," Say spoke first.

That comment made me draw a blank. "I don't think there is such a thing as a good kind of fisting, Say."

Say batted his eyes at Milan. The invisible love-sex connection the two of them had all but crackled. My tray clanking against the table interrupted the transmission.

Milan winked. "Guess you ain't met the right fist yet. When they say fits like a glove, umph it'll make you cum like a KO."

That was enough for me. I'd gone from knowing next to nothing about gay man sex to being able to teach a course. "Okay. Well, hello freak number one and freak number two. Say, you don't look like you saw one minute in the hole. Thank you for what you did."

"Bitch, don't tell me thank you. I need some happy in my damn life and fast. And what is this slop? I think I detoxed in that motherfucker. My tongue works again; I can actually taste this shit they call food. No, no, this ain't good at all."

Sayzano pushed his tray across the table with one finger and a frown. Milan patted his hand before going right back to eating what looked like chicken chow mein and tasted like . . . There was no way to describe the taste. I'd given up figuring out what anything was unless it was pizza, which I liked, or those nasty tacos, which I hated. Everything in between tasted exactly the same as everything else no matter what they called it or what color it was.

"Say, what if I have something that'll make you feel better?" I asked.

Milan pointed his plastic spoon at me. "Make us feel better. When my hersband is upset then I'm equally miserable."

"Okay, okay. Something for all of us to feel better how is that?" I asked.

After dinner we had two hours or so to ourselves to watch television in the community room, play cards, or whatever else that didn't involve real fun. I grabbed what I had left from Aeron's stash since I'd be getting more in a couple of days. Smuggling drugs in prison didn't really feel like real smuggling, not yet anyway. As long as I thought about it like Monopoly and play money with play drug railroads everything would be fine. I'd have to reassess my feelings after the new shipment and the people on Aeron's long-tail list came crawling out like crazy ants.

I stared in amazement when Milan led us to a door that should have been locked. He pulled a bobby pin out of his hair and opened it like he had a skeleton key.

"What?" Milan waved us inside. "Do you know how many locks I fucked up learning how to do that? I just make it look easy; don't try that on your own."

We walked into a dusty, dark classroom that smelled like mildew and rotting wood. Say sat down on the desk and I handed him what I'd grabbed out of the cell. It was taped to one of the slats in the light fixture right where Aeron left it. We each took turns watching the shadows that passed in the hallway. The night count was done right before lights out so everyone just wandered around and mingled or showered at this time of night. I did my bump off the back of my hand just like Aeron had shown me.

"Y'all know this is probably the best present anyone has ever given me since I've been in," I told them with a cheesy grin. My body felt light and puppet-like. It was like I was sitting in a control tower far away watching myself controlling my actions based on my eye in the sky point of view.

"Milan, why are you even in here? Y'all know why I'm here but I have no idea what you did."

Sayzano did his bump and then spread a line across his upper lip. Milan did his off of Sayzano. I looked away when they kissed and did their thing smacking all loud and mumbling at each other.

"Eva, you ain't s'posed to ask that shit. But since you my bitch and all . . . I shot my ex-boyfriend. The shit was self-defense though. We had this whole secret life together until his wife found out and you know how bitches, excuse me, I mean how women do when they man got a um . . . man. He got mad, came to my house arguing and pissed off thinking I'd told everyone when I hadn't said a word. When he pulled a gun on me guess he must've forgotten who the top bitch was. My instincts said only one of us would walk out of there. Guess you know who walked out."

"I'm confused, so um how did you guys . . . I mean was he the boy or—"

Milan chuckled. "If you must know he was a vegetarian. Wouldn't so much as flick his tongue across some man meat, but he'd let me get all up in them hips. Sorry, Say. TMI, I know."

Say shrugged, and Milan blew him a kiss.

Milan had caught me off guard with that one. In prison you have murders and thieves all mixed in with computer hackers and fraudsters. You don't know who anyone is until they tell or show you. However, I was more flabbergasted by Say's confession.

"I regret getting locked up before I was supposed to get my snip cut nip tuck," Sayzano blurted out.

My jaw dropped and he nodded.

"Can I see it?" The question floated out of my mouth before I could think it through. Milan smiled a crooked little smile and Say gasped.

"Eva, what the hell?" Say sputtered.

I shrugged. "Your she-man boobs just kind of throw off the mental imagery and on top of that you have a real penis? I don't believe it; the COs know this and let you in here with women?"

"I don't want women, boo."

"Nope, he don't want women; he wants this right here," Milan sang tooting his booty up doing some kind of "he wants this" twerk shuffle. "Go 'head; show her what you workin' with, mandinga."

I looked at Milan confused. "Don't you mean manding—"

"No, mandingos are men. My baby is a mandinga."

I laughed; it was probably my high but I couldn't help it. Sayzano thought I was laughing at him and rolled his eyes. Then he whipped out a damn king snake. My jaw dropped, my mouth watered, and my kitten got oh so excited. Back when I was little my grandma gave me the birds and the bees talk. I didn't remember how old I was but she said, "Girls have a bird's nest and boys have a worm. One day you let a boy feed his worm to the little birdie in your nest."

Say was up in here with a damn king snake. They ate the birds, the bird's eggs; a king snake would wreck a bird's nest. I walked over cautiously like I was approaching an endangered species. Like he'd vanish or realize what I was thinking and explode on the spot to avoid it.

"Milan, don't get mad but will you share your toy with me? Say, I'm just saying, pretend I'm an asshole. All the wet dream y'all want. I took over Aeron's business."

I was in a trance. It'd been, what, over a year since I'd had or even seen a real one, not counting the ones in my dream. I couldn't look up at Say.

I didn't want to see the man boobs or his arched eyebrows or anything feminine. My eyes were on the prize and it looked smooth, thick, and veiny like he had chocolate thunder dildos molded in his honor. *What a damn waste.*

"I think your eyes are bigger than your, um, you know what I mean," Say said.

"I'm just gonna watch. This will go in my super pervy spank bank for a super fucked-up reference," Milan whispered.

That was all the okay I needed. My fingers closed around it and my goodness it was real, felt real, throbbed, came to life and stiffened in my hand. I got wet on the spot. Aeron would be jealous if she could see how my kitten was reacting to something other than her. Say groaned or growled, I wasn't sure which, as he slid down my bottoms. Milan handed him a condom; it was contraband and not allowed. It was also the furthest thing from my mind but I was glad he had it.

I sat on the desk; it creaked and groaned under my weight. The thing was probably a thousand years old. My head was spinning and floating; my heart was beating so hard it hurt. I was thinking Say would probably be a little rusty in the female department so I reached down and slid the head of his thick latex slick tip up, down, and around my clit. He moaned; it was an actual mannish sound like a grizzly bear growl or a Viking before a raid. That was the sexiest man sound he'd ever made. I parted my lips and slid him inside. We both moaned loud and long. Gay dick, prison dick, unauthorized dick, whatever you wanted to call it, it felt slap-a-nigga good. I couldn't even hold myself up. I fell back on the desk kicking off one of my shoes so I could get my legs free enough to wrap around his waist.

Milan sucked my toes while Say drilled me for an exam I didn't study for. His breasts pressed up against mine and I was lost. Aeron's face shot through my mind followed by Vaughn and then Dontay until we were all rolled together in my head. Milan positioned himself behind Say and even though I couldn't see what he was doing, I could feel it. Milan made Sayzano fuck me breathless. Every stroke that Milan gave Say amplified the stroke that dug into me, damn near shattering my spine, making me gasp when I would have normally been fake moaning. I came first. The only reason I didn't scream or make a sound was because I couldn't breathe from how hard it hit me. My walls pulsed clenched, and tightened so many times I was surprised I didn't crush the nigga inside me. Sayzano came so hard it felt like he was gonna bust the condom.

We looked like toppled building blocks. Say collapsed on me and Milan on him. I actually got a coochie charley horse so I pushed against Say's shoulder.

"This ain't Hotel Calipornia; we gotta roll before we're missed," I told them.

Sayzano swooped in for a kiss I wasn't expecting and I returned it as a courtesy. His lips were too wet, like slobby wet not lip gloss wet. His upper lip was damn near up my nose. I cringed, surprised he didn't notice. I'd gotten what I wanted from him and unfortunately it was all below the waist. Milan frowned and straightened his uniform. All I wanted to do was sleep and get the spit smell off my face; after two or three more fake hugs and dodging Say's kisses we all went our separate ways.

Lord, please don't let this fool be in confused gay-hetero love. That would so not be good.

Chapter 29

Eva
Some Misery Loves Company

It was morning and I was waiting for the cells to open when Officer Blakely's stank face appeared in front of my cell. "Hey, princess, I thought you would get lonely so I brought ya ass some company."

Antonia stood close behind her, holding a box filled with her belongings, a smug sneer on her face. "What up, boo? You didn't think big sis was gonna let you sit and cry all alone did you?"

I stood in terrified silence as Antonia and Officer Blakely exchanged glances. I knew Antonia'd pull this crap. I just figured I'd have at least a couple of weeks or a few days before Antonia tried to mess with me. I was in no way prepared for this.

Blakely unlocked the cell door and Antonia leered at me as she walked over and placed her things onto the top bunk.

"Y'all play nice," Officer Blakely said sarcastically as she gave Antonia a wink. "If I hear any yellin' from outta here I'll just assume it's a false alarm."

The key sliding the lock back into place sounded like a death sentence to my ears. I stood frozen, afraid to make eye contact, afraid to sit down, afraid to breathe.

"You gonna just stand there and play mannequin or you gonna get over here and help me unpack my shit?" Antonia's dark presence seemed to take up the entire cell.

"I'm sorry, I'll help you."

I didn't even bother telling her that the top bunk was mine. There was no point in starting any drama this early on. Ephesians says that we should be humble, patient, and gentle, and so I'd try my best to accommodate her intrusion into my world. I walked over and opened her small box of things, removing her hair brush and folded uniforms. I placed them in the spots where Aeron used to keep stuff on a small shelf over the sink in a corner. Antonia climbed up onto the bunk and watched me like a vulture staring down a small animal from the sky. I could feel the heat from her eyes following me. All the tension was making my hands shake and the muscles in the back of my neck were tense. I recited the Lord's Prayer over and over as I busied myself unpacking. I couldn't bring myself to even glance in her direction.

"You ain't that bad looking, ma. 'Cept for them ugly-ass cornrows. When you get done unbraid that shit. I'on't like it." She spat her displeasure with my cornrows as if it were disrespectful to have my hair in a way she didn't approve of.

"If I unbraid my hair, I don't have a flat iron or anything to straighten it out. It'll look crazy."

My body slammed up against the cell wall with so much force I saw bright spots. Antonia had jumped off the bunk and slung me so hard my teeth chattered. She stood in front of me, her fingers digging hard into my shoulders and her nails cutting into my skin.

"Bitch, did you hear me give you a muthafukin' option? You take that shit out. I ain't playing with your little scary ass." She released me from her grip.

I fought to keep my composure. It took everything I had to keep from crying. I nodded okay and walked on shaky legs to sit on the bottom bunk and started unbraiding my hair. This was going to be worse than I thought. I was delivered from the belly of the whale and dropped straight into the lion's den with no weapon, no shield, nothing but the Word to protect me.

When dinnertime came I was nothing more than a walking zombie. Antonia told me what to do, when to do it, and how. Say and Milan stared disapprovingly as I went to sit with Antonia's group of friends in the cafeteria. The most I could manage to do with my hair was run my fingers through it. My shoulder-length wavy afro was a mess and I was too ashamed to make eye contact with anyone. I barely touched anything on my tray. One of Antonia's friends kept smirking at me like my prison whites didn't exist. She stared like she could see me buck-naked and she was enjoying it way too much.

"Ay yo, Antonia. That's a cute li'l toy you done got yourself. How much for me to play with it for a little while?" Her deep, masculine voice echoed into the empty pit in the center of my stomach. It bounced off of my spine and vibrated up toward my ears as I stared down at my tray afraid to look up.

Antonia's arm thumped heavily around my shoulders as answered her. "Shit, you my people. For you, no charge. Just name the time and place."

Everyone at the table laughed and started making offers. Some were kidding while others were very serious. I could feel the tears threatening to come down, but I refused to cry. I stared at the food on my tray so hard I could see every grain in the dry-ass rye sandwich they served and I'd counted all twenty-two of my potato chips at least five times. The nervous tension I was feeling was taking its toll on me physically. My mouth dried to the point that I couldn't swallow. I quietly popped in a piece of gum and prayed it would give me some relief.

It was a torturous salvation when dinner ended. I managed to grab a few bits of fruit and some chips from my tray and put them in my pocket in case I got hungry later. I didn't know when these women would make their trades with Antonia for my body but for the moment I was just happy not having to face them anymore.

Back in our cell I lay on the bottom bunk intending to pray and meditate before the evening count.

"Da fuck you getting all comfy for? I didn't say you could lie down." Antonia leaned up against the cell wall and crossed her arms over her chest.

"What do you suggest I do?" I wasn't sure if she'd take my question as me being a smart ass and I couldn't hide the tremble in my voice.

"I suggest you get ova' here and show me what dat mouf do." She sneered at me, pointing to the ground in front of her, or did she point at her crotch?

My eyes widened in shock. I knew she couldn't be saying what the hell I thought she was. Aeron had never made me perform oral sex on her so I had no idea how or what to do. *Lord Jesus . . .*

"Um, I . . . I don't know how, Antonia." I stammered out my reply as I stared apprehensively down at the white tiles on the cell floor. I could feel the sweat beading on my upper lip and forehead from my nerves. Maybe she would lose interest if she knew I didn't know what the hell to do. Maybe

she'd give up and just leave me alone. I was wrong.
I could hear the fabric slide in the silence of the cell
as she pulled off her cotton pants and panties. I
made the mistake of glancing for just a second and
caught her standing spread-eagle up against the
wall. *Loooooooord Jesus, if you've ever delivered
anyone please deliver me.* I prayed in earnest, fer-
vent silence, my lips moving quickly and silently.

"Guess you 'bouta learn then. Bring ya ass ova'
here."

Never in a million years would I have ever pic-
tured myself in this type of situation. If I said no
she'd have probably beat me to death. If I did it,
I didn't have any idea how to do it right so she'd
have probably gotten pissed off and still beat me to
death. Reluctantly I got up off the cot and kneeled
in front of her. I hadn't made any kind of direct eye
contact with her out of fear that I'd see a punch or
a slap coming.

"Okay. Now, eat dis pussy like it's your last meal.
You ain't eat dinner so I know your ass hungry."
She grabbed me by the back of my head and pulled
my face toward her.

I made the mistake of letting my eyes focus on
her privates and my immediate reaction was to
pull away. My face balled up in disgust. Had this
heffa never in her life heard of a razor or Nair? I
stared in horror at the tangled mass of curly black
hair. I couldn't believe she seriously wanted me to
put my mouth there.

Her hand was painfully tight around the back of my neck as she guided my face closer and closer until I could feel the soft, thick curls tickling my nose and my chin. The praying began in my head even though it felt more like a monologue.

Okay, I take every gay thought I've ever had back; forgive me, Father, because I can't do this. I know this must be some kind of punishment or lesson because I was having thoughts about Aeron but this is just not right. I'm used to a penis, and I can't imagine doing this to whoever whenever and especially not now. Why is it so hairy?

Cringing, the only thing I could think to do was squeeze my eyes shut and move my mouth in a Pac-Man motion. I was trying my best to not taste or get my tongue on anything. Antonia moaned and spread her legs farther apart at the contact of my mouth on her naked skin. I'd been trying to hold my breath and made the mistake of inhaling. I swear the scent of unwashed woman parts stung my nostrils, probably singed off every hair, and stained my upper lip. I felt a gag coming. Trying to hide my dry heaves as I fought for air made me lose all thoughts of the gum in my mouth and there was just so, so much hair. Before I knew it I'd actually managed to Pac-Man-style "nom nom nom" my gum all up into that mess. I stopped and leaned back in shock. Antonia looked down, trying to figure out what caused the interruption.

"What the fuck?" she yelled down at the tangled mass of bright pink watermelon gum intertwined all up in her black curls. I silently giggled as a slow smug smile spread across my face.

That'll teach your ass to try to force-feed someone when you ain't even got the sense to keep that mess tidy.

I already knew the blow was coming before it made contact and the world went black. But at least it was worth it.

Chapter 30

Eva
She Popped My Cherry

When I came to it was dark in the cell. I wasn't sure how long I'd been lying unconscious on the floor. I also couldn't believe they had done a count and didn't notice I wasn't outside my cell. Officer Blakely probably handled that, I was sure. I groaned; my head throbbed as I tried to sit up and I glanced around for Antonia timidly.

"You thought that was real fuckin' cute didn't you?" she asked calmly from her perch up on the top bunk. She sat there and stared down at me with an unreadable expression. It was nerve-racking not being able to tell if she was angry, or feeling vengeful.

"It was an accident. I forgot about the gum. I'm sorry. I . . . I was nervous." My voice was barely above a whisper. Talking just felt like it would make my head hurt worse. Talking could also get me hurt a lot worse if I irritated Antonia.

She hopped down and I visibly cringed away from her.

"Well, princess, it's your turn. So strip the fuck down. I'm gonna teach you what to do, so next time you'll do me right." She shook her head disapprovingly. "Tsk tsk, my sister should have schooled you better than that."

I felt disgusted by the thought of her mouth on or near me. Even though she looked so much like Aeron, her persona and her demeanor made her ugly in comparison.

"Um, I need to pee. Can I freshen up real quick?" I asked nervously. Even though she ain't have a right to say anything, she sure as hell wasn't going to talk about my stuff smelling or tasting any which kind of way.

"Just hurry the hell up."

I was relieved after she barked out her approval with her face scrunched up in a frown. She turned, pulled a magazine from under her pillow on the top bunk, and adjusted so she could see it under a small slit of light that shone into our cell. I slowly made my way over to the toilet as my mind quickly tried to spin up some sort of plan. Curly black hairs were scattered all over the inside of the toilet bowl. Apparently Antonia had no choice but to cut all that gum out of her hair. I couldn't help but smile. My triumph was short-lived though.

"I said hurry da fuck up. I ain't tryin'a be up all damn night."

Antonia's harsh tone snapped me out of my moment. She put the magazine away and started undressing with her back to me, and I took that as a chance to clean myself up and also remove my uniform. I walked over to the bottom bunk and lay down. She stood over me with her arms leaning on the top bunk.

Please tell me why in the hell would she shave her stuff and not take a moment to shave those yeti bushes growing under her damn armpits?

She stood there staring down at me while I fought the urge to scoot as far away as possible. I was worried one of those little white deodorant clumps dangling from her armpit hair would fall and, given my luck, it would land right in my eye or something crazy.

"Damn, girl, you got some pretty-ass titties. Shame they always hidden all up under that uniform." A smile spread across her lips.

I'd started to say thank you, but wasn't sure if that was a real compliment or if I was supposed to take it like one. The entire situation just felt awkward and she didn't help standing over me staring like she was.

Without warning her heavy self fell on top of me and she kissed me while roughly running her hands over my body up toward my breasts. I closed my eyes and tried to find the energy Aeron had sparked in me but it just wasn't there. They looked the same, but nothing about Antonia felt the same as when I was with Aeron. She pulled her lips away from mine and sucked and bit hard into the side of my neck. I winced and involuntarily my hands flew up to push her away.

Antonia just laughed and pinned my hands above my head as she slid her body in between my legs and bit hard into my skin everywhere that her mouth could reach. I clenched my teeth as tears slid out of the corners of my eyes, but I didn't dare scream or cry out.

When she was done with what I guessed was her crude version of foreplay, Antonia released my hands and sat back on her knees between my legs.

"Now, I'm gonna show yo' ass how to eat pussy."

My entire body tensed in anticipation of the pain I knew was coming. She palmed my butt cheeks in each hand and pulled my hips into her face. Her teeth grazed my clit lightly before her mouth fully opened and I was completely caught off guard at the jolt of heated lightning that shot through my body. She stiffened her tongue and plunged it inside me as far as she could and all the air flew out of my lungs. Small white sparks discharged behind my eyelids that got larger each time her tongue slid out and back in again. The woman had to do some kind of oral-strengthening exercises on a regular basis. I could almost guarantee that she must have eaten pudding cups without a spoon damn near every day of her life. I mentally slapped myself to keep from begging her to keep going when she stopped.

"Damn, girl. You taste sweet as fuck. You got that good-good."

Her comments were so out of place. Was I supposed to say thanks?

Apparently, no, she didn't need a thanks. I was angry at myself for even enjoying what she was doing. Antonia moaned to herself like a fat kid in front of an all-you-can-eat candy buffet. She was in it more aggressively than she was a few moments ago and at that point I couldn't help it. Closing my eyes the little evil voice in my head began chanting, saying, *just let it happen,* over and over again.

Repeatedly she alternated between licking my clit and diving into my core with her tongue. Dear Lord, the woman was multitasking like nobody's business. The entire time her mouth was moving, she'd let go of my butt and with one hand spread me open so her mouth could get full access to every inch of me.

Her other hand stayed in motion tugging and teasing my left nipple, then over to do the same to the right. My body wasn't under my control anymore. In those moments every nerve ending under my skin was following whatever orders her mouth gave them, and damn it if my legs weren't shaking.

I pulled the pillow over my face to stifle a moan when I felt that painfully delightful stretching as two or three fingers glided inside me. She started stroking me in a "come here" motion that made the fine hairs inside my ears stand up. My eyes rolled back in my head and all I could do was feel. You could call me whatever instrument you want; with her hands and/or her mouth, she was playing the hell out of me.

My senses were clouded by pleasure and I failed terribly at trying to distract myself so I could listen in case any guards walked through. All I could hear were the sounds of my wetness as Antonia's mouth and hands drove me into a frenzy. All sense of reason completely left me in that moment and I let go and gave in to the throb that had begun to build between my legs. My entire body convulsed and I could feel my walls clench and tighten as I came harder than I'd ever thought possible. The heat from Antonia's mouth was driving me insane and everything felt extremely sensitive. I fought myself to keep from reaching out and pushing her away. She licked and kept licking everything, from my clit downward. I could hear her slurping up my juices. When she covered my opening with her entire mouth and licked and sucked hard the sensation sent me crashing into another spiral of spine-breaking spasms.

Antonia sprang up, her brow creased in surprised confusion. We locked eyes as her hand went to her lips. At first I thought maybe she had a hair stuck between her teeth. She opened her hand and held it up to her lips, spitting a cherry into it. I could see the muscles in her throat working and she licked her lips repeatedly as realization of what I'd done sank in. I slowly slid up from my position and stood beside the bunk. My legs were so shaky, I wasn't sure if it was from cumin' the way I did or from fear of what was about to happen.

"Looks like you got my cherry, Antonia." My voice was a low, shaky whisper as I stared her right in the eyes.

"What. The. Fuck?" Antonia was holding her throat and her face contorted as if she was in extreme pain.

From what little I did know about people with severe food allergies I gave her no more than a few minutes before her airway closed up completely.

"Call for help," she choked out, looking at me pitifully.

I simply pressed my index finger to my lips, and shook my head saying no. "Just relax. I think this'll go a lot smoother if you try to relax," I whispered.

I quietly put my prison clothes back on and slid the remaining cherries from my pocket and laid them neatly on her bunk. What Antonia hadn't realized when I'd asked to pee was that I'd bitten a cherry in half and smeared the juice on my lips, my privates, and even popped half of it inside.

I remembered Aeron once telling me that the only thing she and her sister had in common was their allergy to cherries. Who knew that tiny seed of information would wind up being so colossal?

You started this and now you need to finish it. If you stop now, you know she'll kill you for what you just did.

I grabbed the razor she'd used to shave with earlier and walked toward her with the other half of the single cherry in my palm. Her eyes widened in horror as I pressed the razor to her throat.

"I can finish this off and let you feel this blade run across your throat, or you can eat the other half of this cherry and die quietly."

I didn't have time for her to give me an okay. I didn't want to risk chickening out. I roughly shoved the cherry in her mouth and watched her fight to chew and swallow. If the coroner did an autopsy they needed to find that other half in her stomach so none of this would point back to me.

Antonia slumped forward on the bed, her face turning a pale white in the dim lighting of the cell. Her chest was heaving hard and she was starting to thrash around as her airway constricted. I sat on the toilet of our cell and watched her intently. I'd just committed murder. How lenient is heaven when it comes to letting someone in who's stained with so much sin?

Chapter 31

Dontay
How Much

The wedding was only a couple of days away and I'd been spending my days grinding like crazy looking for work or a loan. And trying to ignore the guilt that stayed with me over what happened on that boat. Visions of Bear on his knees between my legs made my stomach capsize in on itself. When I'd gone back onto the outer deck Toi was clueless about what I'd done. I wasn't into that shit; it was just the fuckin' crack. I can't even believe I did that shit.

I pulled up to the house and took a deep breath to prepare myself. Toi swung open the frosted glass door in her pink house coat, matching fluffy pink slippers sipping what had to be her fourth pink cosmo. She always wanted to fuck or fight when she drank and I had no idea from the expression on her face which one she was in the mood for.

"You take my car all damn day and you don't think to call?" Toi snapped at me the second my foot hit the porch.

I rubbed the knotted muscles in the back of my neck trying not to get irritated with her. I was flipping through the best way to answer her without making an even bigger deal out of the situation. Seriously, she just gave a nigga a boat; now I couldn't use the car? She needed to keep tabs on my every move?

"Toi, I've been pulling extra hours trying to make sure we can do this dream wedding. I didn't know you'd use everything I gave you on the surgery." I lied.

Her tone softened. "There was the funeral too. I'm sorry."

"It's all right. I'll work something out."

I kept my tone cool, scoopin' Toi up into my arms. She was so damn short it was nothing to grab her up making her my temporary hostage. I nuzzled my nose into the curve of her neck. "I thought you'd be okay since you were driving that nigga's Beemer."

I was referring to the red BMW 345i that had miraculously appeared in our driveway one day. I breathed a mental sigh of relief as the tension melted out of her body and she relaxed in my arms.

"He said I can keep the Beemer or borrow the Lex for as long as I want. But I still need to hear somethin' from you whether you have my car or not. That you're alive and you're okay. That you still love me." Toi pouted up at me and I wished for that moment that I wasn't torn between starting this new chapter of my life. She wasn't making it easy for me to continue our story though. Granted Reverend had this crazy pyramid investment crack scheme going on. I couldn't tell if he was trying to recruit me or steal my woman. Every time I turned around she was flaunting new shit in my face with a Reverend Matthews thank-you card. And the gifts kept coming even after I got off that boat after turning down him and his hand outs.

"I told you to leave his ass alone. I'm not gonna keep doing this. We can call the wedding off right now." I glared over my eyebrows at her reminding her for the hundredth time.

Her eyes darkened from their usual glittering peach-pit brown into shimmery snifters of warm brandy like the Paul Masson she loved to slip in her tea. Toi never had an answer when it came to talks about her leaving her current sugar daddy. I set her down and followed her into the house. She was looking fine as ever in a little black dress held together by all these gold chains.

First thing that crossed my mind was a relaxing, long, hot shower tellin' her how much I missed her. The only thing that stood between all of that was the family I'd started and Toi's unwillingness to cut off the old head she had taking care of her. Her place smelled like warm sunsets, sweet pineapples, and coconut piña colada. I looked around: no toys, no coloring books, no Jada.

"Where's Jada? I thought you were going to pick her up from your aunt's while I was at work."

"I didn't have my car." Toi pouted like a spoiled seven-year-old.

"The Beemer been sitting out there all day."

"I don't like red. I wanted my car."

I jabbed the air. Something told me I shouldn't have let her people tell Eva's sister CPS had Jada. Eva was probably worrying herself to death thinking the worst about her. I just didn't want any of her family scoping me out or tracking me down after the sentencing and they would have started with Jada.

I glared at Toi and she silently stepped aside. I sat myself on our brand new ugly velvet gray couch. The material was the color of wet cement with pleats along the back. It instantly brought the inside of a coffin to my mind and I tried to focus on something else. A deep gold throw rug lay on top the dark gray carpet and gold armchairs sat on either side of us. I tried not to make sense out of the gray and gold color scheme. The gold stuff was all new; it definitely wasn't here when I'd left this morning and an instant wave of jealousy went through me. Good old Reverend Matthews aka her sugar daddy was laying it on extra thick. *Damn, so she's fittin' us in like that in twenty-four hours?*

I sneered at her and her stupid color scheme. It was like trying to warm up slate with fake sunshine.

Women definitely did some strange shit when it came to decorating themselves and their houses with colors. I heard chicks all the time sayin' men were color blind. *Nah, y'all just color confused.*

"I see you got some new ugly-ass shit up in here. Your other nigga drop it off for you?" I couldn't keep the anger out of my voice, didn't try to either.

"Dontay, since you've been layin' up in here, have you put any new shit up in here other than your stank shoes?" Toi stood her small self over me with her hand on her hip. "Until you are doing more than driving the gas out my car and bringing it back damn near on E, don't say shit about what someone else does or doesn't do for me."

"Toikea." I used her full first name so she'd know I wasn't playing. "Why would I break myself and offer to do anything if another motherfucka is gonna be rolling up in here reaping the benefits? You already got a nigga taking care of you. You want me to go broke payin' for you too, just like my pops did?" Adrenaline made me pop up off the couch. "I gotta pay for my woman now? Tell me how much the pussy cost, Toi? Another house, another car? Oh, wait you want a boat, boo? How many cars can you drive at one time, Toi?" I pulled my paper out my pocket and flipped it off the palm of my hand: hundreds, twenties, ones. "Is this enough for your time tonight, ma'am?" Every dime I had left to my name was now littered across her floor like trash.

Her ice-cold cosmo splashed me across my face burning my eyes. The palm of her hand connected hard with my wet cheek, and my head snapped ever so slightly. That small, involuntarily movement made me see red. I blinked, furious that she'd even dare touch me; grabbing Toi by the shoulders I flung her little ass onto the couch. It rocked with the force of her landing on it. My pulse throbbed in my forehead, my face hurt, and my hands clenched into fists against her skin. Black mascara streaked tears ran down her cheeks and I loosened my grip. I couldn't, wouldn't ever hurt a woman. That was my pops; that wasn't me.

Toi kicked me hard as fuck in the stomach. I grunted and went from being on top to lying in the floor on my back. She'd done some kind of Jackie Chan stunt roll off the couch landing on my chest. Glass shattered dangerously close to the side of my head and I winced.

"Tell momma you're sorry, Dontay," Toi whispered against my skin; her cosmo-scented breath warmed the skin on the side of my neck.

What I could only imagine to be a shard from the glass was pressed against my pulse on the other side. I took in a shallow breath when it pricked my skin. My hands went into the universal "please don't kill me" position in the air.

"Baby, I'm sorry," I whispered.

Toi's hips wound into my groin, her teeth grazed my skin from my neck up until she was nibbling at my chin and I forgot how to breathe.

"Tell momma what you're sorry for," she demanded still holding that damn piece of glass.

Blood warmed my skin, tickled and itched as it trickled its way down my neck, making my brain go into a confused panic. I could barely move my lips. "Bae, I'm sorry I disrespected you, I ain't mean it. You know I love you. You know I . . ."

Toi ran the tip of her tongue up the side of my neck licking that itch right up to the source of the wound she'd just inflicted. My brain stopped dead in its tracks; the hamster fainted on the wheel. She trailed her lips up to mine and I was dizzy from the adrenaline rush, ready to do some damage of my own. I was feeling like I'd drunk a gallon of the sweet cosmos I could taste on her tongue mingling with the unmistakable taste of my own blood. If that wasn't the sexiest fuckin' shit in the world I didn't know what was. Crazy as hell but sexy.

Everything I knew about love and making love I'd learned from Toi and she'd just stepped shit up to a level no one could ever compete with. I was careful to slide the shard of glass out of her fingers just as easily as I slid her out of her pink housecoat. I treated her like my personal buffet tasting every bit of skin I uncovered. She tasted like jasmine, warm violets, and carnations, like Gucci Rush on shower fresh skin.

She started running her nails over my abs underneath my shirt and the muscles tightened out of reflex. My other muscle started to tighten and swell, too. She frowned up at me pouting her lips.

"Dontay, can we do something new tonight?" she asked dragging her nails lower and lower.

What the hell else could be newer than what just happened? My eyes drifted downward and I got ready to watch some nail porn. Toi's nails was always on point. I'm talkin' about French manicure, French American manicure, it didn't matter. Eva had nails but she ain't never paint 'em or make 'em pretty. I never understood how important it was for a woman to have nice nails until this chick wit' Don Cheadle nubs grabbed my dick and I looked down and yelped. It was like seeing one of my homeboy's hands stroking my business. Not cool.

She had two lit candles on either side of the bed and they had the room smelling like warm pears and butter cream frosting. I laid her down on her stomach and took my time removing my own clothes. My hands were ice cold. I was scared as hell that I'd slip and cut or scratch her up. But that's exactly what she wanted. She got up on her knees and begged for me run the broken glass along her back. Toi purred and growled; it made these ugly red slashes across her skin.

All of that ass sat perfectly up in the air looking like the top half of a thick "come fuck me" heart. *See now that's exactly why dudes be fallin' in love. Get a chick who just toot it up and we be back there seein' hearts. Eva could have definitely used some notes from one of these seasoned broads.*

When I couldn't take it anymore I made her hit that first-stroke note. Some chicks moan so loud their voice cracks, or they let out a sharp surprised gasp. Toi did a combination of the two and I loved it. I realized that I loved her, had been in love with her all along. I loved Eva but I'd made a mistake, and even though my heart hurt at the thought of leaving her, all Toi had to do was say a word or make a sound.

She was breathless now, gasping and grabbing the sheets. I tangled my fingers in her short hair pulling her head back so I could control her arch, make her take me deeper.

"This is my pussy, it bends, stretches and only cums for me."

I flipped her on her back folding her legs like a pretzel in front of me. My fingers were wrapped tight around her ankles. I let her feel the tip before she raked her nails across the sides of my back begging me to vent all my pent-up anger. Closing my eyes I slammed into her over and over; her body shuddered and her climax made me explode.

***

Toi was dozing off on my chest while I traced the shape of her nose with my eyes. It was my mission to make her leave whoever her other nigga was.

"What in God's name is this?" someone shouted, flipping on the lights. I must have dozed off. I woke up momentarily disoriented. I looked for Eva and Jada's crib before I remembered where I was.

"Daddy, what are you doing here?" Toi shouted pulling half the blankets with her.

"Toikea, I told your mother I'd take care of you before she passed. Now, I don't ask nor do I expect a lot from you but no daughter of mine will be running around with some jobless Negro half her age who's barely taking care of his own family," Reverend Matthews shouted.

"Wait what, did you call this nigga Daddy? Toikea, why didn't you just tell me this was your pops?" I knew exactly why as soon as the words left my mouth. Old Rev didn't want to mess up his crooked house. He had more skeletons than I did. I let him feel the full brunt of my rage. "Nigga, I take care of all mine. I don't jerk off or get power crazy over a nigga suckin' another nigga dick either I'm more man than your cracked-out ass,"

"My daughter will not marry any man who is so weak he'll *drop his guard and let* another man suck his dick, Dontay."

Toi was staring at me wide-eyed.

Reverend Matthews glared at me. "You didn't look so manly with another man's lips wrapped around your li'l willie with your soon-to-be fiancée in the next room." He turned to leave and spun back around on his heel sneering as he looked me up and down.

"Who was he trying to show off for? It wasn't me!" I snapped back, launching off the bed without thinking about where I was or who he was. I didn't mean to but nobody insults a man's pride, family, and his dick all in one breath and thinks he's gonna just walk away.

He was not a small dude by any means. We locked up midair and when we landed he had my naked ass in a full nelson with both my arms pinned back behind my head. I was naked and flouncing around like a fish out of water, with a Bible-strong mothafucka on my back. And Toi still thought that was the ideal time to tase me in my damn groin. All my muscles clenched up and kept clenching, in the most painful, tightening feeling. It was like hitting your funny bone except you felt it everywhere. Reverend Matthews let me go and glared down at me as he climbed over me and saw himself out.

Toi's voice was full of hurt. "Y'all crab apple–ass niggas don't roll far huh? Were you gonna tell me or did you want to have me in the dark until the first James family reunion just like your daddy?"

"Toi, it wasn't something—"

"Just go, Dontay. Don't call me, don't try to see me; just forget you ever knew me. You've been playin' me all this time when I trusted you."

As soon as I could move, I got up and started getting dressed to the soundtrack of Toi crying into her pillow. I did that shit, her heart was broken, and I could feel mine breaking with her. Rev didn't have to put me on blast like that. He could have pulled me to the side and said something. The nigga could have at least let me decide how to break the news to Toi. A tear tried to burn its way out of my eye blurring my vision up. I wanted to say something to Toi but I couldn't find my voice over the scratchiness in my throat.

Reverend Matthews was camped out in the living room. "You better find yourself a mop. That's the only way you'll see a dollar in Hampton Roads now," he mocked me.

I cut my eyes at him and kept going. That cocky motherfucka was gonna get his one day. I picked my money up off the floor and balled it up into my pockets. The house rocked when I slammed the front door behind me. I wanted it to collapse on that devil hiding in Christian skin. I was hoping he'd run out and confront me again. I'd rock that ass to sleep with a solid right.

Chapter 32

Eva
I Know Not What I Do

I was awakened by the loud clank and electric hum of the lights coming on. It was morning: time to face what I'd done. I glanced down from the top bunk and stared emotionlessly at Antonia's pale, lifeless hand hanging over the side of the bottom one where I'd left her. I couldn't move her back up top and there was no point in trying to. Anything done to a body postmortem was sure to leave a mark once the blood stopped flowing, and I didn't want to leave any evidence of foul play. I guessed nights of watching *Snapped* reruns on TV had taught me more about being a killer than I'd thought. Mentally I kicked myself for not making her climb back up before finishing her off.

The demon on my left shoulder was mocking the angel sitting on my right.

You did that. You sinned, you've broken one of the sacred Ten Commandments. But it's not like you had a choice. She would have eventually beaten your ass to death if you didn't handle her first. What's done is done. Repent and you'll be back in His good and merciful graces.

"Open up, seventy-three! Open it up!" Officer Blakely rushed in and I sat up wide-eyed and dazed.

"What the fuck happened in here? I need a medic in zone two block 0039, cell seventy-three. Inmate down; we have an inmate down! Get a unit in here now!" She radioed for help and slid Antonia's body onto the floor. She was feeling for a pulse, looking for a heartbeat.

"What the fuck you do to her, bitch? I know your ass did something! You did this shit? What the fuck did you do to her?" Officer Blakely was hovering over Antonia's body, glaring up at me furiously.

Everything happening around me was a blur. Another female officer came out of nowhere and yanked me down from my cot. She directed me to stand outside of our cell. As a precaution I was cuffed: my hands behind my back, and shackles were placed tightly on my ankles. I could already hear the whispers going up and down the block. Mirrors were sliding out of several bars as some of the inmates tried to get a glimpse at all the commotion.

"Yo, yo, you hear that? Church Girl killed Antonia."

"That little scary-ass Jesus freak murked Antonia?"

"She ain't do that shit; she ain't crazy enough to do something like that. Antonia probably tapped that 'til she passed out or something."

I stared straight ahead, like I could see everything and nothing at the same time. My thought process was hell; maybe if I looked a little crazy the other women would believe I'd killed her while the guards would find the cherries and know otherwise.

At that moment Officer Blakely shook her head up at the other CO and radioed for the coroner to come up. She picked up the cherries that were beside Antonia's body and placed them in a Baggie, handing them to the other CO. She got up and marched toward me, scowling, her hand on her nightstick.

"I guess your ass ain't hear shit huh?" Blakely stood eye to eye with me. One hand rested on her favorite weapon of choice, her baton, and the other on her radio.

"I think I might have heard something, but I chalked it up as a false alarm." I couldn't help throwing her own words back in her ugly, fat face. I knew I'd said enough at that point, maybe too much. So I just shut up.

Officer Blakely rolled her eyes at me and directed her gaze back to Antonia's body. "I don't see no marks or bruises; there's no skin under her fingernails. Nothing indicating foul play." She looked at me again, her voice a questioning growl: "She was eating those cherries in there?"

"I don't know, ma'am. What she did or didn't do, eat or didn't eat was between her and the Lord, I imagine." I answered her in a singsong, matter-of-fact tone.

My response almost sent her through the roof, as she leaned her scrunched-up bulldog face in closer to mine. She was so close I could smell her Listerine and coffee-scented morning breath. She roughly poked me in the center of my chest. Inwardly I flinched, but outwardly I didn't even blink at the gesture.

"We'll see what the coroner has to say 'bout that shit. Now, get your monkey ass back in there." Her eyes narrowed to dark slits and she hissed between clenched teeth, "Antonia was more important than you think. You all up on that praying shit. Well you better pray word don't come back that this shit wasn't an accident or I'm going to personally show you hell on earth, bitch." Droplets of spit flew from her mouth and landed on my cheek like flecks of hot lava. She grabbed my shoulders and roughly pushed me inside before unshackling me. I climbed back up onto my cot and lay back, crossing my arms behind my head and staring at the ceiling.

My nostrils flared in disgust but I didn't move a muscle. I just feigned the appearance of complete and absolute indifference. I heard the click-clack of Officer Blakely's shoes as she stormed off. They were carting Antonia's body away and removing her things, and I couldn't believe what I'd gotten away with. Murder.

Chapter 33

Eva
The Butterfly Effect

This would be my first breakfast alone since Aeron's release. My hands were clammy and it felt like I had a gazillion moths flying around in my stomach as we got in line to go to the cafeteria. No one was looking directly at me, but I could tell all the side eyes were definitely on me. I cracked my knuckles; it was bad habit from when I was a kid, but I was so nervous I couldn't help it. Lady, the inmate in front of me, flinched at the sound and glanced back nervously. A sneer spread across my face, and she quickly faced forward.

In the serving line I blindly waited as the servers filled up my tray. My mind was a blur of activity from psalms of forgiveness to the eerie look on Antonia's face as she drew her last breath.

"Bring your ass over here. Hurry up. Hurreeeeee up." Say was waving frantically from a table in a corner the moment I walked out of the serving line. Milan was seated next to him as usual, nudging him in the side with his elbow. I didn't even get to set my tray on the table or put my hind parts fully in the chair before he was going in, whispering questions left and right, his neck and wrist just a-flying and snapping with each and every word.

"Hi, ho. What the fuck? E'rebody saying you nixed Juarez ass. Now I know my darling little boo-boo ain't no cold-blooded killa. What Juarez do, slip on a Ding Dong wrapper in the dark, fall, and bump her head or some shit? Why you ain't call nobody when it happened? Why you ain't tell the COs that shit? Um, why you ain't saying shit? What da hell went on up in that motherfucka last night, woman?"

Say gave me an exasperated wide-eyed stare, crossing his arms flamboyantly across his chest and popping his lips at me simultaneously.

"Bae, maybe it's because you ain't took a breath, pause, flash, or nothing long enough to even give the girl time to blink. She sitting over here looking like Bambi on the highway and you a damn eighteen-wheeler right now." Milan's tone was calm and protective as he addressed Say in my defense.

"Bitch! A: how she looking like Bambi? That motherfucka was a boy; so B: you might want to compare her to the motherfucka who killed Bambi momma. We obviously got ourselves a gorilla, cough cough, I mean killa in our midst. Aeron leaves and this heffa wants to become a member of Murder Inc. Where dey do dat at?"

"Sayzano, Murder Inc.? Really? They ain't even relevant anymore, and who the hell anybody in Murder Inc. ever murder, fool? You need to shut up before I shut you up; you are talking out the side of your neck right now." Milan was starting to turn a bright shade of pink after this last statement.

As funny as their whisper argument was getting, I had to put a stop to it before they got out of hand. Leaning forward, I lowered my tone barely above a whisper. "You two need to stop this right now." I did my best to keep my face blank, barely moving my lips as I spoke. "I did what I had to do and that's all y'all need to know. Okay?" I narrowed my eyes for emphasis, feeling like an angry mother hen, looking back and forth between the two of them until they nodded in understanding.

I was certain no one else had heard me, but anyone with even the slightest bit of common sense could look at Say and Milan and figure out what I'd probably just told them. They both sat there, slack-jawed, wide-eyed, and dead silent. Anyone with a lick of common sense knew the two of them were never quiet at the same time. You would have thought Antonia'd just risen from the dead and sat down at the table with us.

"I need both of you to act normal. Like none of this ever happened. It's a normal day and, Say, if you don't mind, my roots are something else. Can you freshen up my braids later?"

The smart reply that I was expecting from Say never came; he instead nodded slowly and stared down at his tray. Picking up my fork, I scooped up a heap of runny eggs and shoveled the bland-tasting mess into my mouth. Say and Milan followed suit. We spent the rest of the time eating in silence.

"I do have one question, Eva." It was Milan who spoke first as we were clearing our trays, his voice a barely audible whisper as he stood beside me. "What do you think Aeron will do when she gets word of all this? That's still her family. They all members of La Legal De Represalias. Them some stupid powerful, filthy rich, and extremely brutal people when they get crossed. If they don't like the news it's gonna get very bad, very fast," Milan stated as he glanced around nervously for eavesdroppers.

"A member of the La Di La what?" Sputtering the letters, I turned to give Milan a good stare down, my expression showing my obvious confusion. Aeron had never mentioned whatever he was talking about, so this was all news to me.

He gave me a frustrated eye roll, slicing his hand through the air quickly and then through his hair in an agitated nervous motion, pulling it out of its neat ponytail. He fidgeted with getting it tied back behind his head as he explained.

"The Law of Retribution or Law of Talion." He paused, giving me an expectant look, but I still had no idea what he was stalking about. "The Lot. It's like a gang, some kind of underground organization. Why do you think Blakely let Juarez do whatever the hell she wanted to? You might wanna go unite with the sistas or some shit, because you gonna need backup. If any of the Latina members in here find out and they think you seriously did something to her, they're gonna do something to you, sweetheart. Your little ripple might have started a damn tidal wave."

I didn't say anything. I honestly had no clue what to say. Before being here I knew next to nothing about gangs or gang affiliation. The thought never occurred to me about how Aeron would actually react to her sister's death, let alone the fact that either of them could have ties to an actual gang. I shrugged at Milan as if I didn't have a care in the world and ignored his look of exasperation and anger. At this point the only thing at the top of my prayer list was to make it out of prison and get my daughter. Second on my prayer list was my request for an absolutely spotless coroner's report.

Chapter 34

Eva
Demonology

After breakfast I skipped going out to the yard and instead decided to start doing some research. I walked into the rec room and signed in. The correctional officer behind the check-in desk never even looked up. She was too busy with the phone wedged between her ear and shoulder, lost in a conversation about some drug dealer who managed to get another officer to help him escape. His baby momma called asking where he was and the warden didn't want to give her a solid answer. I wanted to listen further but didn't want to catch her attention and get put out. The room was about the size of a small classroom. One wall was covered in shelves of encyclopedias and law manuals; the other was a random assortment of outdated magazines.

There were three raggedy prehistoric-looking Gateway computers side by side on a long table at the back of the room. Fortunately no one was using them. It was just too nice of a day for anyone to want to sit up in this dusty old closet surfing the Internet. Well, anyone except for me that is. With no idea where to start, out of habit I pulled up my Facebook account and logged in. I was thankful my password and everything still worked.

Depression hit me like a tidal wave as my profile picture stared back at me. That wasn't me, couldn't be. The girl in the picture had her hair pinned up with soft curls falling around her ears. There was a golden glow to her light brown skin from the camera flash, making her already large brown eyes look even larger. I looked at a me I didn't know anymore, a version of myself that was radiant and alive and in love with my fiancé and the Word of God.

My friends list used to be around 500 or so people. They were mostly members from the church, business clients, and associates. I didn't have very many friends outside of that. Rejection set in as I scrolled through the names of the fifty-two people still on my list.

Just look at how supportive your church home is now. All the tithing and time you spent caring and praying for those assholes when they were sick or needed a kind word. Where are they now, Church Girl?

The devil on my shoulder was being a real jerk today, giving me thoughts of doubt and self-loathing. Had it been another church member I probably would have done the same thing myself. Deleted them from my life, scared the dirty association might tarnish my name or leak into my livelihood.

My heart skipped in excitement as I passed over Brother Hall's image. He was always such a sweetheart, helping me with the kids during vacation Bible school and always offering to cover choir rehearsals when I had to work late. His profile was a collage of images from things he'd done recently around the church. There was one of him standing in the crowd, towering over everyone around him. His eyes were closed and his hands were in tight fists as he lifted them in praise. Gone was the nappy fro I remembered. His haircut looked good on him; it gave him a dignified, intelligently handsome appearance.

Seek and you will be shown, ask and you shall receive. Right?

It was a far cry, but what other choice did I have? I hit the message button and nervously constructed an e-mail that would hopefully get his attention and get him to give me a little help. I needed money in my commissary and I needed someone I could trust to help me with my legal proceedings and maybe even trying to get Jada.

Brother Hall,
I know you've heard the news by now. No. I didn't do any of it. I need help and don't

know where else to turn. I can't tell you what it's been like for me in here and I can't bear to think of what my daughter might be going through without me. If you have a number I can call you at I'd appreciate it. It would be a collect call of course. Please don't reply to this and tell me you'll pray. I've prayed enough for both of us. Remember how we used to always say it's the real saints who'll get their knees dirty to pray with you instead of sitting in their comfortable home praying for you? Well, I need you down in the trenches with me more than I've ever needed anyone in my entire life.

   Eva

Using my sleeve I quickly brushed the tears from my eyes and hit SEND. I was about to close the page when a picture in the corner of the screen caught my eye. A chill shot through me as I stared at the People You May Know section. There was a dark, blurry image of a couple, like the picture had some kind of filter on it, but I'd recognize Dontay's gray eyes anywhere. The name beneath the picture was Ms. LoveKush Bettathantheythink Bankhead. I squinted at the thumbnail-size picture. The figures were both shadowed out; he was standing behind her and their faces were blurred all except for his eyes. It appeared to have been done intentionally, like with some sort of photo editing program.

My hands were frozen in a claw-like position over
the keyboard and mouse. I was afraid to click on the
picture and enlarge it, paranoid that whoever this
woman was would know I was secretly stalking her
page. A thousand and one things ran through my
mind all at once. *Did they take that picture before
we got locked up? Was he cheating on me with this
woman? If so, how long had it been going on?* My
finger was unmoving above the mouse; my heart
thudded loudly in my ears drowning out everything
around me. *Click that shit. Just do it.*

"Yooooo, you Church Girl, right?"

I physically jumped and probably even died for
a half a second from fright as someone grabbed the
back of my chair and swiveled me around. The room
flew by in a quick blur. I could feel all the blood
physically drain from my face in panic as I sat facing
five Hispanic women I'd never seen before.

"They said cha ass was mute or some shit, but I
don't believe dat. Nah, I think if chu know waz good,
chu gonna talk to us."

The woman speaking was short, squat, and box
shaped. A white bandana held her hair back from
her round face, making her penciled-in black eyebrows and lip liner stand out starkly against her
olive skin. I glanced around nervously looking for
the guard who was at the desk, but of course she'd
miraculously done the unthinkable and vanished.

"Okay. Wh . . . what would you like to discuss?" I sounded like a straight-up punk; my voice was small and shaky.

A smug smile spread across her face and she nodded to a tall, thin chick behind her. It happened so fast I didn't have a chance to blink, swallow, or even recite the Lord's Prayer. Someone grabbed me up from the chair and pinned my arms behind my back. A rough, callused hand slammed across my forehead, craning my head back, fully exposing my neck.

The one who had been speaking all this time walked up to me and held up a small blade. Cross-eyed, I tried to stare down my nose to focus on it, scared if I took my eyes off of it I'd feel it in my ribs or running across my throat. My neck muscles were constricting painfully from the awkward placement of my head. She came up to me as if she were going to give me a hug and placed her cheek right up against mine. Stale cigarettes and cheap body spray filled my nose as the tip of the blade barely touched the side of my throat. Her voice hissed into my ear like a snake that'd learned to speak broken English.

"Ssssoo, Church Girl, one quesssstion, one answer. Chu kill Antonia?" she asked, pressing the shank hard into my neck, and I winced, certain it was drawing blood. She then turned her head, placing her ear almost directly on my lips, waiting for me to reply.

"She did it, Janisa, she know she did. Just slice her ass up like she deserve." The girl holding me provoked my interrogator in an angry whisper.

Bite it! Bite the bitch's ear off! Slam the bitch behind you into the desk so she lets go and grab the shank while the other one's squealing in pain. Stab anyone who stands between you and that door!

"No." My whispered response was directed more toward this inner demon I'd somehow manifested. It seemed to love bloodshed, reveled in revenge, made me think of the most ungodly ways to handle situations.

"Oh. 'No,' she says." She turned to the other women and shrugged, they all started laughing. I didn't get the joke.

"According to her, I guess Antonia just died on her own. Wid no one in the cell wid her but dis bitch."

The girl holding my limbs hostage laughed, tightening her grip even more painfully. Hell, any tighter and I wouldn't have to worry about being shanked; my neck would probably snap.

"I didn't kill her." It was a pitiful attempt to save my life. I began to silently pray and ask God's forgiveness for everything I'd ever done. It was becoming obvious that they didn't care what I said.

You should have done what you had to do to keep your ass alive. Survival is all about fear and the strength of fear. Animals do it all the time. They camouflage themselves to look like something their predator will fear. Tell them you did it. Make these bitches fear your ass! Lie, make up a lie. Tell them you'd kill them all if you got the chance. You could do it, you've already done it!

I tried to shake the little voice that belonged to my inner demon out of my head. I guessed we all had it; some people just called it their conscience. Whatever it was, the only difference between me and these women was the fact that I refused to let my bloodthirsty inner demon control me, and they gave in to theirs every time.

The one with the blade turned back to me, her face contorted in anger at me speaking without being spoken to. She stormed over and punched me in the stomach with everything she had. The air whooshed from my lungs and the feeling of wanting to vomit and pass out at the same time took hold of my body. The girl behind me struggled to keep me on my feet as my body felt like collapsing in on itself from the pain. I'd never been hit before and definitely not that hard.

I was pulled roughly back up onto my feet and Janisa closed in for round two. A cold sweat was running down my neck and torso. I could feel the cotton fabric of my uniform sticking to my skin. Fighting back waves of nausea I tried to focus on Janisa as she closed the distance between us.

"I'll ask you one more time, Church Girl, did you—"

It happened so fast I had no idea how or why. Janisa fell away from me, a horrified scream frozen on her lips. She reminded me of the reaction my daughter had the first time she scraped her knee. There were a few moments where no sound came out, as tears slowly slid down her face. The sound caught up with her actions as if in slow motion as her scream pierced the air. It was all in a matter of seconds but everything seemed to be moving in slow motion. My captor released me in shock and I could hear her bump into the computer desk as she backed away from me.

The warm, rubbery portion of Janisa's ear flew from my mouth as I spat it toward the girl closest to her. She jumped back in terror and I smiled at her reaction, not realizing it made me look damn near insane. Janisa's blood was running down my chin and I could taste its metallic, coppery presence in my mouth, coating my teeth. *Lord, I'd better not get hepatitis or something from this.* Turning to the girl behind me, my intent was to gnaw my way through every last one of their asses and I lunged for her. I didn't expect her to react as quickly as she did. She kicked to fend off my attack, hitting me in the stomach.

"What the hell is going on in here?"

Crashing to the cold, hard tile floor never felt so good. I tried to catch my breath before glancing up to see who'd come into the room and saved my life. It was a white male officer; he didn't look familiar. The Latinas all quietly scurried out the door like a herd of panicked deer. Janisa ran past him, hiding her injury. The female CO who was on duty walked in past him with her head down. She shot me an angry glance out the corner of her eye before plopping back down at her post behind the check-in desk.

The white officer calmly walked over and helped me to my feet. "You okay?" he asked while brushing imaginary dirt off my arm.

"I'm fine, thanks."

"Um, you're bleeding. We need to get you to the infirmary," he stated, his expression showing genuine concern.

"It's not my blood," I replied coldly and began wiping the blood from my mouth on the front of my white shirt.

"Well, are you Evaline De . . . De . . ." He hesitated, trying to get my last name out.

I hated when people messed up my last name. They always did. You'd think I'd have gotten used to it by now. I interrupted him before he could butcher it any further. "You say the first part like déjà in the phrase déjà vu, and just add 'ardin' to the end of that. Yes, I'm Evaline Desjardin; just call me Eva." I smiled weakly, my stomach still sending sparks of pain through my body if I inhaled too deeply.

"Well okay, Eva. I'm from the main office downstairs. Your probation has been approved and you are free to go, under certain restrictions of course. We need to get your clothes and belongings from processing so you can be on your way. I'll act like what I just saw never happened."

I stood there momentarily dazed, certain the Latinas had murdered me. My body was probably lying dead on the floor and I was floating above it. This had to be God's humorous way of ushering me up to heaven. Dumbfounded, I just stood there shaking from head to toe in disbelief, scared my legs would give out on me if I moved. I felt like laughing, crying, and hugging this angel who'd just saved my life in more ways than one.

"How did it get approved? Who put me in, I didn't do anything or—"

He cut me off before I could continue, giving me a look that pretty much said to shut the hell up and go. "I don't do the fine details, ma'am. I just fetch and deliver." He nodded toward the door and I smiled my first genuine all-teeth-and-gums smile since being in prison.

The question still loomed out there. There was no way Brother Hall could have responded to my message that quickly or, maybe, he could have. God's works aren't made for our understanding; He only requires our cooperation.

Chapter 35

Eva
Deleted Delete Delet
Dele Del De D But Not Dead

I stared down into the bin that contained the only remnants of my life, feeling somewhat apprehensive about touching them let alone putting them on. The last time those clothes were on my body I was in a cold sweat, standing before a judge and a jury of my peers as they read my conviction and sentencing. Doom and gloom were the best words I could find to describe the gray and black pinstriped pant suit in front of me. Nothing good came from the last time I'd worn it and my stomach knotted at the thought of wearing it now.

My heart skipped a beat at the sight of my cell phone. Holding it in my hand made the realization of what was about to happen sink in. Joyful tears filled my eyes at the thought of being able to call who I wanted when I wanted to. Finally, I'd be able to sleep peacefully and have my baby girl back where she belonged.

A glimmer caught my eye and I felt instant unease at the sight of my engagement ring. I'd valued it so much that I'd checked it in out of fear of someone stealing it and now it was all but worthless to me. The four-carat princess-cut diamond twinkled at me, mocking me. It was a harsh reality check.

"You ready, Eva?"

Officer James, the man who saved me from Janisa and her hoard, appeared outside my cell door. My hands were ice-cold and clammy nubs as I tried to smooth my hair back into a wild, puffy ponytail. My ass needed a perm as soon as possible and some new clothes. The ones I had on were hanging loosely on my body, making it apparent that I'd lost a lot of weight.

I finally nodded, giving Officer James a polite smile. "Yes, sir, I'm as ready as I'll ever be."

He escorted me down the cell block and for the first time ever it was eerily silent. I could almost feel the hatred and envy like tiny pins in my skin from the eyes that followed me as I was led out. The only two people I felt bad about leaving, Say and Milan, were housed in a different unit. I made a mental note to send them letters and care packages for as long as they were in here.

Everything felt surreal as I stood in the small corridor at the main gate waiting for it to open. Fear crept up on me like a silent little monster. It scrambled up my ankle, and made goose bumps rise on my skin as it traveled up my body in anxious shivers until it had planted itself on my shoulder to whisper doubts in my ear.

What will you do now? Where will you go? You don't have anything or anyone now.

Grinding my teeth and stiffening my spine, I narrowed my eyes in determination. *I'll do whatever the hell I have to in order to find Jada and Dontay. Nothing can be worse than what I've already been through.*

I stared into the rusted steel of the gate's bars visibly jumping when they opened with a loud clank. The short walk past the security point toward the doors that led outside seemed to take years. I wanted to break into a run and fling myself outside but I somehow managed to keep the wings that were dying to sprout from my feet under control.

The doors slowly opened automatically and I was hit with a humid gust of hot air as I stepped outside into a dreary, rainy August afternoon. Raising my face toward the sky I welcomed the cool, misty rain, taking in deep breaths of fresh, free air. I wanted to erase the smell of prison from my memory as quickly as possible. The scent of bleach, metal, and misery clung to my skin and clothes like cigarette smoke in an old jacket. I visualized it seeping out of my pores with every breath I took.

"Eva?" Someone quietly spoke my name.

My eyes snapped open and standing right in front of me was Bishop Tisdale. He was head of my church and had been the closest thing I'd had to a father figure since Deacon managed to fuck up my childhood.

"It's me," I confirmed, smiling as tears of gratitude spilled down my face. He looked exactly the same as I remembered as his face broke into a wide grin. His chubby cheeks looked a little fatter and his mustache was cut with razor-sharp precision. He had a graying goatee last time I'd seen him; it was gone now putting the deep dimple in his chin on prominent display. He pulled me into a tight hug and I couldn't help but notice how fat his belly had gotten.

Look like somebody been eating good; church folk couldn't send any money but they're obviously still contributing to that building fund. The only thing that fund building is Bishop's relationship with the Cadillac dealership.

Shut up! Shut up! I mentally struggled trying to get my negative, mean thoughts under control.

"Eva, I got a call from Brother Hall saying someone was either playing with him or your spirit had contacted him asking for help. The next day I call and they're saying to be here at two-thirty to pick you up." Bishop began walking toward a pristine black Cadillac XTS and I would have laughed if my mind weren't still reeling from what he'd said.

"Bishop, what do you mean by my spirit?" I asked, giving him a puzzled look across the roof of the car as he unlocked the door.

He gave me a nervous smile before answering, "Um, Eva, if you don't mind riding in the back. Only the missus sits in the passenger seat." He'd taken on the dignified tone that he used to address the congregation during services.

He's lying, he don't want you up front because he's probably scared to be too close to you.

Smiling sweetly I ignored my thoughts. "Sure, Bishop, the back seat is fine by me; just get me away from here as quickly as possible."

The air conditioning came out of the vents in a blast of cool new-car-smelling air and I resisted the urge to ask him to turn it off. It had to be close to eighty degrees out and he would probably combust in his full three-piece suit. I'd had enough recycled air to last me a lifetime; all I really wanted was to feel and breathe in fresh air.

"The reason I referred to your spirit is because we'd been told you'd passed on. That you hung yourself after the sentence." Bishop Tisdale's voice boomed over the gospel song playing on the radio. It was a live choir singing "Order My Steps."

I frowned; the old-school choir sound was not one of my favorites. It reminded me too much of being forced through service after service just about every other day when I lived with my parents. Bishop's shocking information combined with the choir music created an arrow that shot itself into my temple in the form of an instant headache.

Pressing my fingers to my temples I rubbed them slowly. "Bishop, who the fuck said . . . I'm sorry." Bishop frowned disapprovingly back at me through the rearview mirror. "Bishop, would you mind turning down the music? I can't think. I just need quiet. And, who told you that I'd killed myself? Why would someone say that?"

"Child, the Lord's music is the best thing for that headache. It's probably just spirits coming up out of you. Your parents told us that you'd passed on. We held a service and everything. They tried to get your daughter but she'd already been taken by child protective services right around the same time that your house went up for auction. You can stay with me and Mirna until you get yourself together; we already prayed over it."

My body and mind felt as if they were both going to collapse from the weight of everything he'd said. Why in the world would my parents tell people something like that? Lord knows how many times I'd tried to call them collect and they wouldn't accept the charges after hearing me speak my name. My house, my baby, everything was taken away from me and I didn't do anything to deserve it.

Someone somewhere had decided to click on my life as if it were no different than a file in a directory and hit the delete button.

Chapter 36

Eva
Opportunity Quietly Knocks but Trouble Always Seems to Let Itself In

The bishop's house looked somewhat similar to a small three-story palace. It was surrounded by huge oak trees that towered above it, shading the yard. Two large pillars framed the entrance to the front door and the enormous window that sat high above it displayed a large shimmering chandelier. Stark white gravel crunched loudly under the Cadillac's tires as we pulled up the driveway and into a massive four-car garage. We parked in between a dark green Jaguar and a white Audi convertible.

I quietly followed the bishop toward the door that led into the house. I felt like a misplaced drifter going to someone else's home and having to use someone else's things. We entered through a pantry and into a beautiful oversized kitchen. A large yellow bowl stood out in stark contrast against the black marble countertop. It was filled to the brim with Asian pears, apples, and oranges.

As badly as I wanted one, I couldn't bring myself to ask. There was no way I'd go from being told when and where to do everything to being released and still having to ask permission for even the simplest things.

"Let me give you a quick tour. Mirna will be here in a little while to help with anything else you might need."

He led me through the kitchen toward the front of the house, pointing out the living room, dining room, and an extra bathroom. It was the briefest home tour I'd ever gotten.

He probably doesn't want you to know where the fine china or silverware is out of fear you'll rob them and run off in the middle of the night.

Tall, faceless African sculptures framed both sides of a door near the main stairwell. They were creepy black wood carvings that stood taller than me with elongated necks and long oval-shaped heads. One held a shield and spear; the other was apparently supposed to be a woman from the large cones protruding from the upper torso.

"Bought those when we opened a mission and school in Kenya. That's the Guardian and she's the Maiden."

His chest puffed out with pride as he spoke about his ugly statues and I was lost somewhere inside my head. There had to be some kind of way to piece my life back together. It wouldn't happen overnight but with determination and faith, I could turn my mess into a mosaic masterpiece. Bishop was staring at me expectantly; he must have asked me something but I hadn't heard a thing he'd said. Embarrassed to admit I wasn't paying attention I stared at him wide-eyed.

"Everything you need is down there; the basement is large enough for you to live comfortably. I'll let you explore, and send Mirna down when she gets in."

"Oh. Okay, thank you, Bishop. I appreciate everything you're doing."

He pulled me into a hug, patting me roughly on my back. "You live here now. Just call me Kev or Kevin. All that Bishop and Mr. nonsense won't fly in this house; makes me feel like I'm not at home."

"Okay Kevi . . . Kev." It felt awkward calling him by his first name but I'd try. "Is there a phone down there?" I asked as he let me go.

Bishop looked at me expectantly as if he were waiting for me to divulge why I wanted to use the phone, and I clammed up. I really needed to call my parents but trying to vocalize the who or why part of my need for a phone wasn't happening. This wasn't prison, he didn't need to have a say in who I talked to unless I tried to make a long-distance call.

"We are getting a line installed for you. It should be around Monday or Tuesday next week." He hesitated and began rubbing the corners of his mouth where his goatee used to be out of habit. "We think you should just lay low for a little while until we get a few things resolved. You don't understand the impact your conviction had on the community and the other members of the congregation. Then to tell everyone you were no longer with us and see devastation on everyone's faces all over again. Eva—"

"No, no. It's fine. Let's worry about what people will say. That's always been the way of the church right?" I snapped sarcastically.

I'd meant to keep the comment to myself but it came out and it was definitely too late to take it back. Bishop simply nodded his head as he opened the basement door. He was probably agreeing to his own silent argument about being crazy for taking me in. I walked past him and heard the door close quietly behind me.

What these people referred to as a basement would have passed for a loft or studio-style apartment. The room opened up to a large dark brown sectional that faced a wall with a flat-screen television. There was the faintest scent of apples and cinnamon and it actually made the space feel inviting. My steps were cushioned by the plush brown and tan speckled shag carpet as I walked past a wall lined with book shelves and curio cabinets. I quietly studied the painted faces of three naked mermaids lounging on a clock shaped like a coral reef. Their fins were varying shades of shiny blues and greens that stopped at their bared waists. All of the mermaids were posed in various positions but it was the one to the right that tugged at my core, making a knot form in my throat.

One mermaid had fiery red hair flaming around her serene seductive face; the other had bright hair the color of a wheat field and sapphire blue eyes. But, the one with the crown of hair blacker than coal billowing around her kept grabbing my attention. Her languid brown eyes were staring back at me as if she could see directly into my soul. She reminded me of Aeron, while simultaneously reminding me of Antonia.

"I'm sorry to put you down here with all of Kevin's unsightly trinkets," Mrs. Tisdale spoke from where she'd been standing on the stairwell, holding a small tray.

I whirled around, quickly wiping away a stray tear. She walked over, giving me a sincere smile.

"Your husband's trinkets are interesting to say the least. Not exactly what I'd ever imagine to find in a leader of the church's home," I replied, giggling at the eccentric artifact collection.

"We weren't always sanctified, baby." She chuckled. "Girl, we had lives and lived just like anybody else. That's why all that fool's foolishness is down here where we can still admire its beauty and value without being judged." Mrs. Tisdale's tone was soft and playful like we were old friends.

The woman barely spoke to me when I worked in the church, and it gave me the impression that she was just like the rest of the elders and their wives. I'd imagined she'd be stuffy and stuck-up, nothing like the sweet, charming person I was talking to. We were about the same build even though she had to be in her mid-forties; the woman definitely kept herself up. There wasn't a single wrinkle or crease in her light brown skin and her hazel eyes sparkled.

She set the tray on a small table in front of the couch. "I made you some soup and sandwiches. Figured your stomach might need to adjust to normal food so I kept it light. Forgive Kev, he's such a man. He wasn't thinking about anything but getting into his study to pour over his next sermon."

"Thank you, ma'am. Um, I don't know which one I want more: the food or a hot shower."

"Baby, eat the sandwich in the shower; it ain't gonna hurt the shower I know that for a fact. And call me Mirna." She laughed and walked toward another section of the basement.

I followed, feeling a little better in her warm presence. The bathroom was past the bedroom and was about the size of a small hotel room. It was decorated in green, white, and black, reminiscent of a comfy day spa. One complete wall was decorated with a large mural that looked like magnified raindrops dripping off of two bright green leaves. Fluffy white rugs were in various places on the floor that matched the equally fluffy-looking towels on a bamboo shelf in a corner. I balked at the steam and sauna options on the glass door to the shower.

"I wasn't sure what size you'd wear so we have a little of everything. There's a bathrobe on the top towel shelf, razors, soap, everything you need is in this cabinet." Mirna glided over to a small cabinet that looked like a fully stocked convenience store. There were so many types of body washes and lotions I got excited just thinking about which one I wanted to try first.

"Clothes are in the bedroom; we passed that on the way in. You need anything let me know. I'll check on you a little later."

She left and I stood momentarily confused as to how a person could feel like a princess and a pauper at the same damn time.

After what was probably the longest shower I'd ever taken in my life, I sat in front of the television, wrapped in the enormous bathrobe. I'd picked a ginger peach–scented body wash and cream that smelled good enough to eat out the bottle. The sandwiches were gone in the blink of an eye. I ate the things so fast it's a wonder I didn't choke. Even though the soup was cold I still crushed it. There's nothing like homemade chicken soup and I all but licked the bowl. Mirna was definitely right about my stomach acting finicky. Not long after eating my stomach turned into a huge painful cramp.

I wasn't used to Miracle Whip and real cheese. I took a second shower, finally understanding why the food in prison was so bland and uncomplicated. They didn't have doors on those cells. The last thing they needed was a cellblock full of shitty folk blowing up stalls with only one toilet to share. I had to wash my hind parts after that foolishness.

A smile spread across my face at the small cup of peppermint tea Mirna had thoughtfully placed on the tray. I had no desire to get up and go to the kitchen to heat it up and sat lost in my thoughts sipping it cold. The flavor reminded me of a Starlight Mint without all the sugar. I didn't mind; my taste buds welcomed something other than water or orange juice out the can. The clock on the television receiver read five-thirty but all the day's activities were catching up with me. Lights out was usually around seven but having real food and a real shower gave me a serious case of the itis.

My sleep should have been restful but it was far from it. I was plagued with replays of Antonia's last moments and she begged for her life repeatedly in my dream.

Dontay walked in and around our cell watching us, jeering Antonia on. He was wildly waving money around like we were nothing more than dogs to gamble on in a fight. Antonia finally slumped forward and Dontay shouted obscenities. His face morphed into Aeron and it was then her turn to chastise and curse me for what I'd done. She cried and yelled and I cried and apologized.

Seeing Aeron so hurt and upset made my heart fragment into hundreds of tiny pieces that fell to the floor. She picked them up one by one and one minute she was handing me back the pieces and then we were alone on the cot just as we were her last night there. She kissed me and I felt shame and excitement. I was confused at my reaction and angry at myself but I didn't want it to end. Her hands were all over me and I timidly began running my fingers along the small of her back.

She began whispering broken sentences in my ear: "I've missed you so much, mami. I want you; let me make love to you."

Lying back in the bed her body slid gracefully on top of mine. Our clothes were gone and the simple contact of her bare skin against mine made me moan in delight. She nibbled softly on my shoulders before kissing her way down to my ribcage and I squirmed in anticipation. Her hair hung over her shoulder and slid along my body like a silky web of tiny fingers. It caressed my neck *and nipples, softly cascaded across my stomach, leaving every inch of my skin that it touched in a raging pool of need. Aeron giggled at my reaction and made a game out of teasing me with her hair. She rose back up, gently kissing my lips before teasing me all over again.*

By the time she made her way down a second time, there was a raging river of need coursing between my legs. Her breath was hot against my skin and then Antonia was hovering over me. I could smell it before I saw it coming and knew she was raising her hairy snatch up to my face. Shaking my head from side to side I tried to tell her no and she ignored me, slamming herself onto my face. Aeron called out to her in the distance and I thought, well now your sister can see what you've done and she can kill you. I won't be guilty anymore.

Aeron called out to me again and I tried to answer her but Antonia was laughing loudly. Each time I tried to open my mouth to call out to Aeron, hair would fill it until I couldn't breathe. It muffled my screams and cries for help.

My eyes flew open and I took a deep, panicked breath. I must have been holding my breath in my sleep; my lungs and my chest were tight from not getting any air. I shook my head trying to clear the dreadful images from my waking mind. My heart literally stopped cold in my chest as the bishop's face suddenly came into focus clear as day, scaring away all traces of sleepiness. I was completely awake and alert. The pressure I'd felt on my chest was from the weight of his body on mine. Sweat dripped from his forehead into my eyes and I tried to scream and push him off but I couldn't move a single muscle. What kind of hellish nightmare had I awakened to?

He was moaning and moving against me but I couldn't feel him inside me. An alarm sounded in my head as I realized that I couldn't feel my legs, my toes, or any of my limbs.

God, help me please. What the hell did they do to me?

My voice was a panicked cry in my head but no matter how hard I tried I couldn't move, couldn't scream, and couldn't lash out. I controlled the only thing I had control of and squeezed my eyes tightly closed. It was like one of those dreams where you're half awake and half asleep. You can see and hear everything and things come out of corners or shadows but no matter how hard you try you can't move and you can't scream. It used to happen all the time when I was little and my auntie would say the witch was riding my back. My momma would say a spirit was trying to get to me and either way I'd be praying and sleeping with the light on for at least a month. Every ragged breath the bishop took had me trying to retreat into the darkest recesses of my own mind. Now, I had a bishop riding my back; the humiliation and helplessness I felt were overwhelming enough to smother me all on their own. Even though I couldn't feel it, a sudden desire to bleach and burn his touch from my skin was overwhelming me. Fury balled itself up inside my chest and sat there coiled around my heart like an explosive cobra.

You will kill this filthy, pretentious motherfucka for this shit! And they wonder why women go and cut off men's dicks; this is why. Slaughter his ass.

The devil on my left shoulder fed on the rage building inside me and goaded me into retaliating; yet, even now, the Christian side of my mind tried to find rhyme or reason with what was happening.

Is this worth going back to prison, Eva?

Yes, it is!

You can't feel anything. Had you not had that bad dream you probably wouldn't have ever known this happened. Tell Mirna to watch him; he's bound to do it again and she can catch him. Let her witness everything with her own eyes.

Compared to this shit, that dream was as harmless as a cartoon. Like anyone would believe a word you said after what happened at the firm? Like Mirna would even believe you; he probably drugs her ass too. It would end up being a favor for her too.

I'd been holding my breath for most of the inner exchange in my head. I was hoping that I'd eventually pass out. It didn't work. Every time I got to the point where bright flashes of light sparked off behind my eyelids my brain would force my lungs to take in oxygen.

"Kevin James Tinsdale! What the hell?" Mirna's voice sliced into my silent nightmare. It was the most welcoming sound I'd ever heard as it interrupted the sound of Bishop's raging bull-like breathing thrashing in my ear.

"Woman. Why on earth are you yelling when you aren't sitting but two feet away from me?" Bishop questioned her through gritted teeth.

I didn't want to see him again, but I had to look. Peeking through my lashes as best as I could without them knowing I was drugged but awake I had a limited view. Bishop's head was turned to my left and I did my best to glance in the direction of Mirna's voice.

"Because the agreement was that I'd let you buy your plaything so you could act out all your ungodly anus play obsessions without destroying mine. In return I get the grand finale, and you were about to finale," she scolded him.

"The hell? I was not about to finale; you making me lose my focus and I'm going to have to start all over again to get him rock solid for you." The bishop sounded agitated.

Fuck no! Dontay only did that asshole thing twice and we never tried again. How dare this fool think he could just ram all up in my ass and . . .

Mirna, don't make this shit start all over or on my life I'll take you out as soon as I can move again.

Bishop's face lowered and I gagged at the sounds of slurping and sucking as he did whatever he was doing to places on my body that I didn't even want to know.

"No. There will be no starting over. It's momma's turn. You making Princess Pinky jealous." Mirna's voice was so close I already knew without peeking that she was lying beside me on the bed.

"That's why all that fool's foolishness is down here where we can still admire its beauty and value without being judged." Her words from our conversation swam around my head like a gold fish trapped in a plastic bag.

How many girls or women had they done this to? It couldn't have started with me. I used to have a youth choir at the local community center. Every few months one of my teenage girls would vanish without a trace. It would be the same each time, a runaway with no family in the area, no one to notice their absence. Except me.

"Whose pussy is this?" The bishop's voice drilled into my thoughts, interrupting any shocking conclusions I might have come to.

"This is Bishop's pussy." Mirna moaned her response and I wished for a mental shutdown valve or off button. The only good thing about him being on her was the fact that his heavy ass was up off of me. I went back to what got me through my first nights in prison and recited my psalms. The ending of every line was accented with a visualization of how I'd get the bishop and his wife back for what they'd done.

Somewhere between Psalm 91 and the image of the two of them tied up, staring at me, pleading for mercy, I fell asleep.

Chapter 37

Eva
If the Eyes Are the Windows to the Soul Your Windows Look Like They're in Need of Washing

Sun filtered through the high, narrow window in the bedroom. It blinded me, forcing the dull, slow ache in my head to increase until it was going at the rate of a jackhammer. My mouth was so parched that even when I tried to lick my lips to moisten them I got no relief. They felt cracked and dry, my tongue stuck to them and several places, stinging where the cracked skin split open. It was hazy but gradually the memories of the night before came back to me. Scared I'd try to move only to find myself permanently paralyzed, I sufficed with lying there motionless, assessing my body.

The cool sheets on the bed hung loosely around me. I could feel them pressed against my legs and arms, but nowhere else. Panic-stricken at the thought of being paralyzed I sprang into a sitting position, shocked at the grasshopper-green nightshirt and matching shorts that met my eyes when the blankets fell away. I hated green. I would have slept in my underwear before I'd have put these nasty insane asylum colors on my body. Frowning, I began searching for anything to prove that I hadn't dreamt the sordid events between the bishop and Mirna.

From what I could tell nothing looked out of place, except the clothes on my body that I definitely couldn't remember putting on. It felt like I was waking up from a long night of drinking, and my one-night stand had decided to sneak out before I could even confirm whether I'd imagined him.

The sensation of pins and needles shooting through my toes made me put off trying to stand for a little while longer.

That big nigga probably fractured one of your damn spinal disks or some shit if that shit even happened.

My suspicions were confirmed when my brain finally decided to join the rest of me in the "what the hell happened" drama of the day as all my nerves came alive at once. The pain was unmistakable. It wasn't like when a guy's gung-ho and he wrong holes it in the heat of the moment. No, someone could have told me my bum hole had grown arms and tried to take down an entire bucket of suicide hot Buffalo wings while they were still in the bucket. I hurt so bad I'd have believed it, just to not have to acknowledge what had actually happened. Tears fell down my face and I cried every tear that I couldn't cry the night before due to whatever they'd drugged me with. Nausea hit me unexpectedly and I dry heaved until I thought I'd burst a blood vessel and my stomach cramped. There was nothing in there for it to expel.

Lying back on the bed, the most I could do was shakily curl myself into a tight ball. With my forehead pressed against my knees, I tried to pray but couldn't find the words. I tried to recite something to calm myself down but for the life of me, I couldn't remember a single word of anything I'd ever read. *What did they think they could do, offer me a place to stay only to use me every single night? I'll eventually have to leave to meet my parole officer and find work. The food was drugged but nothing oral can paralyze a person like that. First they drug you to make you sleep. Then they inject you with something to make sure you can't move and don't wake up; we'll get their asses. This isn't supposed to happen to people like me and not from people like them.*

The sun had gone from the brightness of morning to the dull orange glow of late afternoon before I'd decided to move again. I showered and looked for my cell but couldn't find it from the day before.

Who's the thief now? They up there stealing ass and actual property.

Dressing myself in an oversized pair of blue sweats with a matching shirt I let my legs carry me toward the gate into hell outside of hell, far from prison hell.

To my surprise the doorknob surprisingly twisted and the door opened. I cautiously crept into the foyer, praying they'd forgotten to lock the door. The house was silent as I silently crept toward the front door. The welcoming aroma of what had to have been pot roast, biscuits, and sweet potato pie called me toward the kitchen. It tantalized my nose, making my stomach beg me to follow it like the sound of the ocean calling to a fisherman. As hungry as I was I couldn't bring myself to walk away from my only way of escaping.

The brass doorknob was ice cold in the palm of my hand. I turned the lock underneath the keyhole toward the word UNLOCK on the handle and twisted. My entire body was tighter than a rubber band. My nerves were taut and ready to snap at the slightest sound. My heart thudded like hummingbird's wings in my chest and nervous sweat began to bead on my upper lip. The door didn't budge and I quietly slipped the lock in the other direction, praying it would open, puzzled at the setback. This wasn't frickin' rocket science; did prison make you forget how to unlock doors? I'd had childproof on cabinets more complicated than a simple lock and—

"Aw look who's awake. That door is a little tricky, baby; you want to go out for some fresh air you can step out onto the patio through the kitchen. Actually some kind of stinging bug made a home out there. Best you wait until Kev has the exterminator look into that." Mirna's voice was sickening sweet as she spoke from behind me.

Turning slowly I composed myself, holding back the tears and nausea at having to deal with her. I was in no way psychologically prepared to face one half of the two-headed monster I'd unknowingly surrendered myself to.

Her usual smile was planted on her face.

Look at this fake-ass smile.

Her hands were busy drying a wine glass on the fold of her apron.

That's probably the glass she's going to use to drug your ass. Grab the vase off the table beside the wall and smack that corrupt bitch in the face.

"Hi, Mirna, I didn't hear you walk up. Yes, I've been feeling queasy all morning; some air is all I want right now," I responded, doing my best to conceal the venom in my voice with as much sugary sweetness as possible.

"Well come along. The bishop was in a mighty fine mood this morning. He's bringing home champagne after he leaves his office. We are going to officially celebrate your freedom, sweetheart."

Mirna turned and went into the kitchen, humming a song I couldn't quite make out. The socks on my feet made my footsteps soundless as I treaded across the white tile floor behind her. Gold veins glittered and glimmered in the lighting of the house and it came to my attention how decadent their tastes in decorating were. The living room I'd passed when I'd arrived was adorned with expensive-looking chairs with mahogany arms and those legs with the claws on the bottom.

Those are not Versace cushions on that chair. How the hell they even know what Versace is?

Golden Egyptian statues of cats and scarab beetles were placed in random settings along the way. From the expansive chandelier to the marble and the cars, all of the things they had were lavish and rich. Yet not a single cross, scripture, or biblical reference could be seen anywhere in their house. This was just a modern vampire lair full of treasures, trinkets, and ill-gotten goods.

My stomach growled loudly as I entered the kitchen and potatoes, celery, and brown onion gravy filled my senses. I could almost taste the food in my mouth, see the biscuit soaking up the gravy.

"I know you've got to be hungry. Supper is ready if you want to sit down and eat with me. Kevin won't be home until later so I'll just keep his food warm."

As tempting as her offer sounded I was frightened that she'd drug me again.

The roast is still in the oven. If you stay the fuck with her and help her you can watch what she does. Might even see an opportunity to grab a knife and . . .

"Yes, that would be nice, thank you." I smiled politely and did my best to hide my discomfort as I lowered myself into one of the chairs at the table.

My eyes were on her like a barn owl hunting a mouse. I watched every move she made including where she got the silverware from and whether it mattered if I took the first bite. After she said grace I made a game out of organizing my food with my fork; she began to methodically cut into the roast on her plate.

"My sister called this morning. No one in the church knows I have a sister, two younger sisters actually. Reena and Mona aren't uh, let's just say there's a reason why lunatics and fools are always the loudest." She paused like it was some kind of joke I'd know the end of. Waving her hand never mind she went on.

"It's so you know to turn around and go on in the opposite direction. Mona got checked into an institution." She sighed long. "Well, won't tell Bishop about that; men get enough crud to be right about as is." She chuckled.

I awarded her with one of my legendary fake smiles, pretending to be fascinated with the scenery through the glass panels of the back door while I waited for her to chew and swallow.

Everything tasted like it had been made with ingredients straight from heaven's garden. My eyes closed in bliss and I savored every bite, amazed at how tender the roast was. I caught Mirna staring at me when I reopened them, but her expression was a little unreadable. She quickly resumed eating and I began to wonder whether I'd imagined the brief look in her eye that reminded me of . . .

"Where are my two favorite ladies?" Bishop's voice rumbled through the quiet house and my appetite was instantly gone. He appeared in the kitchen carrying a bottle of champagne and beaming a wide smile in our direction at the kitchen table.

"Champagne or cham-pleasure? Who says church folk can't drink? You just aren't supposed to drink to get drunk. Ha-ha," Bishop shouted out.

"I thought you were working late; we'd have waited for you before we started eating." Mirna's tone was somewhat disapproving.

It was hard to determine if she was upset because he came home early or because he didn't let her know he was coming home early. His back was turned to us as he got glasses and placed the bottle in the wine chiller on the counter setting the timer. My unease grew when I couldn't see the glasses or where he'd gotten them from.

Soup, tea, champagne. Whatever it is they probably hide it in a liquid for your ass to drink. That tea was bitter; soup was cold but the after-taste was bitter. Don't drink a damn thing they give you. Switch your glasses around, dump it out, do whatever you have to do.

The timer dinged on the champagne chiller and I jumped when Bishop shot the cork out of the bottle with a resounding pop. He danced and blew a kiss in Mirna's direction, giving her a wink and a look that I instantly registered as sexual, promising, and absolutely dirty. The dread and trepidation that filled me at having to experience another night like last night made me sick to my stomach.

"If you would excuse me, I'm not feeling too good. Mirna, I think it's gonna take some time for my stomach to adjust to the food. I'm sorry."

Before either of them could reply I pushed away from the table and fled toward the basement, intent on getting as far away from them as possible. I spun in an exasperated circle as I noted every single window in the basement was nearly six feet up from the floor and nowhere near wide enough for me to fit through. I felt like a trapped lab rat and the thought made me run immediately into the bathroom to pretend like I was actually taking a shit. There were probably cameras all down here watching me even now.

I racked my brain trying to think of a way out.
The front door was obviously not an option but
they didn't use it anyway. And I was certain from
what I could see at dinner there was no way to get
off the fenced-in patio if the door was locked. So
far I only knew of the bishop to come in through
the garage into the kitchen. If I could get to that
door and into the garage I could press the opener
and just run. It now made sense why out of everything they provided the only thing I wasn't given
were shoes.

*Routine, get a routine and stick to it. They
won't know what you know or what you plan if
you do the same things and act the same. Take
your shower and be mindful of something to use
as a weapon. Those fucks didn't give you anything
so tonight should be a quiet one. Find something,
anything to get us the fuck out of here.*

For the first time ever I nodded in agreement
with that angry, malicious little voice. Starting the
shower I contemplated any alternatives to escape
without taking a life or causing anyone harm.
They would have to deal with their sins when they
answered to God. Or I could make sure they didn't
have the chance to do this type of shit to anyone
else and take care of them when the opportunity
arrived. Get out of the house, get Dontay's thieving
ass; I was slowly building a mental hit list.

Steam filled the bathroom and I undressed, preparing to get in the shower, when I noticed a bruise on my ribs. Facing the mirror over the sink I stared at what looked like a long oval on my side and four similar markings on my back. I stood there squinting at myself until it dawned on me. They were fingerprints. Outraged I looked for something, anything to smash. A small figurine beside the towel rack seemed like the perfect target and I stomped toward it.

The ground came flying up to smack me in the back of the head. I'd stepped on one of the rugs on the floor and it slid forward, catching me off guard and off balance. My eyes were closed tight as I waited for the pain to hit me. My head cracked against the floor so hard I was sure I'd fractured my damn skull. Waves of pain crashed from the back of my skull into the space behind my eyes and I groaned in agony.

I waited until the waves of pain slowed down into a steady constant pain that spanned across my entire head. My eyes opened and rolled as the ceiling spun above me. They focused and it was in that instant that I found the tiny camera sitting in the ceiling over the vanity no wider than an ink pen top. Its lens didn't fog up like the mirror and from my angle on the floor I could see how it refracted the light from the bulbs underneath it. I quickly looked away, and raised my hand to stare at my fingertips as if my eyes were still not focused.

"Eva. I brought you some tea for your stomach. Are you doing all right, baby?" Mirna's called out to me through the bathroom door.

I bet she did want to give me some more of that damn tea. She was obviously only checking on me because they were probably watching me.

"I'm okay, but thank you. I'm just going to take a shower and go to bed," I called out from the floor, the sound of my voice making me feel miserable.

"All right, baby. Do you want me to leave the tea for you?"

I struggled to sit up and responded, "No, thank you, Mirna. I don't really care for peppermint that much."

The clinking of the tray as she turned and left was reassuring. I climbed into the shower, sighing as the hot water washed over my skin. Glancing at the ceiling I couldn't make out any lenses or shapes that looked like one over the vanity and it didn't seem like it was aimed to see into the shower. Relaxing as I realized showers were the only chance that I'd get some privacy, I lathered myself up, reveling in the fragrance of the shower gel. The smell of the ginger and peach seemed to calm my headache down, but I only made it worst when the desperation of my situation hit me. I was being held captive and used as some kind of personal sex slave. It sounded like the plot to some kind of suspense, drama movie and yet I was actually living it. From what I could figure, everyone who knew me or of me thought I was either locked up or dead.

Everyone except Brother Hall and Aeron.

Chapter 38

Eva
Misogynistic Missionary

"Teach me how the hell to do it then, since you think you're an expert."

"This is the first crash-test dummy that I actually like, so pay close attention because this won't happen often." Two voices bantered back and forth somewhere nearby.

I tried opening my eyes and it felt as if my eyelids were attached to one hundred pound weights. They were so heavy that lifting them seemed to drain me of all my energy. There was no way this shit could possibly be happening again. I exhaled an indignant breath beyond furious at the fun the two of them were having at my expense. None of it made sense. I ate the same things Mirna ate. I didn't touch the champagne or drink anything and still my ass was stuck going through this bullshit again.

As their conversation registered in my head I realized why the fingerprints on my side and back were so odd looking. They weren't the bishop's; they were Mirna's.

"Flip her on her stomach; it's my turn to get this shit going."

The bishop's strained grunting and the sound of sheets sliding were the only indicators that I was being repositioned. Breathing now seemed harder, and even though I'd tried to suffocate myself the night before, the thought now had me in a panic.

"Baby, gimme that candle," the bishop's voice was directly beside my ear and I screamed, cried, and cursed him in my mind, praying for a chance to at least bite him.

Strawberry-scented wax filled the air and as it scorched my back all the way down to the crack of my ass. Searing pain ran along its path and scorching every single one of my nerves. The skin on my back was on fire and I began grinding my teeth together to block out the pain. I could feel everything and the familiar tingling in my toes was evidence that I'd be able to move if I wanted to.

It's time, it's time, it's time.

I waited until he pulled all the way out, leaving my ass feeling equally raw and just as sore as my back. The sound of the Bishop and Mirna kissing passionately beside me riled my temper. I knew I'd only have seconds. Edging my hand up under my hips I slid my fingers in between my legs as deep as I could from the angle I was lying in.

In one swift movement I pulled the wadded up toilet paper from inside myself where I'd hidden it.

Yes, right up in the baby maker like a damn drug mule. My fingers quickly unraveled the paper that had turned into a semi-hardened shell. Turning my head in their direction I could see Mirna on top of the bishop. I dove at them, slicing wildly in every direction, a small razor in each hand. I was hell-bent on revenge and nothing was safe as I lashed out, shredding sheets and pillows.

One, two, three . . .

It was as if they were momentarily stunned at my sudden mobility. There was no fight or flight; the bishop and Mirna were both stupefied. He was sputtering, his eyes bulging out of his head in shock, and I couldn't make out what he was saying over the sounds of my angry breaths and slashes. I'd somehow tapped into a deep and hateful place. It had me growling a low predatory sound with every slice. Controlling my hands was frustrating and I still couldn't fully sit up because the drugs were still wearing off.

Five, six, seven . . .

I counted in my head the number of times I slung the blades in their direction.

An angry red gash opened across Mirna's lower back and she wailed, rolling onto the floor in agony, momentarily escaping my reach. I leaned over, grabbing the candle from the side of the bed, smashing it against the fat pig's forehead. The glass shattered and piping hot wax covered Bishop's face and eyes. He squealed and flounced around on the bed before going into convulsions.

"Oh Jesus Lord no, he's having a seizure. Please help him." Mirna sobbed.

Pathetic muthafucka having a seizure, he wasn't supposed to go that easily.

Well, looks like we've already got one down, I answered my evil inner twin as I pulled myself down off the bed and stalked Mirna as she crawled pitifully toward the bedroom door.

When I'd taken my shower I had no real intention on doing what they'd made me do. I'd broken one of the razors, removing the twin blades and burying them in the center of a wad of toilet paper. In prison I'd seen Aeron do it with razors when she wanted to hide them in plain sight on the wall. She'd wet and then smooth the toilet paper out until it was almost see-through, and it would harden like papier-mâché or plaster. I had no clue if it would even work with a ball of moist toilet paper but what the hell did I have to lose?

This was all supposed to go down in the kitchen when the bishop was at work. I was supposed to get Mirna first and then wait for him to come home and catch him off guard. Thankfully the stuff they gave me wore off early for whatever reason. No one was ever going to humiliate me again and especially not under the guise of helping me. Antonia had to learn, these two needed to learn, and if my dearest, sweetest Dontay didn't give me the right answers he'd damn sure learn as well.

Mirna moaned from the force of my weight as I hoisted myself up and sat on her chest.

Dontay was out there somewhere and he was either thinking he'd pulled off the crime of the century or was sick to his stomach for having to do what he'd done. I should have just stayed with Deacon from the get-go. Aeron said money unmasks people and from what I'd seen of the bishop and his so-called godly wife maybe Dontay wasn't what I thought he was from the jump. Lost in my thoughts, I'd momentarily forgotten all about Mirna as she squirmed beneath me. Sneering down at her in disgust I thought about my life, the things I'd worked and longed for.

"The two of you could have easily helped me or sent me on my way. So tell me, Mirna, what turns good Christian folk into hostage-taking rapists? Is it the lust or the power?"

I waited for her answer and had to give her credit, for even now she glanced in her husband's direction for support. He'd stopped moving and was either dead or unconscious.

She stared up at me as her eyes did that shimmery dance that eyes do just before the tears start to fall. Under normal circumstances when a person cried I'd have felt bad, but her tears only made me impatient and irritated.

Her voice was a quiet, shaky whisper: "Kevin said that he bought you from a man. I don't know which man. I never asked. The man didn't want you anymore and Kevin bought you, that's all I know."

Time stood still as the meaning behind her words settled into my being. Not only had Dontay played me for all of my money and my clients' money, but he'd also sold me? Like I was property? No, wait, like I was his property?

Fuck this, fuck her. Now is just as good a time as any to learn how the game is played. She in the way, Bishop is in the way, they are all in the fucking way. At one point in time Antonia was on that list. You can either handle your business or get handled like business. Sounds like he's trying to handle you like business. I suggest you go handle him.

I couldn't have agreed with myself more.

Chapter 39

Eva
When Ill-gotten Goods Go Bad

I locked them in the basement after grabbing my sweats out the bathroom and went running through the house looking for cash, my phone, grabbing anything I'd need. Upstairs it was pretty obvious which bedroom was the master. Two oversized French-style doors sat facing me at the end of the long hallway. I kept waiting for some kind of combat Christian intruder alert system to go off somewhere. The adrenaline and my nerves had my stomach in annoyingly painful knots. The Bishop had close to $500 in his wallet that was lying out on the dressing table closest to the door. I shimmied open a drawer looking for his rainy day bama. Everybody has one. If the power goes out or a storm hits and ATMs don't work, you should always have cash in the house. Rich folk just keep extra.

There was a small bronze box with weird engravings all over it. It looked important and felt heavier than it appeared. I slid my fingers over the smooth etchings that ran deep into the metal diamonds carved inside squares and circles. A small panel slid sideways. Taking that as a step to open it I slid my fingers gently pressing other places on the little puzzle box sliding panels up and sideways until it bloomed like a square blossom.

I stared down into it at what looked like gum until I realized they were teeth and I jumped. The box slipped from my hand and hundreds of teeth scattered to the floor. Some of them were so tiny that I could almost envision all these tiny faces with happy gap-toothed grins. Bishop and Mirna didn't fit the charity Tooth Fairy profile type. Teeth were everywhere like oversized grains of rice at my feet. My palms got sweaty and my pulse sped away in my neck. Some were chipped others were covered in dried brown blood. They'd done so many things to so many girls and they had all these trophies. I was enraged at them and caught off guard when my chest ached with a dark sense of foolish envy. It was only be jealousy. I didn't dare take anything from Antonia; I'd felt too bad. *There are some sick-ass people who just like shooting fish in a barrel. Time for the fish to start shooting back.*

I grabbed one of Mirna's purses and ran downstairs to get the keys and get myself out of this hell house. The bishop's study was the only place I hadn't checked for my phone and I actually debated on leaving the thing. The door to his study creaked open; the light flickered on automatically from the motion sensor in the wall. Rushing over to his desk I hesitated when it came to opening the drawers scared I'd find fingers and toes next. Holding my breath I pulled down out the center drawer first.

The only there was a small keyboard, beside it a press-button box. *Well where the hell is the computer? I can start looking up how to get Jada back, map out how to find Dontay.*

It took me looking all underneath and around the desk to figure out the keyboard was wireless. That meant his laptop or computer could be anywhere, just like my phone that was dead so I couldn't even call it. Without it, I was lost because I didn't know anyone's number by heart anymore. Frustrated I punched the keyboard and whirled around to face the bookcase behind me. A small flat-screen television was mounted to the frame. Bishop was on the bed, with his hands across his chest like a funeral service. Mirna was kneeling beside him, rocking back and forth on her knees, praying.

I looked down at the push button next to the keyboard and pressed it slowly. Taking a slow, calming breath, I called out in a cold, flat voice, "Mirna?"

She stopped rocking herself and with her eyes closed she slowly lifted her head skyward. She suddenly whipped around with her lips drawn in a thin, angry line. She glared directly into the hidden camera as if the lens were my eyes. I took an involuntary step back from the screen. Her anger was frightening but I was on the other side of the door this time and my guard was now the prisoner.

"Mirna," I called out in a softer tone than before, "I'm gonna burn this bitch down, and then hunt down Mona and Reena just for the hell of it if you don't tell me the combination to the safe."

It was a gamble, but with everything they had I was pretty sure they had one and I didn't feel like wasting any more time looking for it. I could have asked her where the safe was but there wasn't anything to make her tell me and then tell me the code.

"Figure it out yourself."

I rolled up my sleeves and cracked my knuckles. Mirna obviously wanted to meet my bad side. There was some yellow polypropylene rope sitting on a tall red and silver toolbox. It was the plastic floaty kind they used in swimming pools to mark lanes. Grabbing that duct tape, and a socket wrench, I went into the kitchen and spun around in a circle thinking to myself. The turkey baster sitting in the wash rack by the sink gave me an idea.

Minutes later after a few quick breaths I ignored my wobbly legs and charged into the room that used to be my holding cell. The air was thick with the smell of body funk, fear, and Bishop's bowels emptying as death became him on the bed. Caught off guard Mirna shrieked, wild-eyed; still naked on the floor she scooted back, toward the wall. I smirked, stalking her just as I'd done earlier. Now she was the little girl and I was the tooth hunter. But I didn't want teeth.

When I got close enough I lassoed her ankle with the yellow rope and yanked with everything I had. Before she could get her bearings I had her other ankle in a tight tiny harness. Anger and determination kept me from getting winded. Sweat beaded into my eyes and the skin on my hands was red and raw. I dragged her screaming, crying, and cursing across the floor. Using the fortified bedroom door as a pulley I stood on the other side with my foot pressed against it for leverage and pulled until I could hear Mirna's back sliding up the other side.

"Eva, child, this was all a mistake I swear. I know we can work something out if you just calm down and talk to me."

Mirna went from cursing, to praying, to pleading and I ignored it all. I peeked around giving myself a silent high five. She was hanging upside down, just like I intended. After looping the rope around the doorknob, I taped her mouth and her eyes so I could tie her hands to the knob on her side without getting clawed to death.

My nose wrinkled; now that her ass was up in the air, unwashed sex and the aroma of sweaty hot lady bits wafted freely.

"Mirna, you and Kev left me with a bad feeling. You weren't good hosts. Earlier I asked you for a safe code." I tsked at Mirna. "I think it's only fair that I return the favor and show you what it feels like. To be violated. Left with a bad feeling."

My hands were so shaky I had to hold my breath when I lifted the turkey baster from the floor just outside the door. I did my best not to cringe or jump at the muffled gagging sounds Mirna made when my nervous icy fingers parted the lips of her sex. I undid the bulb on top of baster. The plastic tube was slick from the cooking oil I'd used to lube it with but it slid neatly inside her. Our little insemination was going torturously smooth. She was still for a breath of a second; her brain was trying to understand what was going on. It was the sensation of thousands of tiny legs running into her and all around inside of her at once.

"Fire ants, Mirna. Stay calm and I think they'll be calm, they think they have a nice new warm tunnel to explore. Tell me the code and I'll let you down and you can try to get them out before they start biting. One bites, they all bite. Okay?"

She barely nodded and I peeled back a corner of the tape on her mouth.

She rattled out the numbers shakily: "Thirty-six, thirty-seven, forty-three, sixty-two."

I memorized her shaky rendition before putting the tape back over her mouth and patting it in place. I then turned and left humming to drown out the sounds of her muffled screams, and her body slamming into the door. *Too many baby teeth up there for her not to feel some teeth.*

The study was the first place I checked. After clumsily knocking a painting off the wall and pulling hundreds of books out of the bookcase I gave up and moved to a different part of the house. The Maiden statue was no nicer close up than it was from a distance. There wasn't anything odd about it either except up close they weren't wood they were some kind of stone. Walking around the Guardian I flexed my fingers to ease some tension. Angry hopelessness was trying to sneak its way back into to the picture. *Maybe I should have yanked some fingernails until she told me where it was, too.*

My eyes roved down the Guardian pausing at his crotch. Giggling, I rolled my eyes. *Up in here eye molesting a statue. Wonder what he'd have going on up under there if he was real though.* Leaning in close enough to smell acrylic paint mixed with museum musk, my eyebrows came together in a

concentrated frown. There was the tiniest notch
on the side of the Guardian's hip closest to the
wall. It felt pervy as hell but it was the only way
I'd find out if he was a safe or not. Running my
hand along the front, side, and back of the statue
I felt for something that felt safe-like. Something
clicked toward the notch on his hip and the front
of his chest opened. I tapped the numbers Mirna
gave me into the keypad and my jaw hit the floor.
If anybody was embezzling from anywhere it was
this nigga and my cell phone was on top of that.
Grabbing my supply purse I didn't even think. I
just started bagging as much as I could.

The bishop's keys were hanging beside the
garage door. If his study was that high-tech he'd
better have a damn car charger. I pressed the
garage door opener on the wall and headed toward
the car.

A gruff voice called out, "I was expecting Kev."

I jumped so hard the car keys fell out of my
hand and I got an instant headache on top of
the headache I already had. I almost got whiplash
from snatching the keys up and snapping back
to attention. The garage door had made so much
noise opening I hadn't heard or thought to see if
anyone was outside. All thoughts of company or
a concerned neighbor coming over in the middle
of the night vanished when I laid eyes on this
fool looking like Dog the black bounty hunter.

Momentarily stupefied I just stood there waiting for him manifest a bullwhip, handcuffs, and a pistol from underneath his black leather vest. On second thought his vest was actually a little too tight to hide anything, as were his matching leather pants.

He jabbed a long, dark finger in my direction. "You must be Mirna?" he asked when I still hadn't moved or responded. "Grab Bishop for me, let him know Guinness is here."

I offered a timid nod. "Um, Kev had an emergency and—"

"That's that bullshit! I knew he ain't have no girl who could do anal. Excuse my language but a black ho who can take it up the ass on film is like a damn unicorn. Even when they drugged up they ain't believable. Talkin' about he got one already broke in. I got his broke in. Gonna make me have a crew on standby for . . ." His words were lost on warm night air as he stomped craters into the driveway marching toward his black Navigator that was sadly blocking me in.

Did he just say all of what . . . So, what'd they think? They were about to sell me again and have someone making movies wit' my ass, literally.

My stomach did a somersault and I bit at the inside of my bottom lip to hide the instant look of hatred fighting to spread across my face. I could feel my cheeks flushing hot and probably turning red from anger. Guinness sneered like he'd just walked out of a jungle dragging a full-sized panther. The teary-eyed girl couldn't have been older than sixteen; she looked like a baby shuffling along fearfully behind him. *Please, don't tell me he wants to see Mirna do some kind of raunchy kinky mess right now. There's a hammer on that toolbox over there. Gasoline in the cans. I will tear him down and burn everything.*

He all but flung her in my direction. She stood barefoot beside me in her filthy, tattered jean shorts and tank top shivering even though it was warm. It was too dark to tell if she was hurt and it wasn't the time to ask. My heart ached for her and the sooner he left the sooner I could help.

"You tell Kev Mr. Guinness came by. And Mr. Guinness said a deal is a deal." The duffel bag landed with a solid thwap against the concrete. "Hoes who won't be missed ain't cheap, and they sure ain't easy to come by these days. Kev can just call this a custom order." Guinness took a step toward me staring down the length of his round, bulbous nose at me. He ran his tongue over his top teeth sucking like he'd just finished off a whole plate of ribs.

"So, Mirna, if Kev don't get that message I'll be coming to make you a custom order."

"Police; freeze, hands up where I can see them, nobody move."

My knees felt like they were about to give out. The world would have gone black and I was sure I would have fainted if flashlights weren't shining directly in my eyes.

One of the police officers walked over. "There's been a report of a safe break in at his residence, are—"

I jumped on the opportunity. "It's him; get him, please, somebody get him. He's trying to kidnap us. I'm Mirna. I put the numbers in: thirty-six, thirty-seven, forty-three, sixty-two."

Desperation had me in complete hysterics pointing wildly at Guinness with tears streaming down my face. The last thing I needed was for them to find Kevin dead and Mirna with her fire ant issue at the hands of my ex-con self. Add Guinness trying to sell some girl to Kevin and Mirna, and me standing here with the money. The whole thing would look like a complete mess with me stuck right in the damn middle of it. Words and explanations bumbled out of my mouth.

"It's just me and my niece; my husband is out of town. That man blocked my driveway, threatened us, and took my money; look in the duffle bag."

All mayhem broke lose as they rushed Guinness who was in the process of trying to charge at me.

"You set me up! Nah, nah, that bitch set me up!" Three officers had to restrain him.

One of the officers cautiously used his booted toe to push open one side of the duffel bag so he could shine his flashlight into it. He nodded at me and called out to the others, "Yep, looks like we got him, boys."

"This Navi belong to you, sir?" an officer asked.

"Nope," Guinness barked back.

"That's funny because the name matches your ID and it looks like you've got warrants out the wahoo."

Guinness was put in the back of a squad car and a tall, younger officer with hair so blond it looked almost silver came over. "Ma'am, I'm Officer Pierce; how about I see you all back inside?" he asked, looking at the girl with a bit of concern.

I tried to sound normal but what came out was a nervous, high-pitched guffaw. "Oh no, a friend just dropped her off from the beach before all this craziness happened. Praise the Lord everyone is okay. I was about to have her take those sandy play clothes off out here and throw them in the laundry before we go inside so we don't make no messes."

"Okay, if y'all need us call. Get all that money put back up for your husband thinks you went on a shopping spree." Officer Pierce chuckled and walked down the driveway.

I was doing my best Susie Homemaker wave and fake smile routine. The girl even offered a tiny good-bye.

"You okay, sweetheart?"

She nodded slowly.

"The good news is I'm not Mirna. I'm Eva."

There was still the matter of Guinness's duffel bag. No sooner had I leaned down to pick it up than I was shielding my eyes from high beams blaring in my face. *Oh, no. What if one of those cops needs an ID from me for a statement? As soon as they realize I'm not Mirna, there's no way I could ever explain what I did in there.*

Still blinded from the headlights I didn't have any time to brace myself. The concrete met all of my back with unforgiving roughness. Momentarily stunned, I was actually waiting for the officer to flip me over and slap cuffs on me.

"Bitch, I saved you and this is how you repay me?"

Her voice and the sound of her hand connecting with my face echoed in the garage. My left ear started ringing; the salty, copperish taste of my own blood pressed against my tongue, and coated my teeth. Shocked, I stared up at Aeron and had some kind of guilty outer body pity moment. I couldn't hear whatever she was yelling into my face. There were dark half-moon shadows under her eyes that were raining fat tear drops down onto my skin. Too shocked to defend myself while she was busy trying to choke the life out of me, I calmed myself down trying to ignore the reality of what I'd done. That was prison. That was survival.

Chapter 40

Eva
Eye Spy

The girl screamed jumping on Aeron's back to protect me. She scrambled to her feet pushing her away. I pulled myself to my feet, cursing my wobbly legs. Aeron stood there with her chest heaving, nostrils flared and I glared right back. The tiny leap of excitement my heart made at the sight of her was squashed as all my energy went into faking courage I really didn't feel. Thunder cracked the sky open all around me making me jump. The sound rattled my eardrums and bumped my heart up against my ribcage. My eyes shifted from Aeron to the pitch-black, starless sky outside and even that second was a second too long. When my eyes darted back, her finger was doing that sideways come hither on the trigger. There was nowhere for me to go, no time to move. All my thoughts drained from my head right along with the color from my face as I went pale. I even forgot to ask for forgiveness for all my sins.

The muzzle flared and I saw the thunder before the sound reached my ears. Fear had already stopped my heart. I stared down at my chest like an idiot trying to figure out why the ringing in my ears was so annoying. Gradually the sound of Mirna shrieking in pain behind me became clearer. I was pretty sure I was momentarily deafened from being inside a makeshift gun range. My hearing came back in bits and pieces. Steel clattered to the floor somewhere behind me. Aeron's voice finally broke through.

"I can't believe I'm doing this shit but somethin' tells me you have one hell of a story. We need to get out of here Eva, now."

Nodding in agreement I grabbed the duffle bag and purse, and motioned for the girl to follow as I climbed in the passenger seat of Aeron's Escalade. A spotlight glared in my face from the back seat blinding me for the umpteenth time in one night. Aeron threw the SUV in gear and squealed the tires wheeling us out of there.

"Eva, this is my cameraman, soundman, and jack of all trades, Nigel. Nigel, meet Eva, the woman behind the infamous cherry scene," Aeron announced.

Nigel grinned proudly displaying a gold tooth. "I thought ye looked a tad familiar, glad to see ye can take a wallop, too."

Nigel almost made me swallow my tongue. His unmistakably coarse accent was either English or Australian but he was dark onyx ruggedly easy on the eyes with shocking platinum-blond hair. He gave me a crooked thumbs-up and I fought the urge to tell him that I had no idea what a wallop was but he could wallop me. Since Aeron had all but saddled and mounted the elephant in the room, I took a breath and womaned up.

"How did you find out about what happened?" I asked her quietly.

She glanced at me out the corner of her eye before leaning on the door and propping her chin in her hand. Aeron stared intently at me over her arm on the steering wheel. The girl whispered to Nigel in the back but I couldn't make out what they were saying.

"What exactly do you think I do for a living, Eva?"

"Um, Latina gang model extraordinaire?"

Aeron rolled her eyes. "I run a reality show."

"OMG, it is you!" The girl squealed, "Aeron Villanueva!"

It was the most unexpected excitement, given what we'd just gone through. Her face lit up with the brightest smiles as she reached over the seat timidly touching Aeron's shoulder. Aeron looked up winking through the rearview.

"Nigel, start recording. Eva, messing around with you I almost forgot why I was at that house in the first place."

"Villa who? Wh . . . recording what? Am I actually on camera? Wait, you mean you weren't there for me at all?" I sputtered.

Nigel maneuvered the spotlight from me to Aeron to the girl finally resting on Aeron. He spoke over the side of the camera. "Sorry, cherry chew, we were actually hooking bigger fish when you got caught on the line."

Aeron fluffed her hair, did her eyeliner, and touched up her lip gloss all while steering with her knee. "I have a Web-based reality show, *Garish Lies*. We uncover truths and the shit private investigators can't and we go where the media won't. End of the day they pay for my footage."

Aeron's voice went from sweet, motherly "tell me everything" to expert commentator in a matter of seconds. She didn't even have that damn accent I remembered as she turned and started talking to the camera. I'd stepped right out of prison and into the Twilight Zone. Nobody and I mean absolutely nobody was who they said they were. At this point in my life I'd need to walk around doing background checks before I could even have lunch with someone. I tried to roll some of the tension out of my shoulders. Dontay, Aeron, Kevin, Mirna, everybody had a script except me. Nigel planted his elbow in my boob and I slapped him away.

"Sorry, love. Got to get a good shot."

"I'm Aeron Villaneuva, and for a while we've been tracking the local abduction ring. Most of the girls disappear from shelters and are never seen again. Others are taken from bus stops and after-hours programs. I have a brave young lady named Destiny Vasquez who's going to tell her story."

Aeron paused for dramatic effect and the girl started sniffling. Aeron held up a finger toward Nigel who flicked the light off on the camera. I was surprised that my own eyes were getting damp at the melodrama unfolding in front of me. The sooner I could hug and squeeze Jada the better. This could have easily been Jada and for once I felt thankful for being in the wrong place at the right time. She didn't even look that young; the bishop and Mirna would have destroyed her.

Aeron's voice was barely above a whisper. "Okay, my love. This is your chance to say whatever you want. Tell exactly what happened. I can edit this before it goes online so you have plenty of time to change your mind. No one will hurt you, I promise. I'll have you home by the time you're done."

She nodded.

"I was walking down the sidewalk picking up flowers from the cotton candy trees. They ran up and down both sides and after it rained the petals would cover the ground like snow.

"'Those are called cherry blossoms, *bebé*,' Ms. Lita, my nanny called out. I don't know how she kept up, but no matter what Ms. Lita was always smiling. Daddy said she was the only person other than Mommy who he trusted with me or the keys to our house. He said it was because she understood the value of loyalty. In high school when he was a janitor working at the bank Ms. Lita was supervisor. When Daddy went to college and came back she was a manager and hired him as a supervisor.

"One day Daddy drove me around and showed me all these buildings with our last name on the side. He'd bought those banks. Well on this day I skipped and sang all up and down the block in our neighborhood until I was hoarse and sweaty. Ms. Lita smiled down at me. 'Let's head back to the house and see about ordering pizza for dinner okay?'

"I nodded, skipping and singing my way back home. Sometimes I'm clumsy and I'd tripped skinning my knee and was crying when we walked in the front door.

"'What the hell is all that noise? Is they usually this loud?' some lady called out.

"'Toikea, meet my daughter Destiny.' Daddy introduced me with a big smile, puffing out his chest.

"'She smell like outside. And what is that?' Toikea asked pointing at Lita.

"'That, uh, I mean she's Lita. The nanny,' Daddy rocked back on his heels, answering with a sigh.

"Toikea frowned even harder. 'We don't need that. Nannies is for white folk with disposable income and if it's disposable all like that'—she kissed his cheek—'how come you ain't taking me shopping with it?'

"She started giggling against his cheek and Daddy started blushing like his whole brain just fell out of his ear. Me and Lita exchanged confused looks. I wasn't feeling his little 'toy car.' Nobody treated Lita like that; she was basically part of the family. Since she'd been so rude I got rude and asked, 'Does Mommy know that's here?'

"Daddy choked and Toikea tried to melt me with her eyes. After that we learned about this thing that grownups do called 'breaks.' Mommy had needed one and supposedly Daddy had found Toikea. She made Daddy give Lita a break, too, and that's when he got sick. One day, Toi was all we had left.

"Then she dragged me to her nasty house, made me call her Mommy. And she lied telling some nice man with pretty gray eyes I was his daughter, making me call him Daddy. He cried and was sad all time, he kept telling me sorry. I wanted to tell him so bad. But Toi said she'd have somebody kill my mommy if I messed things up. So we went and did whatever the test was, but Toi's friend worked there and gave him fake results. I kept pretending to be sad so he'd give Toi money and marry her.

"None of it was fair. I did what I was supposed to and I kept begging her to see Mommy. That's when the man in the smelly black truck with the spinning rims came. Toi told me it was too late, that she'd died. Guinness came and got me right before Toi and the sad man's wedding."

Chapter 41

Eva
Guess Who

My throat was moving but no sound was coming out. I rocked myself, gripping my arms so tight my nails cut into my upper arms through the fabric of my sweatshirt. It wasn't a coincidence; Destiny's man with the gray eyes stealing money sounded too close to home. Too close to that picture I'd seen on Facebook with him and that mystery woman. We pulled into a large gated circular driveway a little after three a.m. Destiny was drooling all over Nigel's arm who was snoring with his face mashed against the glass. I sighed and looked over at Aeron with sad eyes as she put the car in park.

"I'm really sorry about Antonia," I whispered. "Can you pull up Dontay's Facebook on your phone please?"

Without a word she nodded and nudged Destiny. "We're here, sweetheart. You're home. Before you go . . ." Aeron held up her cell.

Destiny yawned and squinted at the picture; her face gave away the answer before the words left her lips. "That's him. He's marrying Toi."

The front door swung open and a tiny Puerto Rican lady rushed onto the wide porch in a floral bathrobe. She fumbled with her glasses before finally managing to slip them up on her nose. Her hands flew up to cover her lips; tears cascaded down her cheeks. She took the steps one at a time and couldn't get to Destiny fast enough.

"Ms. Lita!" Destiny rushed into her arms nearly knocking the poor little lady down.

"*Niña,* my baby girl, they found you."

I watched over wiping my nose on my sleeve as Aeron got out and went over. Ms. Lita must have hugged and grabbed Aeron's face at least a hundred times. Nigel sighed behind me and not too long afterward the staccato of his snores was buzzing in my ears. One world was pieced together while simultaneously splintering mine into even tinier slivers. It didn't even matter that Dontay had been tricked into his marriage. The numbing kick in the gut came from knowing he was willing to throw me out of the plane without a parachute to save someone else. After everything I'd seen there was no telling what the people who had Jada were doing to her, or if they were treating her right.

Aeron walked toward the car with a bounce in her step and an excited gleam in her eyes. The roaring in my ears from my blood rushing and my thoughts churning was making me hot and pan-icky. I felt trapped and lost all at the same time. I picked at a dangling thread on my sleeve clamping my teeth down hard on my tongue ignoring the cheerful waves Ms. Lita and Destiny sent our way as we pulled off.

"Destiny's father left everything to Ms. Lita as the girl's guardian. She was really the only person he trusted with everything. I guess Toi found herself shit out of luck and in need of a new sponsor. So she used her as bait for a new bank account."

"Yeah, mine," I huffed.

"Calm down, angel. You're lucky I wasn't close to Antonia. The only part of my made-up bio that was real was that we really did hate each other. She was a bully from day one and she stole all my girlfriends. I'd have all these bruises and shit. My own sister was constantly beating my ass. When she got picked up for that robbery, she tried to say it was me who did it."

"So what were you doing in prison?"

Aeron giggled. "I'm dating the warden. I didn't know Christine was the damn warden when we met. It wasn't like we talked that much. Just lots of rough, drunk um . . . Anyway, when I found out what she did I asked her to let me take my show inside for a few months. See if I could find all that corruption bullshit you hear about. Sometimes Antonia helped; sometimes she hurt."

There wasn't enough invisible lint or errant sweater strings in the world to distract me from the melting pot of mass confusion mixing around in my head. Glancing at Aeron out the corner of my eye I chewed and processed over a million questions at the speed of light. Even though I'd told myself repeatedly that what happened in prison would stay in prison, it was different when it came with a side of feeling dirty and used. It fell into the same category as Kev's, Mirna's, and Dontay's betrayals and so far I'd been doing a pretty good job at exacting an eye for an eye.

"So it was all acting then? Harassing and bullying me, all that?"

"Hmm no, I liked you and I wanted to make Christine jealous for having my celly before you nixed. She'd gotten into the habit of doing that."

My jaw dropped. "You could have gotten me shanked by your psycho warden girlfriend?"

She just shrugged. "You're free now aren't you? Who do you think got you pardoned? These lips are good for more than talking but you already know that."

I turned and stared out the window, feeling my face flush hot.

"Anyway, I did try finding Jada when I first got out and I kept hitting a brick wall. They wouldn't or couldn't help me. Someone's hiding something and I think that someone for starters is you." Aeron's tone was accusatory.

"What do you mean me? After everything I've been through I don't have anything to hide, Aeron. You know that." I didn't. All of my dirt had been laid down in the sandbox for everyone to sift through, climb over, and play in. There wasn't anything else.

Aeron tapped her chin with her finger. "Where did you get the money to start your business?"

Except that. "If you're asking then you already know."

"I want to hear little Miss Eva say it."

"I always say it was a business loan. But my family had some pretty crazy things going on at one point in time. The money was willed to me by a man named Psion Burner or Papa Psion. It was part of my marriage pact when I was ten. He never got a chance to change it because Ava, my mom, kind of killed him before we could get married. When I turned twenty-two all of his assets came to me. I didn't even know until an attorney called me to disburse it."

"Okay now you're being genuine. But there's a gap that I'm stuck on. I researched your case and even have an idea where to find Dontay, but I snooped into his accounts using one of my connects and he's broker than broke Eva."

"Listen up Blues Clueless." Nigel popped up from the back seat. "Out of curiosity I just tried pulling up all the remaining relatives of this Psion

Burner." He flipped his phone towards us. "Destiny Burner came up in the birth certificates same day and year as our little one, but her name was later changed to Vasquez when she turned six."

Aeron whipped a u-turn that nearly sent us all flying out of the windows. The tires kicked up dirt as we broke the sound barrier to get back to Mrs. Lita's. We all were wondering the same thing. If Mrs. Lita was connected or maybe even married to Papa Psion and why hadn't Destiny mention any of it. We squealed to a stop back in front of Ms. Lita's place.

The lights were off and it was obvious they'd gone to bed.

"Should be come back a little later, maybe breakfast time?" Nigel asked.

I shook my head. "We need answers, my daughter is still missing and someone is getting away with a crime I was in prison for."

I was too wired to feel sleepy or even think about anything other than questioning this little girl until I had every piece I needed to find my baby. The light on the doorbell flickered as Aeron pressed it with her thumb. We could hear the deep chimes echo throughout the dark house. I stared up at a crystal chandelier through a window on the front of the house. It glittered and sparkled from the morning light like one of Jada's old mobiles. I missed my baby so much it hurt.

Aeron pressed the doorbell again and by the third chime I'd screamed so loud it's a wonder I didn't shatter every window on the place. I stumbled down the steps with my eyes paralyzed by the rope hanging behind the chandelier. It was tied to the banister and what looked like Ms. Lita was hanging from it.

Nigel kicked in the door and the air from outside made her spin in a slow circle. I couldn't bring myself to move any closer than the bottom step. Aeron's face was sad and drawn as she came over and pulled me into a tight hug. It felt like hours passed as he ran from room to room searching the house for Destiny or whoever might have hung Ms. Lita. Aeron was in the SUV grabbing her cell to call the police when the entire back side of the house was lit up with a bright orange fireball.

I fell backwards into the grass. This couldn't be happening, it couldn't be possible. The fire spread so fast from the back towards the front Nigel almost missed his chance to get out. He stumbled out the door with his face covered in soot coughing the way I did when I was in that box so many years ago. Aeron rushed over and helped me up.

Nigel coughed and hacked his way towards us. "Was headed towards the basement, saw a little pipe bomb with a detonator I got spooked and started to head back. Grabbed this though, it was on the floor near the banister." He handed Aeron the crumpled sheet of paper. Squiggly blue letters that were drawn out in crayon spanned across the paper. It reminded me of Leslie's first scribbled out notes I'd hang around my bedroom. I folded my arms tight across my chest scanning the wooded areas around us. None of Leslie's notes were ever as dreary or eerie as to say something like, *"Burner Burns Everybody."*

Chapter 42

Destiny
Three Lost girls

2004

Still dozing, I squeezed my hands tight in between my legs and groaned. Rocking in place, I tried to drift back to the dream I was having. The mattress springs creaked and popped underneath me. The pops made me think of plops, and plops made me think of drips. My bladder sent a code yellow flash flood warning up my spine. Ava would whoop me until I forgot my own name if I got up while she had company. She'll do a lot worse if I pee in this bed though.

With a huff, my toes hit the cold floor and I started a half-asleep, knock-kneed marathon walk through the dark house. Hot droplets of pee were already tickling their way down the inside of my leg. I flew into the dark bathroom and whirled around thankful Ava never put the lid down. It was one of the many random things she didn't do, like dusting or eating in front of people.

There wasn't time for me to close the door, fight with the light switch, or worry about the water monster. The water monster dripped down from the ceiling to steal little kids. Ava never told me where he took them, and I sure ain't want to find out.

Launching myself the last few feet into the bathroom, I fumbled with my panties. Eeew. My bladder let go early, wetting up my own fingers. I sighed and went full stream ahead onto what I could only register in my mind as the water monster. All the hairs on the back of my neck stood up and probably fell off as my booty planted on something warm and smushy.

"Hey now! What in the . . ." His deep voice boomed through the house.

I shot up like a leaky yellow bottle rocket. That didn't sound or feel like water. Struggling with my panties I teetered toward the door, trailing pee on the way like Frito. Frito was Ava's half-senile teacup Chihuahua. He would forget who we were, bark like crazy, then remember and excite-pee while running all over the place. She had Frito put down.

"Psi?" Ava called out from the hallway.

"Bring me a towel please?" He replied from behind me.

A porcupine burrowed deep inside my chest. All of its little spikes stabbed me when I tried to breathe. I stopped just inside the door with my shoulders hunched praying she'd go get a towel so I could make a run for it. Ava didn't stop to get a towel; she kept coming.

"A towel? I'll get you one in the morning. I need you to come back in here and fin . . ."

The bathroom light clicked on. If I wasn't so sure I was about to die, I'd have made a face. My eyes shot down to the shiny pink points of her high heels. No amount of blinking could make me un-see it. Brown silver dollar pancake–sized circles down to the dark bushy triangle all showing through her pink shimmery nightdress. Not only did I see all her naughty bits, but I saw the smile come crashing down off her face, too. A crease appeared in her usually smooth forehead.

Ava didn't like her boyfriends to see me. I don't even think anyone knew she had a third daughter, especially since she didn't even like me to call her mommy. My other sisters didn't live with us. Ava said they stayed up in some fancy house with Eva's daddy. Since Eva's birthday would be in a few days, I was finally going to meet both my sisters for the first time.

"Destiny? What are you doing out of bed?" Her fingers wrapped around the back of my neck like an eagle scooping a fresh mouse out of a field.

Air hissed in between my teeth. She snatched one of the dusty dark green towels off the holder *flinging it in Psi's direction and pulled me by my neck. Those towels weren't even meant for using. They were for decoration and had been hanging there so long the sun had faded spots on them. Either way, it meant she was super pissed. We went down the hall headed in the opposite direction of the extra bedroom. We were going toward the cellar.*

"Ava?" Psi caught up with us in the kitchen. "Hold on, woman, calm down. I would have closed the bathroom door if I knew we had company," he said in his smashed pea's accent.

All his words ran together in one long smashed-together sentence, reminding me of peas on my dinner plate. I frowned because I hated peas.

Ava spun around. I winced at her nails digging into my skin. She wouldn't put me in the cellar with him watching. It might make him wonder what was down there. Standing in the dim kitchen he looked a big, bald lady. His man boobs were bigger than Ava's. The towel barely fit around his big belly.

"It's fine, Sugar Bear." Ava's voice was sugar-coated venom. "Go back to the bedroom. I need to deal with this. I won't be long."

Psi ignored her altogether. His eyes were glued to me. The corner of his mouth lifted in a lopsided grin making me uncomfortable. He started studying his nails on his right hand. His voice was so low I could barely hear him over the buzzing and clicking sounds coming from the fridge.

"Don't you owe me a birthday present, woman?" he asked, picking invisible dirt from under his nail beds.

Her fingers against my skin. He looked up at her when she didn't answer. I tried looking so far up out the corner of my eye at her that it made my head hurt. The look on her face made something heavy and hollow plunk down into the pit of my stomach. I studied the cracks in the floor trying to figure out why her chin was shaking and her eyes looked like liquid glass.

"Why am I never a good enough present?" Ava snapped.

Psi looked around the room in a full circle like he was searching for the answer.

"It's bad enough you get Eva after she turns sixteen, but now you look at my youngest like she's up for . . . for that bullshit choosing you all buy into with Deacon."

I'd seen Ava mad before but never like this.

"I've dealt with you for six long miserable years. The only thing I've ever thought about since the day you claimed me and got me pregnant was the day I'd take you out of this world."

Psi's head swiveled from Ava back down to me. "But, how? At the hospital the doctor told me she was stillborn."

"No idiot, she's right here, six about to turn seven and better off without you. It didn't take much to keep that joke with a degree from believing I thought you'd hurt her. He said exactly what I told him to, and I brought her home that night. Y'all weren't gonna take this baby away, and when that doctor got a little too high on himself, trying to force me into sucking and fucking. I threw him in the smokehouse right along with your brother D.J. We about to have a family plot back there."

Before Psi knew he was in danger, she was across the room with a meat cleaver in her hand. It sunk into his chest cracking against the bones. I crawled under the table to hide, shaking worried that she'd come for me next. Psi dropped to the floor and tried to pull himself up using the leg of the table. A river of blood was running from his mouth. It was on his hands that he smeared everywhere and pooling underneath him.

"I'm sorry Destiny, baby. But this bitch-ass nigga is really your daddy." Ava stood over him breathing like she'd just finished running laps around the house. "Now, ask daddy why we're out here poor as fuck while Eva and Leslie are living it up. Ask Daddy how much fancy shit he bought Eva for her sixteenth birthday with all that filthy money he got."

Psi's eyes made a lazy line towards Ava. He looked like a wind-up whale on the floor that finally started running out of power.

"*Ava, I can change everything," he wheezed. I just need to sign—*"

"*You already signed your life over to the damn devil. Now tell him I said hi.*"

Ava swung the cleaver and I squeezed my eyes shut.

I climbed into the backseat of the car up the road, remembering the sound of Ava hacking away at Psi over and over. She even made me help drag pieces of his body to the smokehouse. I never went inside, not since the day I'd gotten bored and wandered in. That was the day I found the pieces of the first two bodies.

Ava was crazy but she loved us in her own sick twisted way. I stood in the part of the basement underneath the kitchen table. It was the only part of the house where I could see through the floorboards. Eva, had looked right at me and still didn't see me. They'd all burn for taking Ava away from me, Eva even more so because she had all of my money.

Dontay turned and stared at me over in the backseat his eyes were full of confused happy tears. "When you called I thought someone was playing on my phone. I almost didn't come out here tonight."

I'd called him from Ms. Lita's right after I'd gotten dropped off. I wasn't dumb enough to stay where I could be found. I had every intention of running away and not looking back. Ms. Lita was an accident. She tripped on her way upstairs to check on me falling into some new decorative gold and red braided ropes she'd started hanging from the banister. Her neck got caught in one of the loops and she was too heavy for me to pull back up. It made my stomach hurt to have to leave her like that, but I didn't have a choice.

"On the phone you were saying Toikea set me up and Eva was involved with it? How could they have worked together without me knowing?" He asked before staring off into the distance shaking his head.

I gave him a minute to get mad at the story I'd told him. I hadn't had the time to think through the part of my lie involving Eva. I leaned back against the seat stretching the tight muscles in my lower back.

"I'll tell you everything even how to get back what Toi took, if you help me. Once she finds out I'm not in that sex-slave house, she'll start looking for me. She has to pay for what she did to my step-parents." I told him in a strong even voice.

Dontay was the only one that was like me. He was innocent. But I'd use him to help me get to all the names Ava would curse every time she'd beat me. We'd find Deacon, and Derian, and then Aunt Rose, Toikea, Leslie and last but not least Eva. Everyone would burn for the part they played making my life hell and in return I'd get back whatever was left of my inheritance.

Dontay pulled away from the side of the road while I studied him from my seat. He was still fine as all hell even though he looked a little skinny. All the stress of dealing with Toikea was probably taking its toll on him. My tongue wet my suddenly dry lips and I wondered how hard it would be to break him into fucking me. Ava would always say that you should use what you got to get what you need. Right now, I needed a hot bath, warm bed, and somebody as fine as Dontay to help me bust a quick one so I could fall asleep peacefully.

Leaning forward I turned on my daddy's girl voice. "Dontay, you ever thought about being with someone other than Toi? I mean, you deserve better than that."

He jumped when my finger grazed his ear.

"What are you talking about girl, and sit back. Put your seatbelt on. How old are you anyway, Toi had me believing one thing and —"

"I'm sixteen but looks are deceiving I can pretend to be eighteen, twenty-three, whatever you want." I traced his ear with my index finger. "Now that you know we aren't related don't you feel even a little relieved? I do. It was hell walking around that house thinking damn my *daddy* is sexy as fuck."

His grip tightened on the steering wheel as he shifted in his seat. Stop was no parts of that kind of body language.

"So, are you gonna come put the seatbelt on me or no? We can talk about everything afterwards."

I leaned closer letting the tip of my tongue replace the pattern my finger had been making. When he didn't pull away from me, I kissed my way down his neck until we pulled over to the side of the road. I could see how Toi manipulated him so easily. It only took a few cute words and he was climbing in the backseat. Shit, at this rate, I might not even have to get my hands dirty. If I gassed this fool up good enough, I could just throw the match and let him take everyone out.

ORDER FORM
URBAN BOOKS, LLC
97 N. 18th Street
Wyandanch, NY 11798

Name (please print):_____

Address:_____

City/State:_____

Zip:_____

QTY	TITLES	PRICE

Shipping and handling-add $3.50 for 1st book, then $1.75 for each additional book.
Please send a check payable to:
Urban Books, LLC
Please allow 4-6 weeks for delivery

ORDER FORM
URBAN BOOKS, LLC
97 N. 18th Street
Wyandanch, NY 11798

Name (please print):_____

Address:_____

City/State:_____

Zip:_____

QTY	TITLES	PRICE
	16 On The Block	$14.95
	A Girl From Flint	$14.95
	A Pimp's Life	$14.95
	Baltimore Chronicles	$14.95
	Baltimore Chronicles 2	$14.95
	Betrayal	$14.95
	Black Diamond	$14.95

Shipping and handling-add $3.50 for 1st book, then $1.75 for each additional book.
Please send a check payable to:
Urban Books, LLC
Please allow 4-6 weeks for delivery

ORDER FORM
URBAN BOOKS, LLC
97 N. 18th Street
Wyandanch, NY 11798

Name (please print):_____

Address:_____

City/State:_____

Zip:_____

QTY	TITLES	PRICE
	Cheesecake And Teardrops	$14.95
	Congratulations	$14.95
	Crazy In Love	$14.95
	Cyber Case	$14.95
	Denim Diaries	$14.95
	Diary Of A Mad First Lady	$14.95
	Diary Of A Stalker	$14.95

Shipping and handling-add $3.50 for 1st book, then $1.75 for each additional book. Please send a check payable to:

Urban Books, LLC

Please allow 4-6 weeks for delivery